Second Chances

a novel

E.F. James

Book Design by David Nash

Cover photo provided by Rebecca Nash

ISBN 978-0-6151-9258-1

Printed by LuLu.com. First Edition printing Jan 2008.

I'd like to take this opportunity to say a very heartfelt and sincere Thank You to everyone who has supported me during my journey in seeing this novel to completion. It has been a dream to see my writing in print and with all the love and support of my friends and family, that dream has become a reality. I hope you enjoy reading it as much as I have enjoyed writing it.

Thank you!

E.F. James

Chapter One

"This is the first day of the rest of your life," she whispered as her eyes scanned the crowds that were weaving all around her. It was like watching a busy ant hill on a warm summer's day. Mattie was still reeling from the changes her life had taken. Here she stood in the sunny State of California, not once ever setting foot out of her small hometown, much less the state of Kentucky. Mattie fought the urge to pinch herself, yet again, because it all still seemed so surreal to her. The scene before her was like something out of a movie. The reality, however, was close to overwhelming. Never in her life had she seen so many people crushing together, touching, and breathing the same claustrophobic air. The old fear she'd spent her life fighting was pulling at her with relentless determination. The closeness of people and the unwanted brushing of flesh increased the tightness in her chest causing every breath to weigh heavily within her lungs. Relying on her inner strength she fought for control over the anxiety attack she knew was taking root within her very core.

Following through with the promise to continue her education had proven to be easier than what she had expected. In all honesty getting to this point couldn't have been any easier. The scholarship she was under offered full tuition benefits that would cover her education as long as she continued to fulfill her obligation within the guidelines.

Mattie's life had undergone so many changes in such a short time that she felt consumed with uncertainties and misgivings. With such turmoil ruling her life she felt it hard to remain grounded and forced her focus on what she knew was going to be a promising future. Mattie was trying her hardest to disregard the suffocating sensations that had her throat tight and her breath shallow. The familiar battle she often lost was building as the minutes ticked by and the crowd grew closer.

Being from a rural area only fed her fear of crowds and what their closeness represented. Mattie Collins, however, was a fighter and she would not risk her chance at a new life by letting the fear rule her as it had in the past.

1

Keeping focused on the positive aspects of her life, no matter how hard, was going to see her through.

Mattie had learned a long time ago that self-pity was only an anchor around her neck. Liz, her momma, and her best friend Gracie Jones, the old woman who lived on the ridge, had always tried to teach her that 'pity is, as pity does'. For those reasons, and a promise made to Gracie, encouraged Mattie to focus and succeed with the new journey her life was taking. Albeit, she wanted this with every fiber of her being and had worked very hard to get where she was, didn't lesson the bone deep fear that was threatening to take her to a place she didn't want to go. Just getting here from her distant home had been hard enough, but standing among the crush of bodies without losing her hard won control was becoming harder to endure as time slowly ticked by.

California was a far cry from her little hometown in Kentucky. Changing her life may have started out as a promise to her dying friend, however, that promise wasn't made to only Gracie it was also one she had made to herself. College registration was like an open flea market where some made it a point to stand out and others just waited patiently for it all to be over soon. Mattie preferred being part of the background where plain was overlooked and ordinary was ignored. Gracie and her mother had always told her she was pretty, but she never believed it. Not that her two favorite women would lie to her. It was just their love for her that blinded them to reality. As far as Mattie was concerned blending into the scenery was her solace from interacting with all the strangers that surrounded her.

The sun was shining steadily creating natural warmth and the salty breeze from the ocean offered a welcomed coolness. Some of the bored students had been tossing a football or throwing a Frisbee around offering a diversion from the monotony of standing in line. Mattie kept to herself and didn't socialize with those who mingled around her in all directions. She didn't look up, attempt eye contact, or initiate anything remotely interactive with any of them.

Mattie's gift for making herself invisible was an unconscious art form that aided in protecting her. Being an only child had prepared her for the solitude she now craved. Her body language screamed 'hands off' by keeping her head slightly bowed, back arched at the shoulders, hair restrained in a tight French braid, and a loose fitting dress to prevent eyes from lingering. She wore no makeup to enhance her looks and felt her appearance, actions, and lack of people skills kept contact with others to a minimum. Mattie figured they just considered her to be one of the odd ones and for that she was grateful. As long as they kept their distance from her she would continue to remain a plain Jane among the masses. She was an observer, not a joiner, and had no intentions of changing for anyone. Mattie was so lost in her own thoughts that she hadn't noticed one young mans attention being fixed solely upon her.

Jackson Woods had been watching the amber haired young lady with a mild interest. He couldn't help thinking how she would shatter if anyone were to touch her. Curiosity had always been his weakness and watching her had piqued his interest. Jackson wandered what her face looked like and what color her eyes were, or what her voice sounded like. He had played this game all morning but this was the first and only person that kept grabbing his attention. The pretty auburn hair was the first attribute that had caught his eye as it swayed with the gentle breeze against her perfectly rounded hips. The hair was braided like a thick rope with a length that amazed him. It was such an odd occurrence to see hair fall past a woman's waist in this day and age, not with all the short do's being so popular. Jackson couldn't help automatically thinking that the woman was either vane as hell or some religious nut. He brushed the vane angle to the side based solely on the clothing and the 'don't touch' body language rolling off her like invisible waves.

The only other option left was the religious aspect. He had given her a very narrow avenue of categories but in his mind it was the only two that seemed to fit. Jackson couldn't help thinking she was a contradiction of sorts. She was making a visible statement yet he found his focus drawn to her more than anyone else all morning. He knew just by looking at her that she was rather tall no matter how she tried to hide that fact with the slumped shoulders. He would have remembered a tall, amber haired woman if he had seen her before, since tall women were not very common.

He didn't understand this pull he felt each time he looked at her, but he was intelligent enough to admit it existed. He was puzzled by the need to keep seeking her out, because she was so not his type, yet he found his eyes drawn to her repeatedly. How weird was that?

Jackson thanked the schedule screw-up for the first time in his college career. What was usually a big pain in his ass was turning out to be a blessing in disguise, since that was the reason he was stuck here in the first place. Making a vow to find out who this newcomer was he took in all the details of her appearance and committed them to memory. It should rattle him that he would focus so much attention to this girl, but for some odd reason it didn't.

Jackson's attention was redirected with the business of getting settled into his forced lifestyle. Again. "Yes," he acknowledged, "forced," but not unacceptable. It had been an inevitable road he'd planned to travel anyway. Jackson figured of the two options he had been given that, obviously, college outweighed jail time any day. Hard to believe he had taken that u-turn with his life three years ago. It turned out to be more of a reward, than a punishment. He was saddened it had taken such a drastic step to get his act together, yet he was thankful that it had. Of course, having a very influential family whispering in the ear of a close family friend, who happened to reside on the Judges bench, had ensured the desired outcome. So, his college career had begun and he was grateful his parents had pulled in some favors forcing the changes his life had taken. He had been agreeable and successful with his education, so far, and was pleased he had only a year to go before he graduated. Looking back now he could admit his parents couldn't have made a better decision where he was concerned. His relationship with his parents had been rocky for so long it was taking time to smooth out the bumps that he knew he was responsible for. Play-acting for his parent's attention had always motivated his destructive tendencies and those actions were what had landed him here in the first place. It was a shame he could only admit that now that he was older and apparently wiser.

Pretending to be someone else wasn't anything new for Jackson. He had been doing it all his life. The family being the cast and the wealth they shared being the stage. Yeah, 'pretty boy,' was a description he'd heard more than once, as well as, 'poor little rich kid.' Little did those small-minded people know what it was like to be a non-existent possession in a world of wealth and privilege? Jackson felt like one of his parent's acquisition's that required being polished to perfection when it was time to impress the elite snobbery. Otherwise, you got shelved, just like the silver and fine china after the guests left. He knew now that those were only his feelings and not the actual facts, but when you are young everything feels like a personal attack. Jackson tried to fit into the mold cast for him with little success. Now, he could honestly say, the mold set for him no longer fit, he'd come out on top, and in charge of his own life. He was thankful that his relationship with his parents was not the same as it had been when he was a teenager. This was his chance to succeed on his own merit and he wasn't going to waste it being stupid and resentful with his misguided anger.

Realizing his thoughts had drifted in a direction he didn't want to pursue, he refocused on the task at hand. Jackson was anxious to get his schedule lined up for this last year and the future that awaited him. No longer focusing on the amber haired woman he redirected his attention to the slow moving line ahead of him and the list of classes he hoped still had openings.

Chapter Two

Mattie carried her sparse belongings in a small, worn duffle bag and her guitar in the ratty case in which it was cradled. The guitar meant more to Mattie than anything she had ever owned and considered it her most prized possession. Her precious friend Gracie had given it to her before she died, along with a host of memories that she would always treasure.

Gracie may have been in her seventies, blind and arthritic, but she had meant the world to a lonely girl with no other friends. Gracie knew more about her than her own mother probably had. Not that she would have ever said such a thing to her mother, but it was true, just the same. Of course, her mom had always worked so many hours that it had been natural for Mattie to turn to Gracie for companionship filling the lonely, empty hours she faced each day. Mattie couldn't stand her step-dad Frank, so when he stayed out all hours it kept her free of his unwanted company. Her mother slaved for little wage, while her useless husband drank and gambled it away. How he always made it look as if he were the breadwinner of the family was a joke to everyone who knew him and his nasty little habits. He gave new meaning to the terms lazy and shiftless. Needless to say, she learned her life lessons from the two women she adored and nothing from the man who used and abused all of them. She had learned one thing from him, she amended, how to stay away from anyone of his kind. A lesson she would never forget.

Gracie had always told Mattie, "Girly, you've got to spread your wings and fly, don't fall into a trap of foolish notions made by foolish people. You got to grab hold of the brass ring with both hands and hang on for dear life." Gracie always had such good advice and Mattie chose to take it every time she had offered it. The best advice Gracie had given her was "winners don't quit, and quitters don't win." Liz, her mother, told her over and over again, to always keep true to herself. The advice from both her favorite women had kept her going when all she wanted to do was crawl into a hole and pull it in after her. Their encouraging words had kept her sane during the trying times she had suffered over the last couple of years. Mattie no longer had the luxury of her mother or Gracie, so her memories and the lessons they taught her, kept her grounded and focused.

When Mattie finally made it to her dorm room she began unpacking the few worldly goods she cherished. The only photo's she owned were of her mother and Gracie and she proudly displayed them in new, untarnished frames on the little table by the bed. Her belongings, such as they were, came to her as compliments of the local Good-Will store. She was thankful she had managed to save enough money to buy the meager belongings needed for her transition into college life. Mattie had decided on comfortable clothes that she could change the looks of with a belt or a scarf. With limited finances, she had to be selective in her choice of outfits. College was a place she didn't want to stick out like a sore thumb. She wanted to blend into the background. Clothes were never a concern for her back home, but it would be in this place, so she had chosen several flower print tea length skirts with coordinating blouses, loose fitting shorts for the warmer weather, jogging pants to run in, and other items she felt were necessary for her college career. A career, she had only dreamt about before, was now her current reality.

When all her belongings were put in their prospective places, Mattie began to change her focus. Finding a job was her main concern right now and she needed to get busy looking into possible openings in the area. Her skills had been limited to working for the local grocery store, operating the register, and stocking shelves. That had been the only public job she'd ever had. There wouldn't be any problem if someone were in need of a tobacco hand, a housekeeper, or a cook. There was her talent with music, but Mattie knew without a doubt, she could not perform in public so there would be no job for her in that particular area. Mattie hadn't given much thought to how limited her choices were going to be until that very moment. Quick on the heels of that thought she felt the nerves knotting up in the pit of her stomach and the uncertainty that came with it.

With a deep resolve and gritting determination Mattie headed out and down the brick lined walkway that at present was rather crowded. Bumping into other college students and residents of the small city only heightened her fear of not finding a job. Mattie knew her scholarship would cover her educational expenses but the extras were going to be her responsibility. Gracie had always said, "When life gets tough, the tough get going," so with courage she didn't truly feel, she took a deep breath, and faked tough.

The day waned with empty promises of, "I'll let you know if a position opens up," or "Don't need any help," or the occasional, "Sorry." Mattie continued on her search for the remainder of the day. No opportunities presented themselves. Mattie didn't get angry, and he refused to give up. Tomorrow would be a new day.

After job hunting all day she felt the beginnings of fatigue come over her and sought out a park bench in the shade to rest a little before making her way back to the place she would be calling home. The sky was turning a brilliant red orange, as the sunset skimmed along the horizon, dipping down to kiss the edge of the earth. The sight of such beauty caused Mattie's breath to catch and had her missing home, all the more. There had been many days she had spent on her mountain mesmerized by the colors of an ending day and this gorgeous sunset reminded her of those times. After several restful minutes and feeling rejuvenated Mattie began the task of making her way down the crowded sidewalk. She was surprised that the setting sun could be just as beautiful as the one she loved to stare at in her meadow and found it reassuring in such a foreign place. It must be a sign from above that she could find home in a place so far from it.

Mattie headed home at a slower pace than she had started out at to keep from abusing her sore feet anymore than she already had. She had no job to speak of but as she placed one foot in front of the other she prayed that tomorrow would prove to be more fruitful.

Chapter Three

Mattie felt at peace and relaxed. The crowd had lessoned and the suns gentle descent made for a cooler walk home. It was a welcomed reprieve from the earlier heat. Gazing into the store windows as she passed by, unleashed her imagination, as it often did. Proving her momma was right in saying she was a dreamer with her head in the clouds. Gracie said it was a sign of artistic ability and infinite intelligence. Mattie preferred Gracie's comments because they provided her with the excuse to daydream without feeling guilty about it.

Searching the storefront window of an antique shop Mattie found herself gazing in and letting her thoughts drift, as she took in each object. Traveling in her head was her way of escaping reality. Imagining people and places with the objects she saw encouraged her to press her nose against the dusty window. Her eyes locked onto a well used rocker in the corner of the shop. It was almost identical to the one Gracie often sat in on her porch. The back of the chair was high and made of willow reeds, with a swayed seat from the many hours of use. If she closed her eyes she could see Gracie smiling down at her. Mattie loved to see that toothless smile spread across Gracie's age-lined face as she finished telling one of her many stories. A feeling of deep, dark loneliness swept over her, creating a surge of heat behind her eyes from the tears she knew were always close to the surface. Emotions welling up inside her forced Mattie to pull away from the shop window and redirect her focus on getting home. She couldn't face the emptiness that always pulled at her, dragging her into the abyss that beckoned her. At the crosswalk, while Mattie waited for the light to change, she was unaware that she had become the sole focus of one young mans total interest.

Piercing blue eyes, the color of the ocean, were focused on the mystery girl, again. Jackson had been casually watching for her, not expecting to see her so soon and yet there she was, right in front of him. He had no idea why he was so fascinated with the plain, ordinary, obviously shy lady but he found himself thinking about her at the oddest of times. He didn't understand the attraction he felt toward her but accepted it for what it was. There was just something about her that reached out to him on some emotional level and he felt he had to get to know her. The mere thought should have surprised him because she was not the usual type that he sought out.

Jackson had spent the afternoon working at the boat shop and found, no matter what repairs he was focused on, his thoughts would drift. The woman was constantly redirecting his attention from his work, to her. Now, here he was, staring at her with the compelling need to approach her and begin a

8

conversation. His curiosity was getting the better of him and it was time to replace fiction with some facts. That hair of hers was just as mesmerizing as it had been the first time he saw it swaying in the breeze. The color, the length, the way it shimmered in the sunlight, reminded him of the warm fall colors of autumn leaves. Long firm legs, that only an athlete could own, carried her tall frame with such unconscious grace she appeared to be gliding along the walkway instead of walking. He suspected she had a slim figure, but it was hard to determine with all the loose material covering her from waist to ankle. Jackson thought she purposely hid herself with the loose fitting clothes she seemed to have an affinity for. A deliberate ploy, he was sure, she implemented with great thought. She was such an interesting combination of beauty and simplicity he couldn't help but be intrigued by her.

When the wind kissed the material of her skirt it lightly caressed her thighs like a lover. The shy lady had a figure any model would envy as far as he was concerned. Jackson found himself gravitating toward her like a moth to a flame. "I must be losing my mind," whispered through his foggy brain, and yet he continued following the same path she had chosen without realizing he was doing so. His entire focus was consumed with the auburn haired beauty. He picked up his pace, shortening the distance between them, by weaving in and out of the meandering crowd trying to get even closer. Her long stride was graceful and fluid, like that of a dancer. Her movements were feminine, and purposeful, yet she kept her eyes averted from the crowd surrounding her. Actions, he felt, she had implemented to avoid interacting with anyone else. Making his way to her side he experienced a jolt seer through him like a lightening bolt. The true beauty of the mystery girl came into full view causing Jackson's stride to falter. The full impact of the package she presented registered in his brain so fast he almost staggered with its impact. His mystery girl was absolutely breathtaking. Sonnets were written about such beauty. Music was composed for such women. Stories were written so accolades would resound for years to come. Nothing he had heard to date could even begin to describe the face of an angel.

Had he, himself, almost dismissed her as mousy? God in heaven was he ever wrong, and in this case, he wasn't a bit ashamed to admit it. Her skin was satin smooth and the color of fresh, sweet honey. Jackson's assumption about her height was right she was rather tall, but still shorter than his six-two frame. Her lashes were long and thick, carrying the same color as her hair. Jackson surpassed being compelled to follow; he demanded to know more and forced his feet to move. His heart thundered in his chest and his breath caught in his lungs, as he walked by her side, hoping to get her attention and fearing he wouldn't. To his disappointment she didn't notice him. Ok, he thought, a little more directness was in order. "Excuse me?" he hesitated and waited far

9

longer than reasonable. He wondered briefly if she had a hearing disability. He hadn't given much thought to that possibility and was a little surprised that it didn't really matter to him. So the straightforward approach may be the only way to get her attention. "Hello," he waited again. Damned if he didn't think she was snubbing him. That wouldn't work with him, for he had been weaned on snobbery, and the upper class attitude, that went with it. Fate was working with him as the light changed, forcing the foot traffic to stop at a crosswalk. Jackson felt his luck begin to change with that act of intervention, by the powers that be. Never one to be accused of passing up an opportunity he swallowed his waning pride and tried again. "Hello there. My name is Jackson." He drew in a patient breath and continued to wait for her to respond.

Chapter Four

Mattie had heard every word he'd spoken to her, but to initiate a conversation by answering him? No, she wouldn't do that. She couldn't. Her only defense was to continue ignoring him. It had always worked in the past and she hoped it would work again with this persistent man. She remained silent and waited. Mattie liked his name and the voice that revealed it. He had a husky, slightly deep voice that sent a shiver down her spine with each word he spoke. Every nerve ending in her body tried to react at the same time causing the 'Flight or fight response' to kick into full gear. Talk to him? Not on your life!

Feeling his anger rise he couldn't contain the briskness he heard in his own voice. "Listen lady, all I wanted to do was introduce my self to you. What's your problem?" Jackson felt a deep disappointment that such beauty could have an ugly side to it. He really did want to talk and get to know her but Jackson was only willing to take so much. He usually wasn't a bad judge of character but it seemed he was in this instance. Maybe he didn't want to know her after all. Yeah, and who did he think he was fooling with that lie?

Mattie was battling her own mental war, what to do? What to say? How was she supposed to handle this? With her back ramrod straight and her nerves dancing a jig, Mattie forced herself to stop and face this man once and for all. "Good-bye," was all she could get past her constricted throat. This Jackson was a Greek god and here he was talking to her. She had always had the ability to memorize things easily. With a quick glance she could retain whatever she saw. Using that skill now she noted every detail she could before she dropped her gaze back to the walk. That ought to do it, she thought dejectedly as she continued walking away.

Jackson was left awestruck, tongue tied, frozen in place, struck dumb, and left totally breathless, just from the sight of such pure innocent beauty. Brush off be damned. He'd get over it. Jackson stood there with his mouth agape and stared as his goddess rapidly walked away. Shaking off the shock of seeing her up close and personal for the first time, he forced his feet to get busy, openly mumbling as he did so. "Feet don't fail me now! We are on a life or death mission here."

Did she really have eyes the color of whiskey, with flecks of gold and maybe a hint of silver in the irises? The colors reminded him of a tigers and he was sure there were other shades he couldn't even name. Jackson knew his heart was pounding so hard that it had to be visible from the outside. While he was demanding some foot action, he replayed the blatant brush off she had just bestowed on him. A major brush off, to be sure, yet he couldn't let her get away without finding out the reason for it. She could hear and she could obviously speak with ice-laced bitchiness, but Jackson wouldn't let that deter him. He just had to know her, had to talk to her, just had to everything, with her. He wouldn't give up so easily when he knew there was something between them, whether she knew it or not. Determination that bordered on stubbornness had been used to describe him often. Reality came crashing in on him when he realized that he still didn't know what her name was. A condition he would remedy and soon.

Mattie bolted like a pent up thoroughbred. Wasting time hanging around was not an option to her and getting away was her main concern. Mattie's heart was tripping like a jackhammer impaling itself with each beat. She was too scared to look back in the direction she had just left. She was afraid he would be on her heels. "I can't deal with this, I just… can't." Mattie muttered to herself as she continued on her march toward her new home, at such a pace that her muscles cramped, and her feet ached in the low-heeled sandals she cursed herself for wearing the second time today. A runner, she may be, but even her muscles had limits to the abuse they could take. Gathering her courage like a cloak, Mattie risked a quick glance over her shoulder to see if he was still there. Much to her relief, he wasn't. What she didn't understand was the odd sense of disappointment that followed on the heels of that relief.

A small sigh escaped her unpainted lips as she slowed her brisk pace to a more normal gait. She felt safety envelop her again. A zone she preferred to be in verses the fear and uncertainty she'd felt with Jackson's nearness just moments ago. Mattie couldn't stop her wandering mind from that beautiful man. He was so pretty to look at. Momma and Gracie would laugh like loons if they had heard her call a man pretty, but the description fit him well. She never paid much attention, or thought, to the opposite sex, never felt the desire to. Until now, that is. The tall, handsome man said his name was Jackson. It was a name she wouldn't forget anytime soon. She couldn't think of a time when a man had pursued her the way he had. Mattie liked how he was taller than she was. There was just something about a man being taller than the woman. With her being five-eleven in her bare feet he had to be over six foot as he had looked down at her when he faced her. He had the most beautiful, dark blonde hair she had ever seen on a man. Not that she had ever noticed such attributes on the opposite sex before, but she had noticed it on him. It was long, unbound, and draped over his shoulders, curling at the ends. Those shoulders were well defined, not overly broad like some weight lifter, but from hours of hard, physical labor she assumed. Jackson was the definition of a perfect male body. His eye color resembled the clear, blue ocean that seemed to take everything in at a glance. What surprised her most of all was the fact that she recalled anything at all. She had never noticed a man in the

12

way she had noticed Jackson. The way a woman notices a man. Usually, the fear of getting close to the male species would shatter any whimsical thoughts she may have entertained. Mattie never understood what made her the way she was, but Gracie always said, 'Time will tell Mattie girl, time will tell.' She was plagued with thoughts of broad shoulders, and deep blue eyes the rest of the way home.

Jackson was giving himself a real ass kicking for not moving a little faster behind her. He had no idea what her name was, or where she lived. The decision to find out had been made the minute he looked into those deep, troubled eyes. With an unexpected lightness in his step, he began to softly whistle a familiar tune, while endless possibilities for a new future drifted through his thoughts. "Yeah red, whoever you are, we will meet again. I promise you that."

Mattie was deep in thought when THE voice echoed and intruded on her private thoughts. She felt instant fear that ran bone deep, when his voice penetrated the warm feelings she had briefly enjoyed. Frank, the man she had never accepted as her father, had married her mother after a very brief courtship. She thanked God every day that it was not his blood that ran through her veins. He was a real bastard and she didn't like him, but kept the peace for her momma's sake. Words, she discovered, could hurt just as bad as a fist could. The hitting she could deal with, but the words were the worst of his abuses. Words could play over and over in your head like a CD stuck on repeat. She could still hear his sick taunts and hurtful comments. "Mattie you best keep them long legs of yours locked at the knees and keep them young pups from sniffing around here. You understand me missy? I won't stand for a floozy living under my roof, and by God you'd better pay me heed girl, because if ya don't there'll be hell to pay!"

Mattie shivered as if she'd been stripped to the skin and was left standing in three feet of snow. Her reaction to HIS voice was always a visceral one. It was terrifying and maddening at the same time. "I will not let you ruin my time here, not now, not tomorrow, not ever again!" With that said Mattie began to ease into a casual, steady pace as she made her way home. The overwhelming urge to run and hide had begun to ebb with each step she took, an urge she fought with great skill. Mattie soon found herself at her door and softly humming as she unlocked it, and swung it open. She almost screamed when she was greeted with a loud squeal that erupted from a short female standing in the middle of the room.

13

"A roomy! This is too good to be true. Here I was feeling sorry for myself and then you just waltz in here big as you please." A petite brunette bounced across the room and introduced herself as Rachael Hastings as she offered her hand for a welcoming handshake.

"Mattie Collins," she replied as she offered her own hand. Mattie felt herself smiling at her new roommate's enthusiasm and bright smile. Rachael was a little-bitty thing, being five-feet tall, give or take, with well toned muscles. Her hair was short and the color of midnight black, with large corkscrew curls covering her head. She had eyes the color of dark chocolate with long sweeping lashes that enhanced her pixie features.

A quick survey of the room revealed an excess of CD's, spandex, dumb bells, and several pairs of sneakers. Her roommate was a fitness junkie with all those accessories and a well toned body to prove it. Mattie would bet that even though Rachael was tiny she could take care of anything that came her way. She envied that quality, especially in a female.

While Mattie inspected Rachael, Rachael was inspecting her in return. Noting Mattie's natural beauty and her understated attire, she wandered why she hadn't enhanced what she was born with. Guys probably fell all over her and on the heels of that thought, she decided that was exactly why she dressed down and wore no makeup. Rachael wandered what had happened in the girl's life to cause her to hide such pretty assets. Bet I'll have you figured out in a week or less, she thought smugly. It was obvious that her new roommate was shy and quiet, but that was ok. She had an endless supply of chatter for both of them. She had always been open and friendly with every one and wandered what she was getting into with this tight-lipped beauty that she would be living with for quite awhile.

Mattie's suspiciousness kicked in without warning, making her words sound harsher than she had intended. "Why are you here?"

Rachael having a quick temper and a sharp tongue answered just as curtly. "To get an education just like you, I would imagine, and what might your problem be?"

"I'm sorry... Rachael." Mattie stammered. "I didn't mean to snap at you."

Realizing how much effort it took Mattie to apologize, cooled Rachael's anger somewhat, and she managed a tight-lipped smile. "Apology accepted. What kind of degree is it you're going for? I plan on finishing my degree in sports medicine, or I may still decide on physical therapy." Sighing and shaking her head she hated being undecided. "I'm still thinking about it. Either way it will involve fitness. It's what I love to do."

Rachael heard Mattie's answer, with great effort, that she was entering into early education. She couldn't help but notice the nervousness Mattie exhibited. She always liked a good challenge and Mattie, it appeared, was going to be a huge one. All the more fun, she thought, as she smirked at Mattie. The room fell into a companionable silence.

Rachael realized the conversation was over as she watched Mattie meticulously put away mementoes that consisted of some small photos and knick-knacks. She knew beyond a shadow of a doubt that she and Mattie would become good friends. She had a sixth sense when it came to people and she had a positive feeling about her new roommate.

Mattie quietly watched, with an eerie intensity, as Rachael placed many of her family mementoes on the bare shelves.

Rachael was feeling a little like a germ under a microscope. So being who and what she was, decided to handle this in her usual straightforward manner. Turning to face Mattie she casually spoke of the college and the classes, area interests, local attractions, and anything she could think of, including family. It was obvious that subject was off limits, so she changed the subject, and continued carrying the conversation.

Once Mattie left for the bathroom Rachael felt an overwhelming need to snoop, openly though, with no real digging. That was too personal. She immediately noticed the limited number of personal objects Mattie had put on her dresser. Small photos of an old woman and a much younger one decorated the surface. The younger woman had to be Mattie's mother because the resemblance was uncanny. She could see where Mattie got her looks. Rachael couldn't help wandering if there was a father in the family unit but dismissed that thought since it was a common occurrence these days, but if there was one, he didn't warrant a place on her shelf.

Rachael felt the need to help Mattie with her new transition into college life since she was an old pro with all its props. She knew she could help Mattie adjust, especially since she seemed so shy and withdrawn. Rachael took it as her personal goal to discover the real Mattie Collins.

Upon re-entering the room Mattie came to an abrupt stop. She wasn't used to people looking at her things.

Rachael must have sensed her unease, because she began apologizing when she saw the look on her roommates face. Mumbling "sorry" must have done the trick because the coldness left Mattie's face and she smiled at Rachael. "It's ok," she whispered.

Rachael noticed the hint of an accent before and yet she couldn't place it. "Where are you from Mattie?" Her curiosity always got the better of her. Mattie spoke so softly Rachael felt herself leaning toward her so she wouldn't miss the answer.

"Kentucky," came from her as a sigh at the tail end of a gentle breeze.

"I should have picked up on the accent somewhat since my parents and I used to go to the Kentucky Derby when I was younger. Your accent sounds a little different from the ones I remember hearing at the track though, why is that?" The silence stretched as Rachael waited for Mattie to answer her question. Finally, when Rachael thought she wasn't going to get an answer, Mattie spoke. "I'm from Eastern Kentucky and most people say the accent is stronger there than some of the other areas. I never noticed it myself since we all sound alike."

Pride was evident when Mattie spoke. Rachael could only smile. "Oh, I like it. It has a rhythm to it, musical almost." Mattie smiled and turned to her side of the room again. Rachael didn't see the smile turn into a frown as a faint memory of her long forgotten stepfather seeped into her thoughts only to be replaced with lightening speed by the thought of her mom and Gracie. Mattie didn't understand exactly why she had an overwhelming sense of fear take over when her stepfather skidded into her thoughts, but she knew not to dwell on it as Gracie had taught her to do.

Mattie's thoughts also consisted of this little dynamo she had for a roommate and she decided she really liked her. Mattie knew she would be a good friend if given the chance and a chance was what Mattie was going to take with her new life. Mattie didn't want to waste any new chances that came her way.

Rachael interrupted Mattie's thoughts with more questions and she smiled because she had known there would be plenty more. "Mattie you said the Eastern part, right? Well, um, is that like the hills and hollers you hear about so often? Like the Hatfield's and the McCoy's kind of thing?" She worried her bottom lip waiting for Mattie's reply hoping she hadn't offended her.

"Yes, that's right. Why?" She was curious as to why Rachael needed to know.

"Way cool!" The excitement was thick and heady and Rachael was grinning from ear to ear. "You mean the moonshine, and shooting, and revenuers and all that kind of stuff?"

"Well, yes that's the way history has it and in some areas stills are said to be in full operation to this day." Mattie quickly shied away and wouldn't face Rachael. Rachael understood the sudden change in Mattie and quickly worked at ridding her of any negative thoughts or fears she may have. "Don't worry Mattie, I won't say anything. I was just curious and besides I think its terrific being from a rural area with such great history."

"You do?" Mattie's surprised expression made Rachael chuckle.

"Yeah, I do. The hills of Ky. are famous, interesting to study, and besides, that was a vital way of life to a lot of people." Rachael hoped she hadn't offended her further.

"There was no other way of surviving the hard times for some. Simple living, farming to make ends meet, and raising your family was part of the history not many were interested in. Most of the time that's what made the hills home to a lot of us." Mattie ended the conversation with that and went to her side of the room to sit on her small bed leaving Rachael to wander what brought such a lonely, sad expression to Mattie's face.

Rachael decided to talk about herself so the subject was changed to her own loving family. Her family consisted of her mom and dad because she had no other siblings. She was a native Californian, among many other interesting tidbits, including the fact that she had been in this college area for the past couple of years.

Mattie couldn't help feeling a little excited with that information because if Rachael had been here before she must know if there were any job openings somewhere around town that was close to the campus. Asking her was going to be hard for Mattie because she had always depended upon herself for everything and didn't know how to ask for what she desperately needed. While lost in her thoughts Rachael finished her unpacking and chatted about things that Mattie hadn't heard.

"...Isn't that what you think, Mattie?" As she was brought back into the conversation she had no idea what it was Rachael had been saying. "I'm sorry what were you saying?" She tired to pretend she had heard what Rachael had been saying to her but Rachael knew by the faraway look on Mattie's face that she wasn't paying attention. Most people would have been bothered by that, but not Rachael. So she teased Mattie. "Weren't you listening to me?" She pouted with an extended lower lip, pretending hurt feelings.

"I must be tired; it's been a long day for me." Mattie lowered her head as if she were ashamed of being caught. Rachael regretted the teasing the second she saw the look that crossed Mattie's face.

"Hey, don't sweat it. First couple of weeks is a real drag for everyone." Rachael continued to chatter about classes in a week and settling in, but what caught Mattie's attention was the last statement about a job. If Rachael didn't have her attention before she sure had it now. "I work at a local popular hang out and have since I started college here. I'm a waitress there. Joey, he's the owner, is always in need of some dependable help if your interested in a job. The pay is pretty good, you keep the tips you make, and the place is clean. The most important two things are is it's an alcohol free hangout and the boss is the greatest you will ever have the pleasure of working for. So Matt, I can call you Matt can't I? Are you interested in a job?"

17

Mattie's head shot up, as she couldn't believe her good luck. She spoke with some reservations. "What's this place called?"

"Oh, it's called Waves and if you knew Joey you'd know why. You see, he was and still is a professional surfer and trainer. Since he loved to hit the waves so much he thought the name was perfect for his hangout. So, hence, the name he chose was Waves. Listen, if you're interested in the work just let me know and I will put in a good word for you."

"I've been looking all over the place for a job and haven't had any luck yet. How is it this place has openings and no one else does?" Mattie was a little apprehensive with the sudden job opportunity after searching all over with no openings to be found.

"Well, that's easy enough. The work is pretty tough at times and a lot of the kids around here don't want to work if they can get by with it. It's easier to let their parents support there lazy butts," the last statement being said with a snicker since Rachael could easily do the same thing. However, being overly independent she wanted to work and support herself as much as possible. The socializing alone was better than the money she earned. Rachael had always been a people person and so Waves was the perfect place to work. "So are you interested?" Pouncing on Mattie's silence she quickly added "Joey even provides all the employees with a free lunch during your shift."

Rachael didn't mention the long hours on your feet, the constant ribbing by the rowdy bunch, and of course the frequent need of covering for the 'no-shows-who-work-when-they-want-too-employees,' as Joey referred to them. Rachael didn't want to discourage Matt before she even took the job. Reading people was always a skill of Rachael's and she had a feeling about this girl. She knew the job would be Mattie's if Joey were to be asked by the right person and that right person was Rachael.

"Well, I've been looking for a job ever since I got here and waiting tables or cleaning doesn't scare me one bit, I like to work and I'm dependable. I'd like the chance if the job is still available." Mattie was almost giddy with the thought of having a job just fall into her lap and she would owe Rachael for that opportunity. "I really need a job Rachael my money is low and I can't count on my scholarship for every thing I need." She didn't want to sound so desperate but a job meant security, which meant survival, and surviving was what she did best.

Mattie said that with such truth it touched Rachael's heart. "Don't you worry about a thing Matt," and she smiled brightly, "Joey, the boss man, Sharp will be happy to have you come to work for him. I'll talk to him first thing tomorrow but in case he asks do you have any experience?" As soon as she said it she wished the words back into her big mouth as she watched the gradual disappointment slide onto Mattie's face. "No matter, waiting tables is

18

not so bad and is easy enough to get your own rhythm set into place the longer your there. I aught to know I had no experience when I was hired either and now I'm one of the best there, if I do say so myself. And I do!" The smile on Mattie's pale face was enough to lighten the mood and to let her know that it was ok for now. Mattie was relieved that there might be some light at the end of the tunnel and with that relief came the near exhaustion she felt. Gathering her meager toiletries and her old flannel gown she headed for the tub for a nice hot bath.

In the small apartment they shared Rachael watched as Mattie headed toward the bathroom and couldn't help thinking how beaten Mattie had looked. To Rachael's way of thinking she seemed lost and so alone it was almost heart breaking. Rachael couldn't figure it out. Mattie was a very nice person. Shy yes. Quiet definitely. But why did she seem like she didn't have a soul in the world? Most people would kill for the looks she had, hell even she would. Mattie had long runner's legs, waist length hair the color of autumn leaves that either had the remnants of an old perm or she was one lucky chick if that curl was natural. Mattie was at least five-ten, five-eleven in her bare feet and that alone made Rachael drool since she herself was a scant five-two and that was only when she was wearing her tennis shoes. The looks added to the body were like the icing on the cake. Mattie had the oddest eyes she had ever seen because they were golden with yellow flecks, almost cat like. To top it all off the girl had dimples and moved with feline grace that she was sure made the guys do a double take. Yet, Rachael had the impression that Mattie wasn't aware of herself or how others saw her. She was sure Mattie had perfected the means for hiding her outer beauty with great skill and wandered about the 'why' of it for the second time today.

Most girls Rachael knew of who had that kind of package usually were very aware of what God gave them and shamelessly flaunted it. Rachael wandered what could make a beautiful woman like Mattie keep people at arm's length when she could easily have a flock of followers. It appeared she didn't like having her personal space invaded because she would discreetly pull away as soon as Rachael got too close for comfort. Being a people person and a hugger Rachael knew when to keep a distance and it appeared Mattie was one of those people that just didn't need the physical contact as she did. That was the only thing that could be a potential problem working at Waves but she would worry about that when the time came.

Enough already, she thought as she continued with her housekeeping and adding her own personal touch to the limited living quarters. It was amazing how quickly she transformed her area into a personal den but as her eyes drifted to the other side of the room she couldn't help focusing on the scarce material objects that were Mattie's. There were secrets about her roommate and Rachael was determined to figure out what they were. Eventually, she would find out. She always did.

When Mattie came back into the room she couldn't help notice how much of a change had occurred with her roommate's side of the room. The bookshelf almost transformed into a video rental alongside the TV/VCR/DVD combination that Rachael had brought in with her.

The wrinkle in her brows got Rachael's attention and of course she commented on it. "Is there a problem Matt?" She noted the shift in Mattie's attention to the floor and the slumping in her tall frame. She swore she saw bleakness fill her eyes and a shadow crossed her face before she could avert her gaze. "Matt, you don't mind about the bookshelf do you? I mean I can clear off a lot if you need the space. Really, it won't be a problem, just say the words and it'll be done." Rachael waited patiently for an answer she wasn't sure she would get.

"I was just looking at all those exercise videos. Do they all belong to you?" She was such a soft-spoken person that Rachael had to strain to hear most of what she said when she spoke.

"Remember I said I was into fitness? Well, this is one of my pastimes. I watch a lot of videos for new moves and to keep in shape; it's just what I do. You don't mind those do you?" Rachael watched and waited. She didn't count on a roomy that would have a fit if she were to do her workouts. This was her daily routine. Sports medicine was her goal in life and fitness had always been part of her. Even she had a hard time remembering when she hadn't crunched, twisted, and stretched.

Mattie finally answered a low voiced "No," and went to her bed.

Rachael shrugged her shoulders because she knew the conversation was over and accepted it. Making her way to the shower herself Rachael noticed the guitar leaning along the far wall and figured what the heck and looked over her shoulder to ask, "Do you play that thing or is it for looks and luck?" Well that certainly got her attention.

"Huh?" Mattie had never met anyone who just blurted out every thought that jumped into her head and she wasn't sure she cared for it much.

"Never mind, I was just curious if you actually played." With that said she headed for the bathroom but after two steps she heard Mattie's low voice in answer.

"Oh, well, yes I do, ever since I was a little girl back home."

"Hey, that's great! I love music so you'll have to play for me sometime. Look at my collection over there." Mattie's attention was drawn to a huge stack of compact discs that Rachael was pointing at. Nodding at the sight she told Rachael she would be glad to play for her sometime.

Chapter Six

The following day proved to be a little warmer than predicted however Mattie didn't pay much attention to the heat. Her focus was on the beauty the day offered. The sun greeted her with a warm kiss and a casual embrace. The breeze was light and mildly fragrant with the scent of roses. A beautiful day that reminded her of her meadow back home and the thought made her smile just a little. Thoughts of home filled her mind with long ago days spent with her mother and Gracie. Closing her eyes she allowed herself to feel their presence with her but that feeling was soon replaced with the pain that always came. The pain of being alone brought with it the all too familiar tightening in her chest and the burning behind her eyes. The threatening tears demanded a release that Mattie would not allow. Holding her head up to the bright sunlight she took several deep breaths and opened her eyes to new beginning's and new tomorrows.

Rachael being unable to go with her today promised to call Joey about the job first thing and she did just that. Before leaving the room Rachael was on the phone with Joe as it appeared he liked to be called the shortened version of his name. Rachael gave her the thumbs up as she hung up the phone. "Looks like you're on your way Mattie. Joey said to ask for him when you get there and you two could discuss the job, pay, benefits, and all that other stuff." With directions in hand and a wave in the right direction Mattie was on her way.

Rachael wasted no time dialing Waves again when Mattie left the small room. She wanted to talk with Joey while Mattie couldn't hear her. "Waves, how can I help you?" He answered in his usual baritone voice. Rachael smiled at the sound of Joey's voice because he was a great guy, friend and boss. "Hey, Joey listen I...,"

"Rachael didn't I just talk to you? What's wrong? Are you sick? Are you calling in for tonight? Speak up damn it! What gives?" Joey could feel his pulse pick up. Rachael was his best girl and this would be one of his busy nights. Joey really liked the little whirlwind and she carried more than her fair share of the workload; more than any of the other staff she worked with and he could not do without her tonight.

"Is that concern I hear in your voice Joe, are you worried about little ole me?" She couldn't stop the wide grin from creeping across her pixie face even if she tried. Which she didn't!

Joey coughed a little to hide his slip of genuine concern and informed her he just couldn't find a descent replacement on such short notice. They both knew it to be the lie it was, but neither commented on it as such. "So, why a second call, miss me so soon?" He couldn't help teasing Rachael she was always such a good sport and she usually gave as good as she got.

"Of course I miss you pops, but now is not the time to flirt. I have a huge favor to ask of you concerning the girl I told you about a couple minutes ago." Waiting, and twisting the phone cord around her fingers, she wandered if he heard her.

"I'm so crushed Rachael, 'pops' that really gets a man where it hurts." Smiling into the phone when he heard her sudden gasp. "Gotcha," he thought with a little satisfaction.

"Joey, you know I was only..." she trailed off at his sudden burst of laughter. The weasel was teasing and he'd got her. "Damn," she swore and smiled from ear to ear.

"Oh yeah, I got you and you know it. Ha! You're getting slow Rache. Now who's the pop's in this conversation?" Joey loved it when he could get her at her own game since it didn't happen often. Rachael was a damn smart young woman and besting her was not easy.

"Ok, ok, but listen. I really do need to talk to you about Mattie before she shows up there. I know she really needs this job and she's so shy I don't think she can get a job anywhere else. Mattie told me she looked for hours yesterday and she had no luck so I was wandering if you could hire her in Wendy's place. I know she's not experienced and she's shy but there is something about her. Well, she seems lost and almost empty Joe. Just try to keep an open mind, please?" Enough said, she had never asked this of Joey before and she hoped he wouldn't be angry for the asking of it. Rachael didn't think it would be a problem since Joey did a lot of volunteer work at the shelters. He was a giving man and he would never turn his back on someone in need.

"Rache, it's true I need the help with Wendy blowing out of here without notice but you of all people know how hard the work is and how long the training takes. I always like to help out but why are you pushing this girl? You haven't before, so why is this one so special?" Joey would have hired Mattie anyway since he needed the help but his curiosity was demanding him to find out why Rachael was pleading this girl's case and to him of all people. Everyone on the down and outs was always his priority. He knew what it was like to be in dire straits and always helped when he could.

"I can't put my finger on it Joey but when you meet her you'll see what I mean. Mattie has had some history that wasn't too good. I'd bet my future on it. I just want to help her out and if a job will do that then it won't hurt to ask for a favor to accomplish it."

"You really like this Mattie don't you? I've never had you go to bat for anyone before. If it means so much to you then I won't disappoint you." Joey

22

was proud of Rachael for helping someone in need but it didn't surprise him in the least. She was an open, loving person and she gave it her all in everything she did. This situation was no exception.

"You're a good man Joey. Thank you. I like Mattie and I'd wager my next paycheck that you will to. She has some quality about her that pulls you to her like a magnet to metal. Let me know how it turns out. Better yet, don't. Mattie will tell me in her own way, and Joey thanks, for being such a good friend." With that the phones were put in their usual resting places and thoughts were centered on one young woman with a need.

Mattie had no trouble finding the place Rachael called Waves. The building was bigger than she had imagined and the bigger the building the better her chances were of getting a job. Ignoring a major case of nerves Mattie entered the brick building and tried to avoid her hearts attempt to jump out of her rib cage. "I can do this," she told herself on a sigh and continued on through the heavy mahogany doors that bracketed the opening to Waves.

Mattie was on cloud nine as she walked out of Waves into a much brighter day. Mattie had not only gotten the job but with good pay and benefits. Rachael was right about the boss. Joey was a real nice person and he didn't make her feel uncomfortable at all. Mattie felt she was making progress. Life was improving with each day that passed. If she had been able to see herself she would be surprised at the expression she was wearing. She had a job. A job, a roommate, and two people who have gone out of their way to welcome a stranger that had the potential of becoming good friends in the future. That appealed to Mattie, as nothing else had. The idea of having friends caused her heart to warm and thump a pleasant rhythm. Without conscious thought there was a bounce in her step and lightness in her soul, that was lacking before. Mattie's goals and determination were easing her into a life she had only dreamt about or overheard in someone else's conversations. She hadn't realized how badly she wanted to succeed or to fit in until this very moment in time. It was an uplifting sensation and she welcomed it with arms wide open.

Mattie was excited to tell Rachael she had gotten the job and to thank her for her help. Mattie was still reeling from getting the job but was totally knocked sideways that Joey expected her to begin work tonight. Mattie could still hear those words as they left Joey's lips. It made her nervous just thinking about the moment he had asked her.

"How about starting tonight?" Joey had asked.

"Excuse me?" Mattie swallowed hard and whispered her response.

"Well, you wanted the job and I'm short handed tonight since Wendy quit without any notice. So, how about giving a guy a break and start the job tonight?" The look on her face was total disbelief and fear all rolled up into one. "Since Rachael is working too, it'll be a perfect time to start your training with my best employee." He couldn't keep from smiling at her. Rachael, as usual, was right about Mattie. She was skittish and extremely shy but there was something about her that appealed to him, not anything bad, but there was something. He knew it would come to him in time.

"Ok, if you're sure I won't be a problem for Rachael. I would be happy to start tonight." Mattie was still feeling a little queasy that she had agreed without giving much thought to it.

Joey thought that whispered tone of hers would eventually be wiped out in the crowds and he hoped she wouldn't let it be a problem for her. He couldn't help admiring her looks; she was a knock out in his book. "If only I were about twenty years younger," he whispered to the empty room. Shaking his head at his own foolish thoughts, he continued to watch as Mattie walked out the front door.

Mattie took her time walking back to her new home savoring the weather and her good fortune. She felt the happiest she'd been in a very long time and she just couldn't keep from smiling. Something she didn't do much these days. Mattie thought about the interview and the new boss she had. Joey was very nice and easy to talk to. Not one time did he make her feel uncomfortable like most men did and she liked him almost immediately. She hadn't experienced the wariness that usually accompanied face- to- face conversations with strangers. Joey was a handsome man and he wasn't too old, probably in his forties, she'd guess. He was tall like her and very much in shape. He had a muscular build, trim waist, and long legs that made her wonder if he ran like she did. His hair was still black but the gray was beginning to show through at the temples. He had a strong face that had smiled often if the laugh lines were any indication. "I like him," she whispered in the breeze as she made her way down the walk.

Joey was cleaning the bar top off when the shrilling echo of the phone rang in his ear. A full bodied smile crossed his face as he could almost guess with certainty that the caller was none other than the little busy body right on schedule. "Waves, what can I do you for?"

"Well," in a sing-songy voice, "how'd it go, Joe?" She wasn't quite breathless but he would recognize Rachael's voice anywhere. Feeling the need to tease her for her nosiness he began the game.

"Who is this; do I know you young lady?"

"Now cut that out Joey you know exactly who it is and I'm dying to know how it went." Rachael couldn't keep the amusement out of her voice.

Joey started laughing deep in his throat, "Yeah, nosy rosy, I know who it is and what is it you want to know, huh?" He was still chuckling at the huffing sound his little dynamo was making.

"You should be ashamed of yourself, a man your age taunting young defenseless women of my stature. Shame on you." She even tsk-tsked several times for the added wounded effect she hoped to achieve. "The weasel," she thought.

"Did I, no I didn't hear you say, it couldn't have been, defenseless, could it? Rachael honey you are anything but defenseless, so drop it little munchkin and one more word about my age and I wont tell you one single thing leaving the telling to Mattie who, as I can tell, isn't much of a talker and probably wouldn't tell you much." He knew that would get her so he waited. It didn't take long either.

"Awe hell! Ok, I'm sorry. Now, on with business, what happened? You did hire her right? Please tell me you..."

"Hold it, who's doing the telling you or me? Now hush up so I won't have to repeat myself." He loved cutting her off because it always unnerved her a little. He couldn't hide the smile if he tried, so he didn't. Rachael growled at him. That was her I'm getting pissed sound so it was time to quit bugging the girl. "Ok, ok don't blow a gasket. Before you hang and quarter me I'll tell you I really like Mattie and it went fine, she got the job. But what I don't understand is why you didn't tell me?" He tried for serious but failed at it miserably.

"Uh, tell ya what Joe?" She was going to give as well as he could.

"That, that girl was positively gorgeous that's what," and in that he didn't stretch the truth a bit.

"Now Joe why would I want to tell you something you were going to see with your own eyes anyway?" She caught the tone of appreciation from him. He may be in his forties but he still appreciated pretty women and treated them with respect.

"Well that's true enough, but..." a little warning wouldn't have left him staring like some damned fool teenager.

"Mattie is pretty but I don't think she's aware of it. I mean no make-up, her clothes say 'Hands Off,' and she's as skittish as a new colt."

"I got the message Rache, I'll watch out for her while she's here when you're not. Speaking of which; she will work with you tonight but don't let on that you know, let her tell you the news. On that note I'll see you two at six o'clock sharp."

"Hey, Joey thanks. I know you won't regret it. You're a great guy. I just can't believe someone hasn't snatched you up yet." This was an old comment and an area he didn't talk about. "Now Rache you know you're too young for me," was as his usual reply.

"See ya later Joe." She sighed as she hung up the phone. Thinking how happy she was that she could help someone in need Rachael went about her routine while waiting for Mattie to come home.

Mattie was making her way further down the walkway not really thinking of anything in particular. Wandering and window-shopping not intent on one thing and smiling at her good fortune; she was employed.

Chapter Seven

Jackson was making his way back to the boat shop after a side trip for a sandwich and a drink for lunch. He really loved working at the boat shop. Boats were his passion. Not just sailing them but fixing them, selling them, admiring them, hell everything concerning boats was his idea of a great way to spend his time. Since his move here he thought it would be hell on earth however, Jackson soon discovered this place was exactly where he needed to be. Finding Shorty's had been the best discovery that could have happened to him. He was prepared for the College scene but finding this shop with a great boss was what made it all the more enjoyable. The boat shop turned out to be his constant refuge and Shorty was great to be around. There wasn't much he didn't seem to know about boats and the operation of them. He admired the old man greatly and excelled with the confidence Shorty had in him. Something he had rarely felt when he was growing up.

Today Shorty had asked Jackson to man the shop while he went out and that proved to him that Shorty trusted him. Jackson absorbed the attention like a dry sponge and he was sure his boss and friend knew it. Jackson hooked up with Shorty when he first came to live here and they had hit it off immediately. Shorty had allowed him to use the back of the shop when he wanted to so he could work on his own schooner. That is when he was free of his chores for the shop. Shorty had good ideas for his boat and helped him with those ideas when time allowed. Jackson smiled to himself when he thought of owning his own company one day and selling his own boats, made from his own designs. For now, being an assistant, served him well with his education on the business and how to make it a successful one.

"Man it's still hot as blue blazes out there Jackson," words rushed out on a puff of hard earned breath by the very man he was thinking about. Jackson couldn't help the smirk on his face since this was the same greeting Shorty had almost every time he ventured outside. Shorty may have been an old seabird but he certainly didn't like the heat of the sun beating down on his balding head.

"Bad is it?" Knowing full well what the answer would be but Jackson asked just as he had every time Shorty had said it.

"Man, I bet you could cook an egg on the sidewalk. Landlubber's hell! Give me the water and the cool breeze she carries, any day," he said with full-faced grin behind a solid white beard. Same old comment always brought on that grin of his and Jackson couldn't help but smile back at the old man. Shorty had the mind of teenager and the actions of one as well.

"Well, Heat or no heat, I need to get going. You call me if you need me before Saturday ok?" That being said Jackson headed for the door with his designs stuffed into the back pocket of his Levis, a brand he'd favored all his life. With a little bounce in his step, as there usually was after working at the shop, Jackson headed down the sidewalk toward his apartment. A good cold beer would do him well after the busy day he'd had at the shop.

Turning down Main Street, Jackson took a few steps and froze in his tracks without warning. A heavyset lady wearing a flowered moo-moo and house slippers plowed right into his back knocking him forward like a child's ball. Jackson's site never wavered even though he staggered like a drunk to avoid a potential fall. The look the fat lady gave him could have frozen sherbet but it didn't phase Jackson one bit. He had eyes for only one thing at that point and time. In passing all he heard was a mumbled complaint about blondes and good sense. Good sense, he had. Jackson had enough good sense to keep his eyes fixated on the one object that had consumed his every waking hour.

Chapter Eight

Mattie stood gazing into the wide store front window admiring all the antique displays arranged in such a way as to catch the passerby's attention. So intent on all the objects before her, Mattie didn't witness the commotion taking place at the end of the sidewalk or the steady stare of the blonde haired man. She smiled at the site of the little antique doll swaddled in a crocheted blanket lying in a little wooden cradle. Mattie remembered cradling one almost identical to this one when she was just a little girl. She had spent many hours in the meadow rocking and cuddling that baby doll and her heart warmed with the memory this doll had brought back to her. Time surely changed things, even if age didn't.

"That's her," he whispered to himself as he continued to stare. Focusing intently as he slowly moved with the crowd of shoppers he could see a dimple kissing the side of her luminescent cheek. In the background the squeal of tires and the honking of horns barely registered in his transfixed state. The sounds apparently caught her attention though and as the girls face turned to the direction the sounds had come from, it was as if Father time slowed her movements to enjoy her beauty in slow motion. Jackson's breath caught in his throat and seemed to lodge there. The only coherent thought he could manage was how breathtakingly beautiful his auburn haired angel really was. The hair had caught his attention the first time he saw her but her face outshined that by leaps and bounds. Jackson hadn't realized he had even moved until he found himself standing right beside her. It was as if his body knew what to do when he couldn't even think straight.

Mattie began to turn her attention back to the store window only to come face to face with a god. "It's him," she thought. Mattie felt the air whoosh out of her like she'd been hit in the stomach. He was starring right at her. Mattie stood transfixed by the depths of his deep blue eyes. Her heart began to pound out a beat so loud she could hear it in her ears. People bumped past the two young lovebirds, they thought, and yet neither Jackson nor Mattie could seem to move out of the way. Movement of any kind seemed to be impossible.

Mattie mentally tried to recall one of her usual commands that she would use in this type of situation and yet none seemed to come to mind at the moment. She just couldn't seem to move or blink or even breathe for that matter. Mattie thought he was the most handsome man she'd ever seen. He had looked angry the day she had met him before and she had made herself not look at him. She'd had her own problems at the time. Now, she could only look at him and think her earlier assessment of him was accurate, as well as, lacking. Mere words could not have done the man justice.

Jackson felt as if he had died and gone to heaven. He was far from dead and he was definitely looking at heaven. "Never have I seen anyone as beautiful as you," he whispered as he drank in the picture of her. Who needed beer to drink when the sight of her quenched a deeper thirst?

Jackson could see she was experiencing the same feelings as he was and yet she was fighting it for all she was worth. A shout brought an abrupt change in her. She suddenly stiffened and fled as if the hounds of hell were on her feet. Jackson attempted to call her but the sidewalk was too crowded and he could feel her slipping away with every step she took. The back of her was ebbing away like the tides of the ocean. "Damn it," he cursed loudly. If he had moved faster he would have caught up with her but he had been so mesmerized by her that he'd stood frozen to the spot. Frustration like none he had ever experienced took hold of him when he realized he still didn't know her name. The chance of finding out was much less than it had been just minutes before. "Who the hell are you?" He said to himself not realizing he had spoken out loud causing some on-lookers next to him to stare as if he had grown two heads. Shaking his head and smiling Jackson continued along the walkway with the rest of the civilized cattle.

Mattie ran like the wind but felt as if she were weighted down. The man's voice barely penetrated her frozen mind as he called to her. Mattie knew she wouldn't answer him, she couldn't. Too many years of ingrained fear and demands from her step-father kept her from it. Mattie kept going without any destination in mind except to escape. After several blocks had passed with each of her hurried steps she felt she could finally slow her pace down. Knowing her retreat wasn't enough Mattie ducked into one of the shops that lined the street and to her surprise she had landed in antique bookstore. Leaning heavily on the shops door she tried to catch the breath that she lost either due to the pace of her escape or from the nearness of Jackson. Such a beautiful name for such a handsome young man and for those reasons alone she wondered why he was after her? Mattie smiled to herself and said his name again in a hushed whisper and then realized with a start how she had treated him. A sadness she couldn't explain gripped her and she sincerely hoped that he wouldn't hate her for running away from him. Jackson wouldn't have given someone like her a second thought so Mattie's concern, she felt, was wasted. Mattie knew she was a nameless face in the crowd. Deep in her own berating thoughts Mattie hadn't noticed the movements at the counter in the center of the room.

"May I help you young lady?" penetrated Mattie's thoughts. She realized she wasn't alone. Mattie forced her attention on a little old lady who was bent

30

with age and looking up at her. Mattie found her attention drawn to a hazy pair of gray eyes shrouded with the wrinkles of life and laughter. The little women's smile wrapped her face like a package at Christmas, filled with mischief and joy. Mattie found her eyes drawn to the old women's solid white hair that trailed down her shoulder in a fascinating braid that brushed her waist. Mattie felt comfortable in her presence, a feeling she rarely experienced in the face of a stranger.

"Miss, can I help you with something?" The shop owner asked again with knowledgeable assessing eyes.

"No thank you," she whispered past her dry throat as she gazed out into the little shop. "You have a very nice shop here. Would you mind if I looked around? I just love books because you can see the whole world and experience it without ever leaving your room." And that was what Mattie had always felt. She could be anybody, anytime she wanted to, when she read a novel. What she didn't experience in her empty life she did experience through the written word.

The shopkeeper grunted. "Miss, books are my business look all you want and if there's anything you want just give a yell and I'll be right there. Of course it will take a while to get there since I'm not as young as I used to be." The old woman chuckled.

"Thank you Ma'am," whispered Mattie.

"The name is Sarah sweetie, just give a holler if you need me, I'll be over there" she pointed toward the counter smiling up at the pretty young thing that looked as nervous as cat in a room full of rocking chairs.

Mattie began to make her way along the stacks of the books contained in the wide shelves that reached up to the ceiling. Just walking among the familiar bound novels unraveled the nerves she had been experiencing when she first snuck into the little shop. Making her way toward the back of the building Mattie noticed that Sarah had a large selection of used books too. Some were worn and some looked almost new. Mattie smiled at the site because to her they were more affordable with the limited budget she had. Thumbing the faded spines of the volumes so closely packed had a relaxing effect on her. Intent on the volumes at her height she almost missed those located in the corner towards the floor. Bending at the knees Mattie squatted and carefully eyed each worn book scanning the titles. Just as Mattie began to look at another shelf of books a small, much worn, hand sized book caught her eye. Without hesitation Mattie pulled the little red book out and caught her breath. Homesickness for her meadow and her flower fields and the good parts of her past assailed her causing the all too familiar pain to creep in. The little book was a relic but one that Mattie frequently read as a young girl. Poetry and short essays about the beauty of Kentucky and what it offered only gave the reader a mild glance at what she had grown up in. Reading from this little book had kept her sanity intact for many years and now she was holding her book again and she knew she would have to have it even if it meant asking Sarah to hold it for her until she could pay it off.

Intent on her new found treasure Mattie hadn't heard the shop door open or close, nor did she hear the mumbled conversation at the counter. Mattie rose and thumbed through the familiar worn pages and taking the scent of the paper deep into her senses. The memories this little treasure had rekindled were some of the best memories she had locked away in her memory vault. Carefully turning the pages Mattie turned to one of her favorite poems and scanned it with misting eyes, remembering the times she had read this very work to Gracie while sitting on her sun warmed porch. Feeling better than she had just moments ago she held the little faded red book to her heart. The little treasure wasn't what was making her saddened it was the memories of all she had lost long ago that was weighing heavily. The little book just reminded her of her mom and of Gracie. Oh how she missed her little family, especially now with all the changes in her life and no one to share them with. The heaviness that was weighing her down began to lighten as the good memories washed through her. Mattie heard a faint mumbling coming from the front of the store and realized Sarah must have a customer. Trying to remain unnoticed Mattie eased around the outer shelf and focused her attention toward the register. The site that greeted her caused her to freeze in place and clutch at her little book; the lifeline she needed for stability. Sarah was looking up, way up, into the familiar, handsome face that had her hiding in here in the first place. Sarah was nodding as she answered his questions

"Jackson," she whispered to herself and felt the fear begin anew. Making a quiet backward motion she eased behind the wall of books. Mattie felt she had to stay where she was because she could not face him again. She just couldn't. Clutching the little book like a talisman Mattie felt her heart thundering in her rib cage again and her breath was coming in short puffs. Her self-talk to calm down had little effect on her, but she continued to keep her eyes closed, and forced her concentration on breathing and steadying her nerves. How long she stood there she had no idea but when she felt a light touch on her arm she almost bolted and her heart must have skipped an entire row of missed beats. Breathless, Mattie slowly opened her eyes hoping it wasn't the blonde man who made her feel so, so... whatever it was.

"Honey, are you all right? You've been standing there a while and I didn't know if there was a problem or not." Sarah had a feeling the little beauty was hiding from that nice young man but she didn't ask that question since she felt confidant in the answer she would have gotten.

"Oh, I'm fine." Mattie hesitated, and then continued her train of thought, because she saw the unasked question in Sarah's eyes.

"I found this little book over there," pointing to the shelf right behind her, "and I was curious, how much it would cost?"

Just barely breathing Mattie waited for the answer and hoped it was within reason.

Sarah saw the reverent way the young girl held the old book and she knew the girl would buy it regardless of the price she put on it. That was when she decided the love of the book by the young woman was more rewarding than the money in the register would have been. Choosing the right way to say what she wanted to, Sarah quoted a low price that had Mattie's head swimming. She could not believe her good fortune at such a low amount for such a treasure. Walking toward the cash register Mattie pulled out her meager eight dollars and paid for the book. Mattie couldn't stop the question from tumbling out of her mouth and asked, "are you sure of the cost? It's not a mistake? Realizing what she had said Mattie bit her lip and held her breath.

"I'm very sure Miss, this is my store and I call the shots when it comes to the prices." Sarah tried to hide her amusement but didn't succeed. Mattie only shook her head and smiled at the kindness this little woman easily bestowed upon a complete stranger. Mattie wished to have that kind of ease with people.

"You come on back here anytime Miss, my door is always open and don't make it too long an old woman gets lonely for company."

"Id love to but can you please call me Mattie?"

Laughing softly the old lady told her only if she would call her Sarah. Both agreed and while one felt she had a new friend the other felt she might have the daughter that she'd never had. It seemed like a promising future for both women.

Chapter Nine

Jackson could have sworn he had seen HER go into the little book shop, but there wasn't a sign of HER anywhere. He had looked. Requesting a book on boats, and boat repair, was an acceptable excuse and one no one would question. Not that he needed an excuse but running in and looking for a scared young woman wouldn't get him anywhere fast and he knew it.

The shops owner, Sarah, told him she would order the book he had requested and took his number for her to call when it arrived.

Jackson continued to make his way home with his thoughts revolving around a frightened, mystery woman with auburn hair. He couldn't believe that she had slipped away from him twice now and he still didn't have a name to go with the lady. Jackson had prided himself in the past with the ability to associate with anyone without so much as asking twice and here he was chasing a girl who had made it very clear she didn't want anything to do with him. Why was this woman so intriguing to him? He couldn't answer his own question. He knew it was more than the face and the features, or the hair that was almost alive when she walked and more than the body and what a body it was too. Even with a voice that was laced with glacial undertones had revealed a sultry, silk wrapped voice that was musical. Jackson knew he had to know her in no uncertain terms and he refused to acknowledge the nagging little voice telling him that he may not see her again. "I won't think about that," he whispered, as a smile creased his face. Jackson was determined to find his mystery woman and began to feel much better about the whole situation as he made his way home.

Mattie slowly edged her way out of the little shop carefully monitoring her surroundings like a hunted animal would. She never thought about her actions anymore since they had become so ingrained in her and her basic survival. Avoiding the opposite sex had been a part of her normal life for so long she never gave it a second thought when she repeated the same actions and reactions to them. With her little red book in hand Mattie made her way home letting the blocks of pavement roll behind her knowing solitude was ahead of her. Arriving at the apartment she shared with Rachael she soon realized her roommate wasn't home yet giving her the perfect opportunity to read some of her poems. Making herself comfortable on her little bed Mattie began to thumb through the very familiar pages she had memorized but never tired of reading. About a third of the way through Mattie found one of her favorite poems that reminded her of her meadow back home. Serenity was the only word to describe the look that washed over her features almost peaceful if someone were to see and describe her.

34

The all familiar title was centered in front of her. Finding the sites in her mind, Mattie devoured the poem, and clutched her little book to her chest as she drew in an unsteady breath. The hot rivulets of streaming tears ran down her cheeks as she remembered a long ago past when things had been peaceful and happy. This poem always made her cry when she remembered all the unanswered wishes she had made for herself, her mother, and the family they should have been. Mattie had never given up on those secret wishes, except now they would be wishes that only she would enjoy, if they were to be granted.

Rachael came bouncing in, full of energy, like a mini-whirlwind. "Oh, Hi Matt. I didn't realize you were home or I wouldn't have stormed in here like a bat out of hell." Rachael talked non-stop jumping from place to place in the room not really lighting in one spot for very long and she continued to talk with an un-bridled tongue. She hadn't noticed the stillness in Mattie or the silent tears she shed until it occurred to her that Mattie wasn't answering to anything she said. Pausing for breath Rachael looked at Mattie, really looked, and she didn't like what she saw. The emptiness she saw was palpable and it unnerved Rachael. Making her way to where Mattie silently sat she knelt before her clasping hands with her and drowned in the sorrowful pools of unshed tears lingering in Mattie's golden eyes. Rachael ached to take away the pain she saw in Mattie as she always wished she could when faced with this type of situation. "What's wrong Mat?" Sincerely wanting to help her new friend with what ever it was that had taken the shine out of her eyes.

Mattie hadn't ever had anyone so concerned for her since her mother and Gracie and she didn't know how to react to that kind of attention. She found she didn't like clouding out Rachael's sunshine with her tears and sorrow and tried to tell her so. "I'm ok, really. I was in this bookshop today and I found a little book on poems about home and I realized how I miss my meadow; my home. I didn't mean to worry you, I'm sorry."

Rachael, being the curious cat that she was, picked up the book and read the poem Mattie had left the pages turned to. Reading the poem pulled at her heartstrings and she whispered to Mattie how beautiful it must be where she was from eliciting the saddest smile she had ever been witness too.

Being a true city girl, it was hard for Rachael to feel the way Mattie did, but it didn't cause her to feel any less for the place that seemed to be kissed by angels, or to appreciate when someone else did. The only thing Rachael had seen was the concrete jungle with exception to her trips with her parents. The animals she had witnessed were on two legs where fear came with the sunset and paying toll came with the sunrise. This was what she had told Mattie and what she had grown up with. Rachael couldn't contain the snickering at her own analogies for city life.

Mattie had never lived in that type of environment before and she had no idea what kind of life it would have been. Shoring up her courage she softly offered the only thing she could. "If you'd like maybe we could go some time." She whispered to her new friend and she doubted her offer as soon as it crossed her lips. Home no longer existed for Mattie except in her memories. A peaceful quiet fell over the two young women in the small apartment each filled with their own thoughts and concerns. "Matt?" Rachael asked and then realized she had shortened Mattie's name again, without asking, a habit she hadn't learned to break yet. "I'm sorry. I didn't mean to change your name without asking first?"

Mattie felt heat wash up her face with the new version of her name but found that she liked it. "I guess its ok. I never had anyone to call me that before" pulling her bottom lip with her teeth she asked Rachael the same question. "Would it be ok if I could call you Rache? I won't if you don't want me to."

"Shoot Matt I've been called that most of my life by my friends anyway. My mother would have a king sized fit, as she usually does, but sure it's ok with me. I wish you would it's less formal that way and it makes us closer friends don't ya think?" Rachael felt they were making progress considering how shy Mattie was and the way she always kept up her guard. With the new encouragement Rachael felt her question about that beat up guitar creeping into her thoughts again and hoped it would be ok to ask now. "Matt, can I ask you a question?"

"I guess so." She answered holding her breath hoping the question was one she could answer without monitoring her every word.

"Can you play that guitar for me now? I love music and I was kind of hoping you'd be able to play some today. I mean I can't play a darn thing no matter how many lessons my mother tortured me with."

Mattie smiled and her whole face lit up like a Christmas tree. "Actually, yeah, I can play, it's one of two things I can do well."

Curiosity antennae jumped to attention at that comment. "Ok, if that's one then what is the other thing you do well? You've got my attention Mattie so don't stop sharing now."

"Uh, well, the coach and other folks say I can run really fast. That's how I got to come here on a full scholarship. I won the scholarship through track. I love to run, especially cross country. I mean, I can do most any of the events, but running on the uneven ground, trails shaded by the forest, and feeling the earth beneath my feet reminds me of when I would run back home. I didn't have manmade tracks to train on so I would run in the woods or in the meadows. I almost feel guilty getting my education provided by doing something that fills me with so much joy and gives me peace of mind."

Mattie had a deep crimson pink creeping up her neck that proved Rachael's earlier assessment about the girl being the genuine article of humility. Rachael smiled and told Mattie the college prided itself on it's ability to provide an education in return for all the hoopla they get with the wins in the sports departments and that Mattie wouldn't have gotten the scholarship if she didn't have what it took.

Somehow Rachael eased the guilt Mattie often felt regarding the way she was getting her education. Mattie realized she liked Rachael even more in that moment than she had before. Rachael didn't make her feel poor or that she just tolerated having her around like most people, who had money, tended to do.

Rachael smiled at the relief she saw on her friends face. Feeling the need to explain her own situation she shared her personal information regarding college. "I was just lucky that my mom and dad had a college fund set up when I was born. My mom and dad always earned excellent incomes and managed their investments wisely so that my funds were ready for me when I graduated high school and came here. I also know for a fact my parents contribute donations every year to this school and others for the sole purpose of helping those with a financial need. My parents are adamant that everyone should have an opportunity to get an education and if money is all that is standing in the way then they do what it takes to accomplish that goal." This conversation in Rachael's mind was getting to deep and it was time to lighten up so she refocused on the request she had made earlier. "Think you could play for me Matt?" gesturing toward the guitar that rested in the corner to emphasize her request.

"I haven't played for anyone outside of family Rache. I don't know if I can." Mattie hung her head letting her nerves dance like water on a hot griddle. It wasn't that she didn't want to play for her new friend. She just didn't think she could.

"Hey! Wait a cotton picking minute, I'm not a stranger to you anymore. Granted, I'm not family, but we are friends and we live together like family. We're like sisters now, so can't you try to play a song for me?" Rachael was hoping if she could lay on a little guilt she could get Mattie to try to play something. It always worked on her parents when she would lay on a little guilt and voila they would do what she wanted; most of the time anyway. She hoped it would work with Mattie as well.

"Well, I guess you're right, if you look at it that way." Shoring up her nerve, she straightened her spine, and nodded for emphasis that she would try. "I'll give it my best shot."

"Fantastic!" Without hesitation Rachael leaped off the stool heading for the instrument before Mattie could even think of changing her mind. Guitar in hand she made her way to Mattie's side and plopped down like an eager teenager. Grinning from ear to ear Rachael knew she looked as eager as a puppy waiting to have a ball thrown for a game of fetch and would have wagged her tail if she had one.

Opening the much worn case brought the familiar feeling it always did. Mattie couldn't hold back the heartfelt smile as she ran her fingers down the neck of her treasure. The precious gift Gracie had given her meant as much to her as the woman herself did. The guitar had been handmade of cherry wood and had the most precious carvings of hummingbirds flying along the base.

The red and gold wood grain had such beauty to it even Rachael sucked in a gasp when she saw it resting in the bed of red material lining the tattered case. All this time she had thought it would be a worn, beaten piece of wood resembling the case that kept it safe. When Mattie pulled her cherished guitar out of the ratty case Rachael was shocked by the total beauty. After gapping at the beautiful piece she realized it had been cared for with loving hands. Rachael was sure it represented Mattie in many ways with one being visually obvious. Beaten and battered, yet functional, with exceptional beauty.

Sitting in the straight back chair she used to sit at her battered desk Mattie began to lightly stroke the chords like a lover would caress a mate. The warmth began to wash over her body as it always did when she began to stroke the chords of her guitar. The music, she so often felt in her soul, flowed through her fingertips with each stroke of the chords. Closing her eyes she felt the music wash through her, pulling her into that place of peace and comfort that she so often dreamt of. The meadow, the bubbling brook, the sun on the grasses, the wildflowers filling the valley with a beautiful scent that the gentle breeze carried, began to fill her senses. Mattie was one with the music and her voice revealed that connection. Soothing and caressing the listener in such a sweet embrace that you couldn't help but sway as the feelings flowed through your every pore.

Rachael was a lover of music and she was astonished at the beauty of Mattie's playing. Matt not only played it she breathed it; she was one with it. Rachael thought it couldn't get anymore beautiful until Matt opened her mouth and honeyed words spilled out. The song was not one Rachael had ever heard but it was unbelievable to listen to.

Gracie had taught Mattie this song when she was little but it was her favorite and it always took her home when she sang it. Mattie became so consumed with the music she never listened to herself sing. She just let the melody take her to a place where no other person was allowed and it showed every time she played and let the lyrics flow from her mouth.

Rachael sat Indian style with her mouth agape, blinking her eyes and slowly shaking her head side to side. Who would have ever guessed her roommate, who was so shy, could sing like a goddess? The rhythm and cadence of her voice held Rache's rapt attention. Not only did her voice not break or quiver it was fluid and smooth and lightly stroked the listeners ears like the beating of butterfly wings. It didn't take a genius to know Mattie wasn't in the room by the serene look on her face.

Mattie finished the song and slowly opened her eyes. Feeling such peace always filled her soul when she sang or played a song that meant so much to her. The look on Rachael's face told Mattie she had done well. A sudden wave of self-conscientiousness hit her and she realized she was the focus of attention, a position she never liked. Mentally berating herself for causing the unwanted attention had Mattie pulling herself into her rabbit hole of shame. Dropping her head and focusing her attention to her shoes she found she was unable to say anything. Out of habit she found herself waiting for the verbal attack that she was sure would come. Just who was she anyway to think she could fit in, she didn't belong here, and was only there because of a free ride she didn't deserve. The familiar run down her step dad had pounded into her still rode her hard anytime she got out of place. This was one of those times it seemed. When Rachael hadn't said anything Matt risked lifting her head waiting for the verbal blow that hadn't come.

"Mattie, my God. I have never heard such sweet music and your voice is like liquid gold. You should be a professional! I've heard my share of music, some good, some bad, and some I couldn't bare to listen to, to even judge, but you, yours took my breath away.

Mattie, to say the least, was shocked. Gracie and her momma always said she was talented, and some of those who heard her when passing the house, but Rachael, her new friend, the city girl, liked what she had heard. She had a vast amount of knowledge with music and a comment like that was a heady thing for the shy, withdrawn, country girl. Mattie only smiled her thank you to Rachael and lovingly wiped down her guitar.

The silence was a companionable one and easily accepted between the two women. It was a silence filled with deep thoughts and ideas that remained unvoiced. There seemed to be no further conversation coming and both women eased into nightly chores as a new closeness seemed to create a sisterly bond that hadn't been there before Mattie sang. It seemed as if the song had melded them in more ways than either imagined.

Chapter Ten

Lyle Johnson roomed down the hall and was cussing a blue streak for having to listen to the hick crap he had to endure. Rock and heavy metal were the only music forms that should be allowed on the market. Lyle had been pacing his room for the past ten minutes and had decided that if the hillbilly hoedown didn't stop soon he was going to march down there and make them stop. Lucky for them it stopped before he had to take action. It was a repeat of the same old thing, just a different semester. Why was it every time someone new moved in they had to drive the whole place crazy with their idea of descent music? Pacing like a caged panther Lyle swore. "Where the hell is he anyway? Can't that rich kid get his ass anywhere on time?" He grumbled to the empty room. I guess when your dripping with money time is always someone else's. Lyle had known this rich twerp for the better part of his life and they had always had a good relationship as far as friends went. A difficult feat considering they were from different sides of the tracks. Rich and poor, rarely, if ever mixed, but in this case they did and it worked. Lyle couldn't have handpicked a better friend. However, he was at his patience end if Blondie didn't get his butt here soon. Lyle decided his buddy was going to pay and pay dearly. Just thinking about it brought a smile to his face.

Little did Lyle know, said friend, was closer than he would have ventured to guess. So close, in fact, if Lyle were to open the door he'd see him frozen to the carpet. The friends had agreed to meet in Lyle's room to discuss repairs on an old sailing boat he'd bought. Lyle was great with his hands and his work with wood could make him a very nice future. This particular boat had Lyle's name all over it, a project he knew they could do together, as they had before. Hearing the music and the angelic voice had frozen him in place. By the time he'd really listened, the tunes it had stopped and he couldn't figure where it had come from. Just hearing the music gave him the sensation of being in a warm sunlit meadow with birds singing overhead. He couldn't shake the feeling that his joints were turning to liquid. Before he could move his large frame from the spot he'd stopped in, the door to Lyle's apartment swung open and a very angry Lyle glared at him. He knew it was going to hit the fan by that look and all he could do was shoot an all knowing smile back at him.

"Jackson, what in the hell are you doing standing in the hall like some mentally challenged idiot? I have been waiting on your rich ass for too damn long now and here I find you standing in the hall like the village idiot. What's the problem with you Blondie?" Lyle's mouth quirked up at one corner trying real hard not to smile. Jackson never took him seriously no matter what he

40

said and that only helped their friendship more. Goading the guy was such fun. "Didn't daddy ever give you a working watch or are using your sundial again?" The rich jokes and jabs rolled off Jackson's back as did the poor and destitute did from Lyle's. That was what made their friendship work neither took themselves to seriously being open and honest with each other had always been a priority. "My sundial is dammed heavy and I couldn't get it in my pocket this morning, so back off!" Jackson had to smile; Lyle was a good friend. Making his way to Lyle's room he was grinning like the cat that swallowed the canary.

Lyle spoke with a hint of laughter in his voice, "What in hell were you doing over there like you needed a breather? Have you been drinking? Using some illegal drugs? What? You looked like a real fool standing in the hall looking all sappy. So spill it man, what gives?"

"Don't be a bastard Lyle. I was listening to that music, did you hear it?"

"Too late on the bastard part Mr. Jackson, Sir, and you'd have to be deaf not to hear that country crap wailing down the hall."

"Do you know who was singing?"

"What do I look like the headmaster of this fine establishment? I have no idea who it was but I'd love to put them out of my misery. That so-called music sounded like a cat caught in a box fan."

As they walked onto Lyle's apartment Slipknot drifted from the CD player. Jackson couldn't help himself and let out a real gut wrenching laugh. Lyle had an idea what he was laughing at but he'd bite anyway. "What is so damn funny?"

"Uh-huh, cat in a box fan you say. Have you really listened to that stuff Chief? I mean really listened? Hey, don't get me wrong I like all kinds but what I heard was much nicer than what I'm hearing."

Music was one of the few things the two ever really disagreed on. Lyle's taste in tunes usually left a lot to be desired, considering all you could here was the screaming, unintelligible, paint peeling wails that had no style or meaning compared to the stuff he liked. When it came to sharing work and music together they would compromise and listen to rock or hard rock since it was on even ground and both seemed to enjoy it.

Lyle only grinned and walked over to the stereo to turn his music down but he wouldn't turn it off of which Jackson knew anyway but turning the stuff down was a great relief.

"So... Who was that singing?" Jackson refused to let it go.

"Hell, I don't know man, that's the first time I've heard anything like that around here and trust me if I'd heard it before I would have remembered it."

"You didn't see anyone come in with an instrument?" Jackson was determined.

41

"Listen Jacks I don't stick my nose anywhere except on my face, now can we talk about something else a little more interesting, like the boat?"

"Yeah, well, I got it stored at Scotty's Place, are you free to go look at it?"

"Let's roll" was the only response he gave as he reached for his Levi jacket and his motorcycle keys. Jackson was used to the way Lyle would just drop things and head out with him on a second's notice. Something his parents never did and it still amazed him when his friend did it. Lyle never was the type to waste time on trivial talk or wasted his time unnecessarily. Jackson respected Lyle and his opinions even though most people looked at him as if he had horns and a pointed tail. Ever since Lyle saved his skin he had known Lyle to be fair and often misjudged because of his appearance and the way he carried himself.

People rarely saw the real Lyle. Society only saw a roughneck or a troublemaker. Lyle's looks alone caused stares and only added to the defiant air in him. He stood six-one, had jet black hair that hung between his shoulder blades, a well muscled body, and always observed those around him with untrusting deep chocolate colored eyes. The obvious asset was his Indian heritage that seemed to unnerve people. He never let what people said about him bother him. He always seemed so confident and positive of where he was in life. Lyle probably added fuel to the fire himself by wearing his signature black color all the time. Jackson knew what few people did about the big Indian and that was he worked hard to get where he was. Bigotry and ignorance, often cruelly aimed at him, should have caused him to be just what he was accused of being. A savage by others definition, yet he was far from being anything resembling that. Lyle was determined to prove the idiots wrong and in Jackson's book he had done just that. His Indian heritage and the beliefs he shared with others of the same tribes often kept Lyle on the right track and of course his own sheer stubbornness but he had done his ancestors proud. He didn't fight as they had in the past with a multitude of weapons he still fought and won. Lyle was the greatest friend anyone could ask for and Jackson was proud as hell that he was his. Lyle was not the brother he had hoped for by genetics but he was a brother by spirit. He had always thought they had been brothers in a previous life and it just carried over into this one.

Making their way down the hall resembling a pair of line backers side by side they were a site that could put fear into the weak kneed college crowd. They headed toward the stairs matching their steps as if they practiced it on a daily basis. Instead of visions of his boat dancing in his head Jackson found his thoughts drifting towards the music he had heard earlier. That voice, whoever it belonged to, sounded like the voice of an angel. He found himself wondering if she was as beautiful as her voice had been.

Lyle made it to his Harley and jumped on. His modern day horse Jackson supposed and it was Lyle's pride and joy. Lyle was very talented with all things mechanical and his hog was a prime example of his ability to turn trash into a treasure. He had found the bike at a junk yard discarded after it had been twisted like a pretzel from a wreck. Lyle never saw it as a pile of junk, as most people had. He saw the classic with potential for restoration and he wanted to be the one to repair it. Repair it he did and it was a gem. The black he insisted on painting it was so shiny any woman could put makeup on using it for their reflection. Lyle's pride and joy also had the most awesome grizzly painted on the tank. He'd had other small pieces of his heritage embellished along the sides of it enhancing the lineage he was so proud of. That grizzly was a sight to behold though. Jackson had asked Lyle, after he'd had it painted on the Harley, what it represented to him. He knew it had to do with his ancestors but he knew it was more than that. Lyle was reverent about not scratching it and putting in such a place of honor had more of a personal reason behind it. Lyle told him that he'd had it painted there by an Indian artist who specialized in nothing but Indian objects and ancestral representations. Not only did it represent some of his heritage it was also his Indian name "Big as Grizzly" that his great grandmother had called him when he was a little boy. Most people didn't know that and never would because they only saw what they wanted to and didn't take the time to know the big Indian in black.

Chapter Eleven

Rachael moaned as she heard the deep ripping noise outside in the parking lot. After a couple of loud ear splitting rumbles and a squeal of tires, the motorcycle roared down the street. Mumbling under her breath, as she often did, "No respect for other people, I swear. Ever since I've been here I have heard that bike rip out of here but I haven't the slightest idea who it is. I wish I did. I would give them a piece of my mind. Saturdays were invented to let people sleep in especially those who put in a rough night working."

Groaning as she rolled over she knew sleeping in was a fantasy now. Her curse in life was once she was awake she might as well get out of bed because she would never get back to sleep. "Hope you're happy," she mumbled on her way to the shower, "I'll have to thank you when I find out who you are." A feral grin spread across her face as thoughts of revenge danced in her foggy brain. Rachael had often tried to find out who the guy was but it was like trying to catch a ghost. No one knew who he was or what his name was but one day, she vowed, she would find out. She wanted to confront him about his selfish actions. Of course with her class load and the hours she spent at her aerobics classes and working at Waves, there wasn't much time to socialize, much less find out that recluse of a neighbor's identity. Rachael vowed she would find out who he was this year and then there would be a reckoning. Smiling to herself Rachael made her way into the bathroom for the wake up shower she was in desperate need of as thoughts of revenge danced in her head. After she had dressed Rachael entered the little area beside the kitchen and felt her mouth gape open. She stared at what Mattie had been doing while she was in the shower. "Did you do all this?" Stupid question, she thought, who else would have done it, elves?

Mattie had been so intent on her meal making she hadn't heard Rachael come into the room. Spinning around at the unexpected sound Mattie almost lost her balance. Rachael caught her breath at the instant depth of fear she saw in her eyes. "God, I'm sorry. I didn't mean to scare you. I was just surprised to see you up so early and to see all this" as she gestured toward the breakfast Mattie had spread out on the tiny dinette table.

"It's ok Rachael" she whispered as she clutched her chest and taking in deep gulps of breath, "I didn't hear you come in."

Trying to make light of the situation Rachael headed for the food not having the heart to tell Mattie she didn't eat large meals. "What a spread, you must have been up since sunrise."

"I don't sleep well so I when I can't I play my music or I cook. You don't mind do you?"

"You're kidding right? Mind at having all this? No way!" And she meant it. Mattie had fixed a lot of low fat things and she had fruit, which was her usual meal for breakfast with some yogurt. Rachael noticed that most of what she saw were her favorites and wandered if it was a coincidence or if Mattie was that perceptive with people.

Mattie felt she had done well. Rachael wasn't mad and she had been able to do what she missed doing, taking care of someone besides herself. Mattie smiled a heartwarming smile and Rachael realized it was the first time she had looked happy since she arrived on campus. Rachael thought she would eat a muddy boot before she caused that look to disappear. Mattie hadn't had much in her life to smile about and Rachael refused to be the one to remove that look now.

"Mattie you are saint. You have all my favorites, are you trying to get me fat?" Smiling like she had a secret.

Mattie's heart skipped a beat; she had messed up big time. Slowly raising her head to look at Rachael she realized her roommate was joking with her. Relief washed over her like a warm spring rain and it felt good so she smiled back and whispered "yep" hoping Rachael was in her kidding mood as it seemed she was. Mattie didn't joke with people and she hoped she was doing it right she didn't want to make her friend angry.

Rachael had to steady herself. Not one time since she had been here had Mattie joked about anything, but here she had. Rachael felt it was about time this solemn friend of hers could enjoy life a little more. "Oh, you are huh? Well missy I'll have you know I have a wonderfully high metabolism and I work out a lot so chances are it won't work."

Mattie liked this girl she was fun, full of energy, and she kept people on their toes. "Do ya wanna bet?" She said as she walked closer to Rachael with an outstretched hand.

Shock registered within Rachael as Mattie made her way closer to where she stood. She could only nod because her voice seemed to have gone on vacation. She grabbed Mattie's hand and shook on the bet to seal the deal. Rachael hadn't expected Mattie to come this far in such a short period of time. Knowing that Mattie felt comfortable enough to joke around with her was such a satisfying feeling. Mattie had always avoided touching people so for her to openly offer to shake on a bet was a giant step forward and that made Rachael very happy. "It's a bet my friend" she stated as she shook hands and headed for the spread of food waiting to be sampled.

Mattie knew she had just crossed a roadblock that had been in her path for years. It had taken every ounce of her will power but she did it and it felt great to joke with Rachael. Mattie felt she was on the right track to get her life in some normal balance; she was tired of being an outsider in her own life.

Waging her own inner battle to keep taking baby steps in changing her life Mattie took a seat at the small dinette facing Rachael she shored up her nerve, took a deep breath, and initiated the conversation she only hoped she could continue without losing it. "Rachael, have you lived here long?" Ok, now that ought to start it. Rache loved to talk so now she would listen which was what she did best.

Rachael froze suspending the grape at her open mouth when Mattie spoke. She thought she was hearing things because Matt never opened up a conversation with her or anyone else. After a brief hesitation she let her hand still holding the grape drift back down to the plate as she answered the question she'd just been asked. "Yeah, I've lived here, in different dorm rooms mind you, but in this same building since I started College. I kind of like it because its convenient to town, its affordable, and I don't have to worry about being alone with all the other people coming and going at all hours.

Mattie realized that just sitting and talking wasn't going to be as bad as she had originally thought. As a matter of fact she was finding she liked sharing a conversation with Rachael. "Do you know any of the other people that live here?"

"Well, let's see...she tapped her lip feigning deep thought and smiling. We have across the hall Miss Bulimia, that's Casey Allen. Obsessed with her weight she makes it her goal in life to binge and purge which is pretty disgusting if you ask me. Her bag, not mine. I personally prefer to exercise and be fit, not to lose the meals I eat. So un-lady like putting your finger down your throat to...well you know."

"You mean she does it...on purpose?" Mattie shuddered at the thought of it.

Laughing at the way Mattie was looking with the mere thought of such an act caused Rachael to answer as honestly as she could. "Casey uses that as her form of weight control and it's the 'in vogue' thing to do these days with college girls. Shoot Matt they are proud of doing it and it's a joke among the upper class. I say it's a warped way of thinking if you ask me."

"How sad," was the only comment Mattie could make. "Why don't they just work out like you do?"

"And sweat? Oh heavens" in her mock snob voice. "Buffy and I must not perspire, how preposterous. Ladies do not aspire to that he-man stuff." She stated with her nose raised in the air of pure snobbery. "People like that think they are better than anyone else and physical exertion is not in their general scheme of things. Yet, sticking your finger down your throat is an act disgusting, in and of itself. Hurling your guts up being very un-lady like is an acceptable norm verses the alternative of improving your body with a little effort."

"Now, let's see, where was I? Oh yes, Mary Jo, she lives next to us on the left. Talk about being a brain that girl got hers and half the colleges when they were handed out." She was shaking her head and smiling. "That girl is going places. She has a sweet personality and is kind of quiet, like you."

"Roberta is two doors down. She often acts as a study buddy for those who ask for help and then there is Cheryl and Meryl, the twins who are inseparable, they live a couple doors down and the other 'couple' and I use that word loosely is Beth and Janie. They are always the hot topic around here. They do everything together" she said as she wiggled her eyebrows with an all-knowing smug look on her face, "if you know what I mean." There's supposed to be some drop dead gorgeous hunk living here but in all the years I have spent here I have yet to see this god. My guess is he doesn't exist and the story is just for us unattached females to fantasize about."

Mattie began cleaning the table and putting away the leftovers giving a clearly unvoiced end to the conversation they'd been having. Rachael wasn't upset over the abrupt change in Mattie or the end to their first real discussion. She was just happy that they seemed to be getting closer and were starting to share more than just a living space. Rachael followed Mattie's lead and crossed the room to her small stereo. Flipping through her vast collection she chose one of her favorite warm up tunes and began to stretch out her sleepy muscles. Rachael needed to get ready for the class in aerobics she taught every Saturday. The weekend aerobics class was her baby and that baby called her often during the week but her favorite time was the Saturday class. Everyone seemed to need to work off the week's burdens and that gave Rachael the freedom to really push and burn.

Mattie watched Rachael and decided that her own exercise was lacking. Since arriving she had been so intent on settling in and finding her job she hadn't been around the track in a while, so to speak.

"Matt, I'm leaving now I'll be gone for several hours since I have the responsibility of clean up and lock up. I'll see you tonight then." Rachael stated as she was closing the door.

"I'll be out running, so I'll see ya." Mattie liked the feeling of having someone care where she was and cared enough to tell her where they were and when they would be back. They were beginning to feel like a family and that appealed to Mattie like nothing else had. Pulling out her own jogging outfit and well worn Nikes Mattie quickly changed her clothes and swept her hip length hair up into her favorite scrunchie. Mattie always kept her hair in a tight braid except whenever she ran because she liked the feel of it swishing across her back with each footfall. It was a wild, free feeling she never denied herself even during her meets on the field. That was one thing she would not bend on even when her coaches demanded it she never 'got that hair out of her

47

way' as they often screeched at her. Once they realized it was part of who she was they didn't push the issue. Especially when she would take the lead in most all of her competitions and winning the meets she was a part of they would allow her that one defiant act. It was the only thing she would not waver on.

Running was one of her loves. Cross-country was her forte even though the coaches pushed her to the paved track. Mattie didn't like paved running surfaces but she tolerated it just the same. Cross country running always gave her the sense of home with the light filtering through the trees and the uneven surfaces of the ground beneath her feet. Mattie's ability to run was developed years ago as her only escape as a child which turned into a passion as she got older. Developing and improving her natural skill was as effortless and natural as breathing. Sometimes she felt guilty for being compensated to do what she enjoyed doing but she needed the scholarship for her education and they needed someone who could win for them. Fair enough trade she thought. Making her way to a wooded section of the large park Mattie discovered she could create her own track here where it appeared no one had been before. This was definitely turning out to be her lucky day. Mattie felt her heart soar with the knowledge that she would be the first person to run among the pure, untouched undergrowth of the forest. It would be like running through the woods back home and to find a semblance of that joy here lessoned the homesickness she suffered all too often.

After edging through the brush that lined the woods Mattie felt the peace begin to engulf her, as it usually did, and she began to pick up her pace. Mattie never took the time to monitor how she ran, nor was even aware of how she moved. She only felt the rhythm and freedom each step offered. Mattie was as graceful as a gazelle as she sailed through the air with the speed of a tiger and the agility of caribou. Wild and free she moved like the wind.

Mattie's spirit soared like eagles over snow capped mountains. Living was freedom and this was the only time in her life she felt both. Adjusting to the terrain she was one with her surroundings. Contentment settled over her as it always did and she was at peace with herself and her world, only two things could do that for her, music and running. The two things she could lose herself in and she excelled in them both

The sun was beginning to set drawing Mattie's attention to how much time had passed. Changing her direction in mid- stride she ran toward the outer edges of trees. Mattie was feeling the all too familiar burning in her lungs and the ache in her muscles. It was the sensations she strived for because it meant she had reached her peak. She was alive and in control. Very few things in her life had ever been in her control and she welcomed it with her running.

Making her way to the out skirts of the woods Mattie began to slow her pace, breathing deeply and sweating profusely with the afternoon's heat yet she felt like a million bucks. Self worth was limited to her and it was during these times in her life she felt she was worth something to herself. Mattie burst out of the forest into a grassy knoll heading in the direction of home. Feeling truly lucky she was at college, she had a job, a new friend, and she was safe from the fear she often felt burdened with. Mattie had a new life and she knew Gracie was right when she told her "Good things come to those who wait." Well Mattie had waited her whole life and now she was expecting all those good things Gracie had told her about. The only fear in that was she hoped she would be able to handle it.

The days turned into weeks and life for Mattie had settled into a comfortable rhythm of classes, working, running, music, and her growing friendship with Rachael and Joey. Never having any real close friends she felt blessed that she now had two. Mattie hadn't realized that her life had been so empty until now. For the first time in her life she had true friends that meant the world to her. Realizing that she had lived a lonely life of solitude she shuddered to think what her future would have been like. Entering adulthood with only flecks of warmth and sunshine in her life had Mattie appreciating the abundance she now enjoyed, all the more. She didn't want that old life back. She didn't miss the empty hours, the lonely minutes, or the endless seconds that had consumed her world. Working at Waves had been the best thing that could have happened to her. She was forced to deal with people, something she would have avoided at all costs before. Mattie could admit she still had a long way to go. She could not handle being touched without suffering a panic attack but she could distinguish accidental from intentional without totally losing it now. So far she hadn't been put to the test of someone putting their hands on her and the mere thought made her throat constrict with panic. Mattie held the small hope that she would be able to handle it when it happened. She just hoped it didn't happen anytime in the near future, she wasn't that secure yet. Mattie was becoming a different person and she welcomed each and every positive change greedily. Raising her eyes skyward she softly whispered to the two women who had meant the world to her, that she was trying her hardest to make them proud.

Chapter Twelve

Joey had witnessed Mattie's confidence grow and blossom everyday for the past couple of months. He knew she battled with her shyness and fear of physical contact, but she didn't let those insecurities hold her back. She had become stronger, more resilient, and could hold her own in dealing with the public. He knew it wasn't an easy task turning her anxieties into working tools, but she had, and very effectively as far as he was concerned. Mattie was turning into another Rachael and that was the highest of compliments in Joey's opinion. He had given his girls the title of 'The Dream Team' because they were so in tune with one another that without a word passing between them when one fell short the other picked up the slack. In his eyes they were amazing.

Mattie worked hard and she hadn't missed a day since she started working for him. Joey liked watching her work because she had a quiet, fluid grace that was like poetry in motion. Of course, her looks only enhanced the beauty of her movements. Joey caught himself fixated on her several times during her shift without conscious thought. He had never found himself reacting to anyone the way he did with Mattie. It wasn't a sick or twisted kind of reaction, but more like the response of a father and considering he hadn't ever been a father it was an odd feeling for him. There was something about her that called out to him and he found the need to protect her and keep her safe.

He was a handsome guy or at least he'd been told he was often enough. Someone who was used to double take action from females of all ages, but to his surprise Mattie didn't react like any of the other women he'd met. Young girls often flirted openly with him, an act he tired of long ago, but she never had and he appreciated the difference. "If only I were younger" he muttered to himself. Mattie was like a multifaceted jewel that was beauty personified yet she wasn't bold, brash, or tried to flaunt herself. If anything she was exactly the opposite. That in itself was such an alluring quality yet she never seemed to be interested in anything except her work, school, and running. "Yep, If I were twenty-two Mattie, if I were twenty-two," he sighed while he watched her work her tables. Joey didn't have any designs on her but he sure wished he'd met her at a different time in his life. He would watch out for her just as he had promised Rachael and when he made a promise it was not something he took lightly.

Waves had been filling up again as it had been every night this week. The drawback to being the boss was when problems reared their ugly little heads he had to step up and take care of them. No matter what issues he had to deal with Joey still loved this place. He had even named it after his favorite hobby of riding the waves. His place was clean, affordable, and popular with the college crowd. If truth were told the place kept him young and that alone was a great incentive for keeping it in the green. Not that he encountered any problems with keeping it afloat because everyone seemed to like his place and kept coming back. Joey found contentment in his ownership of Waves because he could open or close when he felt like it, he could make the rules, and if he needed to take off he could delegate temporary leadership to his trusted staff.

Focusing on Rachael brought a smile to his lips; she was his favorite employee. He knew he shouldn't play that game, but she was. She had taken him by storm a few years ago, demanding a fair chance at a job. He hadn't thought she could handle the duties, being such a pint sized little woman and he wasn't a bit ashamed to admit that she had proven him wrong many times over. Joey had given her a chance that day and never regretted it.

Rachael had become a very good friend and employee. She had an uncanny ability of reading people and that talent had landed him some of the best employees to be found among the masses. Mattie was just one of many she had seen potential in. Had anyone other than Rachael gone to bat for her he wouldn't have bothered with an interview. He doubted he would have hired the girl otherwise because he would have judged her and made a snap decision that she wouldn't be able to handle the work. Joey would have been totally wrong and would have lost out on an excellent employee and friend

Waves had been hopping busy, and a little short staffed, but as usual, his girls were handling it. Rachael had the energy of two people and it was a good thing too. His staff worked well together and when he needed them they would work extra without argument. Mattie was diligent just like Rachael and those two were running like a well oiled machine. Waves had been busy before but tonight seemed even more so. This was the busiest it had been since Mattie started working and he couldn't help wandering how his little introvert was going to handle it. Joey watched and wandered if she would cave in with the space growing smaller but she never faltered, she didn't like it, he could see that, but she kept on. That won points in his eyes. He wandered if having such a looker working here had increased his business. Joey doubted Mattie even knew how truly pretty she was. He only shook his head and continued with his work noting how she shyly smiled at some antics the college kids were up to across the room. "Yeah," he whispered "she has no idea."

Joey knew he would keep a fatherly eye on her, especially since Rachael told him she had no family. He often wandered if that was what caused the look of sadness that crossed her face so often. It was more than shyness and it was in her expressive eyes all the time, even when she seemed peaceful.

Mattie Collins had a history that he was sure wasn't a happy one. Joey and Rachael had talked before and they both agreed Mattie needed people in her life that cared and watched out for her. They had become her family as she was a part of theirs.

Mattie was working her usual shift and loving it. She didn't think working at Waves would have benefited her, but it had, and she found herself looking forward to every shift she pulled. She never was much of a crowd person, but she was quickly discovering she enjoyed being around all the different people that came into Waves. She got to observe people as she worked and she could listen to their conversations. Always absorbing, always learning. She had learned so much in the past couple of weeks. More than she would have if she'd stayed back home and she was surviving on her own.

Some of the things she had heard would have curled Gracie's hair. She couldn't contain the smile she felt pulling at the corners of her mouth with that thought. Gracie and her mom had protected her from bad things happening and had her leading a sheltered life. So the things she had heard and seen since her move to California were shocking at first, but now she accepted them as the norm. She often wondered if they hadn't been so overprotective if she would be less shy and fearful of people. It never angered her, the way they sheltered her, she just wondered if it had been more harmful than good.

Rachael was watching Mattie make her way to the grill with her orders and smiled to herself. Mattie was working out real well and she knew Joey was pleased with her work, shoot she was getting a raise and didn't even know it. Rachael was happy things were working out so well for everyone. She knew in the beginning that Mattie was shy and withdrawn, but she was doing very well here. Rachael found it hard to believe how indifferent Mattie was to the young studs that stared a hole in her and practically drooled as they watched her. It seemed as if she couldn't care less and went on with her work as if unaware of her effect on the male population and the angry, jealous looks from the females. Rachael thought to tell her and then decided better of it. Mattie would only get nervous about it and she would be too self-conscience so she kept that information to herself.

On their way home from Waves Rachael was talking on and on in her usual manner and Mattie tentatively listened to the non-stop chatter. When she found her mind wandering she noticed her thoughts were drawn to Jackson which was odd considering she never thought of the opposite sex in any form or fashion. Exhaustion had robbed her of the ability to fight the memories of him and just let the thoughts fill her weary mind. She remembered how handsome he was, how he had searched her out, and how he had spoken to her several times even though she hadn't encouraged him, he still pursued her.

Mattie had always viewed herself as plain, average, country girl, yet he hadn't given up trying to get to know her. A small lifting at the corner of her mouth threatened the beginning of a smile that she quickly wiped away. She didn't encourage him. If anything he probably wouldn't ever look for her again. That should make her feel good, not having to worry about running into him again, instead it made her feel sad and more lonely. She never doubted her actions in keeping men away, so why did she doubt herself now, with this particular man, at this particular time in her life?

Rachael was going on and on, without pause, about some "touchy feely creep at table five" when Mattie brought her wayward thoughts into focus. The description of that group caused Mattie's previously restrained smile to fully erupt into a genuine grin. Rachael always had a way of making her smile and she was thankful this was one of those times. Especially, when she didn't feel like smiling at all.

After such a tiring night, they just didn't have the energy for a full meal and agreed on a small snack of fruit and cheeses. It was during the meal that Rachael told Mattie of Joey's plans for a new local group called "Slam" to come in and do some live stuff for a change of pace. It was all supposed to happen on Friday night.

According to Rachael he did that kind of thing every so often and the customers seemed to enjoy the change of pace. She also told her that Joey would send out an informal invite to some of his contacts in the music business if he thought the band had a sound with potential. The man was always trying to help people, be it with a job or getting the right contacts to come and listen to some unknown kids play at his club. Joey was the kindest, unselfish man she had ever known.

Mattie couldn't remember ever actually hearing a live band before and since she was already scheduled to work that Friday she would get her chance. Just thinking about the upcoming concert caused a nervous excitement to flutter in her stomach. It was another new experience to add to her ever growing list.

Chapter Thirteen

The week went by unusually fast. Mattie had aced her algebra exam and made an 'A' on her psychology paper. Track was great and the coach was pleased with her times. Coach Sanders had said they were some of the best she'd clocked since she started coaching. She was the happiest she could remember being since she had been a teenager and Gracie and her mom were still alive. With all her good fortune, tonight was beginning to feel like a celebration of sorts with the band scheduled to play at Waves. Mattie's excitement didn't go unnoticed.

Rachael saw the radiant glow in her friends face, and the lightness in every step, and could not control the urge to comment on it. "You look like the cat that swallowed the canary Matt, so tell me young lady what's up?"

"Oh, Rachael I'm just happy. It has been a good week for me and tonight we are going to see a live band. It's a perfect way to end the week, don't you think?"

"Well, Miss Mattie Collins, I believe you wear that look quite well and I recommend you do it often" Mattie flushed from neck to hairline with that statement, and not knowing what to say, she just looked down at her feet

"Oh honey, I'm sorry. I didn't mean it in a bad way I was just glad to see you so happy for a change. You looked so alive that you're just glowing. Usually you're so quiet and reserved. I was just glad to see you opening up more. That's all."

"It's ok Rache, I'm just not used to being teased I guess. I grew up by myself, and I didn't have anyone my age around, so it's not your fault, really. But you know what Rache? I am excited about tonight and I can't wait. Do you think the band is any good?"

"Joey wouldn't let them on the stage if he didn't think so. He's always been real selective and he asks around the young crowds to see if they've heard of any new groups and then he searches them out and makes his own decision. Now, if we don't get moving we will be late and Joey will have our hides." That was a running joke where Joey was concerned since he would never 'have your hide' usually all he would do was talk to you. You'd get his point without feeling like a failure.

Waves was packed and as busy as a pack of beavers with a river of twigs. Mattie thought she had seen it busy before, but never as busy as it was tonight. As Rachael and Mattie made their way to the bar Joey was smiling from ear to ear. The music was loud and thumping causing the floor to vibrate with each beat. The rumble of voices trying to talk over the music was almost deafening. Mattie and Rachael were regretting coming in the front entrance since it was next to impossible to get to the back. They needed to get to the back where they kept their royal blue tee shirts with Waves logo on it, aprons and order pads. "Can you believe it's so crowded in here?" Mattie had to scream above the noise level, to be heard, as they made their way through the crowd.

"Yeah, I've seen it like this before. Isn't it great?"

After making their way to their workstations they rapidly began to take orders. It was a feeding frenzy. Mattie was thankful that Waves didn't serve alcohol because it would certainly make their job difficult, and crowd control a nightmare.

The globe hanging from the ceiling flashed multicolored lights across the room creating a menagerie of tiny rainbows. The dance floor looked alive with so many bodies bumping and grinding in every direction. Mattie couldn't stop smiling as she made her way to the grill with her orders. She had never seen such sheer abandon and fun and it surrounded her.

Joey was pleased with the turn out and it appeared his favorite staff was handling it well, even Mattie. He had noticed the awed expression on her face and not the fear he had witnessed frequently in the past. He watched her make her way through the crowd toward him trying to avoid contact with the patrons. Joey told her she was doing great and he was proud of how she was handling such a large crowd. She blushed at the compliments and went on with her work.

Mattie was proud of herself for handling the crowd and keeping the food orders straight. She hadn't worked in such chaos in all her life and this was new to her in more ways than one. If her mother and Gracie could see her now they would be surprised at how well she handled herself with all the young people and the closeness of each body to hers. She couldn't have seen herself in this situation just a few months ago without having a panic attack, but now here she was and she was surviving it. Mattie knew she owed so much to Joey and Rachael for opening up her world and being the best friends a girl could ever have hoped for. One day she hoped to repay them for all the opportunities and life changing experiences they had given her.

Chapter Fourteen

Rachael had been keeping an eye on Mattie and she was pleased with how well she was handling herself. Mattie was dealing with the tight spaces with relative ease, as if she were an old pro, and to Rachael's surprise she seemed to be enjoying herself. Rachael headed toward the grill to get her new orders placed. On the path to the grill she had to fend off disgruntled comments and demands on where the band was. A valid question considering they were extremely late in arriving.

"Hey, Joey when is the band going to get here 'cause the natives are beginning to get a little restless, if you know what I mean."

Joey was beginning to get a little worried about the band himself. He had spoken with them only this afternoon and they assured him they would be here. Now, here it was an hour after they were scheduled and not one phone call of explanation. He didn't like this type of unexpected surprise, especially with a crowd of this size. It could get real ugly, real fast. Trying to reach the band was useless. He had called the number they had given him several times and getting no answer.

Rachael cornered Joey again, half an hour later, wanting to know where the group was, and he had to tell her what was going on.

Rachael rarely saw Joey unnerved and seeing it now didn't sit real well with her. Finding something to keep this size crowd pacified until Slam got here wouldn't be an easy task, even for him. She was racking her brain for a solution as she gazed out into the crowd with the staff weaving in and out amongst them. Her eyes lit on Mattie and she froze stiff when the idea hit her. "I've got it" she said with a snap of her fingers. "Joey, I've got the perfect solution for you and boy are you going to owe me big for saving your bacon!" Joey knew by the smug look on her face that he was really in for it.

"Now, since when do you have a band in your back pocket, Miss bossy boots?" He couldn't resist the tease even with the situation being as dire as it was.

"Watch it smarty-pants or you'll really be in it." She started chuckling at the thought.

"Ok, so what's this life saving plan your going to apparently pull out of thin air?

"It's a name you are very familiar with my man. Mattie." She saw the shock flit across his face and thoroughly enjoyed the look since she never had the pleasure of seeing him knocked off balance before. She patiently waited for the information to sink in.

"Mattie? Our Mattie? That Mattie over there?" He pointed in the direction of his ever shy employee, and then he asked if she had lost her mind out in the crowd.

Rachael's smugness turned to gloating, as the conversation continued. "Our Mattie, as you put it, has the voice of an angel, and she plays the guitar like she's done it since birth. I've never heard anyone as good as she is, and that my dear Joey, just might save your so exposed butt."

"You mean to stand there, and tell me our Mattie can sing, and play the guitar? I've not heard the girl once even openly hum, so how do you know she's any good, huh?"

"Because mister disbeliever she sang for me, and I'm telling you she is great and she can perform while we wait for the band to show. I don't have to tell you how this crowd will get if they feel they've been cheated, now do I boss?"

Crossing her arms over her chest was the 'I'm right and you know it' gesture he had the displeasure of witnessing more than once and Joey knew she was right. "Damn," he swore knowing she was right, and he was going to have to admit it to her, yet again.

"Ok smart pants tell me this, just how do you propose to get the shy and bashful Mattie Collins up there?" He gestured toward the stage.

"We will have to convince her. Mattie doesn't like to disappoint anyone, especially you and me, so if you help me really pour it on thick we can get her to do it."

"I don't know Rachael. I know she's changed a lot in the past couple of months, but I couldn't stand it if I hurt her by being selfish."

"Mattie won't do anything she's not ready for, and she has come along way since she moved here, and started working with us. This will be a good experience for her. At least ask her; there's no harm in that. I'll go get her and we'll see what she says ok?"

"Ok then bring her over here and we'll give it a shot."

Rachael made her way to Mattie's workstation and gently tugged at her sleeve to get her attention without startling her.

Mattie turned and smiled when she saw it was Rachael who wanted her. "What's up Rache?"

"Joey needs to talk to you for a minute." Concern swept over Mattie's face at the blink of an eye. "Did I do something wrong? Is he upset with me for something?"

"No, it's nothing like that, come on." Rachael knew she had to act fast and pulled Mattie through the crowd before she had time to think of all the possibilities of Joey needing to speak with her, so she refused to give her that time.

Joey was at the back of Waves where it was quiet and was waiting for the girls when they made their way through the crowded dance floor.

"What's wrong Joey? Did I mess up an order or something?" The unsteadiness of her voice spoke volumes of how nervous she was.

"No, actually, I'm kind of in a bind and I was hoping you could help me out."

"I'll help any way I can Joey, you know that."

"Let me explain. Slam was going to play tonight, right?" And she nodded her head in agreement. Joey went on "Well, something is wrong. The band should have been here over an hour ago and I haven't heard a word, nor can I reach them on their phone. This means I'm desperate. With no band, and a crowd this size, it wouldn't take much for it to turn into an uncontrollable mob."

Rachael picked up the ball at that point. "See Matt I told Joey you were excellent at singing and playing your guitar, and we were thinking that maybe you could fill in until the band does get here. What do you say?"

Seeing her immediate refusal forming on that perfect mouth, Rachael pressed on. "Joey is in a real tough spot here. These kids expect a band and if there isn't one we will have a major problem on our hands."

Mattie's heart was working like a trip hammer against her rib cage, and her throat felt like it had a softball in it. Mattie hadn't felt this scared in a long time and she didn't know if she could handle it. How am I supposed to get up in front of those people and sing? I can't do it, I just can't. Mattie was focusing on her apron ruffle unable to look at the faces of the two most important people in her life. They were her friends and they had helped her ever since she came here, but she didn't think she could do what they were asking her.

"Please Mattie?" the plea had come from Joey and she just couldn't refuse to help him. He had taken a chance on her when no one else would. "God give me the strength to do this because I can't do it alone" was her silent prayer as she raised her head and whispered "Ok, I'll try, but I don't have my guitar with me, it's at home."

Rachael was ecstatic and she jumped with a very loud "Yes" and a little dance of victory. "Listen Matt, I'll run home and get your guitar, it won't take me a few minutes if Joey will let me use his car." Focusing on Joey she saw he already had the keys in his hand and smiling at her.

Joey didn't like the fearful look in Mattie's eyes, but he didn't know how to take it away either, so he headed toward the bar after giving a huge thank you to Mattie.

Rachael returned with Mattie's guitar and an outfit for the occasion. She wasn't surprised to see Mattie still standing where she had left her. Rachael stood in front of the dazed Mattie and snapped her fingers repeatedly until she focused on her and the task at hand. "Mattie, come on now, snap out of it, it won't be so bad. All the people who love you are here with you so if you get nervous just look at Joey or me. We would never let anything happen to you, you do know that don't you?"

"I know Rache it's just...well.... I...," she trailed off giving up trying to explain, but she knew Rachael understood and just left it at that.

"Let's get this show on the road Matt. Here is your guitar and a dress for you. Now, I don't want any arguments, you can't get up there in your uniform now can you?"

"I guess not" she whispered as she accepted the beautiful dress that shimmered with every movement. "Where did you get this Rache?"

"Oh, well you see my mother makes it a point to send me 'proper' clothing that a young lady should wear. She doesn't understand that I'm not the type and my choices are..., well you know what I wear. So, I have a closet full of finery that doesn't get used. I think it'll fit since mom tends to think I'm curvier and taller than I am, and sends too large a size. The only problem may be with the length but it should be all right. Now, it's getting rowdy out there, times-a-wasting, and poor Joey looks as though he's going to lose his lunch."

Mattie quickly changed into the dress Rachael brought for her and much to her surprise it did fit. She couldn't stop running her hands down the fabric because she had never felt anything so nice against her skin. The material seemed to have a life of its own the way it moved and molded against her body. Mattie loved the deep burgundy that shimmered in the dull light of the bathroom. When she stepped out into the connecting hallway Rachael informed her it was definitely her color. She had a sense of what Cinderella must have felt when she was presented at the ball.

Rachael caught herself starring. The transformation was totally unexpected but not surprising because Mattie was stunningly beautiful even if she wore a grass sack. She barely resembled the roommate she was accustomed to seeing. The girl was breathtakingly gorgeous and could earn high dollar modeling, if she chose to. Rachael reached up and pulled the ever popular hair tie from Mattie's long braid and informed her that she needed to let her hair down more often as the natural waves cascaded over her shoulders and down her back.

Mattie didn't complain about having her hair loosened because it worked to cover the exposed skin of her back due to the dress being cut so low in that area.

Rachael knew Mattie had no idea what a picture of beauty she presented and she forced her big mouth to remain shut, because now was not the time to bring attention to that fact. The girl worked at keeping her appearance as drab and unappealing as possible. Hell, she had it down to an exact science. Rachael had to bite the inside of her cheek to keep from opening her big mouth.

Mattie had gone along with just about everything without a word, but when Rachael started with make-up she protested. "Rachael I never wear that stuff. I'll feel like even more of a phony than I already do."

"Now Mattie have I ever caused you any reason to not trust me?"

"Well, no your one of the few people I do trust."

"Ok then. Trust me with this. You'll look fabulous with just a touch here and there."

"If you say so" she huffed out and rolled her eyes, revealing how she felt about the whole mess.

"I do say so. Now, sit still for just a minute." Rachael ordered as she began applying makeup. Breathless. Yep, breathless was a word she was sure the men out in the audience would be when they got an eyeful of Mattie. Rachael could only smile and help her to the door. Rachael hugged her and wished her luck as she headed back out to the extremely nervous Joey. Rachael gave him a huge smile and a thumb's up to indicate all was well. Joey smiled back and gave Rachael one of his popular winks.

Joey climbed up the stairs and gave the signal for the music to be stopped. The house hushed into a low hum of whispers and anticipation. Holding the microphone Joey began his revised announcement. "Glad you all could make it out here tonight." Hoops and roaring whistles jeered from the crowd so he patiently waited for the crowd to settle down. "Listen folks there has been a slight change in plans," and he was cut off with boo's and hisses that followed the announcement. "Now hold on, before you lose it, let me tell you what's going on. Slam, for some unforeseen reason, is running late so to keep you entertained while we wait one of our very own here at Waves has graciously volunteered to pass the time with her talent. You're in for a real treat because you paid to see one group perform and you get to see two instead. I'd call that a bargain wouldn't you?" The crowd roared with agreement and Joey sighed with relief, he only hoped Rachael was right about Mattie's talent. "So put your hands together and offer a warm welcome for Wave's own Mattie Collins."

The clapping was loud and demanding making Mattie so nervous she couldn't move, she felt like petrified wood. As she stood there frozen she felt Rachael shove her onto the edge of the stage. She got her first glance of the crowd from this point of view and it was even more frightening that just hearing the welcome they were giving her.

"Come on Matt you can do this, just focus and you'll do great" and she kissed Mattie on the check for luck before she pushed her onto the stage completely. "Now go on, their waiting."

Mattie forced her way to the stool Joey had provided and the place got deathly silent as she moved. Mattie had no idea the effect she had on the crowd, men and women alike. She was scared to death being the center of attention and the sudden hushed quiet was unnerving. She knew everyone in the room was focused on her, patiently waiting. Mattie sat on the stool and closed her eyes as her fingers began to stroke the chords of her guitar. Without conscience thought she began to fade into her solitude of music, lyrics, and her meadow back home where no outside sounds intruded.

Chapter Fifteen

Jackson was with Lyle, as they always were, more-so since Jackson had bought the boat. The last couple of weeks they had spent repairing the sails and the hull. Work on the cabin was proving to be more of a challenge. The boat was really shaping up and soon Lyle would get the engine in top running order. Maybe, just maybe, they could take her out for a trial spin.

During the weeks, since Jackson had seen his girl, he knew he was taking that for granted, he found his thoughts were drawn to her. Jackson had looked for her in the crowds and in the stores, or wherever he found himself, without realizing he was searching faces a lot of late. He even asked Lyle if he had seen her and described her in great detail.

Lyle couldn't figure out his obsession with one girl and he told him so. "What's up with you Jacks? All you seem to think about is some nameless girl you only saw a couple times. I don't think I'd tell you if I did see her if she's such a looker. Hell, you got women dropping at your feet and you're after a chick that plainly ain't interested."

Jackson knew he was ribbing him, but he did have a point. He was definitely obsessing, but could not shake the need to find her.

"Lyle, I don't know what it is about her, I just can't get her out of my head. I have never felt like I had to know someone so bad, in all my life."

"Well, hell, Jacks what are you going to do about it? Run an ad in the local paper? Enough talk about your mystery woman already. I'm so hungry my stomach thinks my damn throats been cut. Let's get outta here and go for a burger or something."

"Waves supposedly grill's a great burger and I heard they're going to have a live band there tonight, what say you? Want to go?"

"I'm not a damn teenybopper and I don't want to go to that hangout. I ain't lost a thing there and if that's where you're going I'm gonna head home and grab a sandwich."

"Live a little, why don't ya? I'll even buy. Come on. Don't be such a stuffed shirt. It could be fun and who knows you might even meet someone." Jackson was determined to have a hot meal and listen to some tunes. He could go by himself but he would rather not spend the evening alone.

"Man," Lyle answered him. "You don't know what no means, do you? All right, all right, I'll go and you can feed me but when I'm done I'm leaving. I have no desire to rub elbows with the local college brats. Got it?"

"College brats? Have you forgotten that those people are your age and you are in college yourself? Don't be such a wet blanket. You've got to eat, I'm buying, and the place is cleaner than some other joints around here, so zip your lip and come on. Besides you might even have a good time."

"Humph, don't count on that my friend."

Making their way through the crowd, they headed toward a corner table, just as the music was beginning. Lyle wasn't impressed with the music, but he was hungry, and he wasn't leaving until he got fed. Wandering why he hadn't heard a word from Jacks about the auburn haired beauty on stage, he glanced over and his friend had his eyes wide open, his mouth agape, and he was frozen to his seat. "What the hell is wrong with you Jacks?"

Barely hearing what Lyle had said he never took his eyes off the stage but he answered with a very unsteady voice. "That's her." "That's the girl I've been telling you about."

"You need your eyes examined buddy if you called that jewel plain." He couldn't believe she was the girl who haunted Jackson. No wonder he was determined to find her. Lyle couldn't stop the bubbling laughter as it escaped his lips. "Jackson, would you stop embarrassing yourself, and me, for that matter and shut your mouth?"

"It's her. I know it's her. She's even more beautiful than before. Do you see why I had to find her?" He couldn't stop staring at her nor could he help being entranced by her voice. He was almost sure he had heard her singing before but he knew that couldn't be right. He'd only seen her outdoors.

"No wonder she has become your obsession, I would have too for that matter. Hell, at least finding out who she is wont be a problem now. Damn Jacks she is very easy on the eyes."

"Watch it chief," Jackson eyed his friend in a not so pleasant way giving Lyle the distinct impression he would kick his butt for any lewd comments so he figured it was safer to keep his mouth shut.

Mattie was in a peaceful faraway place that had been her safe haven all her life. Singing the melodies she had been taught, feeling the sun on her face, and the breeze in her hair. The scent of wildflowers penetrating her senses; she was safe and happy right here. The lifts and the dips in her voice were in perfect rhythm with the swaying grasses that only she could see.

Mattie had no idea how serene she appeared up on that stage or the effect she was having on the people who were listening. Swaying with the tunes she played and smiling the way she was caused Jackson's heart to skip a beat and then run into hyper drive. Today was proving to be one of his luckiest days.

Mattie finished her song and opened her eyes, which she quickly realized was a big mistake. The realization of where she was, and the size of the crowd that was starring at her, scared her to death. All she could say to herself was "Oh my God" repeatedly. What do I do now? Lord I can't believe I let Rachael talk me into this. The crowd hated my music I just know it; I've got to get out of here. Panic was rising at astronomical leaps and the roaring in her ears was deafening. Focusing on the sound soon made her pay attention to what she really was hearing it wasn't roaring but it was clapping. They liked it? Mattie couldn't believe the total acceptance from the crowded room. She had never had that experience before.

Someone started to shout for more and before she could back out of the request another shout followed and then another until the place was booming with it. Joey smiled at the response Mattie was getting he was in awe himself; he never would have guessed it. Joey shook his head giving Mattie the go ahead and mouthed to her. "One more time Mattie."

Mattie didn't question it but just started playing again and the place came to a hushed silence. Choosing a popular tune that she'd heard on the radio rewarded her with shouts and some joined in the singing. Mattie hadn't experienced any thing like it. Near the end of the second song, Jackson was making his way to the stage. Mattie noticed him the minute he moved in her direction and she groaned inwardly. "Not him again" she thought. By the end of the song Jackson was near the stage yelling for her to wait, but the clapping drowned out his words. Mattie quickly got up, bowed, and disappeared. She'd heard him yell at her, but there was no way she could stop her retreat. Behind the stage she saw the group Slam come in making her escape easier.

Jackson saw here slipping through his fingers yet again. "Damn it" he swore knowing that if he lost her now he probably wouldn't find her again.

Mattie backed away with her guitar in hand and made for a quick escape. Grabbing Joey's keys she headed for the back entrance running for the car. Mattie put her guitar in the back seat and fumbled with the keys to open the front door when she felt a hand grab her upper arm and spin her around. Mattie almost wept with relief when she saw it was Rachael. The girl almost caused Mattie to have a heart attack right then and there. She was smiling from ear to ear but lost it when she saw the look on Mattie's face. "What is it Matt?"

Mattie quickly told Rachael about a blonde guy who was tall and very good looking following her and she wanted to get away before he caught up with her and she'd explain later.

Mattie took off just as Jackson was barreling out the back door of Waves. "Well damn! Damn! Damn it to hell! I can't believe I've lost her again!"

Rachael just starred at the very handsome guy that apparently had it bad for Mattie. By the reaction Mattie had the feelings were not mutual. "Problem stud?" She asked in a syrupy sweet voice.

"Huh? What?" Was the only reply Rachael got as he stared off in the same direction Mattie had drove off in. He was intently focused on thin air, as if he could make her reappear the harder he starred.

Rachael couldn't help being amused by the way this guy was acting. Snapping her fingers repeatedly to get his attention she began "Hello, Earth to Blondie, come in space cadet, is anyone home? Exactly, what is it you think you are going to accomplish out here?"

"Who is she? Every time I get close to her she just disappears. What's her name?" He almost sounded desperate.

"Now, why would I want to tell you that? If she wanted you to know don't you think she'd tell you?"

Jackson was beginning to steam at this little bit of a woman. "Listen midge all I wanted was her name. I didn't ask for a bunch of lip."

"If you wanted information you don't get it by being a jerk, and besides it's none of your business." She smiled so sweetly Jackson wanted to scream.

"Well it's easy enough to find out without your help" he stated over his shoulder as he walked away.

"Wait, who are you anyway pretty boy, just in case she asks me?"

"And just who are you tinker bell?" He knew that would get her.

"Why you..." she was cut off before she got started.

"Wait a minute before you get in a huff. My name is Jackson Woods and I've met her a-couple of times since the semester began. I've been trying to find out what her name is but when I get close she either runs off or gives me the freeze treatment."

"What's the matter, can't take no for an answer?"

"Listen pip squeak, I just want to know who she is and if you won't tell me then I'll find out from someone in there" he gestured toward Wave's.

"I could tell you myself, but I won't. It's apparent she doesn't want you to know. So, good luck with that Mr. Woods."

"Thanks tinker" Lord she could annoy a saint.

Rachael watched him storm back into Waves as her anger grew like an inferno. She swore it would be a cold day in July before she would let him hurt Mattie. She was beginning to open up and that man spelled trouble.

Mattie drove home, quickly ran to her room, and shut the door. Her mind replayed the near miss with Jackson. Why was he so determined? It was kind of nice to be wanted, but he was probably after only one thing, like her step-daddy harped on all the time. "Gal, boys and men, same thing, only want one thing off a woman and that's to ease himself between her thighs. No more, no less. So you keep that in your pretty little head, ya here? Remembering his words made her visibly shiver. She didn't believe him, not really, but after years of hearing the same song and dance she couldn't pretend his words hadn't affected her. She couldn't keep her thoughts from wandering back to Jackson. He was the type of man a girl could fall in love with. Not that she was that person, but she was willing to admit, it was a possibility for someone. A woman, who didn't carry emotional baggage or gut wrenching fear, when he got close to her.

Mattie had known for years that she wouldn't be one of those women who found happily-ever-after and it always caused an ache in her chest. It appeared her destiny was to be alone. She didn't feel the hot tears trickle down her cheeks, but she felt the ever present emptiness. She didn't understand the root of her fear, but she accepted the fact that love, family, and a home were to always remain a dream and nothing more. Memories locked up tight held that pivotal moment that had changed her life and she knew it had happened when she was sixteen. She remembered when she was little telling her mom when she grew up she was going to have a real family with lots of babies. Gracie, God love her, had often said that one day a nice young man would change her fears into something grand. Well, she was right about one thing, the nice young man she had met, but instead of her fears changing for the better they had only gotten worse.

Pushing back the dark cloud that threatened to engulf her, she stated into the silence, "I am in control of my own damn life," with a conviction that rang hollow. Even she didn't believe the empty words that echoed within the small room. Her stepfather, who no longer lived, still had control over her life, and she didn't know how to stop it. She felt weary, depressed, and so empty the walls were beginning to cave in on her. Pushing herself from the door she walked straight to her battered chest of drawers, and pulled out her favorite running suit. She was determined to outrun her demons.

Mattie often ran out her troubles and this was no exception. She felt smothered and claustrophobic with the thoughts weighing heavily on her mind. She just had to run from the demons nipping at her heels because she didn't have the strength or will, to stay and fight. She had to feel the breeze on her face, the soil under her feet, and the rhythm of freedom pounding with each step she took. Intent on escape she dismissed the incident at Wave's to be dealt with another day.

Chapter Sixteen

Jackson was pissed. "Damn it to hell and back" he hissed. Fate was having a great amount of fun at his expense because his mystery woman had been right at his fingertips, and yet she had managed to slip away from him, again. He felt as if he were trying to catch a cloud in his fist. As soon as he had her within his grasp, she drifted away with the slightest puff of wind. He just couldn't accept the idea that she refused to even talk with him. He wasn't so conceited to think he was God's gift, but he had never experienced such rejection without cause. He was used to being pursued and the one pushing them away, but to his knowledge, he had not been so cold about it. For a second he entertained the idea that she was gay, but dismissed it. It just didn't seem to fit. It was an experience that should have had him backing off, but the odd thing was he found it only intrigued him more.

The reaction Jackson had toward the beautiful woman should have revealed more than he wanted to admit. Shaking his head to clear the cobwebs, Jackson made his way back to where he had left Lyle. He was relieved that his friend hadn't left as Jackson thought he might. He was waiting, impatiently mind you, but at least he was still waiting. Not a known trait for his buddy.

"Well?" Lyle demanded upon Jackson's return. He was more aggravated at having to stand around waiting, than anything else. After several seconds of silence he continued, "Ok then. Did you catch your angel in flight or not?"

"No, I don't know anymore now than I did before" he growled between clenched teeth. "Hell, I still don't know her damn name."

Feeling rather smug and in control of the situation Lyle leaned against the bar and folded his arms across his broad chest smiling at his disheveled friend. Relishing in his friends discomfort and knowing he held the information that could end his pain was a short lived pleasure. Lyle wasn't one to enjoy someone else's misery, no matter how well deserved it was. "Well buddy, ole pal of mine, what's it worth to you to know it?"

"Exactly what are you getting at chief?" Using the old nickname for his friend should have alerted Lyle to just how desperate Jackson was becoming. Lyle felt he had an advantage and he wasn't about to lose hold of it, not just yet anyway.

Jackson had a feeling he was about to be taken advantage of but at this point he really didn't care. "Spill it Lyle. What do you know?"

"Just hold your water pretty-boy." With an arched eyebrow Lyle studied his friend knowing the nickname was a common jab at Jackson's financial status but it was never a derogatory slur, as most people would think. He had known Jacks for years and their relationship was closer than most brothers. "What's a little information worth to you?"

"Dammit Lyle! I'm so not in the mood for your games right now. Just tell me what the hell you want."

Desperation wasn't a word he would have used to describe Jackson, but at this point it was a fitting description. "Tsk, Tsk, Tsk, now don't get your shorts in a wad. Let's see," feigning serious thought, "I've been eyeing this neat little travel set up for my bike and it sure would complete the pieces I already have." He knew he was pushing his luck to the limit here because the look on Jackson's face told him he was on the verge of murdering him right then and there. Lyle didn't dare so much as a glance at him to know there was danger swimming his friend's eyes, but he kept on. "Yeah, a guy with that set up could go quite a ways without stopping for supplies. As I recall it wasn't too bold, not too brassy, it would be..."

Jackson exploded into the last of his words. "Lyle if you value your life at all you'll spill it now." Seeing the negative shake of his friend's head he knew he'd get no where until he gave in to the blackmail Lyle was good at. "Ok, it's yours now spill it or get hurt."

Lyle shook his head in disbelief because he had never seen Jackson so worked up over a female before. "Man you've got it bad for a chick who runs the other direction when she sees you coming. Are you into rejection now? No sweat off my nose. Her name happens to be Mattie, Mattie Collins and she happens to work here. Now, are you satisfied lover boy?"

If a man ever glowed it was Jackson at the very sound of the woman's name. Lyle saw his face light up like a Christmas tree and the smile was almost blinding.

Jackson repeated her name. A name that had eluded him since he first laid eyes on her was playing in his head like a song stuck on repeat. The name suited her. Jackson liked the sound of it as it ricocheted around his shell shocked brain. Mattie could still run, but she couldn't hide. Not anymore, he vowed. He had a name for his mystery woman, and he knew where she worked. This night had definitely taken a turn in the right direction.

Lyle watched his friend as he absorbed this information and ventured to tell the rest he'd gleaned from the cute little brunette at the bar. Lyle had had his fun already and he was about to get a new toy for his bike, so he'd take it easy on Jackson for now. "Um, Jacks?" He waited patiently to get his friends attention and when he had it he began "what do you know about this apparition of yours anyway?"

"Hell, not anything really as you of all people ought to know. I just got her name from you for heavens sakes. I sure would like to know more though. Why are you asking did you find out anything else from your informant?"

"Well she didn't have a lot to offer, but it is more than what you have now. Want to hear what I got?" Lyle knew it wasn't even a question that needed to be asked, but he was enjoying his friend's unsettled reactions to that red headed bombshell.

"Lyle that is the stupidest question you could have asked me and it only tells me you are enjoying the hell out of torturing me aren't you?" Lyle only smiled and shook his head at him. "Of course I want to know what you found out. So put up or shut up, my nerves can't take much more."

"All right, already, can't a guy have a little fun around here? You're getting too serious in you old age my man. From what the little gal told me she's attending the college on a full scholarship to back her. Apparently, she is not only beautiful, she is one hell of a runner, and she seems to have made honor roll every year except one during her entire education. It appears she is from Kentucky, some small hick town, in the mountains or some such. Seems she's a loner, she doesn't have any friends and now we know she works here. Mattie can apparently sing like an angel; that is if you get into that sort of stuff, and that my friend is about all I know of your mystery woman."

"You certainly got more than I did. How did you find out so much when I couldn't find out didly?"

"You my man didn't ask the right people, in the right way" he was eyeing the shapely little brunette again. Winking at her from across the room he said, "Some women just need a friendly face and an attentive ear to open up to and with that pretty-boy I intend to move into my solo act from here on out. It seems Sam is here all-alone and she likes my company, so beat it rich kid. I've got plans that require an audience of none with the participants of just two."

Jackson backed off and watched as Lyle openly flirted with the woman he had been winking at earlier and found he was a little jealous. Jackson couldn't just walk up and talk to Mattie with no qualms. He was beating himself senseless trying to find the one girl that he couldn't get out of his head. Making his way to the owner of the place he was going to ask a question he knew there wouldn't be an answer for, because an employee's personal information was private, but he was determined to try just the same. "Excuse me!" he yelled it over the music that was pumping in the background. "Excuse me!" he tried again.

When Joey turned to the young man in front of him he realized he was the one Rachael had told him about. He decided he would wait to make a judgment about the young man for now, but he would be cautious since it was their Mattie he seemed to be focused on.

"Yeah, what can I get for you?" Joey had a good idea what the answer would be, but he would play along, as if he didn't have a clue what the kid was after.

"I was wondering if you could give me Mattie's address, or at least her phone number."

The cold stare directed at him had Jackson sucking air through quickly constricting pipes. Obviously Mattie had a very protective following around here. Yet, as much as he wanted to step away from the guy, he stood his ground. A move he might end up regretting.

"Even if I could give you that information, of which I can't, why would I want to? From what I saw Mattie wants nothing to do with you. Now, just why is that? Besides, who are you to be asking anyway?" Joey felt like a protective father where Mattie was concerned and from what he'd witnessed Mattie hadn't been protected much in her young life, she'd had too many of the signs that the women at the abuse shelter expressed. They had all suffered at the hands of the incredibly stupid and he wouldn't jeopardize Mattie's hard won successes for some ass to amuse himself with her innocence. He wouldn't betray Mattie's trust in him for anything.

Jackson sensed the bridled anger simmering below the surface of this very big man and he didn't want to be the one he unleashed it on. He could hold his own in a fight, but he had the feeling he wouldn't get up from one with this guy. "Listen I'm not some low-life-scum looking to harass Mattie. I just want a chance to talk to her. Every time I get close enough she bolts away like there is fire on her heels."

"Just why is that young man? What have you done to Mattie to make her take off when you get near her?" Joey felt it wasn't what the kid had done; it was the potential of what he could do that frightened Mattie, but he wasn't going to tell him that. He was going to help Mattie and if this was the only way then he would do it.

Jackson looked thoughtful like he was measuring his answer to Joey's question. "I have no idea really. I've seen her several times, but she always runs off when I try to talk to her. I wouldn't keep trying to find out who she is if I could get her out of my head" he was almost talking to himself it seemed.

Joey knew the kid was really taken with Mattie and he felt a little sorry for him. It would seem Jackson had his ego tramped on quite a bit since he ran into Mattie Collins. It was up to her to face the kid, if she so chose. "I can't give out information on employees to the customers. Everyone knows that and if you didn't consider yourself informed now."

Rachael had been ease dropping on the conversation and she'd be darned if some horny rich kid was going to hurt Mattie. She was like a sister and Rachael would protect her with all the influence she had or her parents could offer. Shoving closer to the conversation she spoke directly to Joey letting the venom spew with each word. "What's this jock want Joey?"

Rachael knew by his looks, his actions, the way he carried himself, that he was a member of the privileged elite. That meant he was used to getting what he wanted no matter what the pain or cost was to others." Rachael had been drowning in that pool since birth and she would not let the likes of this pretty boy drag Mattie to his level. She had fought all her adult life pulling away from that quicksand to make her life meaningful, and her parents had applauded her for her courage that a lot of the wealthy teenagers lacked. That courage would help to keep Mattie out of his clutches.

"It seems this young man wants some information on Mattie, and since you're her roommate I'll let you deal with his questions. You know I can't give out info on the people that work here so it's up to you." Joey gave her the silent nod of his head and she knew what he meant. No words were needed.

Jackson groaned inwardly when he realized it was tinker that Joey was talking too, and he felt his heart hit the floor. Knowing the impression he gave in the parking lot with the freeze queen and the scathing look she was directing toward him was enough to know there wasn't a chance in hell of finding out anything. He would be better off just walking out as empty handed as he was when he came in. No he wasn't quite as empty handed, since he had her name, and a little information on her.

Rachael's look turned smug as she slowly shook her head from side to side while a leering smile curved her lips. This was definitely a dead end.

Jackson never said a word to Rachael and he didn't say anymore to Joey. He felt too dejected. Turning and walking away was easier than beating his head against a brick wall and that was exactly what he would be doing. Before reaching the door he heard his name being called from the bar so without turning he glanced over his shoulder to where tinker stood. Knowing what she was going to say before she said it still didn't take the bite out of the words. "Back off, she's not interested!" Without replying he shrugged his shoulders and made his way through the entrance of Waves and out into the warm fall evening.

Chapter Seventeen

Jackson was feeling totally down and alone as he trudged along the sidewalk. He found himself confused and the more he thought the worse it seemed to get. He just couldn't figure why Mattie was being so elusive. Maybe he was barking up the wrong tree, as his father would say. He had never in his life chased a female the way he was this one. Mattie's auburn hair, tiger-eyes, and a body with all the right curves had haunted him day and night. He would scan the crowds looking for her, watching and hoping he'd find her again. Jackson felt he had truly become obsessed and it only got worse with each brief encounter he had with the girl. He was baffled by his own actions where she was concerned.

Continuing on the wooded path with his thoughts bombarding him with every footfall, Jackson was trying to figure out what to do next. He could hit on the girls who worked in the student affairs office and get the information he wanted, but he didn't feel right about that somehow, the end didn't justify the means. It seemed underhanded and he would rather hear it from the source herself. He couldn't stop the snort of disgust that escaped his throat at that thought. "Fat chance of her ever telling me anything" he whispered to the air surrounding him.

Mattie was in her element and the freedom she usually felt when she ran was taking away the emotions that had weighed her down earlier. Feeling lighter with each step she began to enjoy the run that had started out as a way to escape the demons and the panic that tried to overwhelm her.

She moved like a graceful animal and she ran like the wind over the rough terrain she favored so much. Her thoughts kept drifting back to Jackson and the way he had looked at her; the way he had been pursuing her. It wasn't a position she was familiar with and it carried an unexplainable fear with it. There was a deep seeded dread that bubbled to the surface every time he tried to talk to her. The whole situation was beyond her comprehension.

Joey and Rachael were running interference for her and for that she would be ever grateful. No one had her best interest at heart, not since her mom and Gracie had passed away, and it was nice to know they cared enough to do that for her. Mattie couldn't really understand her reactions to Jackson, but she knew her step-dad's influence was the major contributor. She felt it down to her bones that he was the reason she reacted the way she did with people in general; especially with the male gender. That man was the deep rooted cause for all the anxieties and insecurities that plagued her. She just wished she could remember what was locked away in her head that would reveal exactly what had happened so long ago.

Mattie couldn't understand why she still let his warped comments rule her life, but she was determined to change that no matter how long or hard she had to fight to succeed. With an unexplainable defiance building deep within her she decided she would speak with Jackson the next time she ran into him. That is if he even bothered after the way she had treated him. Just the memory of how horrible she acted sent a shiver to rival all shivers racing through her body.

Mattie gave herself the well worn speech for confidence building as she continued her run. It was her life and she was not going to let the ghosts of the past rule it anymore. The talk worked as it always had and she was smiling inwardly as she made her way across the trail that she had created. The sunset had turned into a menagerie of dancing shadows and the night sounds were emerging from the canopy of fallen leaves. Realizing the dark would consume the forest soon she began her trek back to civilization. Giving her body a push on its reserves caused the welcoming ache she strived for. She had hit her peak and it was her signal to go for that final burn of achievement. She was pushing toward the edge of the woods with as much gusto as she could muster up knowing her cool down time would come on the walk home. She was flying high and soared out into the opening as if she had wings. Barreling out of the woods blindly was her first mistake and grabbing hold was the second.

A tangle of arms and legs clutching and holding on for the sheer reason of preservation was unnerving for both parties as they hit the ground with audible groans. When the cart wheeling stopped, Mattie found her body pinned under a solid, immoveable weight that she couldn't budge. Her gaze locked onto the deepest ocean blue eyes she had ever seen. The run had caused her breathlessness but the need for more oxygen came from the realization that she was under the weight of a very well toned, male body. Mattie forced her breath between clinched teeth in perfect rhythm with her pounding heart.

Jackson knew he had been bulldozed by a female, he'd have to be dead not to feel those luscious curves, but it was taking a bit to get his body to react to his silent commands to move. This was a compromising situation to say the least. He briefly thought he should have some kind of reaction to being on top of a womanly body but oddly enough there wasn't one. He could think of nothing but Mattie and her tiger-eyes. For the first time, he focused on the assailant, and froze stiff. Jackson blinked to clear his vision, but nothing changed. It was her. He couldn't move a muscle. In fact, all rational thought was gone. His heart slammed against his ribs like a vengeful beast. Mattie was more beautiful each time he saw her. She still had makeup on and her hair was a little out of sorts but still resembled the way she wore it on stage.

Jackson's heart was going to explode. The woman he'd been obsessing over, since he first saw her, was lying beneath him, breast to breast, hip to hip, and leg to leg. Just how lucky could a guy get? He couldn't help thinking how well they fit together. In his fantasies however, there wasn't clothing, sidewalks, or parks with joggers all around.

Panic hit like a familiar fist to the gut. Mattie was trapped beneath the unwanted weight of a man and she couldn't breath. Fear she hadn't experienced in years clawed at her relentlessly. She had shut her eyes tightly waiting for the torture to end and screaming from the depths of her soul, "get off, get off, get off," mixed with tears and lashing out blindly.

Jackson was shocked at the transformation he had the misfortune of witnessing. Never in his life had he seen such a fear as hers and her reaction scared the hell out of him. Didn't she know he would never hurt her? No, she didn't know that because she didn't know him. What the hell did she think he was going to do to her anyway?

Mattie couldn't stand the contact. She was beyond talking. She wasn't even in the here and now. She had retreated to a time and place where her memories were locked away in the deepest recesses of her mind.

Begging and pleading, crying and screaming for him to move registered like he'd been shot. Rolling off of her and scooting back Jackson could only stare helplessly as he watched Mattie's evident suffering over such a small mishap. Somewhere in his mind he accepted that this was not because of him, but it was because of a memory the position they landed in that shook her to the core.

Mattie was rocking back and forth with her arms wrapped tightly around her body trying to keep from shattering into a million pieces. Gut wrenching sobs erupted from deep within her that she had no control over.

Jackson felt his heart ripping apart for her, so taking a chance, he lifted his hand out slowly, without actually making contact, speaking softly he whispered, "Mattie? Mattie, do you hear me? I'm here with you. You're not alone. Ah honey, it'll be all right. Your safe with me, I won't hurt you. Please don't cry Mattie. Tell me what to do to help you Matt." Jackson just kept talking to her trying reach into that black void she was caught in.

Mattie slowly began to regain control over tears and shaking that had taken over. She realized she wasn't alone and centered her focus on the soft male voice that had become her beacon out of the darkness. She knew she could trust that voice, she didn't know how, but she knew she could. Mattie forced herself toward that voice and with it came the embarrassment over her reaction to the situation. She couldn't stop her automatic reaction anymore than she could stop the sun from shining. Relying on her inner strength to come out of the dark fell short, so she chose that soothing voice that kept telling her it was ok, and that she was safe. Mattie didn't know who it was, but she was grateful to him for staying and making sure she was safe.

Jackson talked softly to her over and over watching her every move. He could see the changes in her posture, her chants were small whispers now, and slowly she began to raise her head. It was like watching her wake up in the morning he thought as she focused on her surroundings. When her eyes lit on him he noted how her irises grew round and little gasp she released. Jackson knew she recognized him and he felt her tension ease a small fraction. He felt gratification with that tiniest of gestures. He patiently waited for her to speak first he didn't want to scare her anymore than she already had been. So he sat and waited.

Mattie was so grateful that the person she ran into was Jackson. She didn't fear him the way she would a total stranger and she knew on some level he was responsible for pulling her back from that black void. She didn't know what to say to the man she'd been running from since her arrival. Just as she thought she couldn't say anything to him the promise she had made herself while running suddenly blazed in her mind. Didn't she say she would talk to him the next time she saw him? Well now was her chance, so get on with it, as Gracie would say. "Thank you," she forced out on a whisper. The comment sounded husky even to her own ears, but she couldn't help that. She hoped he hadn't noticed.

Jackson did notice and it caused reactions that had no business happening. "You don't have to thank me Mattie. I was the one that got in the way."

Mattie gapped at him when he used her name and just as quick as she had the thought, she squelched it, realizing everyone at Waves knew her name now. "Yes, I do."

"Why?" Jackson was surprised at her insistence on thanking him for something anyone would have done in the same situation. He couldn't help wondering if Mattie had to deal with things on her own and didn't know how to accept help when it was feely given. The thought didn't sit real well with him. She spoke so softly, Jackson had to lean in close to hear what she was saying.

"You stayed" she whispered around her emotion thickened throat. Here was this man she'd spent a good portion of her time running from because of the fear she carried around inside all the time. Yet, he had stayed with her to make sure she was ok. Mattie felt safe with him, which should have felt threatening, but it wasn't. Gracie's familiar voice echoed in her thoughts with her frequent words of wisdom "You can tell about a person Mattie girl by their actions when it's of no benefit to them and they still help." Here she was in the dark with a man who was practically a stranger, and yet he made her feel safe in his presence. Deciding it was time to get off the sidewalk, Mattie struggled to get to her feet, and winced at the pain she felt in her ankle. Staggering to right herself she felt a warm hand on her waist and without thought she pushed the unwelcome touch from her and warned in a cold steel voice "don't."

Jackson was momentarily stunned at the abrupt change in Mattie. He couldn't have been anymore surprised had she reached over and slapped his face. The shy girl he had just sat with was no longer there. She had been replaced with this hard, cold woman shooting a glacier stare at him.

Mattie gulped in great amounts of air as if she were drowning. She couldn't have stopped her reaction to him touching her anymore than she could change her DNA.

Jackson swore under his breath and wandered what could have happened in her life to cause such a reaction. Mattie's complexion changed colors right before his eyes. Every ounce of color drained from her face turning stark white.

She wavered and teetered like a drunken sailor unable to catch herself and the gut jarring fall was inevitable and she cursed her own weakness and uncontrollable fears. Damn it, why does this have to happen every time? Jackson was only trying to help and here I have to act like some scared little schoolgirl and treat him like a leper. She hated reacting the same way every time someone touched her. She was sick to death of the same old shit.

Jackson was so confused with the whole situation that he felt like he was staring in a scene straight out of that Sybil movie, except this wasn't a movie, it was real and he had no idea how to deal with it. Relying solely on gut instinct Jackson spoke to Mattie as if she were a child. "Mattie?" He patiently waited for a sign telling him she was with him. Willing her to look at him was all he could do without touching her and making matters worse than they already were. "Mattie?" He spoke louder, "are you with me honey?" The blank stare she continued to wear was answer enough. "Matt, I'm sorry I swear I was only trying to help. Come on now you're scarring me." Jackson was being completely honest with her. She was scarring the holy hell out of him so he sat there in the dark encouraging and cajoling waiting for it to end; whatever it was. The only light now was coming from the lampposts along the sidewalk lighting up the now empty park.

Mattie heard the tone of his pleas and the urgency in his voice. She didn't hear the words but she knew he was trying to help her come out of the dark hole that had sucked her in again. Keeping focused on him she felt her head slowly lifting, turning in the direction of Jackson's voice. Opening her tightly shut eyes she found herself drawn into a pair of deep blue orbs filled with concern. Mattie felt that jolt of recognition race through her at lightening speed. Her heart began to race all over again. Jackson hadn't left her, yelled, or made any demands. He had stayed with her and patiently waited until her fight with the demons ended for the second time in mere minutes. Mustering up every ounce of strength and courage she had left Mattie gave Jackson a quivering, off-center, poor excuse for a smile. Slowly shaking her head side to side and looking at her feet. Mattie hated the way she'd behaved and it angered her that it had to be Jackson to witness such weakness in her. She didn't know what to say except what she felt. "I'm sorry." The tears dripped silently from her chin as she bent to rub her swelling ankle realizing she had to get home before it got worse. Wondering, not for the first time, what she had done that was so terrible to have to pay for it for the rest of her life.

Jackson had kept a safe distance watching her. He could read the expressions as they crossed her face and refused to sit there any longer and watch the mental self-loathing engulf her. He moved cautiously and knelt before her balancing his weight on his toes and resting his arms on his thighs as he looked directly into her beautiful eyes. He spoke firmly with authority, but non-threatening. "Don't Mattie."

Mattie jerked her face up to look directly into his. How did he know what she was thinking or feeling? She searched his expression intently seeing the conviction of his statement etched in his serious gaze.

"Mattie if you don't want me to touch you, its ok and I won't, unless you tell me its ok. I promise. Do you hear me? Not unless you say, only if you say."

How Jackson had figured her out so quickly surprised her. She hadn't told a soul of the fears and the panic she felt when someone touched her. No one close to her had known and yet he understood from just one encounter. It should have scared the hell out of her that someone had figured her out so easily, and yet it was a relief. Mattie couldn't stop the slow smile that creased her face. If she had known how liberating it was for someone to share her secret she would have told Rachael or Joey already. Jackson seemed different, it was like he understood. She felt her heart open just a fraction for the young man who wouldn't leave her alone and now she was glad he hadn't. Mattie would follow her instincts just like Gracie had taught her. What doubts she'd had about Jackson and his intentions were no longer at the forefront of her mind and realized she did feel safe with him. A feeling she welcomed with open arms. It wasn't something she ever felt with anyone of the opposite sex. Forcing her focus back to the current problem at hand she tried to move her foot and had to grit her teeth when the pain shot up her leg. Now she had to figure out how to get up from the sidewalk and then make her way back home with a twisted ankle.

Jackson understood her dilemma and he had an easy solution if only Mattie could accept it. He was still squatting in front of her and kept his focus intent on her face as he put voice to the thoughts he had on helping her. Speaking softly to get her attention back on him and not on her ankle he made his offer. "Mattie, listen, I know your hurt and you won't get very far by yourself with your ankle being in the shape it's in." He waited for a response that didn't come so he plowed on. "I would love to help, if you'll let me, Mattie. It's my fault you got hurt in the first place. I know you have no reason to trust me and if you would rather I'll call someone for you. I'm hoping you'll give me a chance to do right by you. I promise I won't let anyone or anything hurt you. You tell me what to do so we can get you home and off that ankle. You can't stay out here by yourself it's too dangerous at night especially for a beautiful young woman." When he heard her quick intake of breath he knew she had been listening to him and she was trying to decide what to do, weighing her options.

Lifting her drying eyes she pinned Jackson with a probing stare. Mattie searched his face intently for any signs of deceit or dishonesty. She didn't trust often or easily and years of honing that craft had gifted her with the ability to spot bad qualities with practiced ease. No matter how well the person tried to hide it or disguise it.

Gracie and her mother were the only people who looked at her the way Jackson was at that very moment. A rare quality in someone who didn't even know her and that encouraged her to lower her guard a fraction where Jackson was concerned. That realization brought a calming peace that she hadn't felt in years.

She felt her heart pounding like a set of marching drums and her nerves danced like water in hot oil, but she knew on some unexplainable level that she could trust this persistent, handsome man. Softly speaking she managed an answer to his question.

Jackson almost missed her answer because it was so softly whispered. He shook his head and looked at her intently because he thought he heard her say "Ok" but wasn't quite sure that was what she actually said or if it was the answer he wanted to hear so badly.

Mattie braced herself and spoke a little louder. "I think I can stand but I'm going to need your help if the offer still stands."

Jackson's face lit up as a brilliant smile emerged. He suspected her request took a lot of effort and he silently applauded her. Cautiously, he eased a little closer to Mattie, giving her time to adjust to his nearness. Speaking in a low tone he asked about her car.

"I don't have one. I only used Joey's that one time."

Running away from the scene at Waves in a blind rush instantly resurfaced with that statement. Remembering her flight from the very man that was now helping her brought a feeling of regret with it. Neither spoke aloud the thought they both just shared and focused on this moment in time instead. Jackson couldn't help his immediate feeling of relief because no car meant he would be able to spend more time with her. "Ok Mattie we need to get you to your feet so I'll have to touch you to help you up and then I'll have to hold you by the waist so we can walk you home." It hadn't occurred to him during his instructions that she might live too far away for her to make it home even with his help.

Jackson saw the look on Mattie's face change the minute she heard the words 'touch'. He knew she would have to work through it in her own time and stood, patiently waiting for her to make the first move.

Mattie was giving herself the pep talk of all pep talks building up the nerve to accept his offer. Taking a deep, unsteady breath, she made her decision. Fighting the sick feeling that was churning in her stomach and the nerves that had her shaking and quaking on the inside, she plunged ahead. "I can handle the touching as long as you tell me first, before you actually do it."

Jackson had suspected as much but he still couldn't contain the surprise he felt when she actually said it. "Did you say...?"

"Yes," she answered before the question had completely left his mouth. Quickly changing the subject she continued without pause, "I don't live very far from here, but I would appreciate the help." She sounded breathless even to her own ears.

Jackson rose to his feet and was standing in front of her with an outstretched hand as he waited for her to accept him.

Mattie felt as if she were moving in slow motion when Jackson's hand suddenly appeared in her line of vision. Cautiously, reaching up, she gently placed her hand in the callused palm in front of her. What amazed her was the fact that she hadn't hesitated in her actions.

Jackson felt an electrical charge surge through his body with the contact of her hand in his. His breath immediately stilled then wedged somewhere between his mouth and lungs. He was so focused on the sensations running along every nerve ending that he hadn't noticed how his gaze had locked on the site of their linked hands. He couldn't remember ever having an experience like this one, no matter how interested he was in the opposite sex. Slowly looking down into the face of his angel he realized she was having a reaction similar to his own. Tugging gently he helped her into a standing position.

Mattie faltered slightly as her weight pressed onto her damaged ankle. The pain forced her to lose what balance she'd managed and in so doing she found herself breast to chest, thigh to thigh, and their faces only mere inches apart. This was almost a mirror image of how they were when she plowed him over only this time they were in an upright position. Mattie's reaction to her body connecting with his was different from the last time and it took her by surprise. She did feel the need to push him away but the biggest shock of all was that she didn't want to.

Jackson felt like he had been punched in the solar plexus. He hadn't meant to pull her hard enough that she would lose her balance. Yet, he thought, fate had stepped in to offer him a small slice of ambrosia. On the heels of the pleasure the position offered him, came the realization of how this was going to affect Mattie.

He braced himself for the screams, the wide frightened eyes, and the trembling he had seen twice already. He couldn't bear the thought of knowing he was the cause, again. Jackson silently cursed himself when he saw that she had closed her eyes to him and the trembling had begun. He steeled himself for a repeat of what he had witnessed such a short time ago.

Mattie's thoughts were filled with dread and impending doom. Yet, she wasn't afraid of being this close to Jackson. She found comfort in his touch and knew her reaction was different from what she had just gone through moments before. Refusing to succumb to the fear and its minions she locked her knees, and braced herself to fight the flood of emotion she usually experienced when she was being touched.

She wasn't a small person, but men typically were much bigger, had more power, and scared the hell out of her. Standing completely still, she waited for the bone-deep fear that was always close to the surface, just raring to rear its ugly head. Jackson was so close she could feel his heart beat, his bodies warmth against her bare skin, and the whisper of his breath against her hair. He was making no effort to move. It was as if he were waiting to see how she was going to react to his nearness. She felt the tiniest whisper of hope growing inside her. It was just a glimmer, but it was there. That budding emotion was a light in her darkened world. Just the thought of a normal life brought tears of happiness to her already puffy eyes.

Jackson was relieved to see the expression on Mattie's face. The look of peace and joy, were at odds with the tiny rivulets of fresh tears tracking down her cheeks. For some unexplainable reason he knew beyond a shadow of a doubt that she had just taken a monumental step and she had made it in his arms. His guardian angel was definitely watching out for him tonight. This was better than any Christmas he'd ever had.

Mattie was aware of every contact point between the two of them and she knew she had crossed a barrier when the all too familiar panic tried to surface, yet hadn't. It was time to take a chance, and she prayed she could follow through with her decision. Cautiously, she lifted her eyes to look into the face of the only man that had ever made it this far with her. Smiling shyly she tilted her head slightly to the side and took in the details of his handsome face from the firm chin, to his dimpled cheeks, and the bluest eyes she'd ever seen. Blue eyes that were burning into her own and the emotion she saw there warmed her soul.

Jackson saw her eyes slowly ascending and the pleasure that filled her gaze as she studied his face. She'd captured him like a moth to a flame. He couldn't help focusing just as intently on her. He felt himself swimming in those unusual multicolored eyes that fit the unique woman he was still holding. Putting words to his inner thoughts he whispered "Tiger-eyes," and the spell was broken. He knew it the minute he'd opened his mouth.

Mattie jerked back and staggered slightly but she didn't loosen her grip on Jackson's muscular arms. She searched his face anew in absolute wonder. Wanting to share with this man the huge steps she had taken for the first time in her life. She tried to speak past the tight throat and parched mouth yet found she was unable to. Licking her dry lips she finally managed a whisper of sorts. "This is the first time I..." swallowing hard she finished, "I'm not afraid, not with you." Her admission was more of a confused question than a statement.

Jackson's face lit up into a brilliant smile because that comment revealed all that was left unsaid. Mattie had been able to succeed with him and no one else. The first two times weren't exactly memorable, but there must be something to the third time being a charm. "I'm glad it was with me. Now will you let me help you home? I promise to keep you safe."

No matter that Mattie was making great strides with Jackson, it was still all new, and she had to struggle with a lifetime of responses. Forcing out the reply she wanted to give, and not the ingrained one. She took a slow deep breath and cautiously replied with her desired answer. "Yes, I'd like that Jackson."

Jackson liked how his name rolled off her tongue and he was ecstatic that she'd even remembered it. Sweeping an outstretched arm in invitation to begin what he hoped was a long journey to her home he patiently waited for Mattie to decide if she truly did trust him. He was pleased that her hesitation was only a brief one and he felt an instantaneous heat radiating up his arm with the contact of Mattie sliding her warm palm into his. Her actions should have been answer enough but he didn't want to risk making a wrong move by assuming anything. He looked directly into her eyes and without giving any thought to it, he winked at her.

Mattie's only response was to begin moving slowly, using Jackson as a support of sorts. Mattie knew this night was a defining moment for her future and Jackson was the one responsible for helping her to take the first steps toward it. On some deep level she wondered if this was one of the reasons she ran from him. Obviously the fear of being touched by him was one reason but the other could have been that she saw him as a threat. He was the face of change, the face of uncertainty, the one man that could pull her from a well known comfort zone. Are you watching Momma? Are you seeing me Gracie? She thought as she limped beside Jackson.

The limp had grown less and less the further they walked and the silence between them was a companionable one. When Lewis Street seemed to suddenly appear Mattie realized home was close, too close. As wonderful as this night with Jackson at her side had been she couldn't let him know where she lived. Not just yet. She would have to take it one step at a time. Stopping under the lamplight she realized she was at a loss for words. This was all new territory for her. She was focused on the sidewalk trying to work out what to say when Jackson spoke for her.

He didn't want this time with her to end, but for the briefest of seconds he saw the fear flash in her eyes, and he understood she'd given so much already and he didn't want to push. "It's ok Mattie. I understand. Maybe we can get together another time?"

He had felt such a connection to her from the very beginning but this night had cemented it for him. It was more than just a need to know her; it was destiny that they had met. Jackson knew on some level that Mattie was going to be a part of his future and if it was destinies plan then he was damn sure not going to question it. He knew he no longer wanted the footloose, fancy-free life style as he had before. Everything he ever wanted was standing right before him with a guarded, but peaceful look on her face, and the beginnings of acceptance in her eyes. Life was definitely taking a turn for the better.

Mattie had taken the plunge tonight and she had survived so far. First, she had managed to get up and sing in front of a huge crowd without falling apart. Secondly, she had managed contact with another human being without feeling as if she'd die by his touch. She hadn't dissolved into a mass of uncontrollable shakes, well that is, after the first two episodes tonight. Refusing to dwell on the negative beginning she focused her attention on the highlights of this memorable night.

Gathered under the streetlight they stood facing each other for several minutes, deep in their own thoughts, before they realized they had locked eyes. Mattie blinked and looked away breaking the trance that seemed to have taken them both under while Jackson lowered his head grinning to himself for the embarrassment of staring at her

He didn't want to leave her alone so he told her softly, "go on Mattie before it gets any later. I don't want anything to happen to you."

Mattie turned to walk away when she half glanced over her shoulder at Jackson in the cool lamplight, "Jackson?" She barely spoke above a whisper.

Jackson looked into her eyes and the longing he saw there slammed into him with such force it almost hurt. "What is it Mattie?"

"Thank you. Thank you for everything." With that being said, she slowly turned away, with only a slight hitch in her step and a warm smile on her face. If she could have seen her expression and the radiant glow behind the smile she would have sworn it was another woman looking back at her. The days of such awe and happiness had long since been washed away by time and lost memories. This night had coaxed the carefree wonder and joy of life back to the forefront of her being. Her heart recognized what her mind could not.

Chapter Eighteen

Jackson longingly gazed at the retreating back of the woman who had literally bowled him over. Even with an injured ankle she moved with fluid grace. He whispered into the night air, "Thank you Mattie" and began humming a tune as he watched until she disappeared into the night.

Mattie hobbled her way to her room, which was still empty. She figured that Rachael was still at Waves. With the crowd that was there tonight she didn't doubt it for a second. She made her way to the tub for a long hot bath to ease the swelling in her slightly blue ankle. When she caught sight of herself in the mirror she stood stock still and stared. The reflection she looking back at her wore a magnificent smile, an occurrence so rare that it initially startled her. She hadn't had a lot to smile about in several years and she realized how much she missed it. The easy smiles and spontaneous laughter had all but vanished from her since she was a teenager. She knew she owed it all to Jackson. He had given her some freedom from the doom and gloom that had consumed her. She had dressed in her modest flannel gown that Rachael always teased her about, and headed for her bed. For the first time in years, Mattie drifted into a peaceful sleep having dreams that were filled with a tall, muscular man with blue eyes, blond hair, and dimple kissed cheeks.

Jackson was full of happiness and knew it was due to one person, and her name is Mattie. Sleep was proving to be an elusive thing and knew it was useless trying to attain it. He needed to do something to ground himself and without conscious thought, he found himself standing in front of Scotty's shop. He dug out the ever present key, unlocked the door, and headed straight for his boat. On the way he made a brief stop by the stereo to turn on some tunes, and Celine Dion greeted him with a song of love and forever. "Nope, too deep for me right now" and continued on surfing the stations running into a Bolton lyric, passing it up, and spun the dial for an oldies station. "Well, hell." He grumbled, "Are all the stations focusing on the same thing or what?" Reaching for his CD collection he thumbed through the stack until he found one with a heavy guitar and pounding drums. "Yep, that ought to do it." While Guns-n-Roses kicked ass, Jackson tried to focus his attention on what he was doing. Working on the boat usually took care of that restlessness, but tonight it was a lost cause. He kept seeing the face of a goddess and what had happened with her in the park. He finally gave up trying to reign in his rampant thoughts of Mattie because in all honesty he wanted to dwell on her and the feelings she evoked in him. On the heels of his warring thoughts was the memory of the terror she revealed when they had collided, and he wandered again what happened to cause her to react the way she had. Deep down, he confessed to himself, that he really didn't want to know. The thought of her being hurt and suffering caused his stomach to roll in defiance. When several hours had passed, and early dawn was peeking over the horizon, he felt the fatigue he had strived for finally tapping on his shoulder. After cleaning up, and returning the tools to their original slots, he caught himself humming an unfamiliar tune, and realized it was one that Mattie had sung at Waves. He shook his head and admitted to himself he had it bad. Heading for the lights and getting ready to close up he heard a rattle at the front of the shop. Before he could form a coherent thought the door swung open with a resounding thud. He grabbed one of the long iron tools off the shelf before it registered as to who the intruder was, and when it did, he was furious.

"Damn you Lyle, are you trying to give me a freaking heart attack?" He demanded of his best friend. Standing in the doorway with a grin reminiscent of Cheshire cat and looking every bit the social deviant he was accused of being. His restrained fright escaped as a forced chuckle as he tried to cover up the scare Lyle had caused. "No helmet again Chief? Pushing you luck again trying to prove your head is harder than the pavement?"

"And a big hello to you too pretty boy." He liked the common banter they had with each other. "Just what the hell are you doing here at this hour anyway? Here I come down the street, after a much satisfying night mind you, to see the lights on in here. I thought I'd have to thump some heads. Lucky for you I look before I leap or you would have been scalped." Lyle couldn't stop the grin any more than he could change his Indian heritage. "I thought someone had either gotten brave enough or stupid enough to break in here knowing what would happen if Scotty caught them. So spill it Blondie what are you doing here at this hour?"

"I couldn't sleep and figured if I was up anyway I might as well use the time to work on the boat, and for your information I was getting ready to leave." Jackson knew just as well as he knew his own name that Lyle would know the real reason he couldn't sleep and he also knew Lyle wouldn't let it slide without a comment. He never had and he didn't expect him to begin now.

"What's the matter Jacks little Miss plain playing with your brain?" Lyle was going to enjoy this.

Nope, he knew Lyle wouldn't disappoint him, he had to pursue it. "Shut up Lyle" he knew that would fly like a lead balloon. "It's none of your business."

"Touchy aren't we?" Yep, this was going to be fun. "Listen Jacks I'm only teasing ya man. Mattie is a good-looking piece of..." he trailed off on that thought when he caught sight of the glacier look coming form his friends normally warm eyes.. Oh yeah, he has it bad, Lyle thought. "Uh... I mean...

85

she's a real looker, easy on the eyes, and hard as hell on other pieces of a man's anatomy." "Hey, what the..." he dodged the sailing piece of wood Jackson sent flying toward his head. "Now wait just a damn minute Jackson. I meant it as a compliment. Mattie is very pretty and it's no wander you were breaking your neck trying to find her." Lyle was enjoying his friend's reactions almost as much as he'd enjoyed his little romp with Sam. Nah, she wasn't as much fun. Torturing Jackson had always made for a great pastime and this instance was no different. The angrier Jacks got the more encouraged Lyle was. "I mean, hey, I sure wanted to change gears from idle to full throttle after seeing her." Wiggling his eyebrows in a suggestive manner that he was famous for had Jackson hands forming into a set of white knuckled fists.

"Ok Lyle, you've had your fun, now back off, and leave Mattie out of your warped fantasies." Jackson was having a hard time controlling his emotions and he didn't like it.

"Mattie is it? You're on a first name basis now? Shit Jacks you didn't even know her name until I told you last night at that kiddy club and now suddenly its just Mattie like you've known her all your life. Get over yourself Jacks." Lyle saw the anger on his friends face drain away like he'd pulled the plug and replaced it with a seriousness he hadn't seen in a long time.

"Lyle, have you ever just known something without really knowing, or understanding the why, or the how of it?" Jackson didn't mean for that to come out and to hear it with his own ears he realized how stupid it sounded.

Lyle knew his friend was being very serious and decided to drop the pestering. Obviously this was not fun and games for Jackson. He had known him a lot of years and the question he'd asked required a serious answer. "Yeah, I have. For centuries my family has followed through with everything in their lives that was based on just a feeling. A feeling that was so strong they knew it was brought to them from a higher power. We believe the spirit world can send you thoughts or warnings to guide you when you don't have anything to back it up except the knowledge that it feels right. What makes you ask me something like that?"

"I don't know what it is about Mattie, but I can't get her out of my head Lyle. It's like I've known her all my life. I mean, hell, she caught my eye that first day at registration even though she did everything she could to disappear in the crowd. The way she was dressed, the way she carried herself, the whole package screamed Hands off in big, bold letters. You know, as well as I do, I've never looked twice at a girl like her, yet she has me twisted in knots."

"Jacks I don't have the answers you're looking for, but I'll tell you what my grandma always told me. There is a soul mate for all of us and to those who are lucky enough to find and accept them as such our lives will be rich in love and happiness. My opinion, for what it's worth, is that you have found your soul mate and that is why you feel this pull toward her. This invisible connection that's telling you what should be as plain as the nose on your face."

"I'm so damn confused. What the hell am I supposed to do?" Confessing this to his friend was easier than he thought it would be.

"Get out of here! You confused about a gorgeous woman, and what to do with her? You're kidding right? This is Lyle you're talking to remember?" It was amusing and yet a little unnerving to see his friend so unsettled. The womanizer he had grown up with was at a loss on how to deal with a female. Would wonders never cease?

"Dammit Lyle, I'm not what people think I am! I'm not the user everyone assumes me to be."

Lyle wandered if he'd voiced his inner thoughts since Jackson's angry comment was dead on to what he was just thinking. "Uh-Huh. Tell it to someone who will believe it. I have seen you with my own baby-browns many times over the years. You, my friend, are the love'em and leave'em sort. So don't get all pissy with me because I don't believe you."

"Get it through your stubborn, unbelieving, hard head I'm not like that at all. People believe what they want; whether it's true or not. You, of all people, should know that."

Well, he had him there. "Geeze dude, alright already, whatever you say."

It bothered Jackson that Lyle still didn't believe him but it was his own fault. After years of honing a reputation, how could he expect anyone to believe in his innocence now? Even Lyle apparently had bought into the bullshit he'd spent years spreading around.

Lyle watched as Jackson picked up the wood he'd thrown at his head earlier. Even in his worked up state he still kept to Scotty's rules of putting things back where he found them. Standing there watching him he found himself puzzled by the whole situation regarding this one woman. He had never seen his friend so tied up in knots over a female before and that in itself was unnerving. "Hurry it up rich kid and I'll give ya ride home."

Jackson smiled. Lyle breathed a sigh of relief that this whole conversation hadn't gone completely sour. "Just a minute, let me get my jacket and I'll lock up."

Chapter Nineteen

Later the next night, in two separate areas of town, there were dreams of a similar nature taking place. For one, the dream was one she couldn't remember ever having. This night held no nightmares or demons, but of passion and desire, emotions she'd never experienced before. Mattie still broke out in a sweat, but it wasn't from fear. She still shook to her core, but it wasn't from terror. She still felt trapped, but not against her will. For the first time in her young life she was experiencing a dream she didn't know she was capable of having and in the dream she saw the face of her future. He had the face of a god and the soul of a saint. It was Jackson and he wanted her. Mattie slept the most peaceful sleep knowing that there was a future with her in it. A future that wasn't lonely and cold, but warm and loving. She couldn't wait. Even in sleep a smile framed her face.

For the other, he tossed and turned as the deep passion took his body over. He was feeling her, needing her, wanting all of her. Mattie had consumed him even in sleep. He couldn't get enough of her. He touched her, felt her, and caressed her. Her body was fluid, pliable, and his for the taking. She moaned with abandon as he worshipped her tight full breasts. She arched her back as he ran his hands down her slim torso to her firm, well-rounded bottom. He lifted her hips as she welcomed him between her....

"Oh God" he groaned as his eyes flew open to the pounding of his heart and the pulsing of a painfully heavy erection. "Jesus," he whispered as he scrubbed the beaded sweat from his face with hands that trembled. In the dream Mattie was naked, hot, and wet. He jumped out of bed and paced his bedroom feeling guilty and desperate, with a side dish of agony and aching, all for a woman who owned him body and soul. He groaned again as he paced back and forth not bothering to cover his nakedness. Heading to the moonlit window he jerked it open, welcoming the cool night air as it hit his hot, flushed skin. Jackson fumbled with the nightstand drawer for his smokes and fired one up. After inhaling deeply he slowly released it with a sigh of pleasure. Smoking for Jackson wasn't a habit and he only used the vice when he was in deep need for calm. And right now calm was something his unruly mind and body needed. He would have to fight for control where Mattie was concerned and he hoped he could rely on his usual restraint. Mattie Collins would be a test every time he got near her because he wanted her, true, but he didn't want to scare her. He had witnessed the raw fear in her eyes and he sure as hell didn't want to be the cause of it again. He finished his smoke and wandered back to his rumpled bed and as he hugged his pillow he swore he'd not put Mattie in his dreams like that again. Little did he know his subconscious had ideas of its own, and as he again fell into a deep dream filled sleep he did have Mattie that way many times, and in many ways. Now, he had no doubts what was meant by fevered dreams.

Days turned into weeks and every hour was filled with thoughts of Jackson and the tenderness he had shown her. She also envisioned his magnificent body of muscles that rippled with every movement. She found her mind drifting to physical pleasures. Acts she hadn't considered in regards to herself especially with her damn fears and insecurities. It was unnerving how she would dwell on that man all hours of the day or night. After accepting that she couldn't control what her mind conjured when she was sleeping she began to look forward to being with Jackson in her dream world; the only world that allowed her to be a different woman without the ingrained weaknesses controlling her every move. Mattie had talked with her momma about love, romance, and sex, but that had been so long ago she wasn't sure she remembered all the details from way back when she wasn't even a teenager. Gracie always told her she would know when the time was right and the right man would come along someday. Mattie didn't really believe it then, but she did now that it was happening to her. Not a night went by that Jackson didn't appear to her in her dreams and she found she was less fearful each time. She often wandered if he had any thoughts of her and quickly doused that lunacy. She knew she had scared him half to death that night in the park, and since she hadn't seen him since she was afraid she was right.

Frank's repeated slurs and hate filled comments intruded upon her warm, fantasy filled thoughts causing her to shiver with dread as his scornful words took root. "No man with half a brain would want some piece of hill trash that's so backward she'd have to have a map just to walk straight. The only thing a man will ever want from you will be the pleasure you give him between your thighs and I doubt if you can even do that." Shuddering at the onslaught of his nasty mouth flooding her memory she shook her head harshly and screamed over and over "No, No, No! Damn you straight to hell for your ugly words and treatment most dogs didn't deserve. I'm not the one that was useless, cruel, and one of Satan's helpers, it was you Frank, You!"

Rachael walked in the room and saw the strangest look on her roommate's face. It was a look she hadn't seen Mattie wear before. Mattie usually presented a face serenity, or at times sadness. Unless she were being chased or crowded, but the look on her face right now could freeze a hot cup of coffee and Rachael couldn't help but wander what had caused it. "What's wrong Matt?" When no answer came Rachael continued "Well, what ever it is you look like you could rip someone's head off and hand it to them on a silver platter."

"Oh, huh, it's nothing Rachael. Really, it's nothing. Just a bad memory, that's all". She stammered and held her breath hoping Rachael would just drop the subject. Her asshole step-dad wasn't a subject up for discussion.

Rachael knew enough about her friend not to push any further. Later Rache would know what it was that caused her friend to react the way she did just to a memory. She knew whatever it was had to be one helluva doozey to make her look fiercely pissed.

Chapter Twenty

After several days of brooding Mattie still couldn't get those hateful words from replaying in her head. She hated the fact that Frank still had control over her and he wasn't even around. A shrilling ring of the phone shocked her out of her dark thoughts. "Hello?" Was about the only thing she could get past the lump in her throat from the scare that shrieking phone had caused.

"Mattie hey listen it's me Rachael are you up to a night out 'cause if I have to spend another evening cooped up in that apartment I'm going to lose what little brain matter I have left. We haven't done anything fun in weeks and I say we are due. What do you say?" Rachael was holding her breath hoping her hair brained idea would pull her friend out the slump she was in. Hoping Mattie was still listening she plowed on, "What's say you we go to the club for an evening out? Come on Matt we need a break to loosen up and relax a little."

"What club Rache?" Mattie didn't want to go to some bar she wasn't that confident yet.

Rachael strained to hear her words but the apprehension in Mattie's voice rang out loud and clear. "Well our club, of course, silly. Joey said he had a group coming in tonight and since we were both off with no other plans he offered us a night out on him 'cause we'd earned it. So are you game? We do need a day to unwind, so... please? Can we?" Rachael hated whining, but she also knew how to get what she wanted. She wanted this for Mattie more than she wanted it for herself. Joey had even aided and abetted her with this scheme for he too had seen the despondency in Mattie lately. This plan had to work. It just had too!

"I don't know Rache. I have such a hard time with people. I mean I can handle work because I have a purpose but to be part of the crowd? I just don't know."

"I know Mattie but can't you do this for me? I really don't want to go alone and it would be fun for both of us. I think it would do us both a world of good," she knew she was pushing hard, but she couldn't stand for Mattie to be in such a state anymore without doing something about it. "We won't even stay long if you don't want to. Come on what do you say?" Hoping she had succeeded Rachael patiently waited for an answer. The silence seemed to stretch endlessly even though it had only been about a minute. She heard an audible sigh and she knew it was a done deal. She had won the battle.

"Well, I...uh...I guess it'll be ok Rache since you want to go so bad and I don't want to hurt Joey's feelings by not showing up. What time should I be ready?"

Rachael was grinning from ear to ear as she gave Joey the thumbs up sign.

He repeated the gesture knowing it took a lot for Rachael to get Mattie to agree, but even he had seen how she had been lately and he didn't like it one damn bit. Rachael finished telling Mattie the details then made her way out of the office. "I take it she agreed with much convincing?" Joey asked as she made her way to where he had himself perched.

"Yeah, It was like pulling teeth, but she finally agreed" with a small sigh she stated what he had already thought. "I just hope it works."

"Me too Rache, me too" he was praying they were doing the right thing because if they weren't he knew it could hurt Mattie and that was the furthest thing from his mind. He had sensed she had enough hurt in her life already and he didn't want to be the cause of more. Walking back to his office his thoughts were filled with one very shy, sweet girl who needed some happiness in her life.

Mattie felt the urge to sing and that in itself was the first sign her mood was lighter than it had been in days. Getting out would be good. She found herself reaching for her guitar as she began to hum a familiar ballad.

Her music allowed her to drift to her meadow, run across the hills, and feel the flower scented breeze as it gently caressed her in the warm evening sun. Mattie could feel the peace wash over her and the happiness reaching into the darkened corners of her soul. She owed Rachael and Joey for so much and the upcoming night was her two favorite people helping her again. She knew without a doubt that her boss and her friend were in cahoots but she didn't mind.

Lyle was lounging in his worn, but absolutely comfortable, leather recliner as he intently watched the race cars completing the final lap. Just as he was accepting the fact that his guy had come in third, he heard the muffled strains of the much hated hillbilly music as it drifted into his solitary space. A groan rumbled deep within his throat when he heard 'that crap'. Why should he have to listen to it? Did he force his music on anyone? Whoever it was should be reported to the manager and he would do it too, if he could figure out who the hell it was. Until then he was forced to listen to it and why was he still listening after a couple of songs? All he had to do was put on his headphones and turn on his MP3 player, yet he hadn't. He thought the tunes sounded oddly familiar but he couldn't quite place where he could have heard anything like it. He knew full well he never purposely listened to that kind of crap. Shrugging off the feeling he passively listened and much to his shock he found he was actually enjoying it.

Much to his surprise Lyle felt some of the tension leave his body and he almost understood why Jackson listened to the stuff. As he sat there he went from passive listening to focusing intently on the music and lyrics. Wouldn't his friends laugh themselves into a seizure if they could see him now?

Lyle felt his eyelids slowly drifting downward as he listened and not for the first time tried to place where he had heard that type of music before. Without warning the answer slammed into him like a gale force wind. "Could that be her? The chick Jackson was all mental over?" Muttering under his breath he jumped out of the recliner, walked over to his door, and yanked it open. He stepped out into the hall and held his breath, waiting for more music to drift down to him. Everything broke the silence of the hallway except the one thing he was intent on hearing. "Well damn!" He said more to himself than to anyone in particular. Stepping back into his apartment he shrugged his broad, bronze shoulders and whispered "Oh well."

Jackson was in a foul mood and he didn't know why. "Liar" he berated himself because he knew exactly what put him in this mood he just didn't want to admit it. He hadn't seen Mattie in too many days to count and his overactive imagination had him in a constant state of arousal. What is wrong with me? He savagely thought. "I've got to get out of here before I go stir crazy," he mumbled as he made his way out of the apartment. "Nothing I do will get Mattie out of my head, not even the boat for heaven sakes. I think I need to go where I can't be bombarded by so many thought's, someplace loud and busy might do the trick." He had to get a grip on his unruly thoughts because he found himself constantly talking to empty space. He knew Mattie wasn't interested in him and he was chasing a fading rainbow. He hadn't heard from her, not one word, since that night when she plowed into him. Now wasn't that a stupid thought? Considering, she didn't even know his last name. "Sometimes Jackson..." he trailed off as he made his way to the shower and told himself a night out was exactly what he needed.

Jackson showed up on Lyle's doorstep beating on the door like it was a set of drums.

Lyle was not happy that some fool was pounding on his door waking him up from a perfectly good nap. "By damn I'm going to break your hands and stuff them up..." stopping in mid sentence with his vivid threat, as he noted, it was his soon to be dead friend, who was grinning like a damn fool.

He spoke in very controlled tones that would have scared others half to death but Jackson kept on grinning. "Have you lost your mind rich boy or do you enjoy being chewed up and spit out?"

Jackson pulled on Lyle's shoulder still grinning hoping he had interrupted something. If he had to suffer then so should his friend.

Lyle looked at the way Jackson was scanning the room behind him and blew out a heavy breath. "No, no-one is here. I'm alone if you have to know my business."

93

"Whoa, are you slipping Chief? You're sleeping and alone too. I don't know if the male population can handle the extra circulating female flesh. Tsk, tsk, tsk, I'm shocked at such behavior. I would have thought better of you Lyle now the image you portray is permanently altered." Jackson's mood was already lightening at Lyle's expense, of course, but it felt good to goad him. Hooking his fingers in the belt loops of his jeans Jackson leaned against the wall eyeing his friend.

Lyle was smiling too. Jackson could always make him feel better. "Can it rich boy." The camaraderie they shared kept their friendship close all the years they had known one another. "I choose to be alone if you must know."

"Yeah, sure you choose to..."

"What the hell do you want anyway pantywaist?"

"Oh, aren't we testy?" Jackson mimicked in a falsetto voice.

Lyle gave Jackson a lazy half smile and proceeded with the banter. "So, get on with it Blondie what do you want or is this just a visit to bug the hell out of me?"

"Much as that appeals no, I just stopped by to see if you want to come with me to Waves. I'm bored out of my skull and whether you come or not; I'm going."

"You know how I feel about that adolescent hang out, but at this point even that sounds like a good idea. Paint peeling has been my past time hobby for the last hour and I can't take it anymore besides someone has to keep you out of trouble. Let me get cleaned up while you tell me why you wanna go to Waves?" Seeing the broad grin slide across Jackson face told the tale without words. He didn't need to ask anymore questions 'cause he knew Jackson was after little Ms Country. Granted, she was a looker, but this obsession he had with the girl was almost embarrassing to the male gender. Shaking his head Lyle headed for the shower feeling sorry for his friend. "Yep, you got it bad, you poor sop."

Jackson was eyeing the CD player and the stack of discs lying next to it. He shook his head at the titles he read. Lyle had a taste for strange music, but whatever floats his boat, had been his motto. They both shared some similar tastes in tunes it was just a matter of finding something in this stack. Absently thumbing through the titles he heard a faint melody that sounded familiar but he couldn't place it. CD's still in hand he made his way to the door and listened. Tilting his head to the side he strained to hear it again and froze when the next line of notes drifted to him. He knew that sound, and that voice the instant he heard it. It was Mattie. As soon as he thought it he quickly squashed it, it couldn't be Mattie because he'd dropped her off well away from here the night she hurt her ankle, but it sure sounded like her. He was proving

94

how truly obsessed he was when the sound of a guitar had him twisted in knots.

Lyle walked out with a towel around his waist while rubbing his long, wet, black hair with another. He saw his friend standing out in the hall and he grinned at the site Jackson presented of a lovesick halfwit with a fistful of his music. "Hey man, if you wanted those CD's so bad, all you had to do was ask. I'd have lent them to you."

Jackson hadn't even realized he had opened the door he had been so hypnotized by the music. "Have you heard it before? The music I mean? Do you know who it is that's playing?"

"You mean that stuff that passes for music? Yeah, I heard it before. As a matter of fact, a while ago, before you showed up. It was kind of nice actually. I almost fell asleep listening to it since it was so relaxing, but if you tell a soul I said it I'll deny it to the bitter end. What's the problem?"

"Lyle I know your going to think I'm crazy, but that sounded like Mattie's music."

"I thought the same thing earlier, but then I didn't think about it anymore. This girl has you in a mess you know that friend? You are pathetic. You hear me Jacks? Pa-the-tic!" Lyle headed for his clothes while he laughed at his friend's expense.

"Shut up Lyle! You're just jealous that's all."

"Ha, Ha, now that's a laugh rich boy. I can have any girl, anytime I want one, and I don't have to chase her all over town to do it either. One crook of my little finger and bang, there ya go. So tell me what's to be jealous of? At least I know my women. All you know is a name and a face, which in some cases is probably too much any way. Question is, what are you going to do about it? Dream the day away or go out and have a little fun?"

Jackson knew Lyle was right and through gritted teeth he managed "out" to pass his lips. While he waited for Lyle to dress his thoughts wandered back to the music and he couldn't shake the feeling it was Mattie's music. She had her own sound and that certainly sounded like her signature tunes. Shaking the thoughts from is weary mind he put his attention on the impending night and the potential it carried. He couldn't help but smile and that was how Lyle found him.

Lyle walked up to Jackson and waved his hand in his face and got no response except that stupid grin. Snapping his fingers and raising his voice "wake up sleepy head the night is wasting and I personally don't want to spend it looking at your pretty boy face. Damnit, Jacks lets hit it!"

Jerking back Jackson was embarrassed to be caught so deep in thought and especially by Lyle who would not let it go unnoticed. "Uh, yeah let's get out of here."

"My bike is easier to park and we can weave in and out of traffic without a hitch so are you willing?" It was a question that needed no answer because they always took Lyle's Harley whenever they went out. Lyle always said the bike was a 'chick magnet' and he wasn't wrong. He never wanted for a date when he showed up, but Jackson knew it was more Lyle's looks as it was the bike. "I'm in the mood for action. Not hinting around about it."

"Ya know Chief you're a real Romeo."

"Yeah, ain't I though?" He couldn't help grinning at the comment since it was one Jackson often used when a night of cruising for chicks was in the wings.

Pitching the keys up and catching them Lyle found his mood much better than it had been a couple of hours ago. Jacks always seemed to know when to show up and when to stay away. He had always shown him respect, which was something most people didn't even bother with. They had been best friends ever since they were kids. What a hoot that was since they both were from different sides of the track so to speak. Rich kid and poor Indian trash just goes to show skin color and money ain't everything.

Waves was packed from wall to wall. Packed to stifling, as usual, the music was pulsing so loudly it could be felt through the floor. Lights glittered across the tabletops in thousands of iridescent sparkles. Rachael was so excited she was sitting on the edge of her chair the need to move was so great she could barely contain it. Looking across the table at Mattie she knew her plan to get her out was worth it. She seemed happy in a quiet way, less troubled, and that had been Rachael's goal.

Mattie felt her mood lift just by coming into the place. Having Rache with her made her feel safe enough to relax. That thousand-watt personality of hers was contagious and Mattie was thankful she came.

Sitting off to the corner was a strategic plan that Joey and Rachael cooked up earlier so Mattie would feel more comfortable. That was the reason they had no trouble getting the table because Joey had it blocked off. Rache didn't care where they were seated as long as they could have a good time and she was determined that they would. Rachael didn't tell Mattie that Joey was sponsoring an amateur night and that she was going to push her friend into playing again. If she had told Mattie that, she would never have gotten her out of the apartment. Some things were better left unsaid until absolutely necessary.

Mattie had noticed the bandstand was set up with instruments of all kinds and she wandered who would be playing tonight. She was surprised Rachael hadn't said anything about it. Being off the past couple of days Mattie hadn't heard anything of a group coming in. Oh well, she thought it was going to be a surprise and where music was concerned she was all for it. When she asked

96

Rachael about it she told her of Joey's plans and that there would be some prize money involved and that was all there was to it.

Rachael felt like a heel not telling Matt the rest of her idea but she knew it couldn't be helped.

Joey made his way to his favorite girl's table and was glad to see Mattie had decided to come. He thought for sure she would have changed her mind at the last minute. When Mattie asked about the contest he told her of the prize money and that there would be a talent scout, who just so happened to be a friend of his, out in the audience.

"How many people are going to enter?" Rachael needed an opening to bring up her plan regarding Mattie, and this was the only way she knew to broach the idea with her.

"It doesn't matter Rache it's kind of a free for all no order, no registration, and no fees to participate. All you have to do is get up there and do your thing."

"Hey Joey ya think Mattie would have a chance at the prize? I mean she's really good, well you know that, you heard her. What do you think?" Rachael didn't dare look at Mattie as she held her breath waiting for a response.

"I think it's a great idea and as for winning? My money is on our Mattie here." Swallowing the lump that was growing in his throat Joey looked directly at Mattie and asked the dreaded question. "Are you going to enter the contest Mattie? I'd bet my last penny that you'll win hands down." The look on her face spoke volumes and Joey could tell that she hadn't even considered such a thing. She really had no idea how good she was. If she did she would have jumped at the opportunity.

"From the look on Mattie's face I think you need some help in convincing her to try. You didn't mention exactly how much prize money was in the works Joey and that might encourage her to at least think about it. Mattie, you would have a shot a five hundred bucks plus an interview with a talent scout.

"I just want you to at least think about entering the contest Mattie because I know you can win it." Rachael kept her eyes on Mattie waiting for some response and it was no surprise when one didn't come.

"I agree with you on that tiny and my money is still on Mattie if she decides to enter. But ya never know what will work its way out of the woodwork when money is involved, plus a talent scout in the wings."

"Now Joey, I have told you a thousand times over I'm not tiny, I'm petite." Smiling up at him with the correction that was as old as their friendship she saw his returning smile.

Joey knew he was the only one allowed to get by with the jibe at her size and that if anyone else tried the little powerhouse would flatten him or her. Rachael could take them on intellectually or physically it never mattered because she could hold her own. He had witnessed her in action before and was thankful he wasn't on the receiving end of her wrath.

"What's say you give me some help we got a lively crowd out here tonight."

"Not on your life. Matt and I are here for fun and relaxation so you're tough out of luck boss."

"Now is that anyway to treat your financial backer? I might just have to start hunting for a replacement with a little more enthusiasm and respect for their employer."

Rachael laughed outright at that comment till her sides ached. Joey was smiling at her honest response to his mediocre comments.

Clutching her ribs Rachael gasped for breath and begged mercy. "Enough already, I'm dying here. I give, throw in the white flag, surrender, retreat whatever you want to call it, enough. Besides, you can't replace me I'm one of a kind."

"You got me there dyno." He really liked to tease her, but he was a little worried about the lack of response from Mattie. She hadn't said a word since they had brought up the subject of her singing. Her silence was eerie and all to revealing. "Listen ladies I have to get to work so let me know what the decision is." Making his way back to the grill he couldn't shake that look that had taken over Mattie's normally serene face. That girl must have had one helluva traumatic past for her to react the way she did with just normal things. Things most people took in stride seemed to shake her to her very core. She was too damn sad for her age. He had his suspicions but didn't want to put voice to them or dwell on them either. Diving into the food orders that were piling up by the minute didn't leave anytime to think about the possibilities.

Mattie didn't hear anything past Rachael's idea of getting up and singing in front of people again. She didn't know if she could do it a second time. Granted the first time wasn't so bad but that was to help Joey out. This was just for cash and an interview. She could sure use the extra money and she didn't care about the interview, but she didn't know if she could handle it. Rachael and Joey were betting on her winning and wasn't that a good sign? Refusing to think about it anymore she forced her focus onto the crowd and listened to the music. Mattie slowly felt herself relaxing and enjoying the evening.

The music was vibrating and loud, but no one seemed to give it a second thought. No matter how many times Mattie was in this place it always felt new each time. The excitement coming off Rachael was like watching rainwater pour from the house eves during an evening storm. She had the ability to make an algebra exam a pulsing experience. She was going to make someone very happy one day, and she was sure it wouldn't be a dull relationship. Rachael's excitement was contagious and Mattie found herself going with the flow. How easy it was to get caught up in the spirit of things with her around.

Joey decided after a half-hour he'd visit his girls again and to find out how Mattie was handling the proposition. "Well how are my two most favorite girls in the world?"

Mattie spun around at the sudden interruption and bestowed a beautiful smiling face upon him. Joey had to catch his breath. That girl had no idea what a punch she packed, and he decided it was a damn good thing too. Society couldn't handle it if she did.

"Oh Joey, it's been great. Thank you for inviting us tonight."

"Well Mattie you're very welcome. Have you thought about singing for us again? You have such a beautiful voice Matt, and I think you stand a very good chance of winning. What do you say? You've sung here before and the kids loved you." Holding his breath and crossing his fingers he waited for her answer; fearing it wouldn't be the one he wanted.

Not having an answer he pushed further. "It's a great opportunely Matt and you could have a chance at a career if that's something you want to pursue."

Unable to look at his pleading face Mattie twisted her fingers in her lap and gave him the truth. "I...I just don't know Joey. I mean before it was an emergency. I don't think I can just for the sake of doing it."

"Mattie?" Rachael saw this door open and she was going to walk right through it. She was not one to let an opportunity pass. "The competition won't start for a while yet and all I want you to do is promise me and Joey that you will at least think about it."

"Ok, I'll think about it." Mattie's stomach was so tied up in knots from nerves that she was on the verge of throwing up. She had managed to get up on stage once before surely to goodness she could do it again. Her life had changed so much already and this would be another way for her to keep on changing and growing. Mattie refused to disappoint her two best friends and would keep her word by thinking about it.

Rachael and Joey exchanged a look as Mattie sat motionless wandering if they were doing the right thing in pushing her. It had to be the right thing.

Joey let out his pent up breath and looked at Rachael beseechingly asking her silently the same thing he was feeling. "Have we screwed up royally here?" Rachael only shrugged her shoulders and was praying they hadn't over done it.

Mattie moved as if in slow motion looking from Rachael to Joey and in the space of a heartbeat a small giggle escaped her lips. Joey and Rachael jumped as if someone had shot a gun next to the table. Mattie giggle till it turned into a small laugh trying to hide it with her hand she found she couldn't contain the sound.

Rachael looked at Joey and they both looked at Mattie in disbelief. They hadn't heard her laugh before. Smiles slowly crept across their pale faces realizing everything was ok.

"You two look like someone had thrown a firecracker on your lap. You should see yourselves" and she laughed again. It felt so good to openly laugh. How long had it been? She couldn't remember but she was enjoying it now. Laughing hysterically she let the tears of release slide down her cheeks.

Rachael and Joey couldn't believe their ears. They couldn't get over it. Mattie was laughing outright and it was the first time they had seen or heard it. The laughter was contagious and soon Joey and Rachael were joining her with the tears of joy streaming unnoticed. No one remembered why they were laughing and they didn't care. The stares coming from surrounding tables went unnoticed as well because this was a stepping stone toward healing and they were sharing it with the one person who needed it the most.

Mattie finally stopped laughing and looked at her two best friends and wiped the tears from her face and told them what they already knew. "I don't remember when I have laughed like that guys, thank you."

"For what?" They both answered at the same time.

"It was the look on your faces, it just sent me to the edge, and it was great. So thank you for showing me that I can laugh again."

"Oh Mattie," how could anyone forget to laugh? Rachael's heart ached for the injustice she must have endured. "We love you. We only want you to be happy."

Mattie shed tears, but they weren't from laughter this time. Never in her life had she ever had those words spoken to her except from her momma and Gracie. How could she be so lucky? She felt so blessed to have such good friends.

"Don't cry Matt" Joey didn't handle tears well. He felt very uncomfortable when he had to deal with a tearful female and he avoided it at all costs. "Come on Mattie your killing me here."

"I'm sorry guy's it's just that I never thought I would have such good friends who cared so much about me."

"Don't be sorry. Besides we're like family now. Your not alone anymore Matt. We will always be here for you; always." Rachael reached over and hugged Mattie without thinking of how she would handle it. Joey stood and bent down and kissed Mattie on the cheek an act she had never allowed before and found she wasn't bothered by either endearment. "I'll catch ya later sweetheart; I have to get back to being boss. Give it some thought ok Matt?"

Asking as he gestured toward the stage. Mattie shook her head because speech wasn't possible yet.

Heading back to the bar Joey was thinking of Mattie. He couldn't help wander why she didn't have a score of friends. Oh he knew she was shy, but that shouldn't stop friendships from forming. He couldn't help wander what kind of life the poor girl had, had. Joey knew the signs of an abused person because he had seen it often in the kids at the shelter. Mattie had a lot of the same tendencies, and he didn't like what it suggested. He had no tolerance for abusers. "What happened to you Mattie? You're such a sweet kid how could anyone hurt you?" He suspected what those answers were and he knew abuse came to all races, colors, or religions. Abuse didn't discriminate. Joey had suspected it all along since Mattie couldn't handle compliments, she avoided eye contact, she tried to fade into the woodwork, she had a major problem with being touched or crowded, and any attention was unnerving for her. That was one of the reasons he was so happy for her tonight, she didn't flinch when she was hugged or kissed on the cheek. Mattie was making great progress and he hoped some idiot didn't come along and ruin for her. Waiting tables was a therapy of sorts, for her, and she handled it well. For anyone who took the time to look they could see the changes she had made since she came here.

Rachael had been asked to dance and the little powerhouse was off in her element. Mattie had refused any advances and was left alone mostly. The majority of the people milling around knew her from working here, and they knew she didn't go out with anyone so that made it easier for her. Sitting quietly watching Rachael, and all the activity around her, Mattie sipped her coke, and hoped for her continued solitude. She had always been a watcher and she found watching the dance floor very entertaining. She had learned along time ago from repeated shouts that her stepfather continually threw at her. "No one wants a loser Mattie Collins so you just go off in the corner and watch the winners along with that no good mother of yours. Don't embarrass me trying to be something your not or ever will be." Mattie grimaced at the unwanted lecture and refused to let it ruin her night with Rachael. "Go away and leave me be." Closing her eyes forcing his hateful intrusion from her mind she went into her routine defense and pushed it away back in the black recesses of her mind, where it belonged.

Chapter Twenty-One

Mattie wasn't aware that she had become the sole focus of unwanted attention from a pair of beady, watchful eyes. He knew who she was and he hated her with a passion so deep it resembled desire. The price she would pay for his hatred was a price he had determined long ago. Things were going to change for him, but first she had to get gone, completely and totally gone. No way in hell was he going to let her cause his life to be any worse than it already had been. He was on his way and by God that little bitch was not going to stand in his way again, not ever again. He would see to it permanently. This was personal and he was going to enjoy getting rid of her once and for all.

Mattie felt the hair on the back of her neck stand on end. A cold chill swept over her like a cold, dead finger. Evil was near and she knew it was directed at her. It was the same feelings she got when Frank was around, and leering at her when she was alone. The feeling was too familiar for her to ignore it. Fear began to creep along her skin and snake into every pore on her body. She refused to go back to that way of living so she fought it with all the strength she could manage. Death would be better than having to endure living every day with fear laced into it. She felt confused. She had been having such a good time and as soon as Frank's words haunted her that feeling came back. "Why can't you leave me alone?" she whispered.

Mattie was struggling to remain in control when a group of young men entered the front door. So deep in thought she didn't notice how they ogled her from a distance. Liquor was so thick on their breath that if a match had been struck flames would have ignited from it. This group of deviants meant trouble with a capital T. Deciding to keep the little gal company they headed for Mattie's table. No one knew them but everyone was familiar with their type, and their type always caused problems.

Mattie finally regained her control and began enjoying the night, again. She was sipping her coke and watching the dance floor determined to be like all the other normal people. She wondered how it would feel to get out on the dance floor with a partner since it was something she had always wanted to do but never got the chance. Oh her and her momma goofed around but that was mom and it was easy to fool around with her. Shoot she didn't know if she could even manage it if she were to be asked, but it sure looked like fun. A smile of pleasure radiated from her serene face as she watched Rachael wishing she could be more like her.

The three creeps, as those they were pushing and shoving around were referring to them, were at Mattie's table before she ever noticed. The tall dirty blonde with the nose ring crabbed a chair and turned it backwards and proceeded to flop into it. He grinned at her and let his eyes run over her body that made her skin want to jump off and run. The guy was tall, lanky, and his eyes were the same cold, empty, leering eyes that Frank stared at her with. She couldn't stand to look at him. That one had an evil streak, she thought. She ought to know she lived with evil for many years and had no trouble recognizing it when it was staring her in the face. It radiated from him like a stench from the sewer.

The second thug slid into the other chair and stared at her with the same cold stare the leader had. They reeked like a brewery and it was all she could do to keep from gagging.

The short one was itchy acting. Like he had to go somewhere and couldn't. His face had been pounded by someone's fists if all the bruises he was sporting were any indication and apparently he had been on the losing end.

Mattie was so nervous her hands were shaking. She felt threatened and the fear was choking the life right out of her. Breathing was becoming more difficult as the seconds ticked by. Her eyes had grown large and her pulse was pounding like a jackhammer in her aching chest. She could feel the sweat trickle down her back and between her breasts. She was past scared now. No words had been exchanged and yet they all knew what was going on. The lust they felt was revealed in their rheumy eyes and it grew with each blink their heavy lids made. Mattie couldn't stand the weighted down feeling. She was literally suffocating just by their presence.

The tall lanky one reached across the table and grabbed Mattie's hand. She attempted to jerk it away but he tightened his grip with fingers of steel. He leered at her and leaned over the table on his elbows staring into her eyes. He let out a whoop; "Damn boys! We got us a little tiger here. Look at those eyes. Baby do you purr or do you hiss and scratch when you're petted?" He licked his lips and undressed her with those eyes of his and she was helpless to stop it; much less to move. His voice was deeper, huskier, and his arousal was unmistakable. "Want to play cat and mouse sweet thing? I'll be the mouse and you can play with me all you want before you attempt to eat me." That brought on the ugly laughter from his sidekicks. Seems they were enjoying it almost as much as he was.

Fear had a grip on her throat like Mr. Ugly had a grip on her hand and her only thought was "God please help me."

"Hey pretty pussy let's get out of here so you can run your claws up and down my spine. My buddies here don't mind sharing such a fine piece do ya boys?" The leering stares and the sickening grins was all the answer they gave.

103

"Go away," with the only voice she could manage the words didn't sound any louder than a mere whisper. No other sounds seemed to find their way through her frozen vocal cords.

"Oh ho, feisty little tigress, ain't ya? Personally I like a little scratch and kiss, so I see no reason why we can't get started right here. Looking around to his partners in crime he sneered, "Any objections fella's?"

"Nope, we don't mind a bit," the excited comment came from the itchy acting one.

Still gripping her hand, the first creep began to pull her across the table to his foul mouth. Mattie screamed as loud as she could but the words never left her mouth. She began to earnestly fight and claw to no avail. The bastard only laughed at her. Her nails found purchase across his un-shaven face and she raked deeply. Mattie began crying and all she could get out was a loud "No."

"You little bitch. That's how you want play, do you? Well have I got a game for you? And I promise you won't forget it anytime soon. No one marks ole Link and gets away with it. No one! He reached across the table and grabbed a handful of hair forcing her closer to his face. He smacked her hard across the check and backhanded her a second time. The force created a small trickle of blood to run down the corner of her mouth. Link forced his mouth onto hers in a crushing kiss. His foul breath made her wretch and she knew she was going to die right here with no one to help her. A room full of people and no one was helping her.

Jackson's heart jumped up to his mouth and back down again. He couldn't believe what he was seeing. That low life bastard hit her. Hit my Mattie across the face. That son of a bitch will die! Without any further thought he bolted in her direction.

Lyle had seen Jackson mad before, but this, this was past mad he was into a whole other realm of mad. He was going to kill that bastard and Lyle was going to enjoy helping him. Never was a woman to be hit and he had no tolerance for it. They looked like a pair of raging bulls with fire in their eyes and people didn't question them as they shoved past the crowd.

Mattie wasn't there anymore. She had retreated to her safe haven in her mind where pain and abuse didn't exist. She didn't hear the loud cracking sound as Jackson slammed his fist into Links face or the muffled sounds of gut punches as Lyle landed his big fists into that loose tissue, nor did she hear the swearing as little doe boy got his nose smeared across his face. Mattie didn't move. The activity around her never registered, she just stayed in her seat, frozen with fear.

Joey had been told by one of the customers what was happening and he knew his worst fear for Mattie had just came true. Barking at the other staff to call the cops as he made his way to the table he soon found the ordeal was over and two huge handsome looking men with fire in their eyes were the only ones left standing. "Damned trash can't be civil to anyone. Thanks fella's. I think I'll throw the trash out now, if it's all right with you two?"

"You do that" Lyle answered "better yet, I'll give you a hand." Lyle wanted more and was really hoping the three stooges wouldn't let him down. He hadn't had a good knuckle buster in a long time, and he was really enjoying himself.

"I think I got it" Joey said with a grin "I think you should stay with your friend there." He was pointing at Jackson and Lyle knew what he meant. Jackson was a piece of dynamite on a very short fuse. "All right, give a yell if you need me."

Rachael heard the news and saw Jackson with some other hunk wipe the floor up with those creeps, but her focus was Mattie. Rachael knew this was going to undo all the hard won progress she had made, and now, some horny no-goods just ruined it. How would she get over this? Rachael saw the linebacker's bloody fists and felt some pleasure that they had done some damage to the idiots who had hurt Mattie. Jackson's friend really was gorgeous. Pushing that flash of a lustful thought away, before it completely formed, she forced her way through the gathering crowd to get to Mattie.

She sat there like a statue, she was too still, and considering what had happened all around her it was not a good sign. There were deep red whelps, the shape of handprints, across both cheeks, and a thin stream of blood trickled down the corner of her mouth. She was shaking and tears were easing out of her tightly closed eyes forming tracks down her now damaged cheeks, but not one sound was uttered past her compressed lips.

It broke Rachael's heart to see her like that. Wasn't it just a while ago she admitted that she could laugh again? Damn those assholes straight to hell! Rachael went to touch her but found her hand stopped by Joey. She knew she was looking fierce and questioning his action but he shook his head relaying a silent "don't".

Joey knew Mattie wasn't ready to be touched. "Not yet Rache, she's not with us now, she's in the grips of fear and a history we don't know about. Just wait, and giver her some time, ok?"

Nodding that she understood she watched as Joey got the onlookers to go on with their evening and that he would provide the next couple of songs on the Juke box if they would make a list of what the requests were. Directing his staff on duty tonight to take care of it he refocused his attention on the problem at hand. He, Rachael, Lyle and Jackson surrounded the small table and patiently waited as they stood guard over the battered beauty. She was lost in a past that only she knew of.

105

Mattie was inside herself as she had done many times in the past. She could sense the threat was gone but she needed to stay in her safe haven where she felt untouchable. The shaking will end soon and then I'll be ok again. When she began to feel it was time to come back she started the ingrained training to help her slow return to reality. "Come on you can do this. Start with your legs, slowly, that's it work your way up relaxing and slowly breathing. That's it you're safe and you know it. Now, slowly, to your stomach and your chest, concentrate. Ok, now your neck, and your head; totally and completely safe and relaxed. You're all right Mattie. She kept up with her mantra and would until she was ready to surface from her cocoon.

The group watching her continued to witness the visible control she was exerting. It was like watching calm wash over her in one steady swoop. They were fascinated at the changes they were witnessing. Jackson couldn't stand it anymore he had to touch her. The silence was deafening him. He began to move but Joey stopped him and questioned him with a look that wasn't hard to interpret. The look Jackson gave back was one from the heart and Joey knew Mattie was going to be in good hands.

Rachael started to protest what Jackson was going to do when she felt a large warm hand caress hers. She looked down to see her hand engulfed and sparks like a live wire ran up her arm. Focusing her gaze up, way up, her eyes locked with a very handsome Indian with a build any bodybuilder would envy. He had chocolate brown eyes, oh she so liked chocolate, and he had hair as black as licorice, yes she definitely liked licorice.

"Get a grip," she spoke in a mental demand. "He's not a candy store. A bronze God maybe, that just happens to tower over me, but whoa what a tower." She had gone from staring straight into lustful gazing at such a rapid clip she almost jerked with the impact. Then he smiled at her. "Yep my heart will explode at this rate," and she found herself smiling back. Forcing her attention back to Mattie took all the self-control she could conjure.

Jackson picked up a chair and sat it next to Mattie very slowly, very quietly. He didn't want to scare her anymore than she already was. With every fiber within him he had to force a calm he didn't feel. The marks left on her face angered him all over again. He controlled his temper with an iron grip and began to speak to Mattie in a hushed whisper. "Mattie?" No recognition. "Mattie, sweetheart, can you hear me? It's me Jackson. Do you remember me? We shared a long walk the other day?"

Rachael jerked as if she had been hit. She looked at Lyle in complete surprise. He hadn't known that little tidbit either. He only shrugged his shoulder and Joey shook his head. Apparently this was something neither of them shared with their friends.

"Mattie, remember what I told you? I wouldn't touch you unless you wanted me to. Remember only if you allowed it." Jackson waited and hoped she could hear him.

"I need to know. Mattie can I touch your hand? Like I did before? Remember, In the Park? Is it ok now? Can you hear me sweetheart are you listening to me?"

Oh my God, it's Jackson! Mentally she answered him, but knew he couldn't hear her. "I'm scared Jackson and I can't move. Please help me." The tears flowed down her cheeks, but went unnoticed by the source. She was focused on Jackson's voice and her need to let him know she was ok. She wanted him to help her. With every ounce of strength she had she forced a slight move of her head for a yes. Jackson saw since he was watching every twitch she made. He was sure she knew he was there and that she had heard him. He knew she needed help to get out of the darkness and he was going to be the one to do it. Slowly, he picked up her hand, and opened her fingers from the grip she had them in. Her nails had dug into her palms and left deep red gouges in her skin. It was a small testament to the fear she had endured.

"Mattie? Just relax honey, I'm here now." He reached for her other hand and repeated the same process. He held both her hands in his and he could feel the small tremors lessoning in her tall, fragile frame. "God Mattie what has happened to you to make you fear so deeply?" Jackson couldn't help the thought that had slipped out of his mouth. He slowly began to lean into her, as he saw no signs of withdrawal or an increase in her shaking. If anything her shaking seemed to be growing less and less as he continued to hold her and talk to her as if no one else was around. He slowly put his arm around her stiff set shoulders and he whispered in her ear. "Mattie can you hear me? It's over now. I want you to open your eyes. There isn't anyone here but those who love you. You're safe with us. Open your eyes honey. You're with friends now."

As slow as molasses on a cold winter morning Mattie opened her tear filled eyes and laid her head on Jackson's very willing shoulder, She heaved a great sigh and openly cried. It was almost his undoing. She trusted him as no one ever had. She didn't like to be touched yet she let him comfort her and hold her. He could feel the heated tears soak through his shirt and her body shake with heart wrenching sobs. He was very content to be her living lifeline. He wouldn't have wanted it any other way.

Lyle was very impressed with his friend because without a doubt he knew his friend deeply loved this young woman. Probably something he hadn't even admitted to himself yet. No wander he was going nuts trying to find her.

Jackson finally let reality creep into his and Mattie's world and lifted his head to find Lyle and the others still watching, still waiting. Jackson noted that know all smile on his friends face and that he still held tinkers hand. He only smiled back to Lyle and whispered for them to go and that he would stay with Mattie.

Begrudgingly, Rachael left with Lyle and Joey. Lyle still held onto her small fragile hand and found it felt as natural as breathing to hold her near him. Shrugging he kept hold of her as they made their way to the bar. They all knew Mattie was in good hands and Jackson would hurt anyone who even looked at her wrong.

Jackson stroked Mattie's beautiful long auburn hair and softly hummed to her as if she were a child who had just had a nightmare. In many ways that was exactly how she reacted. He soothed her and felt as if he were on top of the world. Sitting there holding her he couldn't imagine not ever having known her. When he saw that creep hit Mattie's unblemished face and marked her with those ugly red prints he thought he would explode with the sudden anger that rocked his soul. He couldn't imagine why anyone would want to hurt such beauty and mar it with ugliness. He remembered her not being able to handle being touched and how she had reacted to him when it had happened by accident. He couldn't imagine how she had handled it tonight when it was done on purpose and with absolute malice. How would it affect her? He regretted that she had to go through it but he was thankful that he had been the one to help her. He felt her stir and shift a little and much to his shock she shifted her head more comfortably on his shoulder then sighed just enough for him to hear it. In the space of a breath he heard her whispered "Thank You."

Jackson didn't dare move afraid the magic would end. He kept humming in her ear as he continued to stroke her hair and bask in the gift that she was giving him with her acceptance. Not only did she trust him to touch her but she made no effort to move when the danger had passed. The threat was over and he knew she was aware of it buy her response and relaxing muscles. He didn't think it could get any better than this. She was accepting him, his help, and she trusted him. He couldn't hold back the smile that graced his face.

Mattie wasn't aware of everything that had happened because she had closed off as soon as she felt the first touch of that creeps hands on her. What she was aware of now was that she was leaning on Jackson's shoulder and she wasn't afraid. In fact, she felt safer than she had in years. Instinctively, she knew she could trust him just as she had that night in the park. Mattie was caught in a spell that was winding its magic around her and Jackson. She found she didn't want this special feeling to end. Not yet. Mattie whispered his name because she liked how it sounded, but she didn't realize she had spoken it aloud. Nor did she realize that she was crying in earnest with great racking sobs shaking her like a violent storm.

Jackson heard the husky whisper of his name on her lips and his heart skipped a beat. He thought he could handle the obvious turmoil and the silence, but the sobs were going to unravel his composure like an old sweater and he didn't know how to handle that. His heart ached for her.

Mattie's tears slowed from a cascade to a slow trickle as she struggled to find her voice. Husky, tear filled words began find their way past her dry lips. "Thank you for being patient and understanding."

Jackson's heart couldn't expand anymore than it did at that moment. He would walk through fire and brimstone to have the opportunity to hold this woman, his woman, in his arms as he was right now. The trust she had in him to allow the intimate contact revealed so much more than even she realized. "Mattie, are you feeling better now? I swear I saw red the minute that scum laid his hands on you."

"I think so," she spoke slightly above a whisper and her voice was calmer.

Jackson gently placed his finger under her chin and tilted her face so she was looking up, facing him. "Mattie, look at me." An audible gasp escaped him before he could halt it. Twin red handprints had blossomed along her flawless cheeks with swelling to emphasize the force it took to brutally mark her. A thin trickle of blood oozed from the corner of her beautiful mouth another testament of the power unleashed behind the slap she had been dealt. He wished he had that slime ball within reach so he could give him a little more of what he had meted out with his fists earlier. "Oh sweetheart, I'm so sorry." He didn't know what else he could say.

"It's ok. It's not like the marks make much difference on this face anyway." There were few things in this life that she was sure of, but this definitely was one of them. God knew she had heard her so-called stepfather say it often enough.

"Mattie what in the world would make you say such a thing? You are the most beautiful woman I have ever laid eyes on and whoever told you that lie needs a good smack." Jackson was shocked to say the least. Someone certainly pulled a number on her to have her saying such a thing. He hadn't missed the loathing and contempt that had seeped through with her comment either.

Mattie felt her neck pop from the force she exerted so she could face Jackson. She hadn't been told that by anyone except her mom and Gracie. He couldn't mean it. He thought she was beautiful? No way! He'd just said that to be nice to her. He was the one that was beautiful. She saw that for herself the first time she had met him. He had the bluest eyes she had ever seen and his cheeks revealed the sweetest angel kissed dimples. His blonde hair fell below his collar with a slight curl to the ends. She had thought he was a Greek God before and found nothing had changed her earlier assessment of how gorgeous he was. He was a Michael Angelo original. Shifting nervously she attempted to move from him because her stomach had twisted into a massive knot and the way he was looking at her now made it twist even tighter.

"Please don't," was all he could say around the growing tightness in his throat. The look Mattie had on her face when she looked at him couldn't be mistaken for anything except adoration and appreciation. He didn't want to sever the invisible bond they had begun to share. He was pleased when she had stopped pulling away but he also saw the unasked question in her eyes. He was beginning to know her pretty well in the short time he had known her. "You don't need to pull away form me Mattie. You know I won't hurt you." It wasn't meant to be a question.

Mattie couldn't help but wander how he had become so perceptive in reading her. He had known she was not only pulling away from him physically, but also emotionally. She had stopped her movements as he had asked without giving it any thought. Starring into his fathomless eyes she felt herself being pulled in deeper as each second passed. She was expecting the fear that always seemed to be her constant companion, yet it seemed to have disappeared with this man, for now. She moved back the few inches that separated them and welcomed his inviting heat more than the cold loneliness.

Jackson kept his eyes locked with hers. Tiger eyes full of wander and surprise looked back at him and he found it difficult to breath. He could no more stop himself than he could a runaway train with his bare hands. Tilting her face with a finger under her chin, he brushed a light kiss on her full pink lips and murmured, "So sweet my tiger eyed beauty."

Mattie couldn't breath. She was in total shock and she didn't know what to do. Every instinct she had demanded for her to run as fast as she could, but yet she couldn't move. More shocking; she realized she didn't want to. She had never been kissed before and she wasn't disgusted as she thought she would have been and yet it was so ingrained in her to run scared. She was so confused she really didn't know what to do or how to act.

Jackson knew it the minute he looked into her eyes. He should have controlled himself. Now he'd done it. He saved her just so he could be the one to maul her? "Damn," he whispered. He hadn't meant to do that but she looked so vulnerable, so beautiful, and so damn kissable. He couldn't control himself and now he felt like a heel. The look on her face told it all. He had screwed up royally. Now what was he going to do?

"Mattie I'm sorry. I didn't mean to do that. Please forgive me? I wouldn't hurt you for the world. Please don't be scared." He was nervous. He didn't want to lose her so soon. He had just found her. How could he make her understand? He couldn't lose her. Not now. Not ever!

"It's ok." Mattie felt her heart ache. He'd only kissed her because she was here and she was weak. She was a little scared mouse that needed his help. It shouldn't hurt but it did. She had felt the slight brushing of his lips against hers and thought it was special. Her first kiss with the man who had invaded her thoughts and dreams and now he regretted it. She had been wrong and her stepfather's words ran in her memory like a dinner bell.

"Mattie, ain't no man gonna want the likes of you so just get any notion of that out of your head. No one wants an ugly whining red head messing up his life the way you have messed up mine. If someone is interested then he will only be interested in what he can take out from under that baggy sack you call a dress."

She felt her spirits fall like they always did at his hurtful words and this memory wasn't any different. Her heart felt heavy and began to sink as it usually did.

Jackson saw the change in Mattie just as soon as it happened. What did he do wrong? Surely she knew he wouldn't hurt her. Didn't she? He had to make her understand. "Mattie I liked kissing you but I didn't want to scare you. Do you understand that? I didn't apologize for the kiss Mattie I apologized for taking advantage of you and only for that." He held his breath hoping he had made her understand.

He patiently watched her facial expressions as they went form shock to understanding, to what appeared to be amazement. Did she not realize what an exceptional looking person she truly was? Much to his disbelief he couldn't help but realize that was exactly what she thought. She didn't know nor did she make any pretence about her looks. She was attractive as hell and had no idea. God she must have had a hell of a relationship or a hell of a childhood to make her believe otherwise. What kind of monster could do such a thing? He had no idea, but he vowed he would find out, maybe not now, but eventually.

Mattie couldn't believe it. Jackson wasn't disgusted with the kiss he just didn't want to scare her. That's what he had said and she believed him. He didn't look like a deceitful person. She had dealt with those types off and on her entire life and she knew one when she saw one. He didn't fit the same mold and sudden relief swept over her like sunshine on a cloudy day. She was still reluctant to totally believe him even though she knew he was sincere. There had been too many years of abuse to accept things so easily.

Rachael had been watching the little scene play itself out and she didn't like it one damn bit. She saw Jackson kiss Mattie and she waited for it to turn ugly but much to her surprise it didn't. That didn't make her like it anymore than she did and knew she had to get to her friend. She didn't get very far because she was pulled back with the first step she made. How could she have forgotten all about Lyle and her fingers were still entwined with his? She had only concentrated on the scene that had been playing out at the table. After being stopped so abruptly she slowly brought her eyes up the muscular thighs to the narrow waist and across the wide expanse of shoulders then focused on the dark brown eyes that were full of amusement. He was smiling down at her. Like looking down was a choice! Lyle was every bit of six-foot and much more. And here she was a mere five foot-one. Their gazes locked and she saw more than amusement in Lyle's eyes. She couldn't put into words what she saw exactly, but the look held more than she wanted to admit.

Lyle had been ogled before, groped at, hit on, bribed, threatened, and even teased by a lot more experienced species of the opposite sex, but he had never been so approvingly assessed inch by inch the way Rachael had just scoped him out. It was the headiest experience he'd ever experienced where a woman was concerned. He never went without women. His looks, even though he was Native American, had guaranteed him a date just about anytime he wanted one and times when didn't. Having the approval of this little dynamo, for some reason, meant more than any of the empty, one night stand shit that seemed to be his forte. This little slip of a gorgeous package was straightforward and honest. He knew that much from the gossip around the apartment building. Not that Lyle made it his mission to find out about the little tinker but women liked to wag their tongues when it concerned another female who was in better shape, not only physically, but mentally as well. All he did when she made the move toward Jackson was to hold her back and shake his head negatively. He knew she would get the message without words. He only smiled down at her as light dawned and she grasped his meaning. He knew he was in big trouble the minute she smiled up at him. His heart shuddered and his palms grew sweaty.

Rachael was going to have to re-evaluate her earlier assessment of this larger than life hunk of male. She decided that he wasn't a James Dean wannabe as she originally dubbed him, he was much more. He was showing an obvious interest in her if she was reading his expression right. She never attracted the attention of a man who looked like him, yet he didn't hesitate in making a move on her. To say the least he had taken her by surprise, something that rarely happened. No one ever wanted to be with an over achieving midget who took exercise and health as seriously as she did. She hadn't realized she'd been staring the entire time she had been deep in her own thoughts. It took a lot to embarrass her and rudely starring at him ranked right up there. Being the type to face a challenge head on, she refused to look away from him when she had finally realized her own rude behavior. Her eyes held his unflinching, direct, and doing what came natural to her; she smiled. The kind of smile her mother always said could warm the coldest heart.

Lyle was just as surprised, as apparently Rachael seemed to be. He had been so intent on gazing down at her pixie features and the expressions that had skidded across her face that he hadn't realized he'd been absorbing her as she apparently had been him. He liked a woman who didn't play the coy act and owned up to her own actions. That kind of honesty was a rarity in women but here this little nymph was in all her glory doing just that. He liked her more than he would have thought possible in such a short span of time but then when he'd seen her fierceness regarding Jackson and her friend Mattie he couldn't help but approve because protecting the ones you loved went along way with him. Lyle smiled down at the little powerhouse who had knocked him for a loop letting her know he approved.

Joey hadn't missed any of the action that was playing out in front of him like a PG-13 event. His girls seemed to be enamored with the two young men that resembled linebackers for the NFL. Mattie's rescuers were a site to behold, not that he had any tendencies toward men, but even he could appreciate what was obvious to anyone who chose to look. It made him happy to see his girls doing something besides work and school. He knew they worked too hard and that they needed a social life outside of the clubs work hours. He couldn't hold back the grin that spread across his face. He was still grinning as he made his way to Mattie and Jackson's table. He knew what he was going to ask and what it would cost Mattie but he also knew she had to get past the horror and focus on the positive. Besides, as they say in show biz, 'the show must go on.' "Mattie? Honey, are you feeling better?" He could see her emotional wellbeing had improved greatly and he lifted a silent prayer of thanks to the young man who was responsible for the change. The absent look and the fear seemed to have been replaced with something he didn't want to put a title on just yet.

"Yes, I think so." Looking upon Jackson's face she whispered her response as if she were surprised that she truly was better.

"That's great. Now honey I want you to listen to me for a minute, all right? The show will be starting soon and I was wondering if you had decided to enter?" Joey didn't know how she was going to answer considering all that she had been through already tonight. Knowing what had happened could be used as a crutch and an excuse to back out but he hoped she would at least try. He knew she would do it if he really poured on the charm but he didn't want to have to resort to tactics so underhanded but he would if he had to.

Chapter Twenty-Two

Jackson was a little surprised by the request from the clubs owner. His bafflement must have shown through because Joey went on to explain how he and Rachael had been trying to talk Mattie into signing up for the contest. "Mattie that's great. I apparently have perfect timing to come in here on the night you might sing again."

"I don't think I can do this tonight." Twisting her fingers in her lap she focused on the task and whispered, "Not now anyway." Mattie hated disappointing anyone and she knew she was going to do just that but she honestly didn't think she could deal with anymore tonight.

"Sure you can." Joey wasn't about to let her slip out on her chance without at least trying first. He didn't want her to give that much of her hard won strength to those slime balls that had man handled her. "Just relax while we wait and enjoy the show. You can do it Mattie. I know you can and you have a great chance of winning. Don't decide right now just think about it for a little longer ok? Just think about it, for me?" With that he went about the business of being boss.

Jackson slowly reached for Mattie's hand, stopping the nervous twisting, and offering her his support. She accepted his hand without hesitation and he couldn't have been more surprised. He saw no fear, only acceptance, and he could only smile his pride with the obvious show of courage. With their fingers entwined he felt they had just crossed an invisible threshold together. There was hope for them and he was willing to pursue it with all the strength he had.

Mattie felt the warmth of Jackson's skin against hers and the unexpected calm that came with his touch. She smiled with the knowledge that Jackson could hold her hand and she could accept it.

Sensing Mattie's change in mood Jackson took his other hand and tipped Mattie's face up for the second time tonight and looked in to her mesmerizing eyes. She hadn't resisted his touch and he was struck at the sight of her smiling up at him. "Mattie you should try to sing tonight. Not for me or anyone in this room. You should do it for you. To get over all that happened tonight while it's still fresh. You need to do this for new beginnings." He really was pushing the issue but he knew she wouldn't fight him with much effort. He also knew when she refused it wouldn't be just a token refusal and he was afraid it would cause her more damage if he let her get by with it.

"I...I don't know. I'm scared Jackson," she was being honest with him as she worried her bottom lip. She hadn't readily admitted that sort of thing to just anyone but it had been easy to confide in her guardian angel. That was how she was beginning to think of Jackson because he always seemed to be around when she needed him.

"It's all right Mattie; I'll be here with you and you'll be safe." Jackson knew that meant more to her than anything in the world.

Mattie didn't know how she would be able to get up there and act as if nothing had happened but she knew with this man and her friends cheering her on she could at least try. She didn't want to disappoint any of them and that being the case she knew she couldn't refuse. "Ok, I'll do it but you have to promise you won't leave."

"Not a chance lady. I wouldn't leave if a stampede of wild bulls came through that door." Jackson saw the level of relief that swept across her face revealing the true extent of her fear and nervousness at the prospect of getting up on the stage and being the center of attention. Mattie hadn't realized yet how the people she had on her side were willing to protect her no matter what.

Chapter Twenty-Three

When the music started on stage the stranger continued to watch along with the rest of the crowd. He looked upon her and seethed with every breath she took. Mumbling to the vacant space around him he voiced the thoughts that had been churning in his head. "Still the center of attention huh Mattie? Well, you're about to get my attention and you can bet it won't be the kind you want. You won't live long enough to enjoy the kind of attention you deserve." With those thoughts consuming him, he abruptly stood and turned to leave colliding with a waitress at the same time. Ignoring the young woman and the distress he had caused her he mumbled a profanity unfit for virgin ears and stomped out in search of the three hoodlums that had been mistreated for having a little fun with Ms. Goody-two-shoes. The way they had been treated tonight warranted retaliation and he wasn't fool enough to ignore the potential help they could offer him and his own agenda. When it was all said and done he would finally be on top. A position he was meant to be on but denied all his miserable life. The satisfaction of getting what his old man had lost out on was going to be almost as good as seeing that red headed bitch get what was coming to her. Not quite as good, but pretty damned close as far as he was concerned. Smiling at the mere thought of success he made his way out of baby land in search of some patsies that he was sure wanted to jump on his train of pain.

It was close to the time Mattie was supposed to sing and all the people who had come to mean so much to her was patiently waiting to see what her decision was going to be.

Mattie had decided she was going to get up on that stage and sing like she had never sung before. She would do this for her friends, the friends that had become her family. Mostly, she wanted to do this for Jackson, even though he said to do it for herself, she knew she wanted to succeed for him. Without speaking Mattie rose up to leave, signaling Rachael to come with her, and help her get ready.

Rachael walked Mattie back to the dressing room to fix her hair and to help her change her clothes. As usual Rachael was prepared. She must have known Mattie would do the show because she already had a new golden knit dress on hand along with all the accessories. Mattie raised an eyebrow in silent question as she spoke lightly. "Hoping?"

Rachael only smiled back and nodded in a positive motion. Mattie could only shake her head and smile at her friend who had become like a sister. She really loved Rache for all she was and had been to her since they had met.

They heard her name being announced and Mattie felt the nerves begin. Using her well rehearsed calming tactics she began to hum a favorite Lionel Ritchie tune to herself realizing that she wanted that to be her song for the show. Mattie not only wanted to sing that particular song she wanted to sing it for Jackson. He wouldn't know that she meant it for him and that thought built up her courage enough to possibly do what she intended to do. It was a way she could tell him what she felt without actually saying it directly.

Rachael saw the look of confidence wash over her friends face and with it came a smile so radiant it was blinding. She knew Mattie had feelings for Jackson or she wouldn't have been able to sit with him or touch him the way she had. Rachael suspected Mattie's past carried a load of baggage any normal person would have been crushed under and yet she had managed to still survive. She felt that Jackson still had a long way to go with her friend and she would help if she could, not that she had much experience with men. She would also keep a close eye on the buff blonde because she be damned if she was going to sit by and let him hurt her.

She was finding herself a little off center with the attention Lyle had shown her so maybe they could help each other. "Who would have guessed it?" She mumbled to herself. She heard Mattie ask her what was wrong with a concerned look marring her lineless face. She hadn't realized she had spoken loud enough for anyone to hear her. "Oh, it's nothing. I was just thinking aloud. Sorry."

"Would that happen to have anything to do with Lyle? She had seen Rachael with the very handsome Indian, and she found she really enjoyed the reaction that just flitted across Rachael's face.

"Are you teasing me Mattie Collins?" She said in her mock stern voice with her hands poised on her firm hips. "Guess it could be. He is very gorgeous and he is interested in me!" She was grinning like a child with a new toy. Mattie only nodded and smiled at the look of excitement that went with that statement.

Joey knocked on the door of the changing area alerting them it was time. Mattie took a deep breath and started her litany of 'you can do it's' as she made her way to the curtain backstage. "Mattie girl you can do this so buck up and get to it. Let them know who you are on the inside and you will be the best out of all of them." That familiar voice of Gracie's filled her thoughts and gave her the added boost of courage she needed. She was thankful for the reminder and the support. Holding her smile in place and raising her head she made her way to the stage.

Jackson had made his way front and center. He wouldn't have missed this moment for anything. Waiting with unexplainable nerves he held his breath anticipating Mattie's arrival.

Lyle waited for Rachael to come back from the dressing room and it wasn't filled with patience. That little powerhouse had bowled him over. He wanted her with him and as he scanned the crowd he caught site of her weaving in and out of the tightly packed bodies of anxious on lookers. He couldn't believe he had shared the same apartment building with her and not noticed her before, but then again he always looked for the tall, well-endowed female. He understood now what he had been missing out on with that narrow minded point of view. When she caught sight of him staring at her he was rewarded with a beaming smile. Lyle felt as if he had been physically hit. "Damn" was all he could mutter through his tight throat. He reached for her as she got close to him and pulled her to his side. A possessive gesture he full well performed to ward off any other mans advances. He wanted her marked as his territory and there would be hell to pay if anyone didn't heed the warning he was publicly issuing.

Joey made the introduction and the lights dimmed in preparation for Mattie's appearance. Only one beam of light focused on center stage and as she made her way to the stool she realized she didn't have her guitar with her. A hint of fear began to lick at her nerves but as she got closer to the stool she realized Rachael had already covered all the bases because her guitar leaned against the stool awaiting her. She picked up the instrument that was like an extension of her own hand and felt the strength of its history flow through her lending her the added courage she would need. Sighing Mattie lifted the shoulder strap over her hair and slipped her thigh onto the edge of the stool. It was now or never and so taking a deep breath she began.

Jackson found he couldn't force his lungs to work as his breath stilled in motion. He couldn't think, focus, or for that matter move if his life depended on it. He was totally mesmerized by the site Mattie presented. She was the most beautiful woman he had ever seen. He had thought so before but now she had left him speechless.

Lyle glanced up when he heard Mattie being introduced and even he found he was starring. He heard Rachael whisper in his ear, "Isn't she beautiful?" Lyle jerked his head around like he'd been caught doing something illegal. "Uh, yeah, she is." But when he looked down into that elfin face he only had eyes for her. He was starring at her without apology and kept his focus linked with only her. "Yeah, but so are you," he whispered.

Rachael was thunderstruck by the intensity of his stare. Lyle looked like he was devouring her with his eyes and she felt her heart skip past the aerobic level she strived for during her exercises. "Lyle?" She hesitated, waiting, listening, and watching for a response. "What's the matter Lyle?"

"Oh…um… it's nothing really. I just got lost in the view. Do you know how pretty your eyes are?" He asked with a broad smile.

Rachael found for the first time in her life she could be struck speechless. No words would come out of her suddenly dry mouth. So she slowly motioned her head side to side indicating she didn't. He thought she was beautiful and had pretty eyes? Not knowing where to go with his compliment she wordlessly turned to face her friend on stage. She tried to refocus her attention on Mattie while her heart raced uncomfortably in her chest.

Jackson had suddenly become deaf and blind to everything around him as Mattie consumed his entire focus. With every fiber of his being he knew that Mattie was destined to be the most important person in his life. From a spiritual level to the molecular level he knew she was the only woman for him. Was it possible to love someone so soon after meeting him or her? He most definitely knew you could. The feelings he had for her were intense and soul deep. He knew he wanted her physically without a doubt but it was more than that. He wanted a future with her, to spend his life with her, to share everything until he was old and gray with her.

Mattie began to play the tune she had been humming earlier. Strumming lovingly on the well-worn cords she let the music flow through her, taking her to the place that warmed her soul. She focused intently on Jackson while the ballad she sang from the heart easily escaped her lips. Her eyes were closed to everything and everyone creating a shield from the crowd and kept them diverted to the lone man starring right back at her. The intensity was overwhelming so she closed her eyes to block his piercing blue eyes. She kept her head tilted to the side allowing the thick blanket of her auburn waves to cascade behind the neck of the guitar. She wore the peaceful look of serenity and calm while the music flowed through her fingers. She wasn't so lost in the rhythm that she couldn't feel Jackson's eyes still focused on her. She knew he was watching her just by the feel of his stare. She wanted to open her eyes again, but she was afraid he would know she was singing for him and him alone. The need to see his face outgrew the greater fear of facing the crowd. Finally giving in to her desire, she forced her eyes to open as she got to the last and final verse focusing on Jackson. Their eyes locked and held. No one existed in this place except him and Mattie smiled just as the last notes were played out. Jackson had been her protector, her friend, and she had a feeling he was going to mean more to her than either of those things. She had very strong feelings for him, feelings she couldn't put a name to just yet. It was all too new to her. Being a whole person was the goal she had set for herself and she found that she wanted Jackson to be a part of that wholeness. She was so deeply entranced that she didn't hear the applause or see the crowd; she only had eyes for Jackson and the thoughts of a possible future.

Jackson gave new meaning to the words 'struck dumb.' He knew Mattie had meant for the song to be just for him and no one else that was in the room.

He was sure of it. When she gazed at him with such intensity, she had revealed so much more than mere words could express. He knew at that moment she was meant to be his. Mattie was his soul mate and her love for him was reflected in those warm, unique, multicolored eyes. Falling in love with her was sudden, yes, but not unexpected. He had known it all along but had refused to believe that what Lyle had told him could be true. Her honest expression was nearly his undoing but very welcoming to his lonely heart.

Lyle and Rachael didn't miss the look exchanged between their friends. They were both grinning as they continued to openly gaze at one another. Mattie and Jackson may not admit it but they were so deep in love with each other they couldn't see the forest for the trees. Rachael and Lyle both looked at each other knowing what the other was thinking.

"Lyle?" Rachael whispered up to him.

"Hum?" He had to bend down so he could hear her.

"Do you think they even know it?" Her breath came in short bursts with his face being so close to hers she could smell his spicy aftershave and feel the heat of his body next to hers.

Lyle didn't miss the way she caught her breath and the way it fanned across his cheek or how her voice lowered when she spoke. He wanted to brush his lips across her unblemished skin. He shrugged and thought in for a penny, in for a pound and did exactly what he had just fantasized about. Tilting his face at an angle and lowering his tall frame he captured Rachael's welcoming lips with his own. Fire works and heat radiated to his toes. Never had a kiss singed him and turned his thoughts upside down as the impact of this one did. Forcing himself to straighten a fraction he looked into her heavy lidded eyes and gave her a strangled answer. "Nope."

Rachael felt the whisper soft brushing of his mouth on her overly sensitive lips. She wanted more, much more, but she had to put her own desires on hold. Mattie had to be her main concern, not the building lust she was feeling for this larger than life man. She redirected her focus back to where it needed to be. "Lyle?"

"Yeah tinker?" He used the pet name with out thinking how she would feel about it and sincerely hoped she didn't offend easily. He winked and pulled her body closer to his by positioning her between his thighs, hoping she knew he meant no insult by referring to her compact little body. Watching her expressive face for signs of pain at his words or anger for their use he was pleased to see she wasn't overly sensitive about her size.

Not giving a second thought to the 'tinker' comment she voiced what was of the utmost importance to her. "Please don't let him hurt her" gesturing toward Jackson. "Mattie's got a history that has really messed her up so please make sure he's good to her." She couldn't hold the building tears at bay and as she spoke and one trickled down her cheek. She couldn't stand for people to be hurt. Especially people she considered her friends.

"Mattie is lucky to have you for a friend Rachael." Lyle trailed the lone tear as it raced down her cheek only to be caught by his finger. "Listen honey, Jackson has been gaga over Mattie since he first laid his baby blues on her and I can tell you without a doubt that he would never hurt her. Not intentionally, anyways. If what we saw earlier is any indication of how he cares for her then you won't have to worry about her when she's with him. Did you get a load of those creeps he beat to a pulp earlier? Take my word for it Mattie couldn't be any safer if she had her own personal bodyguard."

Rachael suspected it already but felt relief by hearing it from someone else. She hadn't realized until that very moment that Lyle had her up close against his very broad chest during the entire conversation. The position should have bothered her since she had just met the man but for some reason it felt right. Rachael liked the feel of him against her even though she was dwarfed by his very large size.

Without realizing what was happening Jackson was on his feet and moving through the applauding crowd heading straight for Mattie. The invisible bond was pulling him without conscious thought and before he realized it he was standing at the edge of the stage. He watched, as if in slow motion, as his hand reached for the woman who had captured his heart.

Mattie reached for him as if she were a puppet on a string. As her small, elegant hand slipped into his large, callused palm the electrical sparks ignited with a vengeance.

Jackson gently tugged her hand pulling her toward him. Willingly, she allowed herself to be guided by him. He hoped what he saw in her eyes was a reflection of what was in his own. It was the kind of emotion you only read about or dreamt of. Love at first glance had always seemed to be a myth that romance writers peddled at the book stores and yet here he was living proof that it was real and she was standing right in front of him with a smile so bright it was blinding. His love for this woman was growing at such an alarming rate that it made his chest ache.

When Mattie inched toward the edge of the stage Jackson released his hand and lifted both hands up to her waiting for the acceptance of his offer to help her down. Much to his relief and immense pleasure she bent at the waist at placed her delicate hands on his broad shoulders without hesitation and he felt his heart soar. He wanted to tell her how he felt but knew it was too soon and he didn't want to frighten her anymore than she already had been.

Very carefully Jackson inched his palms up her rib cage without taking his eyes off hers. When his hands stopped at the juncture under her arms he gently lifted her off her feet and swung her down to slide down the full length of his body stopping directly face to face with him.

Mattie held her breath because this was too close and she felt the tide of fear rippling against her control. "Not now," she chanted silently. She refused to let the fear ruin what had been the most wonderful night she had ever experienced in her life beside the earlier ambush from the three stooges.

Jackson saw the look blanket her face and felt his heart sink. "Damn, too much, too soon." He made no sudden moves hoping to keep from startling her further. He knew she had achieved a small victory tonight and didn't want it to end so soon.

The crowd roared and clapped but to those it was aimed at heard nothing but their own heart beats. Mattie's body had brushed Jackson's as he had eased her down in front of him, yet she still made no move to retreat from his nearness. The fire her nearness ignited within him was causing a reaction that she wouldn't understand. At least he had a sense that she wouldn't and he needed to put some space between them. He didn't want to frighten her and if he stayed as close as he was he was afraid he would do more than that. He stepped back just enough to break the contact and knew he had made the right decision by the smile that broke across Mattie's beautiful face.

Mattie knew what he had done and the relief she felt must have shown on her face if the light behind his eyes was any indication.

In that instant Jackson was glad he'd had enough insight to prevent a potential disaster. He would have missed the sweetest smile altogether had he not been so focused on her face.

The crowd roared again and the magic that had held them so intimately suddenly disappeared. Only then did they realize they had become the center of attention. Their faces flushed a bright shade of crimson as the situation warranted.

The fear suddenly roared to life and blindsided Mattie attacking with a vengeance. It was clawing at her with a wild abandon. This was worse than what she was used to because she had let her guard down. She knew her control was gone and the need to flee was great. She desperately needed space and she needed it in a bad way. The ability to concentrate or to think had escaped her without warning. The roaring was so loud in her ears it was resonating in her head like a freight train. The combination caused her to react the only way she knew. Clutching her borrowed gown at the hem she bolted for the exit running at full speed without any sense of direction in mind. Her thoughts were consumed with freedom and open spaces.

Rachael, Lyle, and Joey saw the abrupt change in Mattie but no one foresaw the panic that had taken over her features. They saw her make a dash for the back of Waves and Jackson hot on her heels. Rachael started in the same direction with as much energy as she could exert only to be swung into an iron embrace. "What the..."

"Leave them alone for now Rache. Jackson will take care of her. He was the only one to get near her earlier and I'm sure it will be the same this time. He has a connection with her that we don't. She is fighting some wicked demons and apparently Jacks is the one she trusts enough to let him touch her. Let them be for now. Ok?"

Rachael knew he was right but she had never in her life felt so useless. She wanted to go after Mattie, but she also knew Lyle had perceived the situation perfectly so she stayed in his iron grip with her head cradled against his chest. She heard the steady beat of his heart and felt the warmth radiating through his black tee shirt. She wasn't conscience of her hands encircling his waist it was as if they had a mind of their own. She just knew she liked where she was and had no intentions of moving so she snuggled in a little closer and whispered, "Ok."

The contest continued but Joey didn't enjoy it. His thoughts were on Mattie. He'd recognized that she had a fear so palpable that when you witnessed it the sight scared the hell out of you and that was exactly what had happened tonight. He had wanted to chase after Mattie when he saw her bolt out of the club but stopped after several steps knowing Jackson was already on her heels. He knew the young man had a connection to her or he wouldn't have been able to help her earlier. So, forcing his steps back to the grill, he tried not to worry. Not an easy task where his girls were concerned but he would at least try.

Joey hoped she could work through some of the history that controlled her before it stole her soul and killed the beauty she had on the inside but he didn't know if she would be able to. He vowed he would try to get some information that could help them, help her. He didn't know if anything would make a difference but he didn't know what else to do.

Mattie didn't feel the cold sprays of the waves as they hit the breakers or the cold wind that whipped her dress around her legs threatening to trip her with its caress. She had fled the club with only one thing in mind, to escape. She didn't care where she had gone as long as it was someplace safe and free of people. The cool air filling her burning lungs felt good as it opened up the band that had been tightening her chest making it difficult to breath. She didn't feel the tears streaming down her cheeks. The warm rivulets and the sobs racking her tall frame went unnoticed as she made her way along the coast. As reality began to seep into her clouded thoughts she slowed her long strides. As her steps slowed from a fast walk to a slow glide she began to take in her surroundings feeling a kinship for the turmoil of the waves hitting the beach. The beach began to come into focus and the dampness seeped through

123

her dress bringing the chill with it and mild shivers to dance along her skin. Without warning the realization of what had happened at Wave's came crashing to the forefront of her consciousness. Jackson had been standing right in front of her when she acted like a scarred little school girl and ran from him, again. Mental self loathing for letting such a wonderful night end so horribly filled her with unanswerable questions. How could I just run like that? Why did I let the fear take away a special night? Why? Why? Why? She found herself at the waters edge entranced by the relationship of the calm sandy beach with the hard crashing of saltwater. It was kind of like her and Jackson. He was her calm and she was the unpredictable waves. She could only cry and let the shakes take their toll on her already spent body. She shuddered and yelled into the night revealing the true depth of her despair. "God, why does this keep happening to me? Haven't I suffered enough?" She let her head dip down letting her chin rest on her chest as the tears trailed down her cheeks and dripped onto her already wet dress.

"Yes, Matt you have." Jackson had followed her every step of the way and keeping his distance had been the hardest thing for him to do. He knew she needed the time but it broke his heart to stay in the shadows and watch her suffer. He couldn't take anymore when he heard her plea to God. He wanted to comfort her and let her know she wasn't alone anymore.

Mattie swung her head around only to come face to face with the very man who had consumed her thoughts. She hadn't heard him walk up or kneel down beside her but she was thankful he had come. She wasn't as alone as she had thought. He was her beach and he caught the turmoil she threw at him without complaint. It felt good to have him at her side.

"It was just too much, too soon, Mattie. That's all it is. It will get better." Jackson sat next to her being mindful not to touch her, even though that was exactly what he wanted to do. He hoped his presence would ease some of the loneliness he knew she was feeling. It had broken his heart when she lowered her head and openly sobbed the way she had. Without giving any thought to his actions and going against his earlier decision not to touch her, he lifted his hand to her cheek, speaking softly he whispered her name. "Mattie?"

He tried to get her to look at him only to find she was resisting. He didn't know if he should stop or to try a little harder. He opted for trying harder and was rewarded with a response. He couldn't believe the despair and isolation he witnessed in her eyes. If the eyes are the windows to ones soul then his Mattie had suffered far more than anyone he had ever known. His heart ached for her and the pain she must have suffered. Refusing to let her sit here and hurt all alone he spoke from his heart revealing what he hoped she would believe. "Mattie, if you want to talk I'll be here for you and if you don't then I'll still be here. We can just sit and watch the waves if you like." He waited for her to acknowledge that she had heard him, but no response was forthcoming. "Mattie, sweetheart, please let me help you. I need to know if there's something, anything, I can do? Please Matt?" Jackson waited and waited to the point where his nerves danced along the surface of his skin. He thought she wouldn't respond at all and could only hope she was listening. When he began to give up altogether on the hope she would lean on him he felt the warmth of her body against his as she put her head on his shoulder. Jackson's breathe stilled in his throat when he heard her sigh. Yet, he made no move to touch her, hell, he didn't move at all. He didn't want to risk a thing because he needed her more than she needed him. He felt Mattie's hand slide across his back and his waist a she held on to him as tight as she could. Her unspoken trust and faith in him was more than he had hoped for. She buried her face into his strong and inviting shoulder. In that moment he knew he was lost. This reaction happened every time Mattie touched him of her own freewill.

Mattie knew every movement she made and every movement Jackson didn't make and that only endeared him to her even more; if that were even possible. She knew she was safe right where she was and she whispered a thank you to him as she held him in the dark with only the roar of the ocean for company.

Jackson held back the groan that demanded to be released. He closed his eyes and tried to maintain a calm he didn't feel. Taking a deep breath he decided talking was a good avenue about now. "Mattie, do you want to talk about it? I'm a good listener. You don't have to if you don't want too. Just know that I'm here for you if you need me."

Mattie heard Jackson but she wouldn't tell him. How could she? How can you tell someone something you don't even know yourself? How can you explain fear that swallows you whole and you haven't a clue why? How do you make someone understand that being touched terrifies you or being crowded smothers you till you have to run away? I wish I knew what to tell you Jacks. How can I though when I don't even know?

Jackson felt the change in her but it was different this time. He patiently waited a short while when he decided he would drop it and let her decide what she wanted to reveal or keep quiet. "It's ok Mattie. We can just sit here and watch the waves chase the sand. It's such a nice night out we can just sit here and enjoy it if that's all right with you."

"Thank you Jackson. I just needed some space, but I'm glad you came after me." That was the most she could get out of her mouth and she hoped he was content with it.

"You don't have to thank me sweatheart. There was no way I was going to watch you walk away by yourself when you were so upset. I was with you every step of the way making sure you were safe, and held back until you

125

were ready to have company. Now, if you like, we can stay here for as long as you want because I'm in no hurry to leave and I would rather be here with you then anywhere else." Jackson was content to just spend time with her so they sat side by side with Mattie leaning into him and holding on to him for support with neither saying a word. It was a companionable silence between them. For any onlookers they appeared to be the picture of a young couple in love enjoying the evening with one another. They would have never guessed the amount of tears and unspoken pain that had been very evident only minutes before. That was the scene that Lyle and Rachael witnessed as they made their way to the coast line.

The moon was full painting a picture of muted light across the rolling waves of the busy ocean. Jackson heard the soft footfalls approaching them from behind knowing it was Lyle and Rachael nearing the little slice of heaven they had created. He motioned for them to continue approaching with small unexaggerated motions of his hand. He didn't want them to startle Mattie but knew they were full of questions by the looks they wore on their worried faces. Looking over Mattie's bowed head he mouthed to them "it's ok."

Rachael nodded her understanding and smiled back at him. "Thank you" she wordlessly mouthed back. She was ecstatic to see that Lyle knew his friend so well and that he had been taking care of Mattie just the way he had said he would. She didn't know what to expect as she approached the couple but to find Mattie in Jackson's arms and for her to be calm was more of a relief than a shock. She didn't want to see her friend hurt anymore than she already had been. Mattie was her best friend who was more like a sister and to Rachael, family was everything.

As Rachael made her way to Mattie's side she glanced in Lyle's direction to assure him she needed to see Mattie. He smiled back at her as he remained in the same spot they had stopped in, keeping his distance. Rachael lowered herself down beside her still silent friend. She didn't know what to say or how to act which was not the norm for her. She had always prided herself with ready solutions and quick answers but this was one situation she had no sense of direction with. Taking a steadying breath and shoring up her nerve she attempted to draw her friend out of the place she had retreated to. "Mattie," Rachael spoke softly. "Mattie, it's me Rache, are you all right honey?" No answer came and the people surrounding this sheltered girl were beginning to worry the longer the silence continued. The glances shared by the group expressed the worry and even more so, the concern.

Mattie slowly raised her head and looked around her with fresh tears streaming down her cheeks. She was so overwhelmed with emotion the tears were the only release she had.

Rachael's eyes filled with pools of unshed tears as she looked at her friend. She knew for some unexplainable reason that Mattie had fought some internal battle and resembled the walking wounded. She had an idea the war was yet to be fought and when it was it would be a whole lot worse than this mini battle had been. Mattie's face revealed the emotional strain she had suffered this night and the empty shell looking back at her broke her heart. Rachael was frightened for her friend because she knew no one could know the kind of hell Mattie had lived through to put that battle wary look on her face. Rachael finally wept for her friend and lifted a silent prayer for Mattie hoping her prayers would be answered.

After several minutes of silence Mattie whispered, "I'm all right Rachael, Jackson stayed with me and made sure I was safe."

There was a lot of hidden meaning in that statement yet no one commented on it. How could they? Jackson wandered if she'd ever had anyone protect her only to have the answer hit him square in the face. Her actions alone were answer enough.

Lyle wasn't much for the bonding thing except with Jackson and now it seemed, Rachael. He'd never felt any need of it. Granted he didn't know Mattie but he knew of her and how special she was. She drew him to her. There was an invisible bond they shared without putting words to it. He knew they were alike in ways only they understood because what little he had been around her he recognized the signs. Lyle knew those signs well and he refused to ignore them. He had personal knowledge as to what they could do to you especially if you had no one to help you. Mattie was fortunate that she had several people now that were more than willing to share her burden. He vowed he would help as much as she would let him. This secret bond he was sure connected them would have them also becoming close friends. Not a position he welcomed normally, but in this case he was more than accepting of adding her to his short list of friends. Besides he knew Mattie and Rachael were a group package and he couldn't have one without the other, so it was a done deal as far as he was concerned.

Making his movements slow, calculated and filled with purpose Lyle moved in front of Mattie. The action had Jackson and Rachael both shooting him questioning look that he didn't have time to acknowledge. His focus was totally on Mattie. Crouching down in front of brought his face in her direct line of vision. He hoped he wasn't making things worse but he felt this need to speak with her, to help her. He wouldn't stand idly by watching Mattie lose the ground she had a gained. "Mattie? Would you please look at me?" Lyle spoke stern enough to get her attention because it was the only way he felt he could reach her. He knew she would respond to his authority and she didn't disappoint him. He almost smiled when he saw her lifting her head.

Lyle recognized the empty look her eyes held. He had seen it enough himself to know what it meant. Once their eyes met he saw she recognized him.

Mattie knew he had been where she is now and she thought it odd to feel a kinship with a stranger. Yet, she wasn't afraid of him.

They shared a bond that Lyle could see she hadn't admitted to herself just yet, but she would. The thought that raced through his head when they made eye contact was that she was full of repressed memories.

Lyle continued to stare into Mattie's empty gaze and when he spoke she had no doubt it was just for her. "Mattie, I understand. I know where you are and the fight you've been fighting. I know what it's like and I know where it will lead you. You will survive it. You have the courage and the strength. I can see it. Lean on those who love you and accept the help they offer you. You don't have to do it alone." Lyle then gave her his lazy, best friend in the world smile.

Mattie only stared into those fathomless eyes and she could see the truth in what he just told her. She wasn't sure how she knew but was certain that Lyle knew what she was up against because he had faced the demons too. What impressed her beyond measure was the fact that he had survived it. He was telling her she could too. She felt a surge of hope well up inside her. She wanted to thank him but she didn't know if she could get the words out. Slowly and with effort she forced out a whispered "Thank you." She wanted him to know, for some odd reason, that she believed him. This was the oddest encounter she had ever had and yet it was familiar, and oddly enough, comforting. "I don't know why but I think your right."

Lyle only nodded his head and stood. He was still directly in front of Mattie. He reached down, not for Rachael, but for her. Mattie accepted his offer without thought or hesitation and he lifted her into a standing position. Lyle bent next to her ear and he whispered for her ears only. "I'm available anytime you want to talk. Ok?"

Jackson jumped to his feet as Lyle reached for Rachael. "Come on pixie the night is young and so are we. Let's go have some fun." He exaggerated the wink he bestowed on the little minx. He had plans that he wanted to discuss with her and it was areas that needed privacy.

Rachael felt dumbstruck that he still wanted to be with her. Especially after everything that had happened with Mattie. She could only nod her head and smile up at this beautiful man. They began to move away from Mattie and Jackson before Rachael found her tongue again. She stopped dead in her tracks and whirled around to come face to face with Mattie. "I almost forgot to tell you," she couldn't stop the huge grin that stole across her face; "You won the contest Mattie, you won! Joey will talk to you tomorrow. Didn't I tell you would win it? Didn't I?" Rachael kissed Mattie on the cheek and squeezed her hands before she went back to where Lyle stood.

Mattie was speechless. Jackson was smiling at her. Without warning Jackson yelled into the fading light "Hey Lyle?"

"Yeah, whatcha want?"

"Thanks man. Just thanks."

"Ah man." Lyle replied in mock disgust as he continued to walk away with Rachael at his side.

Jackson heard the fading mumbles as his friend distanced himself with his new lady. He knew Lyle didn't like to be recognized for having a generous heart but that was just too damn bad. Jackson knew Lyle understood Mattie and her problems somehow and he was willing help her. Must be the Indian insight he possessed. What ever it was Lyle reached a higher level of respect as far as Jackson was concerned, if that were possible since Jackson had, had high opinions of his friend for years now.

They were alone again and Jackson caught the faint trembling that was shaking Mattie's body and was afraid that she was crying again but when he looked into her face he realized it wasn't tears but the cold that was making her shiver. The wind that whipped off the ocean waves had a bite at times especially as the sun came to a close. He reached out for her, wanting to hold her to him, but he didn't know how Mattie would react to the closeness. Especially after the night she'd had so he caught himself midway and dropped his hand back to his side. He didn't want to be the cause of a relapse into that darkness that engulfed her so ruthlessly. He faced her with all the love and hope he could manage in a single glance. He prayed she could see those feelings expressed in his eyes because they were already strong in his heart.

The gesture of his intended touch didn't go unnoticed by Mattie. How could she explain what had happened to her wasn't his fault? He had been there for her more than once and seemed to have a knack for picking up the pieces she tended to fall into. She locked eyes with those as blue as the ocean they were standing in front of. She wanted him to know, to understand, how special he was to her. With every ounce of courage she could mange and every positive phrase she could recall from memory Mattie purposefully stepped forward placing her body closer to Jackson's.

Jackson didn't dare move. He didn't dare breathe or bat an eyelash. He knew this was a step she had to take on her own as a show of independence and of courage. Mattie was taking a step away from the bonds that had held her captive for so long. He could only smile as she stepped a little closer wearing such a determined face.

Mattie managed a closeness that could only be considered a breath apart then looked up into a face that was meaning more to her than she ever thought possible.

Jackson looked down gazing into that very expressive face with the golden eyes that had captured his heart in every way possible. Her emotions were so visible that he inhaled sharply when he saw the depth of her feelings. Was it possible she felt more than a sense of obligation or gratitude? The sparks danced between them like fire flies. Without thought Mattie reached out to him with an unsteady hand.

Jackson was frozen stiff as if he were a statue. Mattie's hand slid down his cheek and joined its mate upon his chest. Her touch was light as a feather but it was a touch none the less. He refused to move because he didn't want to break the spell. He didn't dare. Mattie moved closer and Jackson's heart pounded relentlessly against his ribs. He couldn't form one coherent thought or utter one word. Speech had left him and his other senses were rapidly retreating. He felt her every tremble and heard every sigh. Praying the whole time that she wouldn't stop and trying to keep a grip on his responding body. Even though he was deep in his world of sensations he was very aware when Mattie's cool soft lips touched his and she whispered against his very welcoming mouth a soft "Thank you Jackson."

Jackson wanted to hold her so bad his arms waged war with his mental demands. He knew it would be the biggest mistake he could make if he acted on his desires. Mattie had made the move and he knew how hard she'd had to struggle for that hard won freedom. He refused to jeopardize her success for anything. His demanding body would not win this fight no matter how hard it tried to act on his base desire. Once Mattie's whispered thanks left her lips a loud crash of waves broke the trance. He knew they had been in this spot a long time because the crashing of the sea increased as the hour grew late. He patiently waited for Mattie to make the next move.

Mattie knew the minute the spell that had woven around them had broken but the magic continued to dance between them. It lingered like the fragrance of freshly misted perfume. She blushed with this newfound boldness but the darkness hid it from searching and knowing eyes. She was taking new steps in her life and she felt she was going to share it with this man who understood her better than anyone since Gracie and her momma. Happiness washed over her like a blanket and her natural response lit her face like a Roman candle. Her life was changing and she with it. Linking their hands she silently nudged him in the direction of home. It was the steps into a future she had only dared dream of. She lifted a silent prayer of thanks for her dreams becoming a reality.

130

Chapter Twenty-Four

While Mattie was finding a little edge of happiness in her world there were those who were making plans to take it all away from. A small group of men sat around a beat up table in a shack that should have been condemned. Talking into the early hours of the morning was proving a great benefit for the watcher. He didn't even have to search for his needed idiots because they had willingly walked right into his devious plans. Life was looking up for him and he was beginning to see his dreams begin to unfold into reality. That could be a bright spot in his black heart if he let it. But he didn't. He bargained and made false promises in order for the little bitch to get her just rewards. His plans were coming together nicely so he was riding high for the time being. He knew everything was within his grasp and the power he felt in that was a heady experience. He relished it. These three dolts would do nicely since they seemed to be too stupid to pour piss out of a boot with the directions on the heel. Yet, they were mean enough to serve his purposes without many questions. He smiled a smile only the mad possessed and the crazy understood.

He made Weasel's skin crawl just like it did when his daddy used him like a punching bag but the weirdo had money to throw away and they needed some green backs. Work wasn't something they were afraid of but habits cost more that a damn burger joint could pay you. That is if you could get hired to begin with. No one hired scum as they were often referred to. Quick cash and some free tail was usually a good enough offer from where he was sitting. Weasel didn't like this guy one damn bit but money was something they were in short supply of and ignoring his feelings would be easy enough.

He could tell his buds didn't like the weirdo either, but they were in agreement to the money and a little fun on the side. Greed and lust took front seat and the deal he offered them was a sweet one. Turns out the chick that caused him to get the hell beat out of him was the one this guy was after. Some family crap none of them gave shit about. Getting his hands on her would be a bonus indeed. Red made him hard the minute he looked at her. He would have had her too, if her bodyguards hadn't shown up. There must be a God up there after all.

The guy said they could do what they wanted with the babe after he taught her a lesson and that had been the final deciding factor. Weasel could feel his jeans get tight just thinking about having her. Everyone in this room were gonna get a little somthin-somthin and they'd all be happy campers.

The three stooges had no clue that he had an agenda that didn't include them. He was in control and he was calling the shots. His plans were the only ones important and if anyone got in his way he would enjoy taking them out. He felt the thrill of anticipation for what he had planned for the little prissy bitch he had spent most of his life hating. He felt a sexual arousal from the mere thought of accomplishing his goals. Damn he needed a woman and he knew he would have no trouble finding one. He often found a whore more than willing to go with him, but when it came time to get to the seriousness of his sexual enjoyment they would end up fighting and screaming their damn lungs out. Not that that wasn't an added bonus because their reactions were exactly what he wanted all along. Their fear became his aphrodisiac and he basked in it until he had to shut them up. Damn shame for them because they wouldn't do it peacefully. He couldn't contain the low growl that escaped his throat. He was ready for a hunt and the prey would be caught unawares. "Let's get the hell out of here and hunt up some fun boys." Before the idiot squad could open their mouths he was leading the pack out to the van and heading into town. Heaven help the unlucky women who happened to agree to a night out with this bunch. The woman or women would be used in ways no living creature deserved to be used. By the time they figured out what was really going down it already be too late.

Chapter Twenty-Five

Mattie had let Jackson take her home that night three weeks ago and since then he'd sent her little notes of encouragement or sentiment, flowers, phone calls, coming into Waves when he wasn't working on his boat or in class. They had grown so close that her heart filled with an emotion she wouldn't put a name on it but she knew Jackson felt it too. He made no demands on her, he didn't push, and he didn't beg for promises she may not be able to keep. That night had been one of her best and one of her worst all rolled into one. When they parted Jackson had made no effort to kiss her or hug her. There were only shy smiles and hopeful glances. That night helped to strengthen the weak bond that already existed between them. It would be the foundation in which they were building a strong and lasting relationship.

Now, as she stood looking over the churning sea and the winds were whipping her skirt around her legs she found herself smiling with the memories of that emotion filled night. She had never experienced such an emotional roller coaster but it had been such a grand ride since then.

Jackson was so sweet and supportive. He understood and he never pushed. She wandered where he got such reserve, such patience. His parents must have instilled all those wonderful qualities in him. Thoughts of Jackson consumed every corner of her mind day and night and it warmed her through and through.

Unable to stand still Mattie started a leisurely walk along the shoreline. The cool breeze and the warm sunshine had been so calming to her restless soul that she hadn't realized she had walked very far until she found herself standing near the rocky overhang. The site was inviting for a body to just sit and enjoy the show of crashing waves. Listening to the sea gulls cry out to one another as they sought out a meal. She climbed high up for the best view and found the perfect place to sit and take in the scene before her. Pulling her little red book of poetry from her skirt pocket she began to read her favorite passages. They always soothed her and reminded of day's past with the two people she had loved dearly.

Mattie missed Gracie and her momma often, but always felt them watching over her. She always sensed their nearness and it soothed her. It was like an invisible safety net ready to catch her when she stumbled. The empty hole left in her heart after they had passed away was slowly filling but would never be completely full. When she thought of her little family being gone her tears of loss would stream unnoticed down her cheeks. There were no words to express how much she missed them

That was how Sarah had found her while she took her daily stroll. She had always found this spot so peaceful and soothing after a day of living in turmoil and hustling crowds so Sarah wasn't surprised to see Mattie had found her little slice of heaven. She had felt a kinship with the young woman and she was pleased they both chose the same place of solitude.

"Mattie, I see you found my favorite resting place. It's where I come to park these tired old bones from the stress of day to day living."

"Oh, Hi I'm sorry Sarah. I'll leave if you want. I only meant to sit for a while so I could read from my book." She held up the very book she had bought at the bookstore the first time they had met.

"Now girl don't go apologizing. It's a public place so sit yourself down and chat with an old woman for a while." Patting the rock at her side Sarah indicated that Mattie should join her. "You looked like you were in some deep thoughts when I walked up. Nothing too serious I hope. It's not man trouble is it honey?"

"No, no, it's nothing like that." Mattie felt the heat rising from her neck to hairline.

"Ah ha, so that's the way of it? Good. You are too pretty to waste away all alone. You need someone to share your life with young lady."

Sarah's bluntness wasn't such a shock anymore. They spent a lot of time together since that first meeting in the shop. They had shared many a cup of coffee since then and had become good friends. In a lot of ways Sarah was like her Gracie and that created a stronger bond between them. "A good loving man is just what you need Mattie girl. Yep, it's just what you need." Sarah couldn't contain the smile that tugged at her thin lips or the twinkle lighting her cloudy eyes. She already knew Mattie had given her heart away, even though she didn't know it yet. In her opinion the young lady deserved all the happiness she could grab.

Mattie blushed again but she didn't argue the point. She valued Sarah's opinions and her friendship.

Sarah picked up Mattie's hand with her own arthritic plagued one and turned it palm side up. She never flinched at the old woman's touch and she always welcomed the sensation of her thin warm skin next to hers.

Sarah had been taught to read palms and this was the first time she had looked at Mattie's. She nearly gasped at what she saw but she managed to control her response. She didn't want to let Mattie know what she was doing. All she could think was "poor Mattie."

Mattie had seen the brief sadness cross Sarah's face but she made no comment. She just began to talk about how Gracie could read tea leaves before she had lost her sight and how she told Mattie she was to have a long life, marriage, and kids. Mattie watched Sarah trace the lines on her palm and

134

the frown that creased her brow. "What is it Sarah? Am I to grow warts on my nose and have toads for children?" She couldn't help laughing at her own silliness and neither could Sarah.

"Oh, it's nothing to worry your self with honey, just a pair of old eyes and some failing eyesight."

Mattie doubted that since she had seen how sharp her eyes were in the bookshop but she didn't push the issue. It wasn't her nature. So she smiled at her friend and ignored the whole episode. She had no desire to hear any bad news. Her life was on track for a change and she wanted it to stay that way.

Sarah visited with her for a while longer and decided she had to head out before Arthur decided to make her pleasant walk a most un-enjoyable and painful experience. Arthur wasn't nice to an old woman's joints.

She demanded a promise from Mattie to come for tea during the week and a free tea leaf reading to top it off. Sarah's thoughts were focused on Mattie to the point she almost missed seeing her young man running toward the cliffs. Now how did she know he would have been the one? She remembered Jackson. He was the young man from the bookstore. How convenient he had shown up right behind Mattie on that same day when she and Mattie had first met. Interesting, interesting indeed. He was the one that put that sparkle in Mattie's eyes and the smile on her pretty face whether Mattie told her so or not. She just knew he was the one because that girl lit up like a roman candle as soon as she saw him headed her way. Sarah had said her farewell before he made his way to where Mattie was sitting and enjoyed the wayward thoughts she was having regarding her young friend and the man she was falling for.

Jackson had been looking for Mattie for quite some time. He almost lost it when he asked Rachael where Mattie was and she swore she hadn't seen her in hours. Rache thought she was with him and he thought she was with her. His adrenaline kicked into overdrive when visions of what happened at Waves flooded his thoughts.

It didn't take long in his search to figure out where she had gone. People tend to notice someone as pretty as Mattie, especially the male species. He didn't like it one bit, but they sent him in the right direction and for that he was grateful. He let the relief sweep over him when he saw her safe and sound on the rocky cliff with the old woman from the bookstore. He couldn't contain his excitement when he saw her. He closed the distance rapidly waving at Sarah as he ran past her. Almost breathless from the exertion tried to slow his breathing when he stopped right in front of her. His heart always did this crazy flip when she looked at him as if he were the most important person in the world.

Mattie smiled up at Jackson and her heart lightened with his presence.

The smile turned seductive causing her dimples to wink at him from the center of her cheeks. He could only stare at her in wander. How could he be so lucky? All he could do was smile back and gave her a breathless, "Hi."

"Hi," she whispered up to him, as she squinted against the sunlight. Then she lifted her hand and shaded her eyes so she could look her fill. She forced her legs to lift her so she could stand face to face with Jackson.

"Been here long?" He had to force the words through an already tight throat.

"No, not long. Sarah was here a while ago and sat with me."

"Care if I join you?" He gestured toward her rock.

"I was hoping you would." Mattie couldn't believe how easy it was to talk to him now but she was glad for it. It meant they were able to share things and get closer. She had missed him today even though she had seen him almost everyday over the weeks past. He had sent her notes and beautiful flowers everyday since the contest but he didn't pressure her.

Jackson didn't move to sit down next to her as she indicated. Instead he sat directly in front of her. He had wanted to see her more than anything and with this opportunity he could look his fill.

Going home to see his parents had offered some time away to repair his strained relationship with them and prevented him from hovering and smothering Mattie. He knew he had made the right choice. Mattie had consumed his thoughts the entire time he was gone and that didn't go unnoticed by his parents. They were happy that his life had found purpose and direction and the anger in him was gone. They thought if a girl was the cause then they were even happier.

Everything seemed to be working out for him and life at this point was great. "I wanted to see you sooner, but..." he couldn't finish his statement when she looked at him like he was what she had been searching for. She literally stole his breath away. "God you are so beautiful Matt." Did I just say that out loud? He thought to himself. "I sure have missed you."

Blushing profusely she smiled and told him she'd missed him too. "Mattie, would you like to go boating with me today? Lyle and I got my boat finished and I rushed to find you so I could ask you to join us on her first voyage. Will you come? Lyle and I have worked on her for months now. Please Mattie? It'll be fun and you'll love it."

Mattie could only stare at Jackson. She had never been on a boat before and she didn't know how to react to his invitation. "But, uh..." she stammered.

Jackson's heart skipped a beat. He thought she didn't want to spend time with him. He hadn't thought that was a possibility. Could he have been so wrong? "If...if you don't want to go with me I'll understand. It's ok really." He could feel a huge gap ripping through his heart at the thought of her not wanting to be with him when that was all he could think about with her. "What was I thinking," he mumbled under his breath. He dropped his head slightly, looking very interested in his sand-incrusted shoes. He couldn't force himself to look at her face when she answered him.

Mattie saw the defeated expression cross his face. It was easy to recognize since she had the look mastered. Mattie had to make him understand it wasn't him that made her hesitate with her answer. She wanted nothing more than to be with him. It was her fear that held her back not Jackson, never him. "Jacks are you asking me on a date? I've never been on one." She smiled shyly at him as he raised his head to look at her in shock.

How could such a beautiful person not ever been asked out on a date. He couldn't fathom the thought. He smiled up at her and whispered a reverent thank God.

Mattie felt her breath catch in her throat. The way he looked at her and the way he smiled made her feel as if she were the only girl on earth he wanted to be with.

Lyle and Rachael walked onto the scene knowing their approach had gone unnoticed. Rachael bounced up the rocks to where the two lovebirds were sitting and starring at each other. Lyle was right behind her watching her little butt twitch with every step she took. He didn't make any effort to change his point of view and why would he?

"So Matt are we going for a wild ride or not?" Rachael really wanted to go but she wouldn't force Mattie into something she wasn't ready for.

"I don't think Mattie is interested in going. She hasn't answered my question yet." It wasn't hard to hear the disappointment ring in Jackson's voice.

"Come on Mattie. We'll have a great time. Jacks and I have worked on that broken down raft for months now and we finished her in record time with this slave driver." Lyle said this as he slugged Jacks in the arm as close friends often did.

"Broken down raft? What's this? Just this morning you were bragging about her to Scotty and don't try to deny it. I heard you with my own two ears Chief." He couldn't keep the smile off his face.

"I'll deny it if I want to rich boy." Lyle smiled back at Jackson. This was a familiar come back that no one else could even think about getting by with. The same went for those who attempted to call him Chief. Jackson was the only one who could say that and keep his teeth in a straight line.

Mattie watched as the two friends bantered back and forth without any signs of anger. She knew they were real close friends and she couldn't help feeling how lucky they were. She couldn't stop the laugh that escaped her mouth as she listened to Jackson and Lyle throw their verbal punches. Their carrying on just struck her as funny and the laughter just bubbled out before she could stop it. Jackson, Lyle, and Rachael all stared at her as if she had screamed like one of those fabled banshees. She laughed even harder the way they were looking at her. She just couldn't help herself. When she got a hold of herself then whispered, "I'm sorry. I didn't mean to laugh at you but..." She couldn't finish what she had meant to say because the giggles took over again. The group started to laugh with her even though they had no idea what was so funny. When she finally got a hold of herself again she became embarrassed and she whispered she was sorry for the second time. She couldn't even look at them now.

Rachael wrapped her arm around Mattie's shoulders and told her it was all right. "You have such a pretty laugh. You should use it more often." Rachael felt her mistake as soon as she had done it. She didn't think. How could she do that? "Damn it." Rachael quickly removed her arm from Mattie and apologized. "I'm sorry Matt. It's the only the second time we got to hear you laugh out loud like that. We didn't mean anything by it."

"But, I laughed at you." She waited for the punishment that didn't come. Mattie looked at them in wander. Was it truly ok? She had no idea.

"That's no big deal Matt. I'm glad we got you to laugh with us. It's another step and since we are taking new steps why don't you come with us? Lyle and I are excellent seamen even if he doesn't know port side from stern but he manages well enough." Jackson was smiling at the group.

"This coming from a guy who had to put an L on one shoe and an R on the other so he would know which shoe went where." Lyle said with a raised eyebrow and a smirk on his handsome face.

"Hey, I was only five at the time and the idea wasn't mine as you may recall."

"That is of no concern of mine." Lyle winked at Mattie and smiled again.

Mattie covered her mouth to conceal her laughter again when she saw the looks Jackson was getting. Her control snapped. The twin looks on Rache and Lyle's faces were more than she could handle so she let it rip. She laughed till her sides ached. The tears flowed and the pain of laughter felt good. She couldn't remember the last time she had laughed so hard.

Her friends were so amused that Mattie cut loose all they found themselves staring at her. Her humor was just as infectious as it had been earlier and it didn't take long for the rest to join in again. Mattie was the first to let reality steal it's way back in. She slowly stopped laughing and the tears of laughter were replaced with tears of joy. The emotions that coursed through her were so strong it was palpable to those who surrounded her. As the laughter died away the group began to get concerned with Mattie's sudden change in mood. They all hoped she wasn't retreating into herself, as it appeared she was doing.

Jackson couldn't help the concern he felt for Mattie. As he looked at his friends he could tell they were thinking the same thing he was. Jackson sat in front of Mattie as she sat on the same rock as she and Sarah had shared earlier. He didn't want Matt's laughter to end. She had the most musical laugh that warmed his soul to hear. Mattie was such a beautiful person inside and out. Laughter suited her and he hated whatever it was that had stolen that from her. Jackson didn't want her to lose that part of herself again especially now that she had just found it. "Mattie?" He whispered to her as he cupped her face and brought it up to his eye level. His voice was but a gentle rasp. When no answer from her came he spoke again. He felt as if she weren't with him anymore. She had returned to her corner of somberness and lonely exile and he couldn't stand the thought of it.

"Please Mattie, sweetheart, look at me. Tell me why you're crying and why you're pulling away from me again? What is it? What's wrong?" He didn't think she was going to look at him when finally she lifted her tiger-eyes that swam in a lake of salt water and hooded by long wet lashes. The concern he felt fleeted as soon as he was rewarded with that dimpled smile of hers. The brightness of it was blinding. "Oh, honey what a beautiful smile you hide way too often. It's like a ray of sunshine on a cloudy day." He was so relieved that Mattie was happy and not sad he hadn't realized he had spoken aloud the thoughts that crowded his mind.

Mattie dropped her eyes down to her lap and Jackson could have kicked himself. He refused to face the look his comment had put on her face and he chose to close his eyes. He was pulling himself together when he felt the gentlest brushing on his face. Jackson thought he imagined the touch when he felt it again. A little bolder this time but still tender and whisper soft. Jackson didn't open his eyes for the fear he would break the spell she was weaving. She entranced him with her touch. He could feel both of her hands on his face and when he thought his heart would stop he felt her fingers brushing the hair from his forehead. Jackson used every ounce of willpower to keep his eyes shut. He didn't want her to stop the gentle exploration of his face; it felt good, too good. He could feel the passion and the tenderness in her touch, the caresses her fingers weaved on his skin was the most erotic thing he had ever experienced.

Lyle and Rachael were entranced with the transformation in Mattie and her effect on Jackson. She was touching him most intimately and it didn't faze her. Rachael was certain she had never seen such open, raw emotion in her life. She had read about it but never been witness to it or experienced it. If she were a betting person she would call it love, pure and simple. "Those two are practically burning with it," she whispered to Lyle.

Lyle had never seen such a thing before. He had heard from his Indian grandfather that everyone had a soul mate, hell he had even told Jackson as much, but he never thought he would be witness to it. Lyle hadn't believed it actually existed in this day and age but here he was looking at it with both eyes wide open. He knew Jackson had, had it bad but he had no idea it was love and not an old fashioned case of lust. He stood corrected and knew his friend one lucky son of a gun to find his true partner, his soul mate. Even his eyes misted as he witnessed what stories were made of. The fairy tales weren't all fantasies after all. Turning his eyes over to his own little pixie he knew he wasn't far behind Jackson and it didn't unnerve him like he often thought it would. He was ready to accept his destiny with Rachael.

Mattie was in a trance of her own making. She couldn't keep her hands off Jackson. Here he sat in front of her allowing her to memorize his face with her touch and he didn't budge, he didn't flinch, or make her stop. He just kept his eyes shut and let her have her way. She sensed he wouldn't look at her for fear of scarring her. It amazed her how he trusted her not to hurt him. Mattie cupped his face with hands that trembled and leaned in to place a soft kiss on his full, moist lips. The contact was electric and thrilling.

Jackson would have instinctively moved had it not been for her gentle hold on his face telling him silently not to move. He felt her shift and scoot a little closer to him and was determined to return her kiss this time. He was expecting it now and all he could think of was joining in. He had been thinking of kissing her for a very long now but didn't follow that desire because he didn't want to scare her. He had never wanted just a kiss so badly in all his life as he had wanted one with Mattie. He could feel her nearness, her heat, and her warm breath on his face. He thought he heard his name on her lips and yet he refused to open his eyes. He didn't want to break this spell she had them both in. He felt her lips tentatively brush his again with more pressure than before.

Mattie was exploring his mouth and he didn't mind one bit. Jackson tilted his head for easier access and to accommodate further explorations. He couldn't help responding to such sweet torture. For the briefest moment he felt her stiffen and thought for sure he really screwed up. Much to his pleasure Mattie continued to share in the kiss. Jackson refused to move another inch. He didn't want her to stop. He ached to hold her and to tell her he loved her. He had known since the beginning how he felt but now he wanted to share it with her. He wanted to show her how special she was to him. There would never be anyone else for him. Mattie consumed him mind, body, and soul. Jackson denied the greed that welled up inside of him demanding to take what she innocently offered. He new he couldn't do that.

Mattie was surprised with her own boldness in kissing Jackson. Never in her life had she acted so wantonly. She could feel the restraint in Jackson's large, powerful body. He understood her need to take control and didn't push for more. How could she tell him how she felt? How could she let him know he had stolen her heart with his tenderness and his caring?

Mattie was smart enough to know she loved Jackson and that was why she could touch him and not be so afraid. She knew without a doubt he would never hurt her but the fear constantly simmered beneath the surface. When he went to hold her it would rear its ugly head forcing her to a place she didn't want to go. She moved her hands in Jackson's long blonde hair threading her fingers through the warm strands. In all her life she wouldn't have believed she could be in this position with a man as she was right now and Jackson was letting her control the whole act. The kiss continued and deepened with every slide of lips and with each sigh of breath.

Lyle and Rachael began feeling like voyeurs and began making their way down to the beach to give Mattie and Jackson some privacy. Strolling hand in hand they made their way to the shoreline to share their own kisses and unspoken emotions.

Mattie pulled her mouth away form Jackson's and placed her forehead on his breathing in short little gasps. They were both breathless from the long shared kiss. He slowly opened his eyes and found himself looking into his tigress's eyes that were filling with unshed tears.

Jackson's chest felt heavy and his heart was pounding erratically. He felt the burning, stinging sensation of his own tears as they threatened to spill over. Was it possible to feel so much for one person that your whole body reacted to it? A pleasurable pain you couldn't explain but knew it consumed you all the same. "Oh, Mattie," was all he could manage. He hadn't ever felt such love, such soul deep emotion, that it made him want to weep. He could even taste the sweetness of it. He wanted to speak but he couldn't say a word if his life had depended on it.

The intensity of their kisses and the intimate body language revealed more than their conscious minds had control of. Jackson sat with his legs encasing Mattie's and his hands were resting on her thighs.

Mattie's breathing slowed yet she continued to keep her forehead gently pressed against Jackson's. The tears streamed in small rivulets down her beautiful face pooling into her deep dimples like small mirrored pools. She felt she had overcome a huge obstacle that had been holding her back with invisible hands. Taking this step would open doors to her future; a new life.

A life that was full to bursting and complete. Mattie knew Jackson was the one person who could fill the void she so longed to be rid of. "Jackson?" She spoke on a hushed whisper.

His eyes focused on her sweet, rosy, wet lips as she whispered his name in that husky ascent he adored. Gradually he raised his enraptured gaze up to her pert nose and glistening eyes. It was then Jackson knew without a doubt she felt the same emotions that he was. Mattie glowed from the inside out and he wandered if a person could burst from sheer happiness. Gazing into eyes that reflected a love he had only hoped to see.

"Um...huh?" He couldn't form a word if he tried.

"I...uh...I...Jacks?" She barely spoke above whisper.

"What is it Matt? You're not afraid are you? I would never hurt you sweetheart. You know that don't you?"

"I know but I need to..." she trailed off unable to finish her thoughts. She wanted to tell him. She wanted him to know, to hear it from her. Saying a silent prayer for strength she drew in a deep breath and tried again.

Jackson heard her or he thought he had. He was finding it difficult to breathe around his constricted throat and pounding heart. His head was spinning and his heart was on the verge of exploding in his chest. He didn't want to believe he'd heard what he thought he heard and yet he hoped it with all his strength. "Mattie?"

He wanted to ask her to say it again but all he could mange was her name in a question asking what he couldn't. He felt the tension creeping up the hands and arms that still held his. He hoped and prayed she wouldn't lose control. Not now. He wanted to hear it from her mouth loud and clear with no room for doubts.

"Jackson, I....I...uh...Oh Jacks I love you!" There she said it and she was still breathing. All she had to do was brace herself for rejection, if any came. Mattie waited with her eyes closed. The waiting went on it seemed for an eternity. It was then she realized he hadn't said anything in return. When she opened her eyes she found his ocean blue eyes fixed on her. He was starring with such intensity that she didn't need to hear words to know how he felt about her. Tears were flowing freely down his cheeks and he was smiling the sweetest smile.

It sounded sweeter the second time around. It meant even more because she was sure of her feelings, so much so, that she had said it not once, but twice. Jackson hadn't realized hearing her profess her love for him would swallow him heart and soul until that very moment. This was what he had craved to hear. This was what he had wanted for months now and yet he couldn't get past the shock of actually hearing it. His greatest joy sat in front of him, declaring her love for him. She loved him! It was worth more than all the money and power his family could offer him.

Fighting the tightness in his throat with his tear soaked voice he finally spoke. "Mattie, honey, look at me." He wanted to look in her eyes so there would be no doubt. He wanted her to see the love he had for her not only to hear it. "Come on Matt look at me, please." Jackson risked much by touching her but he had to. He lifted her face up to his and caressed her cheek with his palm. To Jackson's relief she didn't resist or attempt to pull away she only leaned her face into his palm wanting more of his touch.

Mattie smiled at him so sweetly Jackson almost lost all rational thought in the process. "Matt, please," he spoke in a hushed whisper and she opened her eyes and looked directly into his. "Mattie Collins I have loved you since the day I first laid eyes on you. I knew you were special that first day. I love you with all my heart Matt...Oh please don't cry. I just wanted you to know how I truly feel about you. I'm so...," he was silenced with her fingers on his lips. Mattie didn't want him to apologize for loving her. She shook her head "No" she couldn't let him think he had hurt her but she had to get past the tightness in her throat first. "Don't you dare," she whispered. "Don't take back my gift."

Relief swept over him. "I thought I had frightened you and I couldn't stand the thought of that."

"I know you would never do it on purpose. I've known it all along. You're the only man I have ever trusted, the only one I knew wouldn't hurt me with his touch, and I hoped that was love I saw in your eyes." Mattie had never been able to talk to anyone besides her mom and Gracie like this and yet here she was pouring her heart out to Jackson. She was relieved to finally tell him and he was happy about it. She could feel a certain freedom and strength and she had purpose somehow that wasn't there before. She felt so weightless she would float away if Jackson hadn't kept her anchored down with his warm sensitive hands. He had been her anchor all this time and realized it at this very moment how much that had kept her sane. Fate had brought her here and love would keep her here. She was happy, an emotion she hadn't experienced since her mom and Gracie had been the focus of her life

Jackson was beside himself. Mattie loved him. Lady luck had finally smiled down on him. He had known Mattie was for him but now it was more than wishful thinking. It was a fact. She loved him and that was a heady feeling that so overwhelming. He hadn't loved anyone before nor had anyone laid that claim to him except his family. He couldn't describe how happy he was at this very moment in his life. "Oh Mattie," was all he could manage as he caressed her face not caring about anything except being able to hold and kiss her. Jackson leaned further into her and kissed her lightly. Testing her response he wasn't disappointed with the reaction. No fear, no withdrawing, no regretting. Mattie returned his kisses as he gave them freely. Both were caught up in the magic of the passion that consumed them. Time had no place in their world. It was only the two of them and what they were sharing that mattered.

Lyle and Rachael had walked and talked along the beach and came back only to discover the heated kisses being shared by their friends. They looked at each other and smiled for they had already shared their own kisses on the beach as they strolled in the midday sun. Both wore a face-splitting grin as they slowly approached the kissing couple. Lyle felt it his unauthorized duty to end the little scene he had to endure watching. After all, if he couldn't be doing the same thing, then neither could Jackson. With humor in his voice he cleared his throat and spoke. "Jacks are you going to come up for air anytime soon or will I need to get you an oxygen tank?"

Slowly and reluctantly Jackson removed his lips from Mattie's to reply briskly, "Beat it, can't you see I'm busy here?" He never turned from Mattie as he spoke and he witnessed the deepest blush creep across her smiling face. To his relief and his surprise she didn't turn away from him or try to hide her face. She was changing by the minute.

"Yeah, yeah, so you're busy. Big deal. I'm ready for that sail and so is Rache. Now put your desire in your wallet rich kid so we can go while the weathers fair." Lyle smiled at Jackson because he knew he was the only one who could get by with those comments and he used them without fear of angering his friend. Feeling bold he pushed a little more. "And while you're at it put the other thoughts you have there too. Times a wasting Blondie so let's hit it."

Jackson slowly turned to his soon to be dead friend because Jackson was about to murder him and smiled a not so friendly smile. If Mattie saw the look Lyle got she would have stepped back. It didn't faze Lyle in the slightest. "Since you're going to be the ass I know you are low rent I guess we had better go. Mattie hasn't given me an answer yet so we'll wait for her to decide. Got it?"

Lyle only smiled bigger for he knew Jackson was frustrated and he really liked watching him squirm. He also knew Mattie had to move slowly and from what he was seeing slow wasn't a word he would have chosen. Lyle knew all to well how a heated body could rule over a well-intentioned mind.

"Oh come on Matt. It'll be fun. We'll have a great time with a picnic aboard and everything. What do you say?" Rachael beamed at her friend. She was so happy to see the sadness gone from her eyes and replaced with such brightness. "Come on Matt. We will have a great time. Pleeeease?"

Mattie was so full of love for these people that she felt like she would burst wide open. How could she disappoint her friends? Yes, they were her friends and her family too. Mattie refused to be the wet blanket. She wanted to live and live she would. This was another step in her new life. A step she was ready to take. "Ok, I would like to go but I never...well, I've never been on a boat before."

"Shoot if that's all that's wrong then there is no problem. We will all be there with you and it won't be so bad. Consider it an adventure Matt." Jackson was still holding her hands trying to reassure her with his touch and the anticipation he emitted was all the encouragement she needed for her much awaited answer.

"I'm game if you are." She caught herself and wandered if it was her that just said that. Well, she decided, it was past time beginning her new role in life because it was changing and she liked the direction it was going. Grabbing Jackson's hand she began to descend the rocky formations not noticing the gapping mouths of the people that followed her.

Before she even realized it they were heading to where Jackson's boat was docked and he was beaming at her the whole time. He was genuinely glad she was there and her heart swelled full with emotion for him and his love for her.

The old man Jackson worked with noticed it and he had a question of his own. "Is this the little Miss whose got you tied up in knots and had your face cracked in the middle so much?" He couldn't help the wink he bestowed upon the beauty, for she was a looker, and he was pleased to see the red creeping up Jackson's neck. Yep, the kid had it bad. He couldn't blame the boy she definitely took your breath away. If only he were younger floated through his mind like a whisper. Regretful thoughts were all that kept an old man company and he sure had some now.

"Yeah, this is Mattie. The woman I love." He noted the odd expressions his friends wore but no one was truly all that surprised by his announcement. Mattie blushed prettily. "Matt, this is Scotty. The old sea dog I told you about."

"How do you do?" He said as he reached for her hand. "It's about time a pretty gal snagged this young pup." Turning to Jackson with a worried look on his face Scotty gave him a message to call his dad as soon as possible. "He sounded a little rattled but he didn't give me any details and I didn't stick my nose where it doesn't belong."

Chapter Twenty-Six

Jackson felt a knot the size of a basketball form in his gut as it did when his father called. It was usually his mom that did the calling so if dad was calling something was wrong. His relationship with his parents had always been rather rocky but he knew they loved him. He contributed to their strained relationship by trying to get them to notice him as their son and not another business venture. He had grown tired of being e-mailed, faxed, and telegrammed. He had only wanted to be a part of their lives and getting into trouble had been his only way of involving them in his life. Over the last couple of months their relationship had improved greatly but they still had some things to work out. He owed a thank you to Mattie for that as well. She didn't even know it but it was because of her own loses that he felt it was time to bridge the gap with his folks. He talked and much to his surprise they actually listened. They had come along way and he felt better for it. Now he was worried. Dad wouldn't call here unless it was serious.

Lyle saw the thoughts cross his friend's face as he had them. Something was wrong. He also knew about the troubles and the problems Jackson had faced regarding his parents. They were working on them he knew but now he didn't know what to think. "Better get to it Jacks or we'll never get out of here." Lyle hoped his lightened tone would help but he doubted it would.

Jackson smiled. He knew Lyle was following the same train of thought. He always understood. "Back in a minute." He squeezed Mattie's hands before he made his way to the phone in Scotty's office. After a brief hesitation taking a deep breath he punched in the number. Holding his breath as the phone continued to ring. Jackson knew it couldn't be good but refused to let it weigh him down until he was certain. "Woods here," he heard the familiar baritone of his father's voice.

"Dad, it's me. What's up?" Jackson gripped the receiver until his knuckles were white.

"Where the hell have you been? I've been trying to reach you all morning."

His dad sounded breathless and desperate. Jackson had never heard those two descriptions regarding his father. Any fleeting hopes of this not being serious flew out the window. "Is there something wrong? Is it Mom?"

He heard nothing in return except phone static. Then when he was about to ask again he heard his father sigh. When he spoke again he could hear the tears in his dad's voice. "We are in the hospital Jacks. It's your Mom. The doctor says she's had a heart attack. Can you come home now? Please?"

In all his years he had never heard his father sound so alone and scared. The uncertainty of the situation grabbed Jackson by the throat threatening to steal his breath from his lungs. He could feel all the color drain from his face. How was it possible to feel on top of the world one-minute and feel as if the bottom dropped out the next? Grabbing Scotty's chair he sat down heavily. "Dad?"

"Mom's comfortable for now but you need to be here." Lyndal knew Jackson was Joyce's bright spot and if anything could make her feel better it would be him.

Jackson knew his father well enough to know this was very serious. His mother had always been small but strong in all aspects of her life. This was her heart and he knew his father was hurting because he would never say 'please' otherwise. He knew now it was not only bad, it was very serious. "I'll be there as soon as I can get a flight out and Dad?"

"Yeah, Jacks?"

"Tell mom I love her and I'm on my way."

"I'll tell her Jacks. Just hurry home. I'll be waiting."

Jackson heard everything his father didn't say and it was breaking his heart. He had always seen his dad as a strong person not this unstable, unsure man he just talked to. He knew his parents loved each other but he never considered how it would be if one were to lose the other and he refused to think the thought now. He had to believe his mom would be fine. He had too.

Everyone who saw his approach knew the news was bad. Jackson looked miserable, as if he carried the weight of the world on his shoulders. Jackson stopped at Mattie's side and clasped her hand in a firm grip without thought or hesitation.

It was Lyle who spoke first. "What is it Jacks? Did dear old dad miss his weakly butt chewing or did he need a boost?"

Jackson knew there was no love lost between his dad and his best friend but Jacks also knew Lyle respected him.

"Lyle, it's...its Mom. They think she's had a heart attack. They have her in Cardiac Care and they are monitoring her. Dad wants me home as soon as I can make arrangements." Jackson knew the news would upset Lyle but he had to tell him. Joyce always liked Lyle and she defended him more than once to those who would make him out to be more than a troubled kid who had no one. Lyle was like a second son to her and Jackson never begrudged that relationship even though at times he felt he was the friend instead of the son. She had always run interference for Lyle where his dad was concerned and because she was who she was Lyle had always been loved, as if she was his mom too.

"God, Jacks I'm sorry. How is she? I always loved your mom and I would do anything for her. If you need anything just ask. I'll go with you if you want. I'll work around your dad if need be. I want Joyce to know I'm there for her."

Jackson knew Lyle would move heaven and earth for his mother but he didn't think she could handle the stress that his dad and Lyle would create when together. "No, Lyle. I appreciate the offer but I don't want mom to get upset because dad can't control his temper." He couldn't keep the small smile off his face as he spoke. Lyle and his dad's arguments were legendary. This was not the time to play referee.

"Yeah, well give your mom my love and if you need anything at all you call me. Got it?" Lyle smiled back. He understood and he didn't want to be the cause of more grief. There would be enough of that without him adding to it.

"I've got to get home and pick up some clothes and I'll need a ride to the airport. Got any takers?" He knew Lyle would do it without him even asking but he wanted to lighten the mood some.

"No problem Jacks." Lyle was ready to do what he could for his friend. He knew Jackson would go ASAP no matter the kind of problems they had suffered as a family. They did love each other and they would stand by each other regardless. The only thing he had ever envied Jackson was the fact he had a family that cared whether he lost sight of that at times or not.

Jackson turned to Rachael and spoke as if Mattie weren't standing right beside him. "Keep Mattie safe. Don't let her out of your site. Make her stay with you at all times, ok?"

Rachael was more than willing to do her part but she wasn't so sure about Jackson's request after seeing the hurt look on Mattie's face. "I'll do whatever I can; you know I would without you having to ask."

Mattie didn't like being treated as if she were invisible. She had that type of treatment too many times in her life and she found herself angry that Jackson would treat her that way.

"Excuse me," she had enough bite in her words that she immediately got everyone's attention. This wasn't the meek little mouse. She was angry. "Jackson don't insult me by talking around me. I may be shy but I'm not deaf nor am I helpless and I don't like being treated that way. I want to help so what can I do? You have always been there for me now let me return the favor. I have no responsibilities and no one who depends on me. Let me go with you." It had just occurred to her to go with Jacks and support him during a bad time when he needed the help. It was the first time she refused to be pushed aside. Everyone was gapping at her as if she had just sprouted a horn in the middle of her forehead and she didn't care for it. "What?" She really couldn't see what the big deal was. Why wouldn't she want to be with him? It was her turn to help Jackson and she wouldn't be ignored.

"Do you mean that you would go with me just like that?" Snapping his fingers for emphasis. Jackson knew he was starring, but he couldn't believe he had heard her right.

Mattie spoke softly into the quiet group. "I love you Jackson and I want to be there for you, with you. Please let me." Mattie forced herself to look into his deep blue eyes and she knew her love for him was reflected there. Mattie forced a weak smile, "Please Jacks?"

Everyone heard her words and saw the look in her eyes. Even though the look was meant for Jackson it was hard not to know what was behind that endearing gaze. Jackson wanted this more than anything he had ever wanted in his life. To have the woman of his dreams at his side, loving and supporting him meant the world to him. He felt his heart stumble when she smiled and her face remained so sincere in her request. He felt he had been given a second gift this day. First, her love for him and second her support for him. He felt like the luckiest man alive. "It would mean the world to me to have you at my side Mattie. I'm sorry I didn't ask you right away and I certainly didn't mean to treat you like you weren't here. I'm sorry." Smiling at her with his heart on his sleeve. It wasn't difficult to see how much he truly cared for her. The group stood there feeling like peeping toms but the change in Mattie and the situation with Jackson kept them rooted to the concrete floor.

"It's all right. I don't have a very good history when it comes to being open with people but without a doubt I want to be there for you. That is if you'll let me." Mattie was holding Jackson's hand and rubbing his fingers with her thumb while anxiously waiting for his answer.

Jackson felt the way Mattie was sensually rubbing his fingers and it occurred to him that she had reached out for him with only concern for him and his family. He nodded to her and smiled again keeping her hand in his. In an unspoken agreement the group headed for the door. There were things to do and arrangements to be made. "Hey, Jackson?" Scotty yelled.

"Yeah Scotty?"

"You keep me posted on your mom. I'll make sure we put her on the church's prayer chain. Every little bit helps you know?"

"Thanks Scotty and I'll let you know when I have some information to pass along. If you don't hear from me I'll have Lyle swing by. I'll see ya around." With that, the group left.

Before Mattie registered the whole impact of what was happening she had found herself arm and arm with Jackson getting ready for a plane ride. Mattie was so intent on supporting Jackson she never gave a thought to the cost of a plane ticket or how she would cover the costs of a hotel once they arrived.

Jackson was so caught up in his thoughts of his mom that he hadn't noticed Mattie's growing apprehension.

Jackson's thoughts were centered on his parents and the fact that he could lose his mother with this heart condition. He didn't think he could bare that. Not with the way things had been no matter how well they were getting along now. He knew his relationship with them had been strained for some time and he was man enough to admit most of their problems could be dropped at his feet. All he had ever wanted was for them to treat him like he mattered, to be the son they loved. He knew now that he always had been but when he was growing up it was hard for him to believe it. In his opinion negative attention was better than no attention at all. Shaking his head to regain focus and put it back on the problems at hand.

Jackson began to realize the change that had slowly taken over Mattie the further they walked. He was hoping she wasn't having second thoughts because he really needed her support. "Mattie is there something wrong?"

"Oh Jacks. I don't think I have enough money for this trip and well I...uh...I have never been on a plane before. When I moved here from Kentucky I took the bus so...I'm nervous."

"Mattie you're coming with me is all that matters to me right now. You don't have to worry about the cost I've got it covered and as far as you not flying before don't worry I'll be with you every second of the trip. Consider it another experience to add to all the other new experiences you've had since you came here." Reaching down he unfurled the fingers she had coiled into her palms and kissed the tips of each finger as he unfolded them.

He knew she was thinking of all the possible scenarios that could play out and have her retreating in fear and losing the positive steps she taken up to now. It would be a cold day in hell before he watched Mattie revert back to the shy, quiet, withdrawn girl he had seen that first day she caught his eye. "Mattie honey, I won't let anything happen to you. I'll be with you every step of the way and that is a promise babe. We will do this together, all right?"

Mattie had complete faith in Jackson and his heartfelt promise to be there for her so how could she not try? He had so much more to deal with right now and she didn't want to add more to it by being a pain in the ass. She still had reservations about the whole thing but she wanted to be there for him the way he had been there for her so many times in the past. Taking a deep breath she painted on a smile that she hoped didn't look as phony as it felt and followed the man she loved to the plane. It took Mattie awhile to realize she had been waiting for the fear to grip her and much to her amazement it didn't happen. If anything she realized she actually liked flying. A sense of freedom washed over her and it made her smile, a genuine smile, as she looked out the window. The cloud's floated past her little window as the weightless sensation had her feeling like she was one with little white puffs floating along. She couldn't help wandering if this was how Angels felt. Mattie could picture her mom and Gracie free as the wind watching out for her. The thought created an inner peace she hadn't felt since she was a little girl. Mattie was so consumed with her own thoughts she hadn't noticed how Jackson's attention was directed on her.

Jackson saw the peace and contentment on Mattie's face and he realized that taking her on this trip with him was the right thing to do. She needed this trip as much as he needed her to be with him. He knew the courage it had taken her to make the decision to come with him and to overcome the fear to get on this plane. He smiled inwardly when he thought of the way she had demanded to come with him and how it had shocked everyone who knew her. Jackson knew he loved her before that moment in time, but with her new found courage and strength, his feelings only grew beyond any words.

Jackson realized for the first time that he hadn't shared much of his childhood with this woman who meant the world to him and he was a little apprehensive about how she would react to his own wealth and social standing.

He hadn't told her before because, well, he was selfish. He wanted her to want him for himself not for what he had. He had known she wasn't like the other girls who were interested in him from the beginning and as time passed it wasn't an issue he thought to bring up. Now, that decision was coming back to bite him in the ass.

Jackson was still selfish enough not to risk hurting her and in turn hurting him with the little bombshell of his social standing. He tried to rationalize his decision by making excuses that it was his parent's wealth, not his. It sounded like a lame case of semantics but he was willing to accept it for what it was. The only excuse he could come up with.

The flight was uneventful and Mattie had loved it. Even that dreaded landing most people cringed at when the descent began. She was the epitome of beauty that was keeping his raving thoughts to a dull roar. She was his rock.

Jackson and Mattie made their way through the airport, to the rental car, and headed for the home he had grown up in. A companionable silence fell between them as the radio of the local station filled the air with soft music. Jackson's thoughts were focused on his mother and her health. She was too young for this to happen he kept telling himself. Jackson's thoughts drifted back to his trouble with the police and the problems he had caused. He knew what he had been doing but in his mind it was the only way he could see to get their attention because talking never seemed to work. Now he realized he had went about it all wrong and instead of his actions bringing them closer it only widened the gap. Well, he decided, not anymore. Not anymore!

Mattie's breath caught at the first sight of Jackson's boyhood home. It was more of a mansion to her than any home she had ever seen. She had never suspected Jacks to live in such a place. He'd never spoken of it but then again, she had never asked. The house was antique white with soft dove gray trimmings. Mattie guessed it had at least two floors maybe three it was hard to tell from this distance. Horses ran along the long white fence whinnying with occasional snorting at their arrival. Mattie thought they were such majestic creatures, so pretty and proud when they ran. The bloodlines of racing horses were very prominent. Something most all Kentuckians were familiar with. The muscles flexed against their satin coats giving the observer just a hint of the power they possessed. Mattie could watch them run for hours.

Jackson had heard her short intake of breath and he was surprised her attention wasn't on the house but on the horses his father fawned over. They were running along the fence line with such grace he could see why she was captivated. He was also pleased she focused on them and not the mansion that was witness to the obvious wealth the inhabitants enjoyed. Jackson would gladly have stopped for Mattie to get a closer look at the animals but his need to see his mother was stronger so he continued down the long drive. Stopping at the end of the drive Jackson shifted in his seat and asked, "What do you think Matt?"

Mattie thought it a beautiful place at a distance but now that she was close she was awestruck with the brilliance of the place. It was a little overwhelming if she were to be honest. Mattie soon realized the place had three stories and it was much bigger that she thought instead of answering his question she opened the car door and stepped out. The expression on her face was answer enough so Jackson didn't repeat his question. He came up to her side mindful of surprising her and he heard her whispered, "Wow!"

Chapter Twenty-Seven

Before Jackson could say anything else the front door flew open. Stepping out into the sunlight was a huge burley man with blonde hair. It was like looking at an older and much taller version of Jacks. This man had to be his father. The likenesses were great. This man may have been taller but he was less broad in the shoulders and more slender in the waist than Jackson was. His body stance commanded attention even if he was casually dressed in gray slacks and a polo shirt. Mattie determined the look suited him. As they approached the man he realized he was also very handsome. She could see where Jackson got his good looks. The thought made her smile. Upon closer inspection she noted the same eye color as Jacks but his hair was a darker shade with some very distinguished gray at the temples. She noted the small amount of wrinkling around his eyes and the laugh lines that bracketed his mouth. Mattie thought he was a man who smiled often. Right now he wasn't smiling or laughing and the dark circles under his eyes told the story of his concern for his wife. He hadn't rested well and it showed.

"Mattie, this is my father Lyndal Woods. Dad this is Mattie Collins. I've mentioned her before."

"Yes, I remember. It's nice to finally meet you after hearing so much about you. I must say you're prettier than I had imagined. Jackson has been singing your praises for months now and I'm happy to finally meet the woman who has won my sons heart. I'm very pleased indeed." Lyndal couldn't help the huge smile he flashed Mattie as he thought of what Joyce had told him. They knew Jackson was hooked and now he knew why. Mattie was absolutely breath taking and he had a feeling she didn't even know it. Qualities he admired greatly. Yep, Joyce was right there would be a wedding in the near future. "I'm glad you two could make it on such short notice your mom will be thrilled you both made it home, even though she will scorn me for telling you to come. She didn't want this incident, as she refers to it, to interfere with your studies."

"I'm glad Jackson invited me to come and as far as my studies go I'm very stable in that area."

"Dad, there was no way I was going to stay away and besides we have a fall break right now. If we miss a few days it won't hurt anything. I happen to have a very good grade point average myself and besides I'm in real tight with a very intelligent female. If I'm real good she will tutor me if I get behind, right Mattie?"

"Sure." Mattie was a little surprised at the casual way they spoke with each other, but then again, she didn't have anything to compare to, well, except her own relationship with her mom and Gracie. "It won't be a problem for either of us since we are both on the Honors roll and it won't hurt to miss the few days that are left before break."

Lyndal couldn't help his wayward thoughts. Mattie's voice was pure honey and whiskey. Damn but this one was a package. Intelligent, drop dead gorgeous, and he be damned if she wasn't shy. "How did Jackson ever find you?" He didn't mean to voice his thoughts but there it was, out in the open, just the same. "I must admit Mattie you are breath of fresh air and Joyce is going to love you."

Jackson couldn't stop the grin that took over his face. He was sure his dad would like Mattie but sometimes his dad was hard to read when it came to his female friends. Granted he was right about almost everyone in regards to their gold digging obsessions. He was thankful he saw the honesty in Mattie. She was innocent through and through and that made her a very special woman. He could tell his dad's comment and straight forwardness unnerved her some by the way she searched his face for answers. "Dad is trying to say he likes you already Matt. Right dad?"

"Oh yes, definitely yes." Especially since she had become his son's main focus these past couple of months, he thought. Yep, romance was in the air and he couldn't hope for anything more where Jackson was concerned. He was glad his son had redirected his life in a positive way. You would have to be blind not to notice the changes he had made in his life. The phone calls were more frequent and lengthy and there were letters now. All of which thrilled his mom, which thrilled him. Jackson was maturing and it warmed his heart to know his son was finally stepping up and being the man he knew he was meant to be. Lyndal couldn't help thinking how having Jackson home with his female friend would brighten his wife's day. Joyce's heart attack had scared the daylights out of him but the doctors assured him with the proper treatments she would get better. Lyndal didn't want to convey any of that to his son when he'd called because he knew this would be a way to get Jacks home in a hurry and the reason was valid. Joyce would feel a lot better if she got to see her son and if this was a sneaky, underhanded way of doing it then so be it. Lyndal would do what ever it took to make his wife happy. "Mattie I'm glad you came with Jackson. It's about time we got to meet the girl who has knocked his socks off."

Mattie couldn't help the shocked look she knew was on her face. She hadn't realized she had been the topic of conversation with the Wood's family. Jackson smiled at her reaction but she still felt apprehensive about what they had discussed and then realized she was being just plain stupid. Of coarse he would tell his family about the person he loved. It just hadn't occurred to her right away since she had no one to tell.

Jackson spoke in low tones, "I've told my folks all about you Mattie. I couldn't keep you to myself. I was so happy I had to let them in on it. Mother was so anxious to see you and she wanted to know all about the girl I couldn't stop talking about. I'm sorry your first meeting has to be like this." Focusing his attention back to his father he asked. "How is she dad? Can we go to see her now?"

"Your mother is stable and the doctors said she only suffered a mild attack and that there was some minor damage but not anything real severe. She doesn't seem to be suffering any residual effects except she's weak and tires easily. Dr. Hayes has transferred her to a private room as of this morning and she is waiting for us as we speak. Now, if you two are ready, I'd say we need to get moving. We don't want to upset her or worry her for no reason. So if you two are ready we'll take my car." With that he headed for the Mercedes parked in front of the garage motioning for them to follow.

Mattie hadn't ridden in a Mercedes before so this was another treat. The silence among the three was an easy silence to bear. There didn't seem to be a need to fill the air with idle chitchat during the drive to the hospital. Her thoughts wandered at how lucky Jackson was to have both his parents and that they loved him. As Lyndal guided them down the hospital corridor she told Jackson so. He only smiled at her and agreed with her even though he said there was a time he hadn't felt so lucky. Mattie couldn't imagine it since she had no one of relation left.

Joyce was dozing when they arrived in her room but it didn't take much for her to focus her attention on her visitors. "Jackson," she motioned for him to give her the traditional hug. Joyce knew he'd said Mattie was pretty but there was no way he could have given her the proper credit for her looks with just mere words of description. "Ya know it's just a shame you didn't get here a little sooner. They just served us what used to resemble food and I would have gladly shared." She wiggled her eyebrows in their direction which was in perfect Groucho Marx style.

"Now Joyce we couldn't take your nutrition. The doctor said you had to build up your strength." Lyndal couldn't keep from smiling even if he'd tried. In this case he didn't bother.

"Nutrition, Humph," she mumbled. "I've seen cardboard with more appeal than that lunch tray had. I don't want to discuss that anyway. However, I do want to be introduced to this beautiful young lady you brought in with you Jacks." She smiled like a cat with a bowl full of cream.

Jackson groaned when he saw her planning face flash in place but he knew she didn't care.

Joyce liked Mattie immediately and she had a feeling Mattie was a good choice for her son. Yep, she could hear the wedding march in the very near future and maybe the lustful cry of a grandbaby or two. This heart problem proved to have a use after all. It wasn't the girl's looks it was how she stood unobtrusive, quietly watched and listened, extremely shy according to Jackson, but there was just something about her that Joyce liked and she hadn't even had a chance to talk to the girl.

"Hey! No, how are you? It's good to see you? Nothing? You ignore your favorite son. I'm hurt." He pouted and gave her his best-wounded puppy look he could muster up knowing she was a sucker for it. Joyce laughed at his antics and that was a sure sign she was feeling better. Jackson had always been able to make her laugh and it was good to see he hadn't lost his touch.

"Jackson Woods you are my only son and don't be such a baby. I want to know the girl who has taken my place in your heart." She knew Jackson would try to deny it but it was of no use. She could see his love for Mattie whether he knew it or not.

"No one can do that mom and you know it. There is plenty of room for the both of you.

Mattie was becoming more self-conscience with each word that passed between them and she was becoming more nervous and isolated as she stood there feeling like an intruder. Joyce appeared to be a terrific person, as did Lyndal. She was very pretty, open, witty, and kind. How could she even fit in with that? Mattie wasn't used to all this personal, fun loving bantering. The loneliness had never felt more oppressive than it did right then. She had no one in this world that was hers by blood or relation of any kind. Not a living soul.

"Mom, this is Mattie Collins. I've told you about her a lot, and Mattie this is Joyce my lovely mother.

"I don't know what you have done to my son young lady but what ever it is keep it up! He's needed a new, positive focus and by God I believe you're the best one he's ever had."

Jackson groaned. "Geeze, mom, you're embarrassing me and Mattie so cut it out will you?"

"Ok. Ok. But a mother has the right doesn't she, hum?" Joyce couldn't help looking a little smug.

"How are you feeling mom? Really? Are you having anymore chest pains?"

"I'm fine. I feel great actually. I'm weak mind you but much better. The doctor says diet and exercise and plenty of stress free living are in order to get better. Your father has already searched out the proper food lists, searched out the proper facility for workouts, and decreased my work load to only a couple of days a week. You really shouldn't miss class Jacks but I'm glad you and Mattie came just the same."

"Mom, you know I would do anything for you and besides we have fall break in a couple of days and I'll have you know my grades are very good. Very, very, good. Your timing, as always, is impeccable." Jackson smiled a genuine smile for the woman who had managed to still love him even after everything he had done. He knew he was fortunate to have been given a chance to make things right with his folks and for that he was one man.

Mattie watched the scene with this family and it made her heart feel heavy as the emotions welled up painfully. She felt a knot in her throat and the burning behind her eyes but she continued to fight it even though she knew it was a losing battle. Mattie thought she was doing a pretty fair job of hiding her emotions but the heaviness was beginning to smother her. She thought she was in control until Joyce focused on her and asked her about herself and her family.

Joyce never got the chance to finish her questions because Mattie bolted from the room. She was surprised at the sudden retreat and asked Jackson, "What did I say?" Joyce hated the idea of upsetting someone or causing anyone pain.

Jackson relayed to his parents that Mattie had lost all her family and in essence she was all-alone and how she has been handling things so far. He had told them most of it before so now he filled in the gaps as quickly as he could so he could find Mattie.

"Poor dear," Joyce's heart ached for the girl. "Go after her Jackson. She's hurting and you need to let her know she's not alone anymore."

"My plans exactly." With that he tore out of the room in search of Mattie.

Mattie didn't know her destination; she only knew her need to flee. She ran down the hall until the sunlight blinded her as she made her way outside. The cool breeze kissed her tear soaked face. Drawing in deep, gulping breaths all she could do was let the freedom wash over her. The oppressiveness was leaving her with an empty hole in its wake. Making her way to a bench she sat down beneath the dogwood that looked as empty of life as she felt. Cradling her face in her hands Mattie sobbed for what she didn't or could ever remember having in her life.

Jackson prided himself on reading Mattie pretty well but he had missed all the signs this time. He was so relieved to see his mother he'd ignored everything else including her. Jackson searched all over the place trying to find Mattie. He was starting to hyperventilate the more anxious he got. He was rushing down a hallway when it occurred to him to look for her outside. Mattie loved the outdoors and if he hadn't been so rattled he would have thought of that right off the bat instead of running around like a damned fool. Making his way to the sitting park near the back entrance his hurried steps slowed to a fast walk when he saw her. Taking a deep lung full of crisp cool

157

air to calm his nerves he made his way towards where she was sitting. She was sitting on a concrete bench beneath a fall kissed dogwood. Her face was pressed into her palms hiding the tears he knew were streaming down her face. Her shoulders were trembling and he could hear the soft sobs escaping behind her hands. He slowly approached the bench trying to figure out what to say to Mattie without startling her. Jackson knew enough not to put his hand on her unexpectedly. Speaking softly as he faced her. "Mattie what's wrong sweetheart?" He stood in front of her patiently waiting as he had before. She appeared too deep in her grief to hear anything he had to say. Jackson sat at her feet and softly spoke again. "Mattie, please look at me." Silence greeted his heartfelt pleas. "Honey, please talk to me."

Mattie heard Jackson but she was so ashamed of her actions facing him was not something she was looking forward to. Slowly she lifted her face to look at the man she loved with all her heart and was embarrassed beyond measure at how she had acted in front of him and his parents. Jackson had seen her fear and desperation but this was pure loneliness and embarrassment. Why would she be lonely or embarrassed with him and his family? "What happened back there, Mattie?"

"Oh, Jackson I'm sorry." What a baby she was and how pathetic?

Jackson didn't worry about keeping his hands off and lifted her chin forcing her to look at him. He was glad she didn't resist him. "What are you sorry for honey? What happened to make you run away?"

"I was watching you with your family and it occurred to me just how alone I truly am. I have no one Jackson, no one." A fresh trail of tears trickled down her cheeks. Now he understood. He hadn't considered that before he had brought her with him, but honestly he was so concerned about his mom he just hadn't given any thought to anything other than getting home to his mother.

"Oh Mattie your not alone. Not anymore. You have me, our friends, and my family is your family now. You wont ever be alone again sweetheart. "I'm sorry Jackson, I've ruined your visit with your mother and here she is in the hospital."

"Now Mattie, don't you dare be sorry and nothing is ruined. We were only surprised when you took off. Everything is fine and my folks are waiting on us." Jackson knelt down in front of Mattie and brushed away her tears with his thumbs. She didn't flinch from his touch so they were making progress. Her reaction brought a smile to his face and he continued smiling as he brought her face closer to his. He lightly brushed his lips across hers trying to assure her with as much feeling as he could pour into the kiss.

Mattie sighed with pleasure and smiled as she continued the kiss. Reaching out she put her hands on his biceps with the lightest of touches.

Jackson's loved how she held onto him. Reaching out slowly he placed his hands on her waist and she allowed it. He wanted to jump for joy. Someone sighed and someone moaned as the embrace and the kiss continued.

Breathing heavily Mattie broke the kiss just as she had initiated it and Jackson pressed his forehead against hers. "Mattie you take my breath away. I love you so very much."

"Me too," she managed to whisper around the smile she was wearing. She hadn't known such heartfelt emotion before this man barged into her life. She was smart enough to know that if he hadn't done just that she would have missed out on the love of a lifetime.

Jackson was thinking Mattie and their relationship was more than he had ever dreamt of and was thankful she was in his life, in his heart. He had heard of earth shattering love and the way a relationship could change everything but this was more than he ever imagined.

Sexual relationships were always available to him but no one ever guessed he hadn't ever breeched that area of a relationship with any one. He had a reputation for being a sexual deviant and a long line of one night stands, but no one knew the truth. He mentally chuckled with that thought because he was a certifiable virgin. It may be old fashioned, but he always knew he would only give himself to the woman he was to marry and no one else. The girls he dated found it hard to come from a date with him untouched. He never felt a need to deny their boasts of having had sex with him because it kept the rumor mill running. Doing a mental shake he brought his focus back to the matter at hand.

"Now my little songbird I think it is time to go back to mom's room and then we can make our plans for the rest of this trip. That is if it is ok with you?"

Mattie was still shocked at the 'home' Jackson so casually mentioned. She felt as if she had walked into a fairy tale and she was the princess. There weren't any places like that back home she was sure she would have remembered it. She was overjoyed at the prospect of spending her time with Jackson at his home. "It's more than 'ok' with me Jacks."

Arriving at the estate two hours later Jackson gave Mattie a tour. The living room was huge and the most elegant place Mattie had ever set foot in. A huge white piano sat at the wall of windows where the evening sun drifted in. A huge fireplace along the farthest wall was topped with a mantle covered in photos and figurines. The room was furnished like some she had seen on the cover of magazines. Mattie was beginning to feel a little overwhelmed with all the things she saw as intimidating and wealthy. Something she had never been. What grabbed her attention weren't the other elaborate rooms or the bulging library that made her want to salivate, it was the garden. It was like

159

being back home with all the flowers, shrubs, and the familiar scents. Everything she had seen before had in some ways made her feel inadequate but here she felt at peace and almost whole. Did Jackson know? She couldn't help but think to herself how inadequate she was for him. He had always made her feel like a part of him but now she felt flooded with negative feelings. Why would he settle for me when he could have all this and more? That question plagued her thoughts all that afternoon and evening. She smiled, she talked, but she felt alone, somehow inferior, this place was too intimidating for Mattie and she didn't know how to deal with it. Deciding to ignore her feelings, a habit she came by easily over the years, because she didn't want to face the alternative.

-

Chapter Twenty-Eight

Joyce came home after the first week of their visit. She was weak and pale but she had kept her sense of humor and used it often to lift the gloomy faces of her family. She also had a knack for picking up on things that weren't quite right with people and she sensed uneasiness in Mattie. Joyce really liked Mattie and she knew Jackson loved her as deeply as any human could but she seemed distant and that was what she brought to Jackson's attention during one of their visits.

"What do you mean distant? Mother are you sure you're reading Matt right? She's just a little overwhelmed with all this," gesturing at his surroundings.

"No, I don't think so Jacks. She closes off right in front of us. It's like watching a door being pulled to."

"Come on mom are you taking up ESP activities now" snickering at his own joke, "or how about a madam. I could get you a crystal ball and some tarot cards."

"Laugh all you want Jackson but something is wrong. I don't know what but there is a problem and you need to help her with it. Call it women's intuition or whatever but I can feel it."

"Geeze, mom you make it sound so urgent. I know my Matt and if she were having a problem she would tell me."

'My Matt' didn't go unnoticed by Joyce but her focus was on the problem at hand so she pushed. "Something isn't right I'm telling you Jacks so would you please talk to her. If I didn't like her I wouldn't worry but would you just talk to her. Please?"

"Calm down mom. I'll go talk to her right now ok?" Jackson had ever seen his mother so worked up before. His mother's urgency was affecting him now that she had planted that little seed. Her shoulders had visibly relaxed and released a sigh that sounded like "Good." She leaned her head back against the sofa and closed her eyes as he started to leave the room. The relief he saw on her face puzzled him. His mother had never been interested in his girlfriends before, so why Mattie? He had told his parents he was in love with her so maybe that was it. Jackson shook away his thoughts and set out to find Matt. He had known her developed pattern already. In the last week she had spent most of her time in the garden so he knew he would find her there.

The sun was warm on the walkway and the birds were singing out to one another. Jackson stopped short at the site that greeted him. Mattie was on her knees in the garden with her hand outstretched to small deer smiling and humming. His breath caught in his throat. "God she is so beautiful." The sun was streaking through her Auburn waist length hair casting blonde highlights throughout the unbound mass. He realized her hair resembled the colors in the little doe's pelt. What a picture they made. Jackson held his breath afraid he would break the magic spell that had been woven around the two. The doe sensed his presence and quickly fled into the wooded areas that surrounded the estate. Mattie was still smiling and she looked so serene he had a hard time getting his legs to work. Forcing his feet to move, he made his way closer to her. She slowly turned to face him as he approached and was struck by the intense emotions she elicited with only a mere glance.

Mattie froze at the site of Jackson coming for her, which still amazed her. Never, in her wildest dreams, would she have thought love would happen for her. Not the kind of forever love she knew she felt for him. Mattie felt her heart swell and increase its tempo with each step he took.

"You are the most beautiful woman I have ever seen." He was in awe of this woman and how she held his heart in the palm of her hand.

"You're beautiful to me Jacks," she stated whisper soft.

"I have been given orders by the big boss lady to come and find you." He grinned at her puzzled look.

Mattie looked quizzically as she stated, "But why? I'm fine Jacks."

"Mattie I've known you for along time and even I didn't notice anything either, but mom did. She said she felt like something was bothering you." Jackson sat down being mindful not to touch her unexpectedly. He had learned how to read her reactions and it didn't escape his watchful eye how she unconsciously pulled away to prevent his leg from brushing hers.

Mattie didn't want to tell Jackson how she truly felt, because she knew he would want to talk about it. Her feelings were what they were, no matter what they all said, she still felt inadequate in these surroundings. She also accepted the fact that she needed to be honest with him. Jackson deserved that honesty, even though she knew it might hurt him. "Well, it's just…I feel…" well hell. Just spit it out. She thought.

"You feel?" Jackson encouraged her to continue.

"I feel like I don't belong here Jacks." There she'd said it.

"Don't belong? Mattie, you belong with me and that's all that matters. This", as he swept his arm in a half circle, "this all belongs to mom and dad. I know it's uncomfortable for you, but I'll let you in on a little secret honey, it makes me uncomfortable too." He was mentally thanking his mother for being a perceptive female because he had no idea she had been feeling this way.

"Jackson, you have had your whole life to get used to all it and if your still uncomfortable, can't you imagine how I feel? It's just that I'm a no-body country girl, from a nowhere town, with no family to speak of and nothing of value to my name. How can I compete with what you have here?" She couldn't face him so she chose to focus her attention on her lap.

"Mattie I don't want to ever hear you say that again. You are somebody to me. You are everything. I love you and that's all it takes to fit in with me sweetheart. This", as he gestured widely sweeping his arms about for the second time, "means nothing to me. It never has. This," repeating his gesture yet again, "is my parent's life earnings, not mine. I've never as if I'm part of it either and have rebelled against it as long as I can remember. All I ever wanted was mom and dads love and acceptance, not the money they had or the social standing that went with it."

He hadn't told her much about himself and realized it had been a huge mistake. He wanted, no needed, for her to understand. All he ever wanted was the simple things in life and made many mistakes trying to achieve it. He didn't want Mattie to walk away from him for the same reasons he had walked away from his parents. He knew she was listening to his every word because she jerked her gaze in his direction.

"Mattie, I was given a choice of jail or school. For once in my life I made the right decision. I resented everything and I thought my parents didn't love me. Stupid, I know that now, but then I felt like I had to compete for their attention, so I got into trouble. I finally realized my parents had always loved me, I just chose to think otherwise. My parents and I have a great relationship now. We talk all the time and we still have family sessions once a month. It's been a hard battle, mending the damage.

You had told me, more than once, how lucky I was to have a family and because of that I have worked even harder to be the son they deserved. Please don't make the same mistakes I did and ruin what we have by feeling inadequate, or in second place. You are everything to me, Mattie, everything."

Mattie whispered his name as she slowly stood and held her hand out for his. She needed to feel the contact of his skin against hers. To tell him she understood how he felt about the wealth and all its trappings.

Jackson accepted her offer and just held her. His admissions must have been exactly what she needed to hear. He only wished he'd had the insight to tell her before it got to this point. It was a moment of acceptance, a bonding, and the knowledge that they fit well together. They shared a special love and nothing else mattered.

Jackson held her close and felt the joy well up inside him. He spun Mattie in a circle and as he slowed the spin he captured her mouth with his in a hungry soul-sipping kiss.

Mattie tried hard not to pull away but the niggling fear was rearing its ugly head. She was struggling to fight the tightness in her chest and her breathing was limited. The familiar chant "let go" rang in her head. She began to squirm and wriggle slowing the spinning to a complete stop, yet the kiss continued.

Jackson was so lost in the sensations of their connected lips that he didn't notice Mattie's attempts to get away. He was oblivious to everything except the feel of her in his arms and all thought and reason didn't exist for him. He had no idea the torture he innocently inflicted on the woman he held tightly to his chest.

Not now...Please...Not now! Without further thought the damn broke and she screamed, "Let me go...Oh God help me. Let go..." she heard her own pleas but they had were only in her own head. She began to cry in earnest. Her struggle against his broad shoulders had caused the hold to grow tighter. Trapped, can't breath, don't touch me, let go of me, she couldn't take anymore and ripped her mouth free. The scream she elicited was heart wrenching.

Jackson knew immediately what he had done. He had lost all sense of control and ignored all her attempts for freedom. Now he would have to watch the woman he loved fight that horrible fear again and he knew he was to blame.

Mattie had pushed him away, gripped her arms, and dropped to her knees as she rocked back and forth.

She was screaming, crying, and shaking yet Jackson didn't know what to do. He kept his distance as he watched her fight the demons in her mind it was a sight he soon wouldn't forget. "How could I have forgotten the rules? Dammit!" He couldn't help cursing his stupidity.

Joyce had managed to make her way to the garden after hearing that horrible screaming that rent the air. She knew it was Mattie and suspected the reasons for it. She had witnessed the scene through the terrace windows and knew what was unfolding. The wheelchair was cumbersome so she abandoned it half way to where her son was standing. Joyce felt a strong hand grip her by the waist and knew it was Lyndal. He didn't let her get far without appearing when she needed him. He didn't say anything and only smiled down at her with his understanding eyes. A lot passed in the look they shared.

Jackson stood back as he watched Mattie lose herself in the misery. It was painful to witness. He felt helpless but he didn't know what to do this time. He didn't even realize he was crying, because his attention was focused on the woman he loved.

Joyce and Lyndal saw and they knew without a doubt where their son's heart was. Jackson didn't see them standing at his side until his mom touched his arm. The tears gathered and fell from all parties and when Jackson looked into his mothers eyes it was there that his unspoken need flowed from son to mother.

Lyndal's heart ached for his son and Mattie as he watched her terror, her fear, and her pain. It was like some of the scenes he had witnessed in Vietnam. Scenes with emotions he thought he would never be witness to again, but he had been wrong. He shared a look with Joyce and a nod between them was all that was necessary.

Joyce went to Mattie and knelt down beside her. She knew all to well what she should do and what she shouldn't do. She placed her hand on Mattie's shoulder to let her feel that reality was still around her. She also knew Mattie was in deep and speaking softly wouldn't do it.

"Mattie, it's me, Joyce. You are safe in my garden with all of us here. Jackson is waiting for you. It's ok to come back now." Waiting for a hint of a response was useless. Mattie didn't bat an eyelash. "Mattie, now you listen to me young lady," her voice harsh with anger she didn't feel, with sharpened words meant to cut. This was the only way. "You get a grip on yourself right now! Don't give that bastard the satisfaction. That is what he wants and you are giving in to him. Mattie you need to fight it for all you are worth. We are here with you and nothing, I promise, nothing will hurt you. Not ever again." Joyce waited.

Jackson was shocked that his mother would treat Mattie so poorly. He didn't understand what she meant by 'he' either. Had Mattie told her something she hadn't told him? It didn't matter right now, he just wanted Mattie back but the more he listened to his mother the angrier he got. Never in his life had he ever felt such rage towards her no matter what had happened. He had never known her to be purposely cruel.

Lyndal felt the tension in his son and he knew what he was feeling. Jackson was watching his woman fall apart right in front of him and there wasn't a damn thing he could do about it. Just as Lyndal had all those years ago.

They wouldn't be alone as he and Joyce had been. When Lyndal felt Jackson attempt to move he placed his large hand on his shoulder to restrain him.

Jackson flashed a cold stare at his father, but when he saw the unshed tears and the understanding in his father's eyes, he realized they were helping Mattie. Lyndal gave him weak smile and shook his head letting Jackson know not to interfere. Not yet.

He only nodded back to his dad and mouthed to him "why?" He didn't get an answer and his dad focused back on their women.

"Dammit Mattie Collins, get a grip. Don't give power where it's wasted. You are strong so stand tall and hold your head up. We are waiting for you. Listen young lady, I'm tired so move your ass and don't be all day about it. Now!"

Joyce was practically screaming at Mattie and Jackson found himself in the iron grip of his father. Never had he heard his mother talk to anyone the way she was to Mattie right now. Did she not understand Mattie didn't need this kind of treatment? That she couldn't handle it? He refused to believe that his mother would intentionally hurt Mattie yet he was witnessing it with his own two eyes. There had to be a reason and she would tell him.

Mattie was deep in the darkness, but she heard the words. Words she had heard throughout her life. Hateful, ugly words, but now she was confused. The voice was different. It wasn't her stepfather's voice but it wasn't her mothers either. "You don't know" she thought. "How dare you." No one knows.

Mattie forced her body to stop shaking by gradual increments and forced her head up. The undiluted hatred that masked her eyes staggered those around her.

Jackson whispered "Jesus" and Lyndal was in agreement. He recognized that look on many soldiers' faces and it still had an unnerving affect on him. Joyce didn't even flinch because she recognized that look. It didn't surprise her that Mattie wore it. It fit with the other signs she had witnessed since she had come home with Jackson. Joyce knew Mattie had suffered and she refused to stand idly by and let it continue. That was one of the reasons she had always worked at the clinic. The fear would not hold her or anyone else as long as she could help them fight it.

Mattie blinked and felt a little confused. It was like coming out of a black hole. "Joyce?"

"Now then, that's better. I want you to shake it off Mattie. We're all here. You're not alone anymore and never will be again. Let us help you. Let us be your strength for a while and if you want to talk we are all willing to listen." Joyce sensed Mattie's decreasing tension. The cold stare was almost gone and the tears streamed down both women's cheeks.

Mattie for the first time in a long time felt a kinship with another person other than Jackson. "You understand because you know," was all she managed before she collapsed on Joyce's lap and wept for all those years of being afraid and lonely. It was like a dam had broken and the tears were all the ugliness washing away. Mattie had never let go as she did in this moment. Somehow Joyce knew the suffering she had gone through and she understood.

Mattie knew she wouldn't be the same after this day. This was what she needed. It was her turning point for a better life.

Joyce just sat and rubbed Mattie's back and soothed her while the shaking took over her slender body. Joyce's body was taxed already with her resent hospitalization, so she turned her weary eyes up to the men in her life.

166

Lyndal knew his wife was at her ropes end and he knew it was time for Jackson to take over.

Jackson hadn't moved he only stared at his mother and the woman he loved. His tears ran unchecked down his cheeks. He wanted to know how his mother knew and all he could do was whisper "how?"

Lyndal grabbed his son into a strong embrace and told him to trust them. How could he not? he wandered.

Joyce motioned for her men to come closer and they didn't hesitate. The emotion on her face was more than either could stand to witness. Jackson's silent tears turned to sobs and Lyndal wept as he bent to help his weakened wife. Jackson slid into her place at Mattie's side and whispered to his parents "I still don't understand any of this, but thank you and I love you."

"Jacks honey, that is thanks enough. Stay with her son. She has just crossed a major bridge in her life and she will need you more now than ever before. Don't leave her." Joyce knew he wouldn't but she felt compelled to say it anyway. She was too weak to cross the distance to her wheel chair so Lyndal lifted her into his strong arms and carried her. Joyce just smiled up at husband as he placed her in her chair as he smiled down at her. He nodded at her and turned to push her back to their home knowing the ghosts would visit them this night.

Lyndal knew his wife would need his strength and his support as she dealt with those ghosts again. He knew his wife needed him this night, as she always had and he was more than willing to be there for her.

Lyndal loved Joyce beyond any words a poet could write. She always said he was her rock and he never attempted to correct her. But Joyce had always been his rock, his strength, his heart. He couldn't live without her and when that statement was put to the test, it scared him more than he would ever admit. He thought he was losing her when she had her heart attack and the thought was unbearable to him.

They were both deep in thought as they made their way to their bedroom. Joyce needed to rest and feel alive and Lyndal needed to feel his wife's love. Silently they undressed and went to bed. Joyce lay in her husband's strong arms and against his naked body listening to his heartbeat under her ear. Joyce never doubted his love for her and he held her again as she lost herself in the grief they didn't have to deal with very often anymore.

Lyndal held his crying wife without faltering or weakening his embrace. Joyce was safe in his arms and he would always protect her even keeping the long forgotten ghosts at bay. Sleep claimed them as they shared in a lovers embrace, knowing for now, that it was enough. When Joyce's health was better they would love each in everyway. Joyce slept with a smile on her face. The ghosts did not revisit this night.

Chapter Twenty-Nine

Jackson knew Mattie was finally with him in mind, as well as, body. The storm had passed and a companionable silence fell between them. He held her head in his lap as she lay in an exhaustive state of calm and acceptance. Jackson stroked her hair and her cheek and traced the outline of her profile trailing his hands down her arm to her slender fingers that made magical music. "Oh Mattie what in Gods name has happened to you?" He didn't break his stroking rhythm as he continued to cradle her. He had no idea how long he had sat there but the sun sat low. When he'd first spotted her it was overhead and shining brightly. Could they possibly have been here all those hours?

"Jacks?" He heard the hoarseness of her whispered voice that was still thick with tears.

"I'm right here sweetheart, right here."

"Hold me?" She shifted her face so he could look into her beautiful tiger-eyes.

"Always babe. Always" the relief he felt was in his smile.

"Can we go now?"

"Yeah Matt, we can do whatever you want to do" he'd give her the moon and the stars if he could gather them.

"I would really like to go to my room now" she hesitated "will you come with me?"

Jackson thought he misunderstood her but answered anyway. "Sure, I'll take you to your room, if that's what you want. I know it's been a very draining day and you're tired".

"I want you to come with me and hold me, because I don't think I can stand being alone tonight. Not after everything that has happened today. Would you? Please?" And much to her surprise she wasn't afraid after the words left her mouth. For that matter, she couldn't believe she had even asked it in the first place. Apparently she was more ready than she realized. She needed him with her and for the first time in her life she wanted him in the way a woman wanted a man. That thought was very telling for her considering she had never, ever, wanted that kind of a relationship with any male. Jackson was different in every way. He had helped her to grow into the woman she was now becoming. That black hole that had swallowed her and kept her imprisoned for years was slowing growing smaller and she wanted Jackson to help her finish closing it off. He was the only man who had given her the time and space she'd needed, he could touch her, hold her, love her, and she had fallen so hard and fast for him that the next step was inevitable. Jackson was wearing a look of surprise by her request. "Please?" Mattie hoped her sincerity and desire showed in her eyes so he would know she was seriously ready for this step. Even after what had happened earlier she felt this was the right move and she was ready.

Jackson was speechless all for about a second before he answered her in a rush before she changed her mind. "That's all I ever wanted Mattie. I love you and I would consider it an honor to keep you safe in my arms."

Jackson's face was filled with honesty and love as he answered her straight from his heart.

They made their way to the house with Mattie's hand clasped in Jackson's and her head on his shoulder. He led her to her room and the impact of Mattie's request hit them full force.

Mattie was the first to speak. "Jackson?"

"Hmm?" He didn't know if he could get a whole word out.

"Will you lay with me?" And she shyly tugged him in the direction of the king-sized bed that suddenly seemed to change from inviting, to an overpowering focus in the center of the room. The antique wrought iron canopy bed held a silent invitation that was growing into a scream.

"I will gladly lay with you Matt but I'll lay on top of the blankets, ok?" He didn't think he could take it if it were more intimate.

"That's fine Jacks. I just need you to hold me. I know with you here I'll be safe and the ghosts of a past I don't remember won't steel my sleep away."

Jackson eased his long frame across the bed with only his feet bare and Mattie did the same. She stretched out beside Jackson feeling a little awkward at first then leaned over and gently placed her head on his very broad, solid shoulder. Mattie let out a contented sigh and without thought she snuggled a little closer. Feeling safe and loved lying next to Jackson's body she knew she could lay like this, with this man, forever.

Jackson's noble thoughts were quickly losing ground. For months he had dreamt of Mattie sharing a bed with him and now here they were and there was no way he was going to screw it up. Not after today. He was having problems convincing his body not to harden in certain areas. He knew he shouldn't think about those things but he couldn't force himself to stop. Jackson wanted Mattie in every way imaginable but now was a time for trust and comfort, not lust. Needing to get his mind off her luscious body plastered to his, he decided to ask Mattie what he hadn't dared ask before. Today things were different, the rules had changed, and he wanted to know what caused her fears.. "Mattie?" He almost hoped she was asleep.

"Yes?" She answered.

"What happened? I mean what causes those episodes of fear and anguish in you? I think if you talk about it you can begin to heal." He held his breath. The topic was laid out and it was Jackson's turn to feel some fear.

"I'm sorry Jacks I never meant...I couldn't even..." she was unable to finish. How could she explain something she didn't know? Couldn't remember? A whole year of her life was lost. How could she make him understand her memory loss when she didn't understand it herself?

Jackson sensed her unease or did she just not want to share it with him? Maybe she didn't feel the need to bring it all out into the open. Maybe she had secrets she would rather keep. No, he refused to believe that. He questioned his wisdom in bringing it up. "It's ok Mattie. You don't have to tell me if you don't want to. I'll understand." He continued to rub her arm in slow rhythmic strokes unaware he was even doing it.

"Jackson, it's not that. It's not a matter of wanting to. It's a matter of being able to. You see, I just don't remember. I honestly don't. I have no memory of anything when I was sixteen. It's almost as if that entire year didn't happen. Obviously it did, but ever since then I have this fear of being touched, of being in crowds, of just about everything that most people take for granted. I have memories of when I was young and I loved being hugged. I was a people person and all the normal stuff that I can't stand now. Life was so different compared to how it is now."

Jackson immediately had a horrible thought and pushed it aside. He was staring at the ceiling with a blank expression on his face hoping he could mask the sudden sick feeling in the pit of his stomach. He hadn't expected this, yet he knew she was being honest with him. Mattie was the most honest person he had ever met. Jackson shifted his weight so they were lying on their sides facing each other then he lifted up on his elbow to see her face better. "You don't remember anything? And a whole year is just gone?" He knew the answer was in her eyes so she didn't have to clarify it. What ever happened to her had to be traumatic enough for her to have completely wiped it away. "No wander you're afraid. Anyone would be if a whole year of their life was missing." Trying humor to lighten the mood, "But then again, there are sometimes a little memory loss would have been a benefit." The horror on her face was a clear indicator that he had said the wrong thing, again.

"Don't you ever say that!" she spat out. Never in her life had she reacted to anyone in such an angry way. The look on Jackson's face revealed total shock with her outburst. Gentling her tone she continued her thoughts. "Please don't ever say that Jackson, it's awful, not knowing, never understanding, and jumping at shadows constantly. It's because of that missing year that my life is so screwed up now.

I know it had to be something awful but the problem is I have no idea what 'it' was. Can you imagine what was so bad that I blocked out a whole year of my life over it? I know I had counseling and that kind of thing but I don't remember that either. I know my mother and stepfather died that year so I always thought it might have something to do with that but I have no way of knowing for sure, since I have no family left to ask."

"Mattie I am so sorry. I wish I hadn't brought it up."

"But don't you see Jacks? It's always a part of me, making me its prisoner every time I'm touched or get to close to anyone. The fear's always near the surface ready to drag me into the abyss."

Jackson was silent. Mattie had opened up so much over the past couple of hours that he was beginning to get a better understanding of the complex woman that lay facing him. There was a moment of clarity with what she said and what he had witnessed himself. Her reactions to people and events were a direct result to that lost time in her life, of that he was positive. He wanted to help her overcome this but it was like fighting an invisible entity. You didn't know when or where or how it was going to strike but when it did it was in total control. It caused such raw pain it was debilitating, paralyzing, and controlling. He only hoped that one day they could have a relationship that didn't have to be so guarded.

"Mattie, honey, I want to be the first to point out that you are lying beside me in your bed and have been for the last forty-five minutes and the fear hasn't reared its ugly head. Wouldn't you say were already making progress?" He was resting his hand on her upper arm and waited for the reality of the situation to meld in her mind. He felt her shifting and thought she was going to leave him when she rose up, propped herself up on her elbow, and faced him.

She could feel his breath on her cheek. "Your right Jacks," she whispered huskily, "I owe it to you and your family," she gazed into his blue eyes seeing the intense love mirrored there. She almost retreated from the impact. Not giving in to the impulse she stayed right where she was drowning in the ocean of this mans eyes.

Jackson felt the heat of his body rising. "Mattie, honey, don't look at me like that."

"How am I looking at you Jacks?" She spoke softly and stayed right where she was.

"Like I'm the only man alive," he smiled at her with a nervousness he hadn't felt minutes before.

"For me you are," and she closed the remaining distance between them brushing her cheek against his. "I love you Jackson Woods; with all my heart," she whispered against his mouth. "Don't give up on me."

Could a man be so lucky? "There is no chance of giving up on you. I have waited all my life for you and I'm not about to lose you now that I've found you. You my dear are stuck with me," and saying that he nipped at her very kissable lips. The comfortable warmth suddenly turned into a fiery red haze with that light touching of lips. Jackson didn't move an inch of his body for fear of her reaction so he let her make the next move. He felt her palm caress his face and he knew she was testing the fragile waters.

Mattie was mesmerized by the sensations Jackson elicited in her. The fear hadn't started yet and hoped she had changed something after what had happened in the garden. Mattie was being swept away and what she felt in the pit of her stomach wasn't fright and she wanted more. How to get it? That was the million dollar question. Not having ever been in this position before she was unsure of what to do.

Jackson kept himself in check refusing to budge. He heard Mattie's low moan as she deepened the kiss and thought his head would blow off. Slowly, so he wouldn't break the spell she had created, he lifted his hand gently caressing her arm, sliding it up to the hand that still caressed his cheek. He was pleased that she didn't flinch or startle with his touch. He was enthralled with this new freedom but kept every movement precise and determined. Trailing her ribs to her hip he waited for the dreaded reaction he just knew was coming and yet the only expression was the feel of warm, moist lips brushing on his own. He was the luckiest man alive.

Mattie's thoughts were centered on this man and what he meant to her. She continued to caress Jacks cheek as she prolonged this heart pounding, soul searing kiss. Mattie felt Jackson's movements and for an infinite second she experienced "it" but disregarded those feelings. She wanted to savor this monumental moment. For the first time, in a very long time, she felt as if she were in control of her life and refused to give it up now.

Mattie relished the feel of Jackson's hands on her. This was a part of their love that they hadn't broached yet. Mattie knew it was her own problems that kept things like friends but now she wanted more than a friendship. She wanted his love in every sense of the word. Slowly she tugged Jackson down and he followed her descent to the pillow without breaking contact as they did. Mattie wrapped her arms around Jackson and moaned loudly. This felt right and she felt ready for it.

Not only had Jackson been kissed senseless by the woman who loved him she allowed him so much freedom that he wanted to shout to the heavens. She had accomplished a great deal. Regretfully, he broke the kiss and nudged against her neck with his lips expelling his warm breath. Much to his pleasure she shifted her head to allow him easier access. He kissed her under her jaw line and along the silky soft skin of her neck. Jackson slowly drew his tongue

172

along the full length of her throat. He barely realized he was laying half on and half off Mattie's chest. The swell of her breasts pressed against him was inviting as hell. As tempting as it was he didn't act on his desire.

Mattie had already made up her mind that she wanted to live, to love, and be loved. Mattie knew she wanted everything with Jackson and she wanted to start tonight with him.

Jackson whispered in her ear. "Mattie, honey, I love you with all my heart. Doing this with you is all I've dreamt of and to be able to touch you, to hold you, to love you is more than I thought possible. Even with that I will stop if you want me too. I won't push, Matt"

Mattie had heard every word he spoke and found she wasn't shocked or scared, but excited. How could she not have known? Never mind that now she thought, not now, not here. She felt the stinging heat behind her eyes and the warm stream of tears slide down her cheeks and trail down her neck. These tears were of utter happiness. There were no sobs or shakes wracking her body. She was happy and she was filled with passion for this man. A passion she knew she wanted to act upon without the worry of whether the fear would try to claim her again.

Jackson felt the tears as they rolled down Mattie's neck and he tasted the salt of her weeping. He didn't want to be the reason for her tears. Not again. He began to pull away and looked down into the most captivating eyes he had ever seen. The smile on her swollen lips spoke volumes of her mental wellbeing. His heart thundered within his chest as the realization of her happiness registered in his lust filled brain. She whispered his name as he looked into her warm, loving gaze. "Yes, Mattie?" He couldn't take his eyes off her lips as he watched her warm, wet, pink tongue lick them. How he wanted to lick those lips with her.

"Jacks don't leave. Ok?" She hinted volumes in that one statement.

"I won't go anywhere as long as you want me to stay with you." He couldn't hide his relief from the observant eyes of the woman beneath him. Jackson lowered his head for another kiss and too his surprise she met him half way and kissed him without restraint. He didn't miss the hunger and passion she was giving him in that instant. He couldn't contain the moan deep in his throat dormant if his life had depended on it. Mattie sighed and left the gate open for entrance into that warm and inviting mouth. Jackson wasn't disappointed when he entered as Mattie's essence filled him to overflowing.

Mattie was swimming in emotions and feelings she had never experience in her life. The newness should have scared her to death and yet all she could think was how much more she wanted. This must be what Gracie meant about "the love of a good man was all a woman needed because with it the sky was the limit, so look for love Matt; always love." Gracie was right.

Mattie began a slow seductive smile that broke the intimate kiss with Jackson. Slowly lifting his head Jackson smiled back. Love was an electrical current that popped and sizzled between them.

Jackson loved the woman beneath him and he was relieved to see a peace and contentment on her face. Mattie had broken free of her prison. The dark barrier that had consumed her for years seemed to have cracked wide open allowing her to become this new Mattie. "What's so funny Mattie Collins? Are my kisses making you giggle? Not exactly the response a man wants from the woman he loves," he couldn't stop smiling.

Mattie's smile grew bigger and her eyes sparkled with humor, "I'm not laughing at you Jacks. I'm just so happy my face wants to show it. That's all."

"Well then don't mind me. I love your smile, your laughter, your loving heart, everything about you," his love very evident to anyone who looked upon his face.

Knowing she was in new, unfamiliar territory Mattie was uncertain on how to breech a subject she never thought she would discuss with any other human being. With her heart in her throat and her nerves dancing she decided to plunge right in just like her momma had told her to do when she was uncertain. "Jackson," she said with a conviction she didn't quite feel. "I've never been in this situation before and well, to be honest, I never really wanted to, but now, with you, it's different. The magic and freedom I feel is because of you and how you have changed my life. I want to be with you in all ways." Haltingly, she pointed to her head and then her heart and reached to touch his chest. Lowering her eyes, she patiently waited, not really knowing what to expect.

"Wow," he whispered. "Mattie, sweetheart, open your eyes and look at me please." He couldn't have been any more taken back than he was at that very moment. Today was the day for changes and she wanted it all with him. Jackson felt the heat of unshed tears as they pooled in his eyes and watched one fall onto her upturned face. How could he love her anymore than he did right then? How could he tell her that he wanted all that and more? Jackson knew he wanted this woman in all ways imaginable and he wanted to spend the rest of his life with her.

Mattie opened her eyes when the first tear drop softly landed on her cheek. The look on Jackson's face revealed more than she had expected to see. He was smiling as his blue eyes swam with unshed tears as his gaze locked with hers.

"Mattie, sweetheart, do you know what you are asking me?"

"Yes, Yes, I do. I love you more than mere words can say and I want to experience everything with you. Unless you don't...don't want me."

"Not want you? Not want you? Oh Mattie you're all I've ever wanted. Since the day I saw you, you have consumed me. I want you to know something first," he hushed her comment with his finger on her lips, "please let me finish this. Never in my life have I loved or wanted anyone more than I do you. I want everything with you. All the possibilities, the future, heart, mind, body and even soul if it were allowed but I want you to know before we go any further," he gestured to the bed they had been sprawled on. "I want you to know I have never been with a woman in that way and I would be honored for you to be that woman. I always wanted my wife to be my only partner, my only lover. There is one thing I want from you before we go any further and that is a promise. I want your promise to be my wife. I can't make love to you without it. I want you to be my wife, my friend, my lover, the mother of my children, and my life long companion. I love you with all that I am and I ache to be with you but you have to promise me or I won't do what you ask of me."

"Oh my God, Jackson I...I would love to be your wife. It's a dream I thought would never come true for me and now here you are offering me what I always wanted. To know you waited for me as I have been waiting for you makes it even more special."

The need to do this perfectly drove Jackson to ask his question again so she fully understood and answered without reservations. "Will you be my wife Mattie Collins? Will you share your life with me?"

"Yes, a thousand times yes!" She wrapped her arms around his neck chanting her answer over and over planting little kisses along his jaw line. Mattie had no fear in sharing this closeness with Jackson. Peace filled her, blanketing her in warmth and security. She felt a sense of home wash over her and in that instant she understood what it was that her mom and Gracie had told her all along. The love of a good man made life worth living. Mattie had found it with this man and hadn't even been looking. She could have sworn she heard him whisper "Thank God" but wasn't sure since the blood pulsed in her ears and her heart pounded against her ribs. She knew her life wasn't going to be a mere existence anymore she had a future and she would share it all with Jackson. The man who refused give up, stole her heart, and gave her a sense of freedom. Most importantly he was the man who loved her without demanding anything in return.

Jackson wanted to worship every little inch of skin on her beautiful body but he didn't think he had that kind of control. He'd been a virgin all these years and... that thought stopped him dead with sex crazed rampant thoughts. Mattie was a virgin too and had so much happen to her that he didn't want to screw anything up by being a callus bastard. Jackson whispered his love for

Mattie as he gently ran his hand up her rib cage and slowly caressed her breast with a butterfly touch and a whisper of what was to come.

Mattie had to remind herself to breath. She couldn't keep from wanting to hold the air in her lungs so she could focus on the sensations flowing through her from head to toe. No one had ever touched her so intimately and yet she wasn't shaken by the strangeness of it. Without thought she felt her back arch into Jackson's touch sending out a silent request for more.

Jackson slowly caressed and rubbed her nipple to a hardened peak through her thin blouse and lacey bra. "Mattie, honey, you could tempt a saint with this body of yours," he said with a low groan.

Mattie remained silent as she drifted and floated in her inexperienced body. The sensations flooding her system silently controlled her every move. She was so caught up in the magic he was weaving in and around her body that she was hard pressed to hear what he was saying to her. Rubbing her hands along his broad shoulders, she slid her fingers down his well defined biceps, eased both hands up cupping his sweet face in the palms of her hands, and kissed him with all the passion she was feeling for him. Containing a moan of pleasure was impossible.

Clothes were becoming a barrier neither wanted. Unspoken agreements to remove those barriers began with the slow opening of buttons on Mattie's blouse. Trying to be casual and relaxed, took an enormous amount of will power.

Jackson began a slow descent from the top button making his way to her waist. As if her blouse were a living, breathing thing, it slid open and fell to her sides, exposing a lacey peach colored bra that held the swelling ivory flesh of ample breasts. "So beautiful," he whispered. "So sweet," he mumbled as he lowered his lips to the edge of the lace and licked her skin seductively. Trailing slow, tender kisses from one breast to the other he realized that the little wisp of lacey material had a clasp in the front. My, oh my, how he loved such modern devices. A man must have had easy access in mind when he invented that little gadget. Grasping the latch he unleashed Mattie's breasts but the lace clung to her swollen curves. Looking upon Mattie's face he saw the seductive smile curving her lips.

Jackson reached up to trace her brow with his fingertip, trailing down her nose, to sweep along her puffy lips. He gently ran his fingers down her neck, along her rapidly beating pulse, turning his hand over to sweep his nails down the unblemished pale flesh of her chest. He was amazed how expressively she reacted to his touch and exploration of her beautiful body.

The clinging peach lace still cupped her swollen breast. He swept his finger under the edge and slowly, seductively eased it away exposing the creamy flesh beneath it, giving her time to make him stop if she couldn't deal with this intimacy.

Realizing he was the first man to be granted this freedom all over again, caused him to pause in his venture toward her pert nipple. Jackson's hand trembled as he circled the hardened nub and gently stroked the puckered skin. Mattie arched upward into his touch, her body understanding what her mind didn't. He palmed and caressed her. Following his desire he bent to taste her. He licked her soft flesh like a cat would a bowl of cream. He encircled her nipple over and over knowing he had to have more and sensing she wanted what he offered. He engulfed the tip of her breast into his hot mouth and began to slowly pull at her with rhythmic motions that sent pulsing blood to his already hardened, painful erection.

Mattie saw exploding stars flare behind her closed eyes. The feelings Jackson created in her had complete control and her mind couldn't form a coherent thought if it tried. She didn't know when her hands found their way to Jackson's lowered head or when her fingers threaded through his blonde locks firmly clutching him to her, a silent request for more. Mattie felt like her guitar and with each touch Jackson was playing her, stroking her.

Jackson thought he would explode when he felt Mattie's hands in his hair pulling him closer. Slowly moving he paid homage to her other breast. The sensations of desire filled the room, overwhelming them both.

Mattie ached with a wanting she had never experienced before. She hadn't realized she was tugging at Jackson's shirt until she felt him helping her. Eyes locked on one another, breathing was labored, lip's red and swollen from deep kisses, keeping his eyes locked on Mattie's he slowly edged the remainder of her blouse away. Skin to skin from the waste up released their pent up body heat.

Mattie lifted her hands to Jackson's chest and the soft patch of curly brown hair that lightly dusted his well muscled pec's. The invitation was there for her to touch, to explore. She ran her fingers into the softness of it and gently scraped the warm skin beneath it. She felt his heart thunder matching her own rhythm. She lifted her head to kiss him where her hands lingered and traced his nipple mimicking what he had done to hers. Mattie heard the quick intake of his breath when she took possession of the small nub. She had no idea he could feel what she had felt or as intensely as she had. She had been wrong. This was, in essence, their honeymoon and they would make sure it was a memorable night of passion and love.

Jackson lifted up on his elbow and watched Mattie's face as he unbuttoned her skirt and tugged at the material. The skirt slipped from her hips and he eased the rest of the material down to her knees and discarded it with their other clothing. Mattie's silky slip began the same descent that her skirt had

177

followed. Lace so small it didn't cover much hid her woman hood. The peach color was the same as her bra had been. Jackson couldn't stop starring at her beautiful body. Playboy pictures were nothing compared to this woman he loved. Her curves, her softness, her long muscular legs were more inviting than anything he had ever seen. He slowly brought his gaze up to her face letting her see his pleasure by the sight of her totally exposed, nude body. He wanted her to see his love for her. Jackson watched the expressions float across her face he began to run his fingers from her ankle to her calf encircling her knee in a slow caress and continued to softly brush her skin with his strong callused palms. He slowly ran his hand up her thigh and it was here that he felt the first hesitation, just a fraction, before he slowly ran a finger over her covered mound. Shivers raced over her skin causing goose flesh to wash over her. He was struck by how her response affected his. When she moaned he knew she was lost in his touch and what he was doing to her. "Look at me Matt," he whispered hoarsely knowing his excitement made his voice sound husky with desire. "Mattie, honey, look at me please."

Mattie turned her head slowly and opened her heavy lidded eyes to him with a huge smile on her reddened lips.

Jackson spoke softly. "Mattie, I want you in every way a husband knows a wife and I want to know if you're sure. Are you absolutely sure you're ready for this, and to be my wife?"

Mattie whispered back around the lump in her throat. "Jackson I want that more than anything. I want to live, I want to love, and I want you. All of you."

Jackson couldn't stand the distance, ever slight as it was, any longer. He leaned over and kissed her breathless while he cupped her soft breast in his palm. His touches elicited whimpers and seductive arching that only enticed him more.

Mattie wanted it all and so much more. She wanted to touch. She wanted to know. She wanted. Reaching for him she stroked his hot flesh. She began to run her fingers down his chest until she arrived at his waist. Moving slowly she made her way to his jeans and unsnapped them with slow agonizing little tugs. The zipper slowly sawed downward releasing the binding that kept her from his skin. Her hands lingered and her fingers brushed his hardened flesh. The brush was inviting and all thoughts flew to the corners of her mind as she caressed him with her palm. The fabric didn't hide much but she was fascinated with his arousal and stroked him, slowly. "Jackson I want to see all of you. Please help me." Mattie smiled when he didn't hesitate and eagerly lifted his hips for her. He smiled so seductively at her. She was overjoyed that she didn't feel any embarrassment or shyness

178

with him or what they were doing. Lifting up she slowly pushed him back onto the mattress and began to pull his clothing off one slow inch at a time.

Jackson was determined to let Mattie set the pace but it was taking every ounce of will power he could manage. He felt her breath against his flesh as she slowly worked his pants down his thighs and he felt her hair graze him like a hot iron. Mattie was branding him with her touch and she had no idea she was doing it. She slowly ran her hands up both of his thighs as she made a path to his ribs and around his chest and then descended to his belly button. He held his breath and he hoped silently asking if she would touch him again and tried to remain patient as she repeated her journey. Jackson was gritting his teeth trying to maintain control. Mattie was torturing him ever so sweetly. Forcing his eyes open he focused on the woman torturing him and realized she was watching him. Mattie was peering up at him with a sirens smile and he watched as her eyes followed the path her hands were taking.

Jackson groaned, as his body grew even tighter. Was there such a thing as death by desire? "Mattie? Please have some mercy on me." He was surprised and excited when she did as he begged. Her hands stopped at the juncture of his thighs then slowly caressed his engorged, aching manhood with her magical fingers. He could feel the pulse pounding in the hardened extension of his body and it was demanding serious attention. He would die a million times over before he would frighten her by acting on what his body was demanding of him.

Fighting those demands were becoming increasingly difficult as his body screamed for Mattie's and the release he craved. She slowly slid his boxers over his throbbing erection, down his legs, and dropped them to the floor to join their pile of discarded clothes. He froze in place fearing how she would react at seeing his exposed nudity and painfully erect sex. When she continued to move over him without pause or fright, he sighed deeply with relief, and sucked in a breath as Mattie's hair cascaded down his body like warm silk. Holding the uncontrollable moan within his throat was impossible. His body was reacting to Mattie so viscerally his control snapped.

Mattie knew by the way Jackson reacted to her touch that he was enjoying what she was doing to him. Reading his responses was all the encouragement she needed. "Jackson sweetheart, look at me."

Jackson instantly thought something was wrong but when he opened his eyes focusing on hers he was reassured by what he saw behind that aroused gaze. "Jacks I want to see your face while I touch you. I want you to see me want to touch you." He understood what she was asking and he could give her, painful as it was to maintain control without looking upon her beautiful face, watching her was going to test him beyond his limits but he would do that and more if she asked.

179

Mattie watched his face as she ran her fingers down the length of his erection. She cradled him and caressed him in the most intimate ways and she wasn't afraid. She couldn't hold back her smile when he told her she was killing him again for the second time. His body was as rigid as granite and desire held him in its fist and to know he maintained that control for her filled her heart with more love than she ever imagined possible.

Mattie didn't stop to think about her actions and focused on the feelings. Desire was pulsing in her veins, ruling her actions. In that moment she bent her head to do what she was being drawn to do.

Kissing the most sensitive area of Jackson seemed as natural to her as breathing. The fall of her hair created a privacy that aided her in what she was doing. Shielding her face from his gaze aided her in this bold act as she set on torturing the man she loved.

Jackson went rigid with the first touch of her sensuous mouth on his throbbing, sensitive flesh. Bursts of pleasure rocked him to the core as lights danced behind his tightly closed eyes. Mattie tasted, tormented, and innocently explored him to the point of losing control.

Mattie knew he was on the razor's edge when he grabbed her and pulled her up the length of his body. "Dear God, Mattie I can't take the torture another second."

Jackson pulled her up and over until she lay beneath him and swallowed her up with his kiss. Tongues caressed, sighs passed, and moans joined in the chorus. He wanted her with a desperation he had never felt before. He trailed his hands down her breast to her flat well toned stomach and continued until he touched lacey panties. How could he have forgotten those dainty little things? It occurred to him he could turn the tables on her and she would be the one wriggling out of control.

Running his fingers along the waistline of the lace and delved beneath the fabric, tugging at the material inching it downward. Mattie moved without him asking buy lifting her hips and shifting ever so slightly. Jackson eased the panties down her long well toned legs, past her ankles, and finally there were no barriers left between them. Flesh to flesh, heat to heat, and a need so deep it dictated their actions.

Jackson maneuvered himself so he knelt between her thighs and began a slow rhythmic stroking of her sensitive flesh from ankle to thigh, from ribs to breasts, and then he started all over again. As he made his last descent he followed closely with his upper body. His hot breath seared her throbbing flesh at the junction of her thighs and Mattie died a little death with the pleasure she felt. Jackson smiled as she wriggled her sweet little body demanding what she didn't understand yet. He couldn't resist softly blowing on her sensitive flesh. While she was caught up in the feelings of his hot

180

breath on her he boldly touched her with his tongue. Slowly and sweetly he tasted her.

Mattie jerked her head up and stared in surprise at Jackson. Eye to eye their gazes were locked and she knew he was doing exactly what she had done. He looked as if he planned to torture her as she had just done to him.

The sweet smile on her face told him all he needed to know so when he tasted her again he grew bolder and that was when he felt her hands in his hair. Was she pushing him away? Holding him closer? And soon realized the passion in Mattie dominated all other sensations and she trembled as his tongue caressed her and loved her. She arched upward with his gentle probing and he could feel her body tense as he flicked his tongue along her folds.

Mattie was the one begging this time. "Now, please Jackson...I.... I can't.... I need you now." She knew he felt the same way and now wasn't soon enough. The magic in the moment sparked and the air sizzled as their hearts pounded.

Jackson rose up above Mattie as she tracked his movements with a heavy lidded gaze. "I love you Jackson Woods." He heard her whispered declaration and his heart filled to the brim for her. He didn't know when Mattie had moved her thighs granting him access but was well aware of the invitation. He felt her soft folds part as his arousal began to breech her. Slowly entering her virginal womanhood he had to grit his teeth, resisting the urge to plunge in because he refused to hurt her. Not now, not ever. Mattie encouraged him further when she wrapped those long legs around his waist. Her innocent movement forced him to surge forward joining them completely breaking the barrier of her virginity in one fail swoop. He stilled himself waiting for tears of pain that didn't come. He was blessed with the sweetest smile he had ever seen and that was the only reassurance he needed.

Jackson lifted his hips and pushed into her welcoming flesh, joining them in the oldest dance known to man.

They rocked together, increasing their pace, as the blood thundered in their ears and the bright lights exploded behind closed eyes. The heat climbed so rapidly between their bodies it was like a flash fire without the flames and the flesh to flesh friction created a dusting of sweat that glistened on their brows and breathing became rapid.

Mutual demands of deeper and faster with increased momentum pushed them to the precipice of completion. Jackson focused on Mattie's face as she focused on his with the building tension of a climax that took them to the brink of together. Jackson felt her tighten around him and he responded with a deep thrust and a guttural cry as they both soared into completion. Jackson was rigid as he spilled his seed in Mattie's welcoming body as her orgasm milked every last drop from his spent body.

Mattie felt boneless as Jackson fell upon her naked breasts trying to control the pulsing sensations coursing through their bodies. Who would have thought it?

When Jackson started to come back to reality it occurred to him he hadn't moved. He must have been crushing Matt. Jackson started to move and she held him in place. "Don't go," she asked as she ran her fingers up and down his spine like little butterfly touches. Jackson whispered into her ear, "fireworks." Mattie only smiled and pretended not to hear him. "Hmmh?"

"I swear Mattie I saw fireworks." Mattie's smile widened, but she didn't answer him. Jackson began to worry he had hurt her. Here he thought she was enjoying their lovemaking as much as he was and she wasn't. He dared to look at her and was extremely relieved to see a smug satisfied look on her face. Mattie was wearing the brightest smile he had ever seen and ventured to ask. "Mattie?"

"Jackson?" She answered with as question.

"What's wrong?" He was beginning to get a little worried by her silence. Still joined Mattie grinned even bigger and tightened her muscles around his reviving flesh and a small giggle escaped her grinning lips.

"What's so funny?" He realized she was playing with him, darn her hide. "Oh think that's funny do you? Well..." he trailed off as he began to slowly move his hardened flesh within her; "two can play that game." He was pleased to see the look of surprise on her face. "You, my little minx, are going to regret laughing at me." The glitter in his eyes spoke volumes.

"Oh Jacks that was so beautiful, so special, so right, and again so soon?" The smirk on his face was answer enough.

Jackson began to move his hips teasing her still aroused flesh. He could feel her tug on him and murmured to her "so tight, I just had you and you're still so ready." Jackson continued to ease into her creating the dance that lovers knew so well and in unison they rocked into the stars and watched fireworks explode yet again and many times during the night until each lay in sheer exhaustion, sated, naked and happy. They slept in each other's embrace.

How long she slept she had no idea. The room was washed in dim moonlight. Mattie briefly wondered where she was and realized the answer as the heat of Jackson's body caressed hers. The smile was automatic. In all her life not even her music or her running could make her feel the way Jackson had by making love to her. Mattie realized she not only lost her virginity but also the nightmares that had plagued her nightly to steel her sleep. She also knew she was free and Jackson was the one who gave that to her. No bone chilling, muscle-freezing fear, intruded on her and it was like being released from a lifelong prison. She sighed heavily and smiled while she kept her eyes closed enjoying the warmth of the very male body that lay next to her.

Jackson had been watching her for some time and he still wasn't sure that everything they had shared was real and not part of his daily fantasy. Mattie was his in every sense of the word and yet it still felt like a dream. He had wanted this all his adult life and now here it was and he still felt it was quite real.

The play of emotions on Mattie's face made him smile. He knew when she awoke; he had felt her body stiffen very briefly then relaxed again. His smile grew wider when her breathing changed because he knew she was awake and remembering what they had shared. He leaned closer and whispered in her ear. "You look so beautiful and content. I can't tell you how much I love you Mattie."

Mattie slowly opened her eyes with heavy-laden lids of desire and smiled even bigger for her soon to be husband. She felt no shame or doubt in her only the love for this man. She lifted her hand to his unshaven face and told him what she felt. "I love you so much I ache at the fullness in my chest. I am so content, so happy, and so free. This was the most beautiful night of my life Jacks and the ugliness didn't come to ruin it." Her eyes swam with unshed tears of happiness and held him in her gaze.

Jackson knew he had to have her again as he lifted her auburn hair and threaded it through his fingers as he spread it across the white satin pillowcase. All his dreams couldn't hold a candle to the real thing and here she was beneath him. She almost felt ethereal, fantasy like. He ran his hands down her shoulders to her fingertips and he couldn't help remembering the touch of those long slender fingers touching and stroking him. "Damn," he mumbled.

"What's the matter Jacks?" She began to worry at the tone in his voice. Was he regretting his decision to make love with her, or asking her to be his wife and her thoughts began to swirl out of control.

Jackson saw his mistake as soon as it had come out of his mouth. "Don't go there Mattie. I only meant to compliment you. Your body is so beautiful it should be worshipped and I am awestruck you gave it to me. I'm lucky and so happy. I love you and don't forget it so soon. Please?"

"No Jacks. I'm the lucky one and I'm sorry I let doubts start to wiggle into my thoughts. I know you love me and I love you." Mattie closed her eyes against his questioning stare.

Jackson's gaze was focused on Mattie willing her to open her eyes to him and as if she knew it she opened them. He found he could only look upon her pretty face and wander at his good fortune. "Oh, Mattie" was all he could manage before he captured her lips in a breath stealing, mind-boggling kiss. A feeling of home washed over them. It was more than just joining bodies; it was a joining of souls. Jackson knew about soul mates for life and possibly through death but never imagined he would be one to experience it.

The day awaited Mattie and Jackson as they slept and dreamt of the future that was to be theirs. When the sun woke them with its warmth streaming through the sheer window treatments they shared their first morning together as lovers. It was the first day of many to be shared. Companionably they showered and dressed together with no awkwardness to be found in the act of sharing such intimate acts. The day was bright and inviting. It was the perfect beginning to share their joy with Joyce and Lyndal.

Chapter Thirty

Jackson's feet didn't seem to touch the ground as he and Mattie searched out his parents to tell them their news. They found his parents in the garden with the sun shining and the birds singing. A fresh new day to go with a fresh new life and they couldn't wait to share it.

"Mom, Dad, we want to talk with you if it's all right." Jackson announced as they approached the breakfast laden table that his parents were seated at.

You would have to be blind not to see the looks passing between her son and his Mattie and that made Joyce very happy. "Sure, what's on your mind?" Joyce shared a look with Lyndal that meant their hopes were going to come true for their son and his girl.

"Well, I have asked Mattie to marry me and she said yes. We wanted to tell you guys first that we want to get married as soon as possible. We know we haven't been together that long but mom you always told me when the right girl came along I would know, my heart would know. Well, here she is and we both know we are meant to be together. Right, Matt?"

Looking straight at Jackson's parents she smiled at them both and spoke from her heart. "I love your son with all my heart and I know he is my soul mate. The only man meant for me. I hope we have your blessing and you understand we want get married as soon as possible."

"Yes!" Was all Joyce could manage as she punched out into thin air with gusto. "We were hoping you two would make a decision. Weren't we Lyn?"

"Yep. As a matter of fact your mother was making a few hypothetical plans just this morning," he smiled at his wife and winked. They had had this discussion for several months. Actually, when Jackson had first mentioned Mattie and her popularity with their son had dominated every conversation.

"We can get the caterers we routinely use for the parties here and then I can call Trisha at the florist and we..." she abruptly stopped at Jackson's laughter.

"Whoa, mom. Hold it just a minute." Jackson was in complete shock at his parent's ready agreement and they were already making plans. He couldn't have been more surprised or for that matter more happy. "Mattie and I want to keep it simple. Can you do that Mom?"

"You want simple, I can do simple. You want elaborate I can do elaborate. What ever you two want we will do. Mattie is there anything special you want?" The look that passed between her son and Mattie didn't go unnoticed. Joyce and Lyndal accepted Mattie early on in Jackson's relationship when they realized she had won his heart and they couldn't be any happier with his choice had they picked her themselves. "It's up to you dears just tell me what the limit is and if you have any preferences. It is your wedding."

Mattie spoke softly but very clearly. "Joyce I have no special requests except one. Would you mind filling in for my mother since I have no one?"

Joyce couldn't speak but forced her voice past the growing lump in her throat as she told Mattie she would be honored and stood for the embrace she knew Mattie wouldn't fear. The tears shed were as natural as rain and a stronger bond was forged between the two women.

No one questioned the desire for a speedy wedding. It was an unspoken knowledge that time wasn't on their side since the young ones would have to return to school and Joyce and Lyndal wanted to sponsor the event here in their home. No one questioned or made demands for them to wait or that they were too young for such a life changing experience to be jumped into on a whim. The four seemed to know life only offered perfect mates and perfect opportunities on rare occasions and went with the feelings of it being the right thing to do. No regrets. No unreasonable demands. No delays.

Joyce offered her wedding gown that she had kept for a daughter she hadn't been blessed with but she would be honored if Mattie would wear it for her wedding and that was what she had told her when she presented it to her. "I know it's a little on the old side Mattie and If you don't want to wear it, it wont hurt my feelings but if you want it its yours for the asking." Opening the dust covered box revealed rows and rows of Irish lace and silk. Mattie had never seen anything as beautiful as the wedding dress she was now being offered. "Joyce, this is the most...I would be honored to wear this. It's so pretty. I bet you were a beautiful bride."

"If I do say so myself, you're right, I was. Here take a look at our wedding day," as she handed a photograph for her to look at. "My mother had that gown made especially for me. It took months for it to be finished. I felt like a princess wearing it and I would like to share that magic with you on your wedding day. Won't you please make an old woman happy and wear it?"

Mattie would have worn the gown if looked like something a court jester would have worn. She had never felt so welcomed by anyone, other than her mom and Gracie. Jackson went without saying, but to have Joyce treat her like a mother would, meant more than mere words could express.

Joyce patiently waited for Mattie to decide if she was going to accept her offer or if she was going to request her own dress.

"Joyce, I would be honored to wear such a pretty gown and the fact that it is older makes it even more special. I love Jackson with all my heart and this day is to be special for him too. I have a feeling by wearing your gown he will be thrilled that I chose it to start our life together, just as you wore it to start yours with."

Just as Jackson had predicted Joyce was a mini tornado when it came to organizing parties and events. Within one day she had arranged catering, florists, phoned everyone of importance about the wedding, and even made arrangements with the local pastor at their church. The real topper was a live band she had arranged for entertainment. Mattie was so impressed by all the arrangements Joyce had made it amazed her that one person could get so much done on such short notice. Mattie didn't mind. All she wanted was Jackson and if it made his parents happy by planning the ceremony then she had no objections and apparently neither did Jackson. Standing back and out of the way they were surprised at the effort his folks put into their wedding. The event would happen the very next day and the garden was being meticulously cared for. The flowers were in full bloom and the garden was Mattie's favorite place so if the weather agreed that was where the ceremony would take place.

That night Mattie had called a very excited Rachael. Her friend was as ecstatic as Joyce and she was a little disappointed she wouldn't be able to come but she was with her in heart. Of course she demanded lots and lots of photographs and insisted she cover that end of the details. Joyce hadn't covered that aspect as far as Mattie knew and so Rachael quickly jumped in and took that over. Rachael informed her that her parents had contacts all over and they had lots and lots of friends that would be able to pull off the request. Rachael had no qualms about using their influence and money for her best friends wedding and so she cut the call short with an "I love you Matt and congratulations. If anyone deserves to be happy it's you."

Jackson was in his room having his talk with Lyle. Lyle didn't seem a bit surprised at the news and even told him he knew already. Jackson didn't ask him how he knew because Lyle would only say "Heritage, what else." Lyle asked how Mattie had handled the cross over and that surprised Jackson too. How did he know about any of it? He only accepted his friend's words and answered him as best as he could. "It was tough Lyle. Mattie suffered something horrible and she doesn't even remember what it was. The good news is she has changed so much in the past few days. It's not just the freedom she has in her eyes it's the freedom she has with being touched or held close. She has lost that fear it seems. I can't explain it, but whatever it was that she conquered she gave herself to me and agreed to marry me the same night. I can't tell you how happy I am."

Lyle heard the pleasure in his friend's voice and he knew more than Jackson thought he did. "You mean Mattie gave her virginity to you and you gave yours to her. That my friend is a bond you will always share. Ok enough words of wisdom. What are you planning to do for a place to crash rich kid? Any plans?"

"Lyle?" He had to know.

"Yeah, what is it Blondie?"

"How did you know?" He knew Lyle understood the question. He never told anyone he hadn't been with a woman so how did he know that.

"Let's just say I had a vision and that vision didn't consist of the rumors those horny little twits liked to spread. Don't sweat it man. You should feel lucky the Gods and Spirits have guided you two together and ensured you were both pure and clean. Now, if you don't mind you're giving me a headache with all the questions and frankly my heritage is beginning to rise at the doubt you have. Ok?"

"All right Chief. I'll quit with the questions and thanks for not letting on. But ya know what? I swear I saw fireworks and if that is any indication of what our married life is going to be like I will be a very happy man."

"Fireworks are good and I'm sure you will have a long happy and satisfied life with Mattie. I myself have idea for a certain little dynamo that keeps me hopping. I never would have guessed such a small package would knock me for a loop but she has. She is my mate and I know it. It will only be a matter of time Jacks and I will be right where you are."

"Really? I can't wait to witness it. I kind of thought you would be a lifer for bachelorhood. I guess when love hits, it hits with a powerful punch. Lyle listen man I have to go. There are some things to get done still and time is running short. Will you take care of things for me?"

"Sure no problem and give Mattie a kiss for me. I really like her Jacks your one lucky SOB to find your soul mate and to have enough sense to marry her before she could slip through your fingers. Congrats dude and enjoy the honeymoon." With that he hung up with a grin on his face knowing Jackson would enjoy every bit of his life with Mattie it was in the stars for them. Lyle always accepted that knowledge for what it was. Truth, and he didn't question it.

The night greeted the four inhabitants with restlessness and unleashed energy. Mattie and Jackson slept in their own rooms on mutual agreement and Joyce tossed and turned in Lyndal's arms fitfully. The anticipation for the day to break the silence of night was more than any one person should have to take. Mattie had thoughts of her mom and Gracie. Jackson thought of the honeymoon and the future. Lyndal's thoughts of future grandchildren for him and Joyce to spoil and Joyce she was remembering hers and Lyndal's beginning and the love they still shared. Grandchildren worked into her thoughts as well and knew they would make great grandparents and so the night continued to tick by with very few inhabitants enjoying it.

When the dawn kissed the night away the mansion broke into a fury of activity. People came out of the woodwork. Joyce certainly pulled in the favors for this event. This was her only son and he would have a wedding to remember. Mattie had no one and Joyce took her under her wing giving to her what a mother would if she had one. Lyndal didn't want his wife to overtax her health and he kept a steady eye on her, helping where he could, and he didn't go far from her side. "You need to slow down a little" he would whisper down to her and she would pat his cheek and grant him a heart stopping smile. They both knew she wouldn't but he had his priorities too and she was it.

Everything was set and no untoward events happened. All the paperwork was cleared and filed. Who said money couldn't buy anything you wanted Joyce mused. The house was decorated in record time the band was set up in the garden and the seating was provided. Her flowers were in show stopping mode as if they knew a wedding was to take place. Everything was set, everyone was ready and thank God the weather was perfect.

Jackson stood in his mother's garden where an arbor had been decorated for today with the preacher waiting. Jackson wore a white tux with the very restrictive, peach colored cumber bun stealing away what little air he could draw in around his constricted throat. The only thought that kept him sane was the fact that his cumber bun happened to be the same color that Mattie's bra and panties were the night they had joined in her room. If not for that his nerves would have torn him a new one. He wasn't nervous about marrying Mattie it was all the hoopla that surrounded it, that had him in knots. As he stood straight and tall as per his father's instructions, his mother would whisper, "Dashingly handsome" in his ear as she patted his cheek. She told him many times how pleased they were with Mattie and how happy they were that they were getting married. The subtle hints for grandchildren hadn't gone unnoticed either. It still amazed Jackson that his mom couldn't wait to have little bodies around for her to spoil. His mother was full of surprises. This wedding and the arrangement of everything from flowers to a popular band just took his breath away and it was for him and Mattie. The garden was the perfect place to start their future since it was also the place where Mattie had buried her past. It was beautiful and fitting for their wedding and everything was a gift from his parents. Jackson loved them more now than he ever thought possible. Their relationship had certainly improved.

Jackson's eyes focused at the back of the guest lined chairs as the music began to play and a little girl his mother "borrowed" for the occasion threw flower petals in the path Mattie would take. When the Wedding March began Jackson had first noticed his dad all trussed up and beaming with pride a blind person could pick up on. Lyndal had agreed to walk Mattie down the isle since she had no family and Mattie jumped at the offer. Jackson's gaze quickly fixed on his bride. She was radiant. Mattie had never looked as beautiful as she did right then as she held onto his dads arm and they made their way down the path toward him. Mattie was wearing his mother's gown and it was beautiful. Jackson's heart swelled with the love he had for her. Mattie's feet didn't seem to touch the path. She floated like a drifting cloud and she was coming toward him. He thought she was the essence of woman. His woman. The white Irish lace billowed with the breeze and kissed her ankles with each step she made. The crown of lace and pearls loosely held her auburn hair away from her face and the length swept down her back. A large teardrop pearl was cradled on her forehead. Mattie carried a fresh bouquet of wildflowers with a long white ribbon secured around them. Jackson never heard the hushed gasps upon his bride's arrival or the oohs and ahs that followed. His attention was focused on his future, the woman he loved beyond all measure.

Mattie was so happy her eyes spilled over with small trickles of silvery tears. This was the day of a fairy tale come true and Mattie was so happy she couldn't contain the joy she felt. Her only regret was that her Momma and Gracie weren't here to share it with her. Their spirits were there. She could feel them with her. Life was the best it had ever been for her. She only had eyes for Jackson as he stood there so proudly revealing his love for her in his eyes, as he waited for her. He was so handsome and strong. He had changed her whole life from a world of darkness and fear, to a world of love, hope, and dreams. A world he wanted to share with her.

The ceremony was beautiful and well orchestrated. The vows exchanged between the bride and groom weren't just words but a life's promise made from the heart. When the time came to kiss the bride Jackson smiled and embraced his wife knowing he didn't have to hold back. He could touch and hold her all he wanted. Now was the time he had been waiting for.

Jackson slowly brought his face down toward his wife's and his breath caught when he saw the heated passion in her tiger-eyes and the tell-all smile she gifted him with. Jackson caught Mattie's lips with his and was lost in the searing passion. He couldn't stop the need to deepen the kiss and so he did what his body demanded. Mattie matched him move for move. Neither one realized the crowd was whistling or making comments about waiting for the honeymoon. The kiss continued. The preacher was smiling and trying to get the young lovers attention. Needless to say it didn't work and the kiss continued. The couple changed positions but didn't break the seal. What seemed like an eternity to the observers was mere seconds for the bride and groom.

Jackson felt the slight nudging on his arm and tried to brush it off. The pressure increased and he began to hear the whispered words from a man. Jackson's fuzzy brain began to make sense of the words his father was telling

190

him. "...Everyone is still waiting. Come on Jacks let Mattie breath." Not that she would notice Lyndal thought. "Jackson, come on son so the preacher can introduce you."

Jackson comprehended what his dad was saying and slowly, with reluctance, lifted his head from a very flushed Mattie. Smiling and blushing the couple ducked their heads and faced the preacher.

"Attention folks, now that we have the bride and groom's attention, I would like to introduce to you Mr. and Mrs. Jackson Woods." As the announcement rang out Mattie and Jackson turned, held hands, and began to make their way down the isle. Joyce and Lyndal reached out for the couple and shared a family hug and kiss. It all felt right and whole. They were a family. A complete family.

As tradition demanded the first dance belonged to the bride and groom. This was a small detail Mattie didn't know about. How was she supposed to do that when she didn't know how? Jackson didn't know as they had never gone dancing and she had no reason to tell him. Now here she stood in the center of a dance floor and had no idea what to do. Jackson was smiling and holding her, waiting. Now what? She thought to herself.

Jackson pulled her closer and immediately noticed the shift from relaxed to tense. He saw the inkling of fear and whispered "Oh Mattie." He leaned down and whispered loud enough for only her to hear. "Mattie, honey, what's wrong?"

"I... Uh..., well Jacks...I don't know how to dance. I never was taught" she whispered back to him and then looked down as if ashamed.

Jackson understood why she was tense. She was frightened because she didn't know how to dance. If that's all that was bothering her it would be easy enough to fix. "Mattie what I want you to do is just lean into me and feel the music. Pretend you are playing and singing. Just feel the music Matt, you can do it." He smiled at her expression of understanding and nodded.

The music began slowly so Jackson pulled Mattie closer and began to sway with the rhythm and the notes. Mattie closed her eyes and felt the music just like Jackson had told her too. She felt like liquid and moved with Jackson. She had no idea she was dancing just as she was supposed to. She was lost in the music as she usually did when it took over. Mattie didn't realize she was humming softly in Jackson's ear.

Jackson noticed immediately and he couldn't help the response his body was having to Mattie's alluring sirens song. He was almost thankful when the music stopped because he didn't want to embarrass Mattie or himself with the reactions she elicited in him.

Mattie tipped up her face to Jackson and pouted. An action she had never performed in her life and kissed his cheek. She knew where his thoughts were. Mattie had an overwhelming desire to sing for Jackson something she and Joyce had already planned but she had to do it now. She didn't want to wait for the agreed upon time. It had to be now. "Jackson I'll be right back ok?" He only smiled and agreed to let her go with the promise to "hurry back."

Joyce knew the change in plans the minute she saw Mattie walk away from Jacks. She knew her role and quickly grabbed her son's waist for the dance that just started. "Happy?" She asked as she twisted him around.

"More than I can ever tell you. Thanks mom. You and dad have made this the happiest day for Mattie and me. How can I ever..."

Joyce stopped his rambling with her finger to his lips. "Don't go there Jacks. Your father and I were happy to do it. Besides I get a daughter out of the deal remember?"

"I remember. I also remember the request for little ones as soon as possible." He couldn't help smiling at the red tint in his mother's cheeks. It was good to see her health returning.

"Well, I don't want to push but." She wiggled her eyebrows at him. "I have to have some grandbabies to spoil rotten in my old age. Besides, with two such beautiful people you will make some very pretty babies. I'm so glad it has all worked out the way it was meant to be. We really do love your Mattie Jacks, she is a treasure and she needs to feel special. I know she hasn't had a very good life and your father and I are counting on you to make her new life with you, and with us, a happy one. Mattie hasn't had the kind of life we have enjoyed and I for one intend for her to have it now." Joyce was doing her job very well as she saw Mattie making her preparations on the make shift bandstand. Joyce only smiled up at her son who was going to be caught unawares very shortly. My how Mattie had changed since the day she let it all go. Joyce was truly happy for her son and daughter-in-law.

Mattie was in place as she watched Joyce dance Jackson away from the band. She had a knack for playing songs by ear and she had heard one on the radio that she wanted to sing just for him. God she was nervous but she wasn't scared. She slowly made her way to the lead singer's position and waited for him to finish his song. Once the song ended the announcement began. "Excuse me ladies and gentlemen. Excuse me. Can I have your attention please?" The crowd began to quiet down and the announcement continued. "I'm honored to present a special woman with a special treat for her new husband and the rest of you can listen if you wish." Stepping aside he left the opening Mattie was waiting for. Gathering all her courage she spoke "Jackson this is for you. I love you."

Jackson made his way through the opening the crowd created with his focus only on his wife. Mattie sat on the stool provided and began to play. The song she had chosen was one by the group Savage Garden. Mattie began singing the lyrics with eyes only for Jackson as he made his way to stand in front of the bandstand. Mattie focused on only him as she put all her feelings into each word. "I new I loved you before I met you. I must have dreamed you into life..." and she went on with the song she had dedicated to her husband, her heart, and her love.

Once the song ended Jackson stepped up to the platform and held out his hands for Mattie to join him. Mattie did just that and was slowly lifted down to descend his full length until she stood on her own. Jackson stared deep into her eyes and was lost. Covering her mouth with his was as natural as breathing and that was exactly what he did. The roars went up like firecrackers at the fourth of July. Jackson poured his thanks to her into that kiss while the quests only watched on. The world ceased to exist between the two as the kiss continued.

Joyce and Lyndal were mesmerized as they had never seen their son as happy and content as they did when he was with Mattie. They were thrilled with the way his life had changed. They couldn't have hoped for any better.

As Jackson and Mattie prepared to leave after the reception Joyce held onto her son with a fierce need. She couldn't keep the tears at bay and let them trickle down her cheeks. Lyndal stood near and spoke what she couldn't. "You have made us very happy and very proud of you Jacks."

"Thanks dad. It seems we have all changed a lot in a short amount of time. Mattie is so good for me and has helped me to appreciate you guys even more than I ever did before."

"Well now that you have captured the love of your life and the wedding part is behind you and Mattie, maybe you can concentrate on making us grandparents. Not to rush you mind, but we aren't getting any younger ya know?"

"I agree with your mother on that one Jackson. You and Mattie here need to start working on a family 'cause I would like a little one around to teach the horse business to." Lyndal decided enough pressure had been dumped on the kids and reached out with his long arms to encase the entire group in a fierce bear hug. He knew it was going to be a long time before they got to visit again. "I'm going to miss having you two at home. Don't stay away too long and call often. Ok kids, its time you two headed out of here. Your mom and I don't want you to go, but your flight won't wait."

As they made their way to the car and the bubbles were being blown into the wind Mattie let the bouquet fly. Jackson held the door open to the rented limo but before Mattie left she turned to Joyce and Lyndal and mouthed the words "thank you both, I love you." Joyce and Lyndal both smiled and kept the tears in check. This family had definitely come together.

The flight home was uneventful compared to the past weeks. Mattie had called Rachael and Jackson had called Lyle before they left so they were expecting them.

Once their two best friends knew when the newlyweds would arrive they made it a point to change out all of Mattie's things to Jackson's apartment. It didn't take a genius to figure out the couple hadn't planned the abrupt wedding and it didn't take much more to realize that living arrangements hadn't been thought out either. Lyle and Rachael took it upon themselves to arrange everything including a welcome home party scheduled at Waves courtesy of one Joey.

Rachael told Jacks and Mattie of all the changes in living arrangements etc. when they picked them up at the airport. "Joyce agreed when I talked to her about it. She said you two were too busy to think of such stuff and to go ahead with whatever plans we had in mind. I hope you don't mind that we did all the rearranging without your approval first."

"Mom would" Jackson shook his head side to side and smiled at Mattie. "This is one time I really am glad she interfered and she was right about us not thinking about the living arrangements. Thank you guys for everything." Jackson hugged Rachael and then Lyle. Lyle was the brother he always wanted and he'd been his best friend since they were boys so hugging him was as natural as breathing. "Thanks chief for everything. I wish you could have been there when we got married but I'm glad you were here to get things ready for us when we got back."

Lyle was speechless for a long minute. He felt a new kinship with Jackson. They had always been close but it seemed now there was more there. A brother-hood between them that was growing stronger the older they got. Lyle didn't know how to respond to such an emotional time so he relied on old habits and quick wit before he wept like a baby in front of all of them. "Yeah, yeah Blondie I can see married life has already turned your brain into mush."

"Oh but it's a great mush to have my friend." Jackson replied with a lopsided grin.

Rachael was hugging Mattie and crying all over her. "Oh Mattie I knew it. I knew you two were supposed to be together. I'll miss having you as my roomy but I already have a potential roommate in the works" she said as she eyed Lyle and wiggled her eyebrows. "I'm so happy for you and Jacks."

They agreed on a time to get together so they could go to Waves for the party Joey had planned and went to their homes. Mattie hadn't been in Jackson's apartment before and really didn't know what to expect but when Jackson opened the door they were speechless by what greeted them. Lyle and Rachael had made his place into a home for them. Those two had fixed everything up and it really did resemble a home not just an apartment to flop in. Jackson still held Mattie in his arms from crossing the threshold and kissed her breathless in the doorway. He had personal plans of his own and he was determined to carry them out starting now. He hooked the door with his foot and sent it home with a shove. Jackson devoured Mattie's mouth without breaking contact while he locked the door. With Mattie still in tow he headed for their bedroom. They hadn't made love since the first time at his parent's home and he was anxious to begin the honeymoon. Apparently so was Mattie, as she gave no protest to being taken to the bed. Rachael had prepared that as well. Candles were placed everywhere and flowers decorated all the tables. On the bedside table were two Champaign glasses and a bottle of bubbly on ice. The fineries would have to wait for they couldn't. Jackson began to remove Mattie's clothes as if he had done it a thousand times. Amazingly enough he did it with a steady hand.

Mattie felt so self-conscious she began to shield her bare breast and pink began to color her cheeks. "Oh Mattie, don't be ashamed of your beautiful body. Don't cover yourself. You're so perfect to me, my eyes ache when I look at you. Don't torture me by hiding what I love to look at, please."

"Jackson" she could barely whisper out to him because the way he was looking at her made her ache in newly awakened places. Mattie took courage in the way Jackson looked at her and slowly dropped her shielding hands to her waist. "I love you" was all she could mouth to him.

Jackson was given more than a sight to behold he was given an undeniable trust and faith. Feelings so strong welled up inside him that made him shake but not enough to deter him and his desire. Jackson found himself reaching for the woman who had stolen his heart. Joining their hungry lips together led their bodies on the same path. Jackson trailed wet tantalizing kisses down Mattie's long slender neck to the swell of her opaque breasts. As smooth as satin he continued his journey to her rosy nipple. As he circled the hardening nub he heard Mattie's intake of breath and felt her heart race beneath his firm lips.

Jackson knew she was being pulled further into the throws of passion when he suckled her breast she grasped his head and tenderly held him to her. He almost lost control when he felt her nudge him to her untouched breast. Praising her flesh and releasing a desire that was in no way a chore Jackson and he savored her responses. He trailed his tongue down her ribs to her narrow waist where her skirt still held its place next to her skin.

Jackson left it intact for now and changed his course to remove Mattie's shoes. Such an act shouldn't be so intense but it was the way Jackson did it.

Slowly, lightly touching, Jackson ran his palm up her naked thigh under her skirt to her lace clad hips, all the while, watching Mattie respond to his touch.

Kneeling as he gently stroked her thighs and calves he encircled her hips with both his hands and slowly squeezed just to feel her flesh in his palms. His wife was erotic and consuming. He could feel the demanding throb in his groin and refused to listen. Not yet he told himself. Not yet. Jackson ran his thumbs over her mound enticing a slow moan from her.

He knew he was driving her to the edge as she began to move her hips silently asking for more. He continued to stroke her thighs and her hips just barely edging her womanhood with his thumbs. His erection strained against his jeans to the point of pain and release was being demanded, not requested, or hinted at. Yet he refused to listen. He ran his hands up Mattie's thighs again to her hips and began to rub his fingers under the edge of her lace panties.

Mattie's movements were becoming impatient and her moans were laced with frustration. Jackson continued to ignore the demand of his own need and chanted to himself "not now." With his forefingers at the edge of the imprisoning lace Jackson began to nudge the garment downward, under her skirt. The movement was torture of the finest; so sweet and so painful all at once. The descent of lace on creamy skin was slow and purposeful until they were discarded. Jackson began his return trip up her calves to her thighs and just gracing her mound with his thumbs again had Mattie bucking at the sensation he had created. He heard her tortured cry of "please" and yet he kept on his path. He would finish it.

Jackson slowly ran his hands down her thighs to the edge of her skirt and hooked it with his thumbs as he slowly moved the material downward. The cool air brushed her thighs with each movement of the skirts dissention. As the material crossed her apex the hottest, moistest, lighting bolt of sensation took hold of her as Jackson loved her with his mouth. She moaned his name as the pleasure took her and rocked her. There was no room for thought only feelings.

Jackson was doing what he wanted to and he knew he was doing it right by the way Mattie responded to him. She was so sweet and wet and she held him to her without shame. He groaned with pleasure when he felt her fingers weaving into his hair and clasping him to her. He felt his body tremble when she experienced her release. He knew he needed her now and she needed him. It was time and he couldn't hold back anymore.

Mattie wanted to scream as her body demanded more. She was pulling at him and tugging at the clothes he still wore. Buttons flew and jeans were discarded. It had to be skin to skin and anything that stood in the way of it was lost. "More" was the only thought they both could make and even it was an unspoken one. Pleasure was controlling their actions now.

Mattie opened for Jackson and he settled his hips where they fit perfectly. She wrapped her long legs around Jackson's waist and urged him to come home. She was waiting for him to enter her when he plunged into her without restraint. Mattie held him so tightly she thought she was going to hurt him. With each thrust and with each pulse she stroked his manhood and lost all thoughts to the sensations filling her. Plunging and demanding was equally shared as the climax began to take over. Mattie opened her eyes to look into his face and he looked down into hers. There was no doubt in what they were sharing and exchanging. When she accepted his deep final frantic thrusts they died the little death of completion at the same time.

Jackson shuddered and trembled as he emptied himself into his wife's willing body and she held onto him like a lifeline. Both were panting for breath, as their body demanded replenishing. Jackson lay still as Mattie clutched his sweaty torso and neither moved. They were sated and gratified. There was no rush to end the magic they had just shared.

Mattie had never thought a man and a woman could share the intensity as deeply as they had. She had definitely been wrong. However the longer she thought the more reality crept in. How in the world could she ever look Jackson in the face after what she had done? And encouraged him to do to her? She couldn't believe she had finished while his mouth was working such magic. Did she disgust him? Berating herself was so ingrained she was quickly losing sight of what they had truly shared and was turning it into something ugly and disgusting.

Jackson felt the change in her body and he knew what she was doing. He would not let that happen. He eased up onto his elbow and brushed the hair off her face. He still caught himself thinking how beautiful she was and that she was his. He refused to let her be embarrassed by what they had shared. The gift of trust and love she had shown in her actions with him. "Matt?" And he waited for her to look at him. She didn't. "Mattie, honey, don't be ashamed of what we shared. Don't be embarrassed by something so wonderful I can't even begin to put into words. Please don't make it ugly and shameful or regret our lovemaking. I'm lucky you would share your body and your passion with me in every way. Please don't shy away. I love you Mattie Woods and there is nothing we have done that we should be ashamed of.

He saw the glistening trail from spent tears tracking down her cheek causing a brief moment of fear to race down his spine. Jackson couldn't stand the thought of being the cause of any pain.

Mattie felt the frown turn into a smile at the words Jackson had just spoken. "I love you so much, that sometimes I think it's all a dream and I'm going to wake up. What we did was special and I won't ruin it with degrading thoughts. I was a little embarrassed because I didn't realize we could, you know, do that. I won't regret something so wonderful. Something you and I shared. I can't seem to stop smiling at you."

"Smile all you won't to sweetheart." He kissed her on her nose. "Mattie" He whispered as he captured her lips again and slowly, seductively began to move in her since he hadn't changed his position. He smiled as he saw her eyes widen with surprise.

"Oh. Jacks" she spoke in a breathless whisper. It was quite some time before they managed to get to Joey's place but oh what a way to pass the time!

Upon entering Waves the cheers drowned out any music that may have been playing. Joey saw the amazing transformation in Mattie. He decided she was positively gorgeous and her face was radiant with the love she showered on Jackson. Any man alive would be a lucky son-of-a-gun with a woman like her on his arm and in his life. He made his way to the front of the crowd as Mattie and Jackson made their way to meet him.

Joey grabbed Mattie's hand and with his expression asked wordlessly if hugging was accepted. Mattie nodded and broke into a face splitting smile. She opened her arms for Joey's rib crushing hug. She didn't flinch or stiffen with his touch and he saw that as a good thing. Mattie was healing. Jackson was good for her. "Congratulations Mattie."

"Thanks Joey." Mattie was so happy it was almost scary. In her mind she sent up a silent thought to her favorite people letting them know she was happy. "Thank you" she whispered again hugging him back.

"Your welcome honey, but what are you thanking me for?" Joey honestly had no idea.

"For being my friend, Joey. Just for being a friend when I needed one. For trusting me and giving me a job and just thanks for watching out for me." She kissed his cheek.

Jackson heard what she said to Joey and he silently thanked the man. My how his Mattie had changed in the past couple of weeks. He was in awe of his new wife. How lucky could a guy get? Just saying 'his wife' should have him shaking in his Nikes, but it didn't. It felt right. The most certain thing he had ever done in his life. His cheeks ached from all the smiling he had been doing because he was so happy.

Lyle saw the glow of happiness on his friend's face and felt duty bound to rib him of his married status. "Hey, choir boy. Turn down the wattage on that grin before you blind me here." He said with a huge grin.

"What's wrong old man? Jealous?" Jackson nudged Lyle in the ribs.

"Fat chance of that rich kid! When I have my own little box of treasure right there," as he pointed to Rachael who was arm in arm with Mattie making their way to the bar chattering like a pair of magpies. "That little powerhouse is more than enough for even me. Who would have thought it?" Lyle shook his head still disbelieving he had found in Rachael what Jackson had found in Mattie. He hadn't even been looking and yet she waltzed right into his life like she had been a part of it all along. "I always looked for the long legs and the chests that a man could use to pillow his head on. Then this little dynamo bowled me over."

"You sure have surprised me. I never would have thought it. Ya know what though? I think Rachael is the best thing that has ever happened to you. She certainly can keep up with you and she is a chance taker which makes you two perfect for each other." Jackson was overjoyed that Lyle was as happy as he was.

"I know it and it doesn't scare the hell out of me as I always thought it would. That little bundle of woman has knocked me every way possible and I survived anyway. She is so full of life she's bursting with it. She says life's too short not to grab all you can from it and she's right. I love her more than I ever believed I could love another human being. I was always the poor Indian trash from the wrong side of the tracks and here she is from your side of the money train and she doesn't care. Her parents don't care. They only want her to be happy and they support her one hundred percent. All this time, I thought wealthy people were the same and here her parents are just like you are. They are completely opposite of what I expected. Can you believe she was afraid her money would scare me away and she didn't want to tell me? Imagine that."

"Lyle you never were all those insults that people liked to throw at you and we both knew it. You have always been better than you gave yourself credit for. I've known it since we were kids and Rachael knows it now. That is probably why she loves your ugly mug." He said with a smug smile and a casual wink.

"Too much sentiment ain't good for a man, so enough already, rich kid."

Mattie was having the same type of conversation with Rachael. "Rachel, I'm so happy I just can't believe how different my life is now compared to months ago. Everything is so fresh and new. It's great!"

"I know you are absolutely beaming with happiness and love. You deserve it honey. Jackson is good for you. Granted, I didn't think so the first time I saw him, but he has certainly redeemed himself. I'm so happy for you Mattie."

"Yeah, Jackson has changed my life. Oh, Rache I didn't know you could love someone so much it takes your breath away."

"You too will make a great life together honey. I hope Lyle and I can be as happy."

"Are you happy Rachael? Are your parents happy for you?" Mattie didn't know how her parents would react to someone like Lyle when you knew his background.

"Well, Mattie, happy is understating what I feel for Lyle. He is everything I have ever looked for in a man and then some. To think I have lived next to all that man for all this time and never knew he lived there. I owe that meeting to you Mrs. Woods. Since he was with Jackson, and Jackson was chasing after you, well it was just meant for us to meet when we did. So, I thank you. My parents absolutely love him and they have given us their blessing. I feel like I'm walking on air half the time."

"The fates were certainly smiling on us weren't they Rache?"

"Our guardian angles guided us and sent them in our direction so, in essence, sent us the men we were meant to spend our lives with. I think we have been blessed."

Joey banging a glass with a spoon interrupted their conversation and the patrons sitting around the place.

"Ok folks. Drinks are on the house for the first round so we can toast the bride and groom. Mattie and Jackson on your nuptials." Raising his glass and waiting for the crowd to follow suit he added, "I wish you the best in your life together and to always be happy."

"Mattie, can I ask you a question?" Joey whispered to her minutes later.

"Sure, what is it Joey?" Mattie began to feel the nerves in her stomach, old habits died hard.

"Well, I know you just got back and all but I was wandering...well...will you do us the honor of singing a little please? It would be great for business." He pleaded.

"Well...uh...I guess I could but I don't have..." Joey cut her off.

"I just happen to have your guitar here." He had a guilty look on his smug face. Mattie had the idea that she had been set up. But since it was Joey she didn't mind so much. Sighing in mock resignation with a smile on her face Mattie stated, "Well, I guess so." She couldn't turn down the first man who had befriended her and given her a job when she'd first arrived. He had encouraged and supported her since that first day. She couldn't turn down his request, nor did she want to.

Joey was so surprised by her teasing manner that he just stood their smiling and whispered to thin air, "Welcome home, Mattie. Welcome home."

Making her way to Jackson and Lyle's side she tilted her head to whisper into her husband's ear of Joey's request.

Jackson was pleased that she agreed without letting her fears rule her. He snuggled her against him and passionately kissed her fears away. "You amaze me sweetheart, ya know that?" he whispered into her ear.

Mattie made her way to the stage as her new family made their way to the corner table. She never was one for public speeches or outward signs of emotions that she could control. So much had changed for her and she wanted everyone to know who was behind it. In a gentle hushed tone Mattie spoke into the microphone. "Excuse me, everyone," she waited and when the noise remained she spoke again, only louder. "Excuse me, please."

Jackson stood with his mouth gapping open at the sound of her voice. He had never heard her speak to the crowd from the stage before and he held his breath hoping she would be able to say what she wanted to without losing control. She was always so self-conscious, and yet here she was, bold as life waiting to be heard, eyes open, mike in hand, and she was a beautiful sight. The crowd became quiet and Mattie was the center of attention.

What a time for nerves, she thought, as her pulse raced, and she suddenly became aware of every breath sawing in and out. Her palms began to sweat.

As she stood there she suddenly felt like she had jumped in too fast and the fear was jumping up and down like a kid demanding attention. She closed her eyes and focused her thoughts and attention on Jackson.

Jackson saw the change and he knew what was happening. He refused to let her lose any ground if he could help it. Forcing his way to the stages edge, he swung his legs over to the top and stood in front of her.

"Mattie?" She didn't respond to him and he knew she had begun that retreat again. He hadn't seen her do that since they were at his parent's house and he would be damned if he would let it happen again. The place became so quiet you could hear a pin drop. "Matt, Honey?"

The paler of her complexion, the signs of retreating, the building fear was all there battling to take control. He wasn't going to let it take her to that dark, lonely place. Jackson stood in front of her and slowly stroked her cheek with his palm as he spoke to her.

"Mattie. Listen to me sweetheart. I'm right here with you. You don't have to be afraid anymore. Remember?" Jackson lowered his head to hers and covered her tight lips with his as he stroked her hair hoping she would use his strength to snap out of it. He didn't think she even knew he was touching her.

Mattie slowly responded to his kiss and deepened it with each slow sensuous stroke of her tongue to his. She focused on Jacks and Jacks alone. Jackson was focused on her and the kiss she was responding to.

Mattie finally raised her hand and threaded her fingers into his soft blonde hair and moaned deep in her throat. The thundering in her ears was not her blood pounding, as she had originally thought it was, but the thunder of applause. Slowly she opened her eyes and pulled back from a very pleased, smiling Jackson. Neither had realized the microphone had been between them or that every word was heard. Jackson whispered to her, "God Mattie I love you beyond words. Will you sing for me?"

Mattie was breathless and whispered back, "I love you to infinity and back. Will you stay here with me? Will you sing with me? I've heard you sing and I know you play the keyboard. Will you share this moment on stage with me?"

How could he turn her down with that look on her face? Jackson didn't know how she knew that about him. He never told anyone but he was sure his mother had something to do with it. Jackson still found himself asking, "How do you know that?"

Mattie smiled at him and revealed what she had already witnessed. "You sing when you're happy and you've been singing a lot lately. Come on Jacks? Sing with me here and now?"

The crowd heard it all and the chants began. "Sing, sing, sing..." trailed off when Jackson kissed her and nodded his head yes.

Mattie sat on the stool with guitar in hand and Jacks behind the keyboard. They only had eyes for each other as they sang like they were totally alone in the room. When the song ended the roar of applause shook the rafters because they were great together.

Lyle and Rachael were speechless. They had never heard those two sing together and now that they had, they were stunned. They were terrific together. Lyle hadn't heard Jackson in years. It was part of his rebellion to his parents. Hell, he didn't know the kid could still play the keyboard. He certainly proved he could and then some. They were absolutely fantastic together even if it was 'that' kind of music. The thumping of glasses on the table interrupted his thoughts and the chant for more roared to life.

Jackson shrugged and smiled at Mattie leaving it up to her to decide. She smiled back and raised her eyebrows in silent agreement. They played again and again. Deciding it was time to bow out. Jackson stood and told the audience it was time for him to pay attention to his wife. They gave their thanks and stepped off the stage into the still crowded dance floor. Congratulations and pats on the back were many as they made their way back to their friends.

Joey was speechless and his mouth gapped open while he shook his head. "Who would have thought it?" All he could say as they approached was to tell them they were hired. Mattie and Jackson were hand in hand and only smiled at the offer. "Right" Jackson smirked. "Mattie sure, Me no way."

"What? You were great together and I'm being serious. How about weekends? Pays good and I can get you a deal on your meals. I'm just like this with the boss" as he gestured with crossed fingers. He waited for an answer but when he didn't get one from Jackson he focused his attention on Mattie pleading with her eyes.

"Jackson," she said "I couldn't do it without you. I won't do it without you!"

Jackson couldn't put two syllables together to form one word.

"It's always been you. Since I've been here and tonight it was us, together. We are a team Jackson. Where you go, I go and where I go you go, right?"

She had him there. He couldn't refuse her or the truth she spoke. "Ok Mattie. If you want to take Joey up on his offer, I'm game of you are."

"No, Jacks. If doing this is what we want. Not you, not me, but the two us. Ok?"

"Alright Mattie, we'll do it together. Who knows it could be fun. Turning to face the man who was still waiting for an answer Jackson shrugged his broad shoulders as he relayed their decision. It was the first decision that he and Mattie had made as a married couple and it was nice to share responsibility on something even if it was a simple thing. "Well, Joey it looks like you have a deal and Wave's gets live entertainment."

"Yeah Joey it looks like your stuck now, cause we are a package deal!" Mattie gave him her hundred-watt smile.

Joey felt his breath lodge somewhere in the vicinity of his lungs when Mattie gave him a smile that could melt rock. Jackson was one damn lucky guy and he'd bet a years salary that the young man was very well aware of it.

Chapter Thirty-One

Weeks passed in sheer bliss for Mattie. Everything she had ever hoped for was now hers. She was married to a man who had changed her life and loved her as much as she loved him. She had a family, friends, and a place to call home. Her meadow was home but this was more so, because everyone she loved was here. Her days were spent going to class, preparing for finals, and looking toward the holidays with Jackson, her new parents, and spending time with Lyle and Rachael. Life was so much more now than it had been for years. Mattie was sure her mother and Gracie were smiling down on her and knew how happy she truly was. She stared off as she focused her new life.

That was how Jackson found her when he made his way into their home. He stopped in mid stride just to stare at her. Mattie was the most beautiful woman he had ever known and she was his. She was starring out the window by the sink and didn't know he had come into the room. He came up behind her and nuzzled her neck as he encircled her waist. Her body went full alert. "Where were you gorgeous?" He whispered as he kissed and nuzzled her exposed flesh at the nape of her neck.

"Oh...Uh..." she had a hard time thinking of anything when he did that to her. "Just thinking."

"Bout what?" "Me?" "Us?" "This?" As he rubbed his aroused flesh against her very tight little butt.

"Actually no, which is amazing; considering how quickly that is the only thing on my mind these days." She turned in his arms and he held her tighter. Jackson picked her up and sat her on the counter she had just wiped down. He fit his hips comfortably between her open and inviting thighs. My how he loved these loose dresses she favored. It certainly cut back on his work, he thought, as he slid his hands up her soft, accessible flesh. She leaned into him and kissed him with great fervor. As moans and sighs were exchanged the temperature in their little kitchen increased by several degrees.

Mattie nuzzled Jacks neck and rubbed his arms. She encircled his waist and proceeded to pull his sweeter up inch by excruciating inch. When the material eased off his shoulders she proceeded to throw it to the floor. Flesh to flesh she stroked his muscled biceps and taut back with her long slender fingers. His body was so beautiful.

Jackson felt like he was being stroked. Mattie was playing him with her musical fingers and he felt like he was going to explode from the sensations she was creating. As many times as he had made love to her it still felt like the first time. The fever couldn't be contained. It controlled and demanded and they responded. Jackson slid his hands up Mattie's thighs and continued to her inviting apex. He stilled immediately when he encountered her wet, open, and uncovered. Mattie didn't have on any panties. There were no barriers and he growled deeply. His control was quickly sapped because he hadn't expected her to be ready for him. "God, honey, what you do to me."

Mattie felt the same about him but she couldn't speak. She could only feel the need. She wanted to scream with a desire that ruled her body. With frantic hands and jerky movements Mattie slid Jackson's zipper down in a slow tantalizing motion that made her want to weep. She had such a demanding need to touch him. She craved the feel of his flesh in her hands. Reaching deeply into the V of his jeans she found what she wanted and cupped him in her palm. The twin orbs were cradled as she slid her fingers side to side. He was warm and soft and so ready for her. She edged closer to him, needing him, wanting him, feeling him. The ache demanded he be inside her and she didn't want to wait any longer.

Jackson was caught up in the sensations of Mattie's magical touch. He clutched her hips and tugged her to him. Forehead to forehead, breath to ragged breath, Jackson whispered, "Matt. Oh Matt, please now. I need to have you...please?"

She knew exactly what he wanted because she wanted the same thing. Lifting her long runner's legs around his half-bare waist she gave him her answer without words. With a loud groan she felt him enter her and all thought escaped as his huge erection, filled her to her core. The ride was swift and demanding and heaven help her she wanted more of what he was giving her. "Now, please, oh...my... God" passed on a gasp as each thrust of Jackson's flesh pounded into her own and the climax that shook her was indescribable. The act stole her breath away. The earth moved. The lightening flashed. The thunder rolled. The thing was there wasn't a storm anywhere except here, in her small kitchen, with her husband.

When reality crept in Jackson spoke. "Oh, Mattie I'm so sorry. I never meant..." but he didn't get to finish what he had started to say because Mattie hushed him with her fingers to his lips.

"Don't" was all she could manage. Mattie didn't want him to apologize for what they had just shared. Emotions were churning and so deep they began to escape in the form of tears. They cascaded down her cheeks like a bubbling brook. How could she tell him what he had done to her? How could you ever put such feelings into words? How could she tell him how much she truly loved loving him? She felt like a raw and exposed nerve and it was all because of what they shared.

Jackson was kicking his mental ass for taking her like she was some cheap, nobody. How could I make love to her in the kitchen for God's sakes? On the counter, of all places!

"Jackson?" she whispered. Mattie felt the change in him as they held on to one another. He was still inside her and she could feel every pulse of his heart beat, every movement his breathing created. She had to tell him. He was thinking too much. "Jackson, look at me please. Don't do that. I wanted this and as I recall I encouraged it. I think the kitchen is my second favorite room in the apartment now. I love you Jacks. I love what we just shared. It was beautiful and special and I hope we will do it again because every time you touch me I feel so full I'm overflowing with the emotions. I can't believe how lucky I am to have you." She lifted his face to hers and smiled through the tears. "Who said the kitchen was only for cooking food anyway?"

She was teasing with him and she was smiling. Jackson still couldn't believe how different she was. How giving, accepting, and open she was with him. He smiled back at her. "Well Mrs. Woods I do believe your joking with me."

"Say it again" she whispered.

"Say it? Say what babe?" He cocked his head sideways trying to figure out what it was he had said that she wanted to hear again.

"Say my name again Jacks."

Light dawned. "Mrs. Woods how I do love you."

"I love you too, with all my heart." She bent and kissed his moist inviting lips encouraging him to open and let her in. She was not disappointed. Mattie felt him stir in their still joined bodies and she grinned into his mouth.

"See what you do to me woman." He was having a hard time catching his breath but it didn't stop him from resuming the action. Before they could go any further a loud pounding on the door broke the sexual tension that had already began to build again. Reluctantly, Jackson pulled his mouth away but remained embedded deep with in her warm, tight folds. On a sigh he said in not so happy tones. "Who do we know that could have the world's worst timing?"

"Oh, no," Mattie whispered. "I forgot. Rachael and I planned a shopping trip for today." Smiling like a Cheshire cat. "Guess I got a little side tracked."

Jackson snickered at the little evil twinkle he saw in her eyes. "Yeah. I'd say you were, just a little." He bent to kiss her and began to move within her again forcing her to moan with pleasure. The pleasure was deep and consuming but he heard the pounding on the door just the same. He also heard Rachael yelling for Matt to open the door before she kicked it in. That would have been funny if he didn't think she would do it. Lifting his head he yelled over his shoulder. "Hold your horse's shorty. I have need of my wife at the moment come back in five. Now be gone with you."

"No problem." It was a damn shame they were having all the fun while she had to wait knowing what was going on. It wasn't fair. Rachael mumbled as she made a tour of the apartment building.

"Jacks. I can't believe you said that. Now Rachael will know what we are up to in here." The humor in her voice only encouraged him to continue right where they had been interrupted.

"Speaking of which," he bent to kiss her neck and rub the nipple of her breast. No more words were exchanged and the body language was all that was needed. Every time was explosive with her and he hoped it would always be this way for them. After another heart stopping climax overtook both parties and a return of normal breathing Jackson lifted Mattie off the counter and slid her down the length of him. "I hate to let you go since we were having such a deep, intimate discussion."

"Me too. But I promised and the shopping is for Christmas presents." She hung on to his neck as she looked directly into his blue mesmerizing eyes. "You have the ocean in your eyes and it sweeps me away every time I look into the pools."

"You take my breath away Matt" and he kissed her on the lips again just because he had too. Pulling away he fixed his jeans and straightened her skirt. "Better put on your panties Matt or I might not let you leave at all. I have suddenly developed a new love of those dresses you wear and without any lace nothings under there the temptation is really strong to have you again. You better get your self ready before shrimp gets here and starts banging on the door again." He patted her very desirable derriere as she headed for the bathroom.

Mattie heard the knock at the door and knew Rachael was back. She had a hard time hiding the blush that rose up her neck as she heard the greeting her friend belted out. "Hey, sex fiends aren't you two tired yet." She was grinning like a fool but she couldn't help it as she saw the looks on her best friend's face.

"You're just jealous tinker. So shut it up." Jackson said. What a little powerhouse she was, he thought, while he looked at his best friend's significant other. He couldn't get over how she had taken Lyle by storm. The poor guy never had a chance. He certainly didn't know what hit him.

"Hello?" Snap, snap, snap, resounded as Rachael purposely clicked her fingers in front of Jackson's face. "Earth to Jackson, come in Jacks." She was grinning from ear to ear. Rachael had found she really liked Jacks since she got to know him. Being the person she was and the history they already had Rachael couldn't pass up an opportunity to goad him.

"Yeah, yeah, yeah. So what are you two up too today?" Trying to cover his embarrassment at being caught daydreaming.

"We, my dear boy, are off to do serious damage to wallets, cash, and any available plastic we might be able to scrounge up. Any form of American currency will do. Right Matt?"

Mattie was smiling at her favorite people's exchanges and her heart swelled. How lucky I am, she thought. "That's right Rache. Serious damage." She answered with true enthusiasm. Something she never felt about shopping before.

Jackson groaned and drew his attention to Rachael. "What have you done to my wife?"

Smiling like a kid at Christmas she only said that Mattie was blossoming.

"Blossoming? Blossoming my foot. You are converting her into one of those females." He said with a crooked grin on his handsome face. No anger or regret in his tone of voice.

"Now you just wait a cotton pick in minute mister rich..." she trailed off as her focus narrowed in on Mattie's face. Matt was grinning and struggling to hold back a huge laugh which found its way out of her mouth in a great resounding rumble. Mattie laughed until she was weak with it. Gasping for breath and holding her stomach to ease the pain. Mattie continued to laugh at the site of them both looking like bulls ready to charge.

Jackson and Rachael only stared as Mattie laughed like a damn had just broken. The sight was something to behold.

This was the sight that Lyle witnessed as he stood in the doorway of the apartment. Mattie had a deep laugh causing her body to shake. He felt the corners of his mouth curve upward then he joined in. Before they realized it all four were laughing like a group of loons. "Enough, enough. I can't take anymore." Mattie wheezed out between gulps of desperately needed air. When the last of the laughter died down the group discussed the day's plans.

"Ok. So the fearsome, twosome is off to shop country. Lyle what say you we take off on a he-man-bonding thing?" Jackson had eyes only for his wife as he spoke. His smoldering gaze said what he really wanted to be doing and the look didn't go unnoticed by the group.

Lyle's eyebrows rose in a questioning motion. What exactly Jackson meant he hadn't figured yet. "We can take off on your bike and check out the scenery." He said as he wiggled his eyebrows in a seductive manner. The scenery was obvious in the way he suggested it. Jackson only wanted to draw the females into a verbal battle. He wasn't disappointed. "Well since that's the way you want it count me in Blondie." Lyle winked at Jackson.

Mattie saw the look and she knew the guys were teasing and she knew Rachael did too. When Mattie looked at her friend she saw that 'you bet' look and knew she wasn't going to let the comment go without a retort from her.

Rachael knew the statement was a baited one and she wasn't going to let the men down. She wanted the scenery to be her and her alone. Sauntering her well-toned lush little body up to Lyle and wrapped her arms around his neck to pull him down to her parting lips. When she let the kiss end she left him with a smoldering comment. "My scenery may be small but it carries one hell of a punch that is only for you. So don't go sight seeing too much lover." Rachael seared him with another breath stealing kiss that knocked him for a loop and she knew it. Trouble was it had the same effect on her.

Mattie and Jackson only smiled at the couple who acted as if they were in the room alone. "Looks like the 'sex fiends' need to cool off Matt." Jacks couldn't help using Rachael's comments back on her. He really liked goading her. She kept life interesting.

When Rachael let go of Lyle he was speechless and unaware of the look he had on his face for the little woman who bowled him over. "Yep, he's hooked," whispered Jacks to no one in particular.

"Uh, yeah, I'll remember that tinker." Lyle whispered for Rachael's ears.

"See that you do tall, dark, and dangerously good looking," and with that she whipped around and spoke in her 'lets get' tone. "Matt lets hit it girl. The bargains are beckoning and time is a wasting."

Mattie did a quick clean up, combed her long auburn hair, and grabbed her purse. After a long slow kiss that had drugged her mind she headed out with Rachael. They had made their way downtown and began to browse and window shop. Mattie spotted a small but expensive compass she wanted to get for Jackson so she drug Rachael into the store with her. Laughing and tugging on Rachael neither woman noticed a small group by the van that had been watching them and their every move. The women had no idea they were being hunted. They never suspected a thing.

Emerging from the little shop with Jackson's gift in hand Mattie and Rachael were deep in conversation about their favorite people. Lyle and Jackson were always the topic and they were consumed with love for their men. Neither one noticed as they continued on their path to the edge of the street that was connected to the dark alley. Continuing on with the conversation they began to make their way across the street when they were grabbed from behind. Before a yell emerged from either woman they were thrown into the beat up white van or what had appeared to be white at one time. Tape was quickly stretched across their mouths and blind folds covered their eyes increasing the fear of the unknown with the thought of why they had been taken. Before any other thoughts were formed their hands were tied

209

behind their backs. "What the hell was going on?" Rachael was frantically trying to rationalize what was happening and who was behind this attack. More concern for Mattie over rode her thoughts. For a second before the blindfold stole her vision Rachael had seen the absolute emptiness in Mattie's eyes. She wasn't there and that look scared the hell out of Rachael.

Rachael had never been a quitter and she wasn't about to start now. Wrenching at the binds on her hands she felt Mattie bump into her. She didn't like the trembling that radiated from her still form or the whimpers of a trapped animal.

The sudden feeling that there was more danger to Mattie than this attack filled her mind. Mattie's history would come to call on her again and damn that wasn't fair. She had worked so hard to get her life into some semblance of normal. How could she get Mattie to help her if she was closed off? Dammit life wasn't fair. She was going to need a plan.

How the hell was she going to do anything? She was tied up, Mattie was in her own world of torment, and she was in the process of getting mauled by some damned creep with an itch for helpless females. The creep was in the back with her and Mattie and she knew she would have to be careful with her movements. Not that that would be too difficult she thought as she tugged at her bonds. "Think, think clearly." If she said it once she had said it a hundred times since they were slammed into the hot, smelly van but Rachael didn't stop trying.

The ride seemed endless and brutal. She had bounced and bumped all over the place, hitting Mattie in the process. She was too still, too quiet and that worried Rachael even more than if she had cried or yelled or something. The stillness was eerie and it was a real worry. Rachael groped for Mattie's wrist and felt for her pulse and it was slow and steady. Her pulse should be bounding, but yet it felt as if she were asleep. This situation was going from bad to worse in a New York minute. "Dear God Mattie where are you?" Rachael couldn't keep the thought from pounding in her brain. She felt totally alone. Rachael didn't like being alone.

The van bumped and the silence remained. Why didn't they talk? Or say something? The silence seemed to go on for an eternity. Rachael knew that wasn't the case but it felt like it when you were the one tied up and blind folded. Rachael had pretended to be out of it in hopes of keeping the-too- big pawing-claws-off-her, but those hopes were only that. Because someone was copping feels like a kid in a candy store. She was so disgusted she was surprised at the loud booming male voice from the front passenger seat demanding for the feely creep to keep his hands off the merchandise or he would lose some important pieces of his anatomy. The hand that had found its way up her blouse suddenly stopped and retreated. Apparently he was a follower but his whispered anger at the guy was very colorful and quite explicit.

"Hey, bitches are you listening back there?" The voice yelled. "Time and patience always benefit those who are willing to accept both. I've bided my time and I've been patient. Now, damn it, I'm going to get what's rightfully mine and you my dear Mattie are going to get all you deserve, too." The disgust he felt laced every word.

Rachael knew she was caught up in some past that involved Mattie and she knew this man only meant to hurt her and Rachael. She couldn't help thinking what the hell Mattie had been into or if she even remembered. Rachael would bet her inheritance Mattie had no idea what had happened and it had to do with the lost year in her life. Damn. What ever it was wasn't good and what was happening was a real bad sign from her past and their future.

After several minutes the van came to a rattling stopped and the silence was deafening inside the hot rust bucket. Rachael heard a door slam and then the screeching of the side door opening. That bossy voice was ordering again.

"Take the shrimp on in, you all can have her as your toy since she was just a bonus anyway. Sad for her. Wrong place, wrong time. Now Mattie? That little cunt is mine and the pleasure I take in her torture will ease some of my years of hatred. She just took and took. Well, now you will take and take until I get tired of giving it and then little precious you'll die a slow and painful death. One I will take much pleasure in.

You see Mattie dear old dad didn't count on me finding out about all that insurance money. Since you and your whore mother were supposed to die and dad was the one supposed to collect on those policies. The bitch of his plans came with your mothers near death, a loaded gun, and damn good aim. As now, as fate would have it, I'll get all the money and you can go stay with mommy in hell." With that he laughed the kind of laugh only the insane could manage.

His henchmen didn't care either way. As far as they were concerned money was money and a free piece of tale was an added bonus. They only shrugged at each other and waited for their crazy boss to figure out what they were to do next.

Rachael knew now, or at least had an idea, of what had happened and yet Mattie was clueless. As a matter of fact she hadn't even made a sound. This was so not good. How was she going to get Mattie to help in their escape when she was so out of reality's reach?

Rachael knew that death was imminent and she was not going to cave in. She would fight and try to save their lives so when she was pulled from the open van she did exactly that. She fought like a demon to get loose and bolted. Using only her instincts she ran as hard as she could.

She managed getting away without being caught at first. No one had expected the outburst and Rachael used the element of surprise to her benefit.

Rachael heard the voices behind her become fainter and then she hit the woods. The temperature change alerted her and then the descent of the ground and the tree branches scraping her face. The blindfold made it very hard to navigate but she couldn't take time to try to get it off because she didn't know how far they were.

Stepping wrong sent her plummeting downward. Her bound wrist burned with each jolt. After the endless freefall Rachael came to a sudden, painful stop at the base of one of the big pines the area was famous for. She was having a hard time catching her breath and the searing pain she felt with each inhalation alerted her to possibly a broken rib. The whack on her head began to throb even more and the blackness began to sweep over her.

The reality of her situation began to fade and Rachael had to force herself to remain alert. The fear grabbed her when she realized she was still in danger of getting caught. With a great effort she moved and a lightening jolt of pain pummeled her from the injured ribs. Maybe she had more than just one rib in a cracked state. Mattie needed her and that thought kept her conscience and moving.

But first she had to get this damn blind fold off before she could get her ass moving. Rubbing her head against the rough bark of the pine, she managed to get the blindfold off after several painful swipes against the tree. The woods were darkened because the dense foliage didn't allow much sunlight and yet Rachael had to blink at the brightness. Once she focused she tried to figure out where she was. "Lost. That's where I am," she answered her own question. "Thank God I'm flexible," she thought as she righted herself into a sitting position. Her head pounded, her ribs ached with a vengeance, and her hands were numb. Working with protesting muscles and screaming ribs Rachael pulled her still bound hands under her bottom so they would be in front of her instead of behind her. As soon as she managed that feat, she pulled the tape off her mouth. Rachael tried to loosen the twine but it was too tight and her teeth could only do so much. She was a little relieved that her balance would be better now with her hands in front of her and she could breathe a hell of a sight better than before. Now she could make some good time. Or at least she hoped she could.

Sounds further up the hill drew her attention. "Where in the hell is she? It's not as if she could see to hide dammit! If you had been watching like you were told the little twat wouldn't have gotten away. We would be screwing her instead of thrashing around like Smokey the Bear looking for her."

"Kiss my ass." One of them answered. "Who would have expected her to take off like that and anyhow, where were you? If you hadn't had your eyes glued to that other whore the runt wouldn't have gotten away."

"Me? You were the one with the hard on looking at her."

"Well I won't argue with you there. She damn sure makes a rise in your Levis. That little cherry that took off would have eased the ache until we got a chance with that one. You know Ray will have his way with her and after seeing what he does, we know there won't be anything left for us to touch."

"Yeah. Maybe we'll get lucky just the same. I'd like to bury myself into that patch of red hair. Damn but she is one hot piece of ass."

Rachael knew she had gone pretty far because their voices sounded distant from where she was hiding. She struggled to pull herself up and leaned against the tree while she fought the dizziness that threatened to take her again. The relentless wave's of nausea and the continual pounding in her head was hard enough to battle but when it was joining forces with the dizziness it was almost more than she could stand. She swayed on her rubbery legs as the bright lights filled her vision and cursed her weakness.

As soon as the assault eased up on her battered body she began to slowly move. Testing her ability to move without kissing the ground again Rachael began taking one step at a time. With nightmarish visions of Mattie crowding her thoughts she began to force her body to move faster.

Rachael knew she had to get help fast and falling apart was wasting time she couldn't spare. The distant rumble of the men who had followed her began to fade with each step she took increasing her hope that she was going to make it out of the woods and find some help. Rachael began to believe she would make it if only she could figure out where she was. She stopped and listened hoping for some signs of town, some traffic, or the water on the beach. Anything, that would alert her, or direct her. She listened hard and held her breath. Waiting. It wasn't long before she was rewarded with the distant sound of a car passing. The sign she'd prayed for. She ran with the speed of the wolves she loved so much and still felt as if she were crawling.

Her heart was pounding in her chest with the same rhythm as the relentless beat in her temples. She felt sick to her stomach and knew throwing up was not an option but imminent when she felt the bile rise in her throat.

Rachael clutched a young sapling and emptied her stomach. "Could I feel any worse," she mumbled to herself. She regretted her own words as she thought of where Mattie was and what she heard those two creeps say this Ray jerk would do to her.

Once her bearings were intact again she headed in the direction she had begun in the first place. Mattie's life depended on her success in getting help. Rachael moved like a cougar searching for a meal. She struggled so much with the pain and exerted more energy than she ever had during one of her workouts. In her minds eye she could see Mattie and hear those gut wrenching screams that only the mad could release and Rachael felt that was what would happen to Mattie, yet again.

Mattie would go mad and quite possibly she wouldn't return this time. Rachael knew that there had been a first and it lay in the past with the man who spoke with such hatred. Each thought only encouraged her feet to move faster. Limbs hitting her went unnoticed as they cut, scratched, or gouged at her flesh. Her arms, legs, any other exposed body part quickly became a bloody mass of bruises. Rachael refused to give in to the despair she felt weighting her soul down. All she could focus on was escape, Mattie, and her own rescue. She had to get help. She just had too.

Chapter Thirty-Two

Mattie, however, wasn't feeling anything at all. She wasn't dead, or at least she didn't think she was. It was black and lonely in this dead space and the scary thing was she knew she had been with Rachael and the day had been sunny. She didn't know where she was or what had happened. If she wasn't in so much pain she would swear that she was in a bad dream.

"Mattie, come over here sweating. It's momma."

Mattie spun around at the sound of her mother's voice. There she was with her arms wide open and she was smiling.

"Momma," she whispered. "I have missed you so much." She hugged her mother for the first time in too many years to count and it occurred to her she shouldn't be able to hug her at all. "Momma, exactly where am I? Is this Heaven? Are you an angel come to take me with you?"

"Slow down baby girl. I have been sent to this in between place to help you honey. I stay in a beautiful place watching out for you and that my dear is Heaven. I'm not an angel so to speak but...it's hard to explain. This place is for those who haven't passed yet and I need to keep you here until you can go back. You have a sweat young man who will be there for you, he loves you very much, and I have to tell you I really like him. He didn't give up on you and he never will. For that I am thankful."

"Yes, he does and I love him. You told me someday I would find my soul mate and I did. I wish Jackson could meet you and you him. You two would get along so well.

"I wish for all those things too honey, but right now we have a situation that we need to take care of. It's a situation that is very grave for you. Honey, you're in danger of being physically and emotionally damaged and the powers that be, sent me here to help you, and to keep you safe."

"Danger?" Mattie whispered. Confusion just washed through her by her mother's words. She was having trouble processing what she was telling her.

"You are in a place separate from your body, where there's no pain. This place is of peace, light, and love where I can keep you safe until the worldly help can get to you."

"Now, you need to listen to me, those men who kidnapped you and Rachael are hurting your body and you need to stay here with me so you wont be alone, hurt, and afraid. I won't let you feel the pain Matt. I'll stay with you until Jackson can come and help you."

"Oh, momma. I remember now. Rachael and I were shopping this morning I think. We were laughing and having a great time and out of nowhere we were grabbed and thrown in the back of a van but I didn't know who they were or what they wanted. Oh my God, mom, what about Rachael? Is she here with us too? They're going to kill us, aren't they mom?"

"Calm down honey. Rachael got away, and she's trying to get some help. That girl is a great friend to you and even though she is hurt she's still trying to get to the police. You picked some great friends Mattie. You are very lucky they all understand you and are always trying to take care of you even when you don't know it or want it. The important thing for you right now, is to stay here with me, so I can keep you safe until help arrives.

The men that grabbed you are pure hate and evil. The leader is a man you never knew existed and neither did I for that matter. One of the many things that horrible man I married kept from us. I should never have married that man, but I thought I was doing the right thing for us Mattie. I'm so, so sorry for what he did to you, to us. Anyway, the man had a son, your stepbrother, Ray. He is the one who grabbed you and Rachael."

She said as she stroked her daughter's long hair while she held her. The gift of being able to hold her baby girl again was like a dream come true.

"It's ok, momma, you didn't know." Mattie whispered as she drifted into slumber. Her mother cradled her head in her lap like she used to do when she was young.

The reality of the aftermath when it was all said and done wouldn't be a dream and it would take more than most people could manage to get past it and still remain sane. Focusing all her attention on her daughter she kept up small talk and humming to keep Mattie's body from expressing the pain that she knew would have already overtaken her had she not been here to stop it.

"Look at her smiling like some damned lunatic. There's not a bit of fight coming from her. Most women would be screaming their damn fool heads off right about now.

Yo Ray? Are you sure she's not some damn nut job and gets into the kinky shit? Not that I mind a bit but I figured she would have given us nine kinds of hell like some she cat on crack. I'm a little disappointed that she's acting like a lifeless blow-up doll. Leon, the dirty blonde, leered down at the unconscious red head with a body that rocked.

Ray was watching and wandering if the little bitch was playing some kind of game. Mattie never fought, or screamed, hell she didn't even whimper for that matter. A good actress his little stepsister made or she went completely mental and shut down. Well dammit she's not going to lay there and ruin my fun. She will feel my anger one way or another. He had waited too long for his revenge that he had become obsessed with it and the least she could do was feel it. He vowed she would one way or another.

216

Ray had a very brief recollection of the little mouse that got away, but he figured she'd be so lost in the woods that eventually she would plunge to her own death sooner or later. This area was filled with mountainous drop-offs where the little bitch could disappear permanently, besides her hands were tied and she was blindfolded. Far as he was concerned it was a done deal. Ray had his prize trussed up like a Christmas turkey right where he wanted her.

Mattie was his trophy, a trophy he had worked hard to achieve all these months. It was like crossing a finish line and was being rewarded with the money and the woman. The thought of his perfect game plan beginning made his crotch throb.

He had never been so aroused by the sheer anticipation of hurting this one and having her scream for him. The boys stood back after they had her secured. Mattie's legs were spread apart and tied to the bed rails by the ankles and her wrists were tied above her head. The bed was more of a cot really but it would serve his purposes and then some.

Ray ripped the shirt off Mattie's motionless body and tossed it to the floor. The gasps that rent the silence in the room gave voice to the combined lust at seeing her perfect breasts. Pure sex radiated throughout the shack.

Ray didn't notice and didn't care. He had a purpose and that purpose was to torture and end Mattie's life. When he was through with her and she took her last breath then he could live the life he was meant to live. It would be his; every dime. The little maggots behind him didn't have a clue what his real plans were and he didn't give a good damn.

Now, who was the white trash? I knew this day would come Sis, and I'm going to enjoy every damned minute of it. Every whimper, every tear, and every scream will be for me Mattie. You're going to know what its like to hurt, to suffer, to feel the kind of pain I had to feel. While dear ole daddy was out screwing and hooking up with your whore mother, I was getting the shit kicked out of me by mommy dearest and her string of ever changing losers. The tables have turned and you aren't going to survive it, while I make a trip to the bank with all that insurance money. I'll be the one living high on the hog and you get to be worm bait!

Ray kept up his ranting and raving but not a word passed his snarling lips. This conversation was meant for family and he knew she could hear him. The voices told him she could and they had never been wrong. They were the only constants in his life and he trusted them.

The other men in the room stood back watching in fascination. Mattie lay on the cot tied to the frame wearing only her panties and her bra. Of which one strap had been cut away. Ray had removed most of her clothing one

217

piece at a time enjoying every slice his knife made into the fabric, and the nicks into pale flesh that were oozing crimson.

Ray's erection was hard as brick. Not from seeing Mattie nude, that didn't do it for him, it was the red rivulets tracking from various areas his knife had sliced so cleanly. The excitement of really getting down too work on her was palpable and the rush of power made him feel like a God.

The look on his face and the evil in his eyes kept his cohorts in check. They didn't dare move in on him.

The group of young hoods watched the lunatic with the babe and how he had reverently cut away her clothes. He acted like it was some sort of ritual. The damn man was crazy and they all knew it.

The huge hunting knife Ray used gave him even more power. Knives scared people and he liked the element of fear he could feel seeping from his victim's pores. The good ole boy's club may be scared shitless with fear, but it didn't stop them from joining in the fun. Money was money and a fine piece of snatch on the side for desert was an added bonus. Ray was intent on his pleasure and no one who knew him would stand in his way.

They had witnessed first hand the amount of cruelty he could dish out for his sexual pleasures. It was disgusting to watch him. He pleasured himself with men and women and he wasn't at all nice about it. He relished in the amount of pain he could inflict or the suffering that followed. The group saw and agreed he was a sick, twisted, son of a bitch.

Chapter Thirty-Three

Rachael was running faster than she ever had in her life. The adrenaline that coursed through her small frame was more than she had ever experienced before. Her heart was racing in such a fury of beats she thought it would simply rupture from the stress.

She managed to get away from the sick bastards but Mattie was still in their clutches. "Dear God Mattie." She whispered breathlessly as she continued running. Never in her life had she felt such misery.

Rachael had witnessed Mattie's responses in the past and they were fierce and heart wrenching to the point she couldn't even speak. Rachael knew when it was all said and done both of them would have been raped and killed without hesitation. She also knew it would be up to her to try to get help.

Mattie had zoned out to her safe haven so she wouldn't be of any help. It was totally up to her. She just hoped to God she would make it in time because if not Mattie would be dead. If not in body she certainly would be in mind and soul. Rachael feared Mattie would never recover if the latter happened. She would never be as she was. Mattie would be mindless, soulless, and a spiritless shell and that thought made Rachael run all the faster and harder.

Rachael finally made it to the edge of the woods and down the road where she found an emergency roadside phone. She banged the numbers so hard her fingers ached. Not that it mattered since she had lost the feeling in her fingers some time ago. As soon as the phone was picked up she had been transferred to three different desks. The last desk belonged to a Blake Spears. He claimed he was a detective. Rachael didn't care who she talked to as long as she got someone to listen and she sure as hell wasn't going to be transferred again!

Blake was not in a good mood and how the hell did he get stuck with basic phone calls that a patrol officer could handle, he wanted to know. He had done his fair share of line duty. He was a detective not a traffic cop. He had worked hard to get where he was and he didn't like it one bit at having to deal with some hysterical female. He had had a bitch of a day and his head was playing bass in his temples with each heartbeat. He had been given the grand ass chewing by the boss for not following police procedure 'again' and he had not had a tiny morsel of food all day. Yep, Blake was not in the mood for teenage drivel. With a calm that didn't reach his voice he barked in to the receiver. "Spears here. Spill it or hang up."

"Listen. I don't give a flying shit who you are mister. My best friend is about to be raped or murdered or both so I need you people to hall ass to the old abandoned shack up in the woods. Do you know the area?"

"Whoa. Listen kid, pranks to a police officer is a pretty serious offense, so I suggest you be certain with your information."

"Damn it! Would you listen to me you uniformed pencil dick. I've had it with this shit. My friend may be dieing and I've got to play phone tag. Hell, I barely escaped from those..." Spears cut her off.

"Just a damn minute here! Your saying you were kidnapped, tortured, and you escaped?" There was enough fear in her voice to get his attention. Either she was one of the crazies on the loose, a great actress, or she was serious. He feared it was the latter, which is why he was still on the phone.

"That is exactly what I've been telling you numb nuts. Would you please get off your ass and help me. Please?" Rachael couldn't hold the tears back anymore. She couldn't get anyone to listen to her and Mattie needed help. How could these people be so dense?

"Where are you at Miss.?"

"The name is Rachael. I'm, let me see," she stepped over to look at the street sign, "on the corner of Walsh and Stevens. The emergency phone booth, please hurry."

"I'll have a squad car there in a few minutes. You had better hope you're telling the truth. I am not in a very good mood."

"I'm not in the habit of pulling pranks on cops. Just move it would you please? Mattie's life is in serious danger."

"You stay right where you are until the cruiser gets there. I'll stay on the phone with you. Can you tell me what happened? Can you calm down enough to start talking to me? Rachael? Your name is Rachael?" He paused, waiting. "Are you still there?"

"Huh. Oh yeah I'm here. God, would you please hurry." Rachael felt herself begin to shake and the tears wouldn't keep any longer.

Blake could only rely on his skill and compassion. He spoke to Rachael softly and smoothly. He didn't need a hysterical female on his hands and this story was, if it were true, was going to be a major feather in his cap. He could feel it. He would bet his badge that this girl was honest and something really horrible had and was still happening. A girl's life depended on his skill and experience.

"The cop car is here; do I wait for them to come over here or what?"

"Just stay there and wave the officer to the phone when he gets out of the car. I want to talk to the officer. They will bring you in. Is there anyone I should call for you?"

"Could...could you call Lyle Johns he's my fiancé and call Jackson Woods he's Mattie's husband." She paused then continued with her now jumbling thoughts as the adrenaline began to drain from her. "I don't think I can wave to the police my hands are still tied. I don't feel so good Blake." Rachael's head began to spin and she began to feel nauseated. "The ground is spinning." Rachael began to fall when the officer caught her.

"Sir, Ramsey here. This little lady looks like death warmed over. I think she's passed out. Sir? Her hands were tied so tight they are blue and she's been roughed up pretty bad. Should I take her to the hospital first?"

"Nooo!" Rachael had heard what the cop said through her fogged up brain and she didn't want to take any more time than they already had. "We have to find Mattie. Take me to Blake. We don't have a lot of time." Rachael forced herself to rise against every protesting muscle and pain she felt. She would not give up until Mattie was found.

"Bring her in. Move it full scale and I mean full scale. We have a situation that time is of the utmost importance and I don't want any more time wasted." Blake could feel his nerves jump knowing this was the real thing.

Rachael moved with less than her normal agility. She was bone tired and sick about Mattie. "How could I leave her there?" The question had been eating at her since she took off but she knew she had no choice. It was run or they both stood absolutely no chance at survival.

The other officer opened the door with his mouth agape. The young man hadn't seen such a site it would seem. Rachael had no idea her clothes were in a tattered mess, her hair was spiked all over her head, and her eyes were swollen and blood shot. Her lip was split and bloody and she had numerous cuts and bruises all over her small body. She must look a fright she thought. Mother would have a fit if she saw how she looked now.

The police officers were gut wrenched at the sight of this young woman. He had a daughter about her age and he couldn't imagine what fear she had experienced or the torture she had suffered. He spoke calmly to her. "Miss. Your hands. Let me free your hands."

"Huh? Oh, silly me. I forgot. Pretty stupid huh?" The smile she had didn't reach her eyes and her lips quivered with the strain of the forced smile.

"No Miss just concerned about your friend and frightened I would imagine." Once the twine was cut away she grimaced and drew in a sharp breath as a stinging pain roared through her hands when the blood rushed to her fingers. Her wrists were raw, scraped, and bloody but she didn't feel the intensity of the severe wounds. Rachael was concerned about Mattie. Not herself. How was she going to tell Jackson? How? Questions she had no answers to.

After the officers settled Rachael into the backseat of the cruiser she was wrapped in a blanket and given a cup of coffee the officers carried with them.

It only took a few minutes to get to the station and shuffled into the detective's office. The Captain, a paramedic, and some other officers greeted Rachael. Everyone seemed to stare but for the life of her she couldn't find it in her to care. Once she was checked over and given some more coffee that man she had talked to on the phone introduced her to the group.

Blake had begun to ask some questions when the door flew open with a loud bang into the wall. Rachael jumped and screamed before she could stop herself.

Lyle and Jackson froze at the sight that greeted them. Rachael didn't look like Rachael and Mattie wasn't anywhere in sight. Lyle was shocked beyond comprehension. He was speechless as he took in the condition of the woman he loved. What he was feeling for his little powerhouse came roaring like a freight train that slammed the breath right out of him. Unleashed furry swelled inside to the very core of his soul. He couldn't move for the shaking that was overtaking his body. What in God's name had happened?

Rachael whipped her head up in Lyle's direction. She hadn't realized her body had moved until she found herself in his embrace getting the breath squeezed out of her. It felt so good to feel his arms around her that the pain didn't register. Reality and the knowledge of being safe washed over her. Safe, safe, safe just kept running through her thoughts. It was that litany that brought her to her senses. Mattie. With her limited strength she tried to push Lyle away. She had to tell Jackson.

Lyle was shocked at first. Why was she pushing him away? "Not now tinker. Don't push me away. I just need to hold you for a minute." He whispered into her dirty hair as he held on tighter.

"Jackson," she squeaked out. Pulling away from the comfort and security of Lyle she turned to face him with the worst possible news.

Jackson hadn't known fear. Not like this. He saw all he needed to in Rachael's eyes. He knew her news was about his Mattie and it was going to be bad. Jackson groaned low and deep as he swayed. The policeman at his side and Lyle at the other led him to a chair and eased him down. His world was shattering like ice crystals in hot water and he didn't know if he would survive it.

Blake cleared his throat to get the attention back to him so he could get this show on the road. Time was running out and Mattie's life was going with it unless they could move fast. Real fast. Rachael focused on the detective and lowered herself into her chair as Lyle covered her shaking body with the warm blanket the officer had given her. Lyle stood behind her and kept his hands on her shoulders. She was thankful he was here. He gave her strength to keep going.

Jackson couldn't feel anything. He was too numb. He only looked at Rachael as she spoke. Blake asked her questions and then told her to start from the beginning. Without hesitation she did just that. "We were shopping together. The buddy system was how we always did it. Mattie preferred it that way." Rachael went on with the story.

Jackson drew in a breath as his head began to spin. He couldn't get past Mattie being in the hands of evil. His thoughts were drawn back to Rachael's story and tried to comprehend what she was saying.

"I think I recognized a couple of the voices but I was blindfolded so I couldn't see them." She felt Lyle's hands digging into her tender flesh but she didn't say anything. At least she could feel. "Remember a couple of months ago at the club when those three creeps were harassing Mattie?" Rachael had directed the question to Jackson since he had been face to face with them. When she saw his nod she went on with her story. "Well, anyway, when I ran off and went flying down the mountain and stopped when a tree jumped in my way I heard them talking while they looked for me. I think it was them Jackson."

Blake jumped on the information and barked orders out to get busy with the artist. He was interrupted with Rachael telling him to look at that old shack. He was so busy with everything he hadn't followed up on that tidbit when Rachael first spoke of it. Stupid, stupid, stupid. "Rachael do you remember where that shack is? We need to find it fast."

"Oh my God. I forgot. It's the shack on... We have to hurry. Mattie, she wouldn't move or anything. Jacks one of them knew her. He said she would pay and he was going to collect on some insurance money. She wasn't with me Jacks. I couldn't get her to communicate with me and when I grabbed her wrist her pulse was calm. It was too scary for her to be so calm. You understand don't you Jacks. It wasn't a good sign. The leader said I was a surprise. He wanted Mattie, Jacks. He purposely looked for her and grabbed her." Rachael hesitated but continued with her train of thought. "You have to get her out of there. That leader, he's crazy. I never heard such hatred in anyone's voice. He made my skin crawl."

Jackson's color drained from his face. He could feel it. His Mattie. How would she survive this? Every nightmare she had ever had was true to life and she had just begun to live a normal life. He didn't have to watch his every touch anymore. Hadn't she just teased him this morning while they made love in the kitchen? How in God's name would she survive this onslaught? This will kill her and take her away from him. Her reality won't be with him. He knew he would lose her in more ways than one if they didn't hurry. "You have to find her!" He demanded. "Now, dammit!"

Lyle heard the desperation, the terror that had gripped his friend. He didn't know what he would do if it had been Rachael still up there. He had never seen Jackson so shaken but then again he hadn't had to go through this before either.

Blake had his voice ricocheting off the office walls. Everyone jumped and went to their stations. He liked seeing them hop to his command. At least in a crisis they didn't question his authority. He focused his attention back to Rachael. He had to have details and she was the only link he had to Mattie's location and her surroundings. While he questioned her further he saw the door open to his boss's presence. He couldn't remember his boss getting personally involved with this type of case but the help would be welcomed. The man had a protective streak when it came to the college students especially females. He had two daughters the same age and he always made sure the frat house was safe. Twenty years on the police force earned him his position but his reputation for being a fair man with his crew was what had him on a pedestal with his fellow police officers, new and old alike. The respect he received was given freely and he said it kept him in line.

Rachael sat sandwiched between Lyle and Jackson. The shaking she was experiencing was uncontrollable. Her body's response wasn't just related to the cold but also to the shock her body was going through from her narrow escape and now wanting to get to her friend.

Rachael had never experienced such fear in all her life and had no desire to experience it again. That declaration was short lived because she knew she had to go back. She had to show them where the shack was. It seemed as though they were wasting time and every second of Mattie's life was in danger of being ended. "Listen Blake. I want to go with you. I can help you find the place."

Blake was shaking his head and mumbling "Negatory. I can't involve a citizen in this take down. I'm sorry Rachael. I know Mrs. Woods is your friend and all, but I can't let you get involved." He recognized his mistake as the words had left his mouth.

"You listen to me. I am involved in this whether you like it or not. Mattie is more than a friend to me and I will be there for her. Now you have two choices you can either let me go or I will go on my own." Rachael knew she was being a demanding bitch, but she couldn't find it in her to care. Mattie's life was in serious danger and she was going to help. Rachael had always been a fighter and she was determined to fight now. "Damn you she is like a sister to me and you don't know anything about her. Don't you get it? There is a lot more at stake here than just a physical survival. Mattie may not survive this mentally. She has a history that she doesn't remember but we all know it was bad. She has a whole year she can't even remember." Rachael

224

glanced at Jackson hoping she wasn't overstepping her bounds. She didn't like the look on his face. "God Jacks I'm so sorry."

And with that her well contained tears broke the dam and spilled down her cold, dirt smudged, scratched face.

"What kind of history are you talking about?" Blake thought he might have some motive here if there was some history with the girl.

Before Rachael could answer the question Jackson spoke up. "Mattie can't stand to be touched. Only a select few of us can. She loses herself and gets completely hysterical. When that happens she fades out. Like a blank sheet of paper. Something happened in her past that she doesn't remember but I know it's brought on by unexpected physical touching. We have to find her or she will be lost in more ways than one."

All Blake could do was stare at this young man. He saw the love he felt for his wife just by looking into his eyes. The other emotion that flitted across his face was a realization that they probably were already to late. The resignation he witnessed was enough to turn his stomach.

Chapter Thirty-Four

At the run down shack the torture was well underway and Ray was getting really pissed. Rarely did he show his true temper but it was on the verge of appearing now. Not only had that damn little midget got away but Mattie was still out. He had planned this for far too long and he had no intention of being denied his pleasure. He had to have a little cooperation from the victim for that though. He wanted her to feel every ounce of pain he was inflicting on her. She had to pay. She had to pay for it all. In his sick, twisted, gelatinous glob called a brain he knew he would get it all once she drew her last breath. He would not be denied his enjoyment of her torture. The leering smile he had plastered on his face could freeze a summer lake. Ray nudged, pinched, hit, and cut her skin, but Mattie just took it. He tried to slap her out of it. He tried to dump cold water on her and still 'no cigar' as the Carney man said at the fair.

Ray was not only twisted he was impatient as hell. He took his large knife and casually ran it up Mattie's bare leg. Blade side down. The blade left a trail of red velvet as it was drawn up from her ankle to her knee, and then her thigh and stopping at her panty line. The blade was sharp as a razor and did a better job than he had hoped it would. Much as he wanted a response from her still form Ray was disappointed when he didn't get one. Determination forced him to repeat the action on her other leg. By the time he made his third stroke frustration encouraged more pressure with the blade.

Mattie's blood trickled faster with the deeper cuts and Ray was rewarded with a low moan that only a sick mind would enjoy the sound of. He allowed a slow curving of his lips because that was what he wanted. The sound of her pain was what he had been trying to achieve. His only fear was that the fantasy would be better than the reality.

Ray could feel the blood surge to his groin and the power of his arousal was what enticed him to do more. A little blood and a lot of pain went along way with him. He needed it, thrived on it and took great pleasure in it. Ray took slow, measured strokes as he ran the razors edge down Mattie's arm from fingertip, to elbow, to under her arm. The moan was louder indicating Mattie was not free of the pain he was inflicting on her perfect skin. The joy he felt with each moan was an aphrodisiac for his pleasure and her inevitable death would be better than anything he had ever experienced. He never had any intention of sharing her with his minions that stood motionless watching his actions in absolute disbelief. They had no idea how far he would or could go with the torture.

The group was sickened at the way Ray was mutilating that beautiful woman's body. Sure they'd hit or bite, but this was some sick, twisted shit even for them. For the first time they began to worry what the crazy SOB would do to them after he was done with her.

Ray couldn't hold back the evil laughter that bubbled out of his sneering mouth. With the speed of a cheetah he threw the Bowie knife into the chest of the leader of his little entourage. It thrilled him to see the wimp fold like a rag doll. The other two were stunned.

Ray had the advantage and he knew how to use it. He pulled a second knife from his waist and deftly sliced open the pudgy ones stomach from rib to rib. The little tub of lard gasped as he watched his insides spill to the dirty floor right where he stood. Last, but not the least victim, tucked tail and ran. His mistake.

Ray's pleasure heightened. The runner only made it to the door before the cabin filled with an ear splitting crack as the back of his skull exploded like a grape under his shoe and he ran no more. Ray took the time to drag his lifeless body over to his buddies. Ray was laughing softly as he pulled his knife out of the chest of Blondie. "A little heartburn can leave you breathless," as he laughed with his own sick humor.

Ray was supremely pleased at how well his plans were working out. He had always planned to rid himself of the little band of idiots he had enlisted for his dirty work but to do it impulsively just now had heightened his arousal. He felt himself through his jeans rubbing the erection that was throbbing with a need for release.

He hadn't been this excited since that little twit in Hardinsburg. It was a fact she had put up one helluva struggle. A long fight that was so arousing he'd almost lost it before he had even raped her. He managed to hold on until he squeezed the last breath out of her while he was buried deep within her. Ray knew she had been good. Real good. Mattie would be the ultimate and he was anticipating every second with her.

"Mattie you can stay out of it if you want, but I will find much pleasure in your torture and resulting death. You will pay for all the crap I have had to deal with for these last shit encrusted years. My revenge will be so sweet." Ray continued with the slicing of her pale blood glistened skin.

Mattie felt the safe haven with her mother begin to slip away and the pain began to register in her numb reality. She wanted to scream but no voice would come. Mattie felt the burning on her arm and her legs. "What was that?" She asked without words. The feeling of danger was tangible. Palatable. Acrid. The fear was the worst she could remember ever having. Except deep down she knew she had felt fear this bad and worse before, but she didn't know how or what made her feel that. Her thoughts went to

Jackson and how she would miss him. "Why now? I just found him. Please don't let this happen again" and she was sure she had been through this before. Mattie didn't realize she had released a low moan. Her face was turned towards the wall and tears trickled dirty paths down her battered face.

Ray didn't see the shimmering silver streaks running down in tiny rivulets to the dirty pillow. He hadn't noticed as his attention was so focused on his brutal work to Mattie's body. Blood lust was an all absorbing, mind controlling entity that had him in its clutches. His feet were riveted to the floor while his eyes absorbed the sight he had imagined hundreds of times. Ray decided that the reality of it was better than any fantasy he had conjured up. He couldn't stop the demented smile that overtook his face.

Mattie knew she had to pretend no matter how she hurt as the reality began pounding into her. She prayed for the oblivion she had experienced before, so the pain wouldn't rack her body. Jackson was her beacon for survival and she clung to that thought with a vengeance.

A small wisp of Rachael crossed her pain-riddled mind and she realized she didn't know where she was. Her heart ached with the knowledge that Rachael may not be alive anymore. She was Mattie's best friend and she couldn't stop feeling that this was all her fault. Terror was gripping her with a fierceness that threatened her every breath. She couldn't think. Her head hurt so badly that her thoughts were choppy.

It was so dark in this place she had escaped to, she was trapped in her own thoughts. Mattie hated the dark. The memory of dark rooms and locked doors swept over her and she knew she had suffered that torture as well. A cellar with a cold damp dirt floor and creepy crawlies all over the place flooded into her memory. Oh how she hated dark places. "Jackson please help me. Jackson? Please?" Her whispered plea found its way out of her swollen lips.

The plea did not fall on deaf ears. Unfortunately, the plea landed on uncaring ears. Ray heard it all right and pictured the pretty boy from the club. "Yeah, once a whore puts out her scent the pretty ones come a sniffing," he thought. As if she could hear him Ray told Mattie her rich boy didn't have a chance in hell and she was going to pay dearly for all the years of his pain and suffering.

Mattie heard him and the loathing tone he used to punctuate his words. She also knew this crazy man would kill Jackson if the chance presented itself and she had to protect him. Jackson had been the light of her life for this past year. She deeply loved him and she knew she was going to die but she would not allow Jackson to follow the same path. She wouldn't let this maniac hurt the love of her life.

Ray tried to arouse Mattie. He wanted to hear her beg and plead and to suffer with each touch, each caress he offered her. Touching her breasts and gently rubbing the nipple he entertained thoughts that made him smile and why not he thought he was in charge.

Mattie was disgusted. His touch made her want to throw up. Pleading with her thoughts she begged for help. Help from his filthy touch. Help from the pain that was wracking her body. Praying her pleas would be answered.

When Ray didn't get the responses he wanted and was striving for the anger overwhelmed him. He wasn't going to let her sleep through his lessons.

Grasping her breast between his work roughened fingers he pinched her with all his strength. He still got no response, which only angered him more. Growling deep in his throat he grabbed a fistful of hair and pulled it out by the roots. He couldn't stop the unwanted thoughts of how pretty that amber hair looked wrapped around his fisted fingers. Power surged within him as he began to saw off all that beauty. He had no room for beauty in his twisted mind and it had to be removed. Cutting that shit off was like cutting away the thoughts. He wanted to hurt her and if a woman had hair like that then it would hurt to have it whacked off. He grinned at his barber talents.

Mattie heard the rasping sound of a knife cutting her hair. The searing-pain of him pulling out a great amount with his work worn hand had only been the beginning of removing the one thing she truly liked about herself. Mattie began to feel an uncontrollable tripping inside of her self. The reality was fading like a projector with slides except the slides were her life.

The safe black hole, her safe haven welcomed her as she escaped him within the safety it offered. Her mind was taking her away from the reality of what was happening to her. Mattie remembered this place. It was quiet and peaceful. She didn't have to be afraid here. Mattie thought of her momma and Gracie as the warmth enveloped her. "Momma, where are you? Where's Gracie? I'm scared! Please come and stay with me. Please?" Mattie felt her fear easing away as a soft light covered her with warmth and safety. The calming effect opened her senses allowing her to hear what she had been longing for.

"We are here child and you are safe. I want you to listen to us and stay as still as you can. Honey let him think you're asleep so you can stay safe a little longer. That's the way baby. We are here with you." Her mother spoke so softly Mattie calmed without hesitation.

"I have missed you and Gracie so much." Mattie's heart felt a moment of ease but her fuzzy brain heard the male voice trying to dominate her thoughts. She tried to fight but the words were demanding and tried to penetrate her new found peace.

"Come out, come out, wherever you are. I know you're in there Mattie and my patience in running mighty thin with you. Come out and play with old Ray. I promise you'll die to regret it." Laughing at his own sick wit was a sure sign of his craziness.

"Mattie honey you need to listen to me baby. You have to stay real still. Don't move. Gracie and me are going to keep you safe right here. Ok honey? Come on now." Mattie was encircled in a warm embrace from her mother and Gracie.

"Ok. Momma I'm not afraid now." Mattie's face reflected the sudden peace and security she felt. She even smiled with the pleasure she was feeling.

"What the hell?" Ray didn't know what was going on but that was not the response he wanted. The fury was boiling in him now and the determination was becoming obsession. He was going to insure she felt what he had to offer.

Chapter Thirty-Five

Was it possible for pain to become so intense that you became numb? Jackson thought as he sat in the police detective's office. He was paralyzed. Was it just this morning Mattie had made passionate love to him? Hadn't she seduced him in the kitchen and taken his breath away? God. What will I do if...?" He couldn't finish the thought. He just couldn't, wouldn't believe it or accept it.

He had to move and jumped up pacing along the tiled floor while thoughts of Mattie raced in his head. Her laugh, her sighs of pleasure, her thoughts and tenderness, everything that was her consumed his mind. He found all rational thought processes impossible. Pacing became the alternative to hitting something or someone.

Lyle held on to Rachael for all he was worth. She had been through hell and yet she sat here with not one compliant to cross her lips. He knew she was concerned about Mattie. Hell they all were. He felt lucky his Rachael had made it out but she was too consumed with the situation to give a thought to her own injuries.

"Rache?" He whispered. "Rachael. I love you sweet heart." Lyle waited for her to look at him. His breath caught in his throat when he saw the look in her eyes. She fixed her gaze to his and they were filled with unshed tears and an emptiness he had never witnessed in her expressive face before. She looked so lost it unnerved him. His Rachael always knew who she was and where she was going. She never looked uncertain before and it took him by surprise to see it now. He knew she was asking the questions of 'why' and 'who' but no one had any answers. Two wonderful people were attacked and no one had any answers. It was a damned frustrating situation.

Blake kept asking the same thing. What was in this girl's past that would elicit being kidnapped? Possibly tortured or killed? What tragedy had happened to her that had her reacting like she had been abused or worse? He had listened to the stories from her friends and husband and his experience told him he had a good idea of what had been done to her when she was so young. What the hell he thought. Maybe there was a connection from that and this mess.

Blake had a gut instinct and he always followed his instincts no matter how far fetched. It had saved his butt many times in the past and he hoped it would save Mattie's this time. While his team worked on a game plan to get her out without causing her death he worked on the computer running search after search on her past. Nothing showed up. Then it occurred to him to look under her maiden name and it was then he hit an invariable gold mine.

"Damn" he muttered more to himself than to those in the room. Printing the information would be useful so everyone could read the report. After scanning the information he soon discovered that there was a connection between these two cases or he would turn in his badge.

That bet revealed the certainty of his thoughts. When the printer stopped its endless racket Blake grabbed it and shook his head. "Hell, no wander she blocked her past out. I would too." Still muttering as he sat back in his chair. Normally civilians weren't privy to the type of info he had, but in this case he would take the chance and suffer the wrath of Khan after the fact. He felt he was limited on choices and if these three could shed a little light on the subject then it would be worth it.

"Folks. I think I have something. I dug into Mattie's past and I'm afraid it isn't very good. At least we know what happened to that missing sixteenth year and how that may be connected to this. Do you want to hear it?" He directed his comment to Jackson. "It may help us out if you hear it maybe there is some piece of info Mattie may have mentioned at some time." He waited and all three nodded 'yes' without realizing it of each other. Blake proceeded to tell them about the information he had and who the assailant was.

As the information was being shared in this office another kind of meeting was still taking place miles away in the run down derelict building that was soon going to be the last place Mattie Collins would draw her last breath in.

Mattie wasn't in any pain just then. She was being held in a warm embrace. "Mattie honey? I know you don't remember what happened to us. To me, but honey, you need to remember now. I know what you have had to deal with over the years and it's time to heal. You will have to remember so you can heal. Do you understand? You can't keep it locked away any longer."

"I don't remember any of it but I do know it was bad. I feel it. I don't want to remember it, please don't make me."

"Matt. Please listen to me. You are going to have to get it out so you and Jackson can have a peaceful future. You need to remember it now Mattie. I'll help you. I'm right here with you. Please Mattie. You have to get it over with so you can live without the fear and restraints. Ok?"

Mattie had never heard her mother demand and plead so. All she could do was shake her head up and down for the yes she couldn't say with her mouth.

"I'm right here honey. I'll help you as much as I can. Now listen. Remember our house and your step dad Frank? Do you remember him?"

"Yeah, I remember him. You weren't too happy married to him were you?"

"No, I wasn't Mattie. Frank could be cruel with his words and with his fists. Now I want you to concentrate on him and what happened when you were sixteen. We were having such a good day out in the meadow. Do you remember Mattie? I want you to focus on that and think real hard. Can you try to do that for me?"

"I'll try momma. I remember we were in the meadow. I think we were walking together and talking. The sun was warm on my face and the breeze was so soft and sweet with the scent of wildflowers." Just talking about it with her mother brought the long forgotten memories to life.

The memories swept her into the current as they floated along like ripples in a still pond. Spring was such a beautiful time with all the greens and gold's. Everything was in bloom and scented with its own perfumes. The animals were out and about making a place for themselves in the grasses. The birds were singing their love songs to all who wanted to listen and Mattie was with her mother.

She loved her mother with all her heart. She was all the family she had unless you counted Gracie. Gracie was their best friend. She may be old and blind, but she understood Mattie and she would spend hours talking to her. Liz, her momma, was talking about all the possibilities available after high school and boys. Not that Mattie showed much interest in that department.

Her momma never pushed her or made comments like Frank did. Her so-called step father, wasn't much of a father figure at all, and he took every opportunity to point out Mattie's faults and taunted her with them.

He liked to knock 'a little sense into her' as he put it. His idea of punishment was with iron fists and cruel words. Mattie never trusted him but she tolerated him because her momma had married the man. As soon as that ink was dry on the marriage license he revealed his true colors. She had always felt he was hiding his true self and she had been right.

Her momma had said the same thing so she knew she wasn't imagining it. Mattie knew Frank was a control freak and always demanded things to be done his way. There was no other way with him.

Liz and Mattie knew how far to push things and when to hold back in a very short time. Frank was a selfish, demanding man. They just let him do his drinking in peace and hoped he would stay gone when he did it. Most times he did and on rare occasions he didn't. The liquor would give him the excuse to show his ass and they were always on the receiving end of his brutality and anger. It was those times they feared for their safety.

Liz had plans for Mattie's future and those plans included leaving home and getting an education. She liked having her mom help her plan the future they both would share and it wouldn't include Frank. They were more like sisters than they were mother and daughter. Even more so now as she got older and they could share more adult matters. Their secrets for the future were theirs alone and it didn't consist of drugs, liquor, or being beaten within an inch of their lives. They had plans for a happy, bright future.

233

After spending the afternoon walking and talking Liz realized it was getting late and they both knew dinner had to be on the table. Frank was fanatical about his mealtime. Not because he wanted to digest his food before he went to sleep it was so he could go out boozing with his friends at an early hour. "Mattie, I need to go. I have to get busy with dinner. Are you coming or are you gonna stay a while longer?"

"I think I'll stay awhile longer if it's ok with you momma. It's such a pretty day out and I want to enjoy it." Mattie couldn't keep the smile off her pretty face.

"Ok honey. I'll be at the house. Don't stay out too late all right?" Liz knew how much Mattie liked the meadow and she didn't mind letting her stay here. It was one of the few things her daughter enjoyed and she wanted her to have that for herself.

"I'll be in to help soon." Mattie yelled out to her mothers retreating back.

As Liz made her way to the house she didn't notice the door slightly open or the rusted and dented car parked down the hill. She wasn't expecting anything out of the ordinary when a fist plowed into her face as soon as she crossed the doors threshold. Before she could grasp what was happening a hand clutched her hair and drug her through the rest of the doorway.

She heard the door slam as she was being pulled along the cold floor. Liz's head hurt and she was seeing dancing white lights. Knowing she had no choice she opened her mouth and screamed as loud as she could for Mattie. She attempted to deflect the repeated blows to her body as she lay on the floor. It was during the kicks she finally focused enough to recognize Frank.

The shock of knowing it was him was a brief one. Liz wasn't surprised by his actions. Ever since she had married him he had changed into a total stranger. He gave Jekyll and Hyde a run for their money. Liz had been able to keep most of his abuse away from Mattie but he had been steadily grown worse and she feared Mattie was next. "What are you doing Frank?"

"Well dear. Let me enlighten you." He kneeled down into a crouch and almost fell. "Damn." He righted himself as he let out a harsh laugh.

Liz could smell the stench of liquor on his breath. It was so strong she held her breath against the offensive odor. "You're drunk. Again," she hissed.

"Sooo what? I figured instead of a divorce your death would be better for my wallet. You see I took out an insurance policy along time ago on you and with your untimely death ole Frank will be conveniently rich. To my way of thinking, that was a much better idea. Aint that right Buck?"

Liz hadn't noticed the other man until that moment. He was a disreputable looking creature. He was filthy and ugly to boot. Unfortunately for her he was muscular and he was leering at her with black, soulless eyes. She could barely hide her revulsion.

"Yeah. Money is a much better idée." He snorted.

"What insurance money are you talking about? You don't have any insurance you fool!"

"That was the wrong thing to say Liz." Frank kicked her in the ribs with a resounding crack. "I'm not fool you bitch. I have had this planned for a long time and it will work. You and your damn daughter provided me with the perfect opportunity. I took out a policy on you over a year ago. The smart thing was I took one out on me too. No sense in drawing attention when its time to collect that wad of cash. We were both named beneficiaries if something happened and to sweeten the pot more I named Mattie as sole heir and recipient if anything happens to the both of us. I wouldn't say a fool would have thought of that would you?"

Liz realized just how crazy he truly was.

"You're insane," she whispered in a strangled tone. Before she had the opportunity to say anything more, he kicked her like a football square in the abdomen. Liz felt something burst from the impact, but didn't have time to discern what it was. The pain was the worst she had ever experienced in her life. Her ability to think clearly was waning, but she had enough processes left to realize her daughter was in as much danger as she was if she were to come in now. God no not my Mattie! Liz hadn't realized she spoke aloud until she heard Frank laugh deep and loud.

"Now dear you're precious little Mattie will be with you. I can't risk her getting what I've planned on for such a long time. Can I?"

Liz groaned as the next assault came. The pounding was making Frank want more than just beating her; he wanted her rough and hard. Something she never allowed, being the little prissy ass that she was. Now was the perfect opportunity and he prided himself on taking advantage of opportunities as they came along. Liz was as sexual as a board in bed but by God he was getting randy as a Billy goat with each blow he inflicted on her. It amazed him what a good sound beating good do for a man's sexual appetite and he was getting mighty hungry.

"Keep an eye out for Mattie will ya Buck? The little missus and me is going to have us a little fun right here, right now, on the floor. You can watch if you want and then my friend you can have her when I'm done. How does that sound to you old pal?"

Buck grinned at the thought of plowing Liz's row and rubbed his crotch in anticipation. "I think that's right neighborly of ya Frank."

Liz felt the bile rise in her throat. "God help me. I'm going to be sick." And she was with a vengeance. Emptying her stomach of nothing but blood didn't ease the sickness. If anything it was worse and she felt herself slipping into the blackness that had been threatening to swallow her whole.

235

Frank dumped water on her determined she would know everything he had intended to do to her. He pulled her to the rug and ripped off her clothes exposing her bruised pale flesh. Shame washed over her. She had never been so embarrassed or scared her entire life. Frank only stared at her and sneered.

"Hell honey, don't look so scared, it isn't like I haven't fucked you before. This time though you will do more than lie there lifeless beneath me if I have to beat a movement out of you. I like it rough anyway so you would only do me a favor by forcing me to hit you. You will work your bony little ass and enjoy it or I'm going to punch you with every plunge I make. Got it?"

Liz was so shocked all she could do was nod her head and let the tears trail down her bloody swollen cheeks. She knew without a doubt today she would die and Mattie would have to fiend for herself if she could get away. If it took her very last breath she would make sure Mattie survived this nightmare. She would live and be happy. Mattie's life literally depended on Liz surviving long enough to stop this insanity she was trapped in.

Frank almost drooled at the prospect. This business was becoming very much the kind of fun he could handle. Who would have thought Liz could turn him on like this? His sex throbbed with desire and the excitement was almost overwhelming. He ripped his zipper down anxious to have her. He didn't take his pants down only slipped then over his hips. He forced her legs apart and plunged into her uninterested flesh.

"Oh yeah so tight," he murmured to himself as he pounded into her. He didn't only hit her. He beat her. The pounding of her flesh was erotic, as it never had been before. Maybe it was the rape factor. He had never expected Liz to be so damn good.

Liz only cried and prayed that the attack would end soon. She had felt her hip pop when he forced her legs open. The searing pain he was inflicting was almost unbearable. Never would she have imagined her life ending this way. Franks thrust became deeper and harder and he began to pinch her breast while he hit her and smacked her.

Her body was shutting down and she didn't notice a change in pain. Pain was pain and she was in the midst of the worst pain any woman could go through. He finally climaxed as he bit her cheek drawing blood with it. Liz barely noticed. Her consciousness was fading.

Frank determined it was the best piece of ass he had ever had as he got to his feet. Wiping the streams of sweat off his brow he motioned for Buck. "Have at it pal. I got more than I thought she could ever give me. Enjoy yourself my friend."

Buck had watched Frank take her and it had him so aroused he could barely think. He was ready to have her but he wanted a little something more than what Frank had. Reaching down he grabbed Liz's legs and flipped her onto her stomach. He barely heard Frank laugh and make his comment of being sorry he hadn't thought of it first.

No amount of preparation could have braced Liz for the amount of pain that ripped through her body when Buck mounted her and plunged in. Liz was numb all over until he assaulted her and this was the worst. He pounded into her and grabbed her breast while her husband stood smirking and watching. "Bastard," she whispered. She closed her eyes as the pain took her. She felt her head snap back as Buck grabbed a fistful of hair. She saw Frank saunter over and smile. "Having a good time honey? Don't say I never showed you the best time a gal could ever have. I know Buck here won't forget this ride. Will ya Buck?"

A deep throated groan answered as Buck emptied himself into her abused body. Once the shaking of his body stopped Buck grabbed her by her hair and slugged her in her ear busting the eardrum. Liz lost all thought as the black swallowed her into oblivion and took the pain away.

"Oh no you don't Liz. You are staying right here with us." Frank demanded as he pulled her to her unsteady feet. The punches he delivered kept coming from everywhere all at once. Liz couldn't hear, she couldn't see anymore, and the pain didn't register as it had in the beginning. She was dieing and she knew it. She barely noted falling as he released her. She was a broken mound of flesh as she fell into her small nightstand.

Liz knew her chance to stop this abuse was within reach, all she had to do was stay alive a little longer. Mattie's life depended on it. That was when she heard the singing muffled with the ringing in her undamaged ear. Liz's body froze and her heart pounded. Dear God it was Mattie and she was coming in here. "No," she groaned through her swollen mouth.

"Shut up," Frank whispered. "Or I will kill you right here and now."

His threat didn't mean anything to her. Liz knew she was already dead. She refused to let her daughter suffer as she had and if being quiet insured that for just a little longer then she would do it. For Mattie. Liz watched Frank and Buck flank each side of the door before Mattie stepped in. "No Mattie." "Run!" But she knew her warning was wasted. Mattie was already in the room.

At the warning Mattie turned to see her mother's naked, battered, and bloody body. She screamed for all she was worth before Buck slammed his fist into her jaw and sent her flying across the room, slamming her into the wall. The men followed the path Mattie had taken and took turns kicking her. She never knew what hit her.

"Depraved bastards," Liz thought. Fighting to keep herself conscience and squinting out of her one useful eye Liz inched toward the drawer that contained the gun she had bought months ago. Little did she know she would end up having to use it to save her daughter from the very man she had married and called husband. Liz knew it was loaded and was thankful now she had kept her purchase a secret. If Frank had known it was there she had no doubt he would have used on her. She could hear the blows her daughter was receiving and she only hoped she would stay unconscious to block the pain they were inflicting on her innocent body.

Frank and Buck were so intent on Mattie and the torture they were bestowing on her they didn't pay any attention to Liz's movements. The hitting finally stopped and the lust was thick in the room. Liz saw the evidence of what their intentions were. They didn't see a teenager's battered body. All they saw was another woman to rape and ease the pressure in their bulging pants. Liz wouldn't let it happen.

Buck was determined he would have her. This young piece made his mouth water. Mattie's clothes were ripped so it was easy to pull off the rags that remained.

Frank let out a deep-throated groan. "Damn, she's fine looking. Never would have guessed with all those damn granny dresses covering her up. Sure makes your mouth water, don't it Buck?" Buck didn't answer he only pulled an unconscious naked female away from the wall for easier access. He was positive she would be better than the mother.

Liz tugged at the drawer and beneath her women's magazines was her .38 fully loaded. Liz was told this was a good gun and it would take down whatever you aimed it at. Liz had seen it first hand at the firing range when she got her training. Now she would have to put that training to use. Her daughter's life depended on it.

Struggling to get up on her elbow she had to lean against the wall. Liz was shaky and she was bleeding out. Nausea assaulted her but she ignored it focusing on her daughter. Mattie lay helpless and beaten with that sick trash climbing on top of her. The sight gave her the strength it took to take aim. The shot rang out in the small A-frame house. The bullet ripped through Bucks back and exited his chest, slamming into the wall. He never knew what hit him and his last thoughts were certainly not on his own death. Bucks lifeless body slumped half on top of Mattie while his blood soaked her.

Frank was shocked. "What the hell?" He whipped around to see Liz holding a damn cannon in her shaky hands and it was aimed at him. She looked near death but her intent was crystal clear. "You bitch. Look what you've done. You've done up and killed Buck."

His authoritative voice lost any edge he thought it had. Frank resorted to laughter because the sight of Liz with a gun unnerved him. He would never have guessed she had it in her and from the looks of it she wouldn't have it in her much longer. He could hear her wheezing and gurgling from where he stood. Time was all he needed to win this hand. Buck could be the scapegoat since he was worm bait already. "Damn Liz. I never would have thought you had it in you to kill a man. You'll fry for murder. You know? You just signed your own death warrant."

Liz never flinched. Never broke her cold stare. She didn't waver at all and that made Frank's skin crawl.

She could feel her life ebbing away. Time for her was running out. "I may already be dead Frank but at least I won't burn in hell like you will." Her voice rasped in a whisper but by the look on his face he understood her words. Liz took aim and fired without warning. The bullet slammed into his chest and the shock of it on his face was almost comical. His heart no longer resided in his chest.

Thank God she had, had training. She would have hated to aim again. The blood pored from the gapping hole and Liz sighed with relief. Mattie would be safe now. Liz slid down the wall at an angle lying with the gun still gripped in her hand. The darkness was consuming her and she welcomed it with open arms. The pain didn't exist anymore and she became calm and relaxed. She couldn't help wandering if she should be feeling something as she slipped into the dark warmth.

Mattie stirred. Her head felt like it had been used for a battering ram. She couldn't open her eyes. Was it nighttime? Where was she? What happened? As she tried to move she remembered.

The attack from Frank and some stranger as soon as she entered the little place they called home. As soon as that thought crossed her mind she remembered the sight of her dear mother. "No!" She screamed from her swollen lips. "Mom?" She yelled into the dim room.

Through the tiny slits of her swollen eyes she tried to focus and couldn't. She tried to move and found she couldn't do that either. She felt weighted down. She couldn't move her legs or her arms and it was hard to breathe.

As consciousnesses came back she realized that something was on top of her and she was naked. Before another thought crossed her dazed mind the pain slammed into her without warning. She tried to suck in a deep breath and regretted it. When she tried to lift her head the room began to spin and her stomach churned.

Once she steadied her swaying head she focused on the weight that had her pinned. That was when she realized there was a man on her. Blood was everywhere. Screams ripped through her tight, swollen throat. Pushing with all her might she shoved at the corpse who was half naked with a hole the size of a basketball in his chest.

Mattie realized what he had meant to do and it sickened her more than the blood did. She scooted and shoved until she could make her way to the wall where she stopped. Mattie found her eyes frozen on a pair of lifeless brown eyes. She didn't want to look but she couldn't turn away either. Her body shook with fear and revulsion. She was confused, scared, disoriented with what was happening. "What in God's name have I done? I don't remember!"

"Momma?" She waited. "Momma?" She screamed. Covering her eyes with bloody hands she became frantic. Breathing hurt. Her body was a massive amount of pain all over, and she was frozen in one spot. She couldn't move. Fear gripped her and held her prisoner. She heard a low moan and held her breath. The first thought she had was that the men were going to start in on her again.

Where was Frank? Wasn't he here? She couldn't focus her muddled, fuzzy mind. Everything was a jumbled mess. Mattie focused her attention and forced her eyes open. Her eyes only opened into slits because they had swollen shut from all the blows she had taken. Looking to the side she managed to bring into focus a bloodied, lifeless body.

Reality was a rude awakening. Frank was dead and she shocked herself when she couldn't find any sorrow at the sight. How could she? She asked herself. The deep moan of someone in pain came again and she realized it was her mother. Where was she? Is she...No! Don't go there. Before she realized it she was standing against the wall trying to remain conscience. If the wall didn't hold her she would fall.

Mattie got a glimpse of her mother on the floor across the room. She couldn't get a deep breath through her tight throat. Her beautiful mother was hurt bad. How could anyone hurt such a beautiful, kind, loving woman the way they had hurt her?

"Momma? Oh, momma! What's happening?" Mattie began to cry as she inched along the wall, digging deep for all the strength she could muster into her beaten, abused body, she flung herself across the room between the two corpses making her way to her mother's limp, unconscious body.

Mattie knelt at her mother's side and attentively reached for her. Lightly tracing her battered face Mattie cried openly by the abuse she had suffered. "Oh, momma," she whispered. "Momma, open your eyes please. Can you look at me? Don't leave me here all alone momma. Please don't leave me."

Mattie lost all train of thought as the realization her mother was going to die slammed into her in a sudden rush. Her mom, her best friend wouldn't be with her anymore. "Don't...die. Momma! She screamed as loud as her strained voice would allow. She rocked back and forth with the agony that was taking her soul and twisting it with a vengeance.

Liz heard her daughter's pleas through the haze of black velvet and the warmth that had cocooned her. She didn't want to leave the serenity and peace, but she had to tell Mattie.

"Mattie," she whispered. "Listen to me sweetheart. I don't have much time. My body is dieing. I know it is. I can feel it."

"No!" Mattie screamed as sobs racked her beaten body. "No, you're not. I'll get help. You can't leave me. What will I do without you? Please don't go. I love you. You need to stay with me. You just have to fight a little longer Momma? Please!"

"Mattie, honey, I don't have a choice now. My body is past help and we both know it. I'll always be with you my girl. In here, she said as she tapped her chest and she smiled through her swollen lips. "Leaving you is the hardest thing I have ever had to do, but I'll be in your heart and in your memories. I'll always watch out for you. I love you more than I can ever tell you baby. Always." Liz's vision began to fade. Mattie's face began to gray around the edges. Tears streamed down her battered checks. "Mattie," she sighed. "Live a happy life with lots of love. You'll make a great wife and mother some day. Make me proud honey. I'll be watching you. Grow to live, grow to love, and grow to be." Her voice was so low now Mattie could barely hear her. "Love you Mattie. Love you." Closing her eyes on the only sight that ever mattered to her Liz floated into the arms of welcoming piece knowing Mattie would survive. Liz smiled as her last breath escaped her pale, bloody lips.

Mattie saw it. The peaceful smile on her momma's face as the light left her eyes. She was gone and Mattie was left alone for the first time in her young life. The room began to darken, her head began to spin, and she moaned with the loss of her best friend and the love of her life. The darkness took her and engulfed her. Her heart ached with the worst pain she had ever imagined. She was completely alone.

"Momma, I remember now. It's why I've been so afraid. Isn't it? The reason I can't be touched without losing it, isn't it?"

"Yes honey. Your mind put up the wall to protect you from the memories that you weren't ready to have. The problem was it closed you off to the world. You have spent your whole life sheltered from the life you can have honey. That was why I wanted you to remember. It is time to live Mattie. You have a life with Jackson and he loves you so much. It's time to live and get on with your life and your destiny with Jackson. A family is in your future Matt don't let your past overshadow the life you're entitled to. You owe it to yourself and to Jackson."

"You know about Jackson?" Mattie whispered her surprise. "We are married momma. I love him with all my heart."

"I know baby. I've known since the beginning. You are soul mates. Cherish your future and have your family Mattie. I'll always be there with you. I'll know wherever you are." After saying that, Liz's voice became harder and more serious. "Now Mattie I need for you to listen to me and do as I say. You are in a bad place right now. Help is on the way. Your little friend Rachael has made it to safety and she has everyone jumping to come to your rescue. I need for you to lie as still as you can. Gracie and me will stay here with you. Do you think you can do that for me?"

"I can do anything as long as you and Gracie are here. Gracie where are you?"

"I'm here Mattie girl. Now you listen to your momma and we'll get through this mess in one piece. I like your Jackson, baby girl. He's a fine young man and we know he will take care of you. He loves you very much. Mattie girl you'll never be alone again. We love you and right now we need for you to pay attention and stay right here with us and you'll be ok."

"Ok Gracie. I will do whatever you tell me to."

Chapter Thirty-Six

The shock and disbelief on Jackson's face after hearing the horrible details the detective just spilled out about his Mattie was more than he had suspected had happened to her. In his worst nightmares he had never experienced the hell Blake just described Mattie had gone through. No wander she reacted so violently to unwanted touches. The fear she experienced was understood. How did she survive such a trauma? No wander she blocked it out. Jackson was surprised she was so balanced. How in heavens name did she manage to survive?

Rachael was drenched with tears. God in heaven, poor Mattie went through pure hell. Here she was again at the hands of more crazies and her sanity may not survive a second round of such brutal treatment.

Lyle had suspected Mattie had gone through some sort of trauma in the past but he certainly hadn't thought it was as bad as what he had just heard. To go through such mental anguish, such physical abuse, and to witness your own mother's death it amazed him she functioned at all.

Lyle knew she was stronger than she ever thought she was and now he understood why he felt that about her. Poor kid had suffered more than the average person had in a lifetime and at no fault of her own.

Blake interrupted the three blank faced adults sitting in front of him by clearing his throat. "Well, now, it's worse. It is happening again. Mattie has been kidnapped and God knows that she may not survive this time."

Jackson screamed. "No!" Looking frantic he had to say his piece. "Don't you dare say it! Damn you! Mattie will be fine. Do you hear me? I said she will be fine! I know it here." He slammed his balled fist into his chest. "Here!" He wouldn't let the tears that threatened to close his throat off to come. He wouldn't be weak. Mattie needed him to be strong and he would if it killed him.

"Ok. Now listen." Blake continued. "Let's figure out what these bastards were after while the men finish getting prepared. We can't just rush in because they might kill her right then and there. Rachael wasn't part of the plan. They watched them until the opportunity came to grab the girls. Now, according to Rachael, the drive wasn't long and she managed to get to help by foot so the place is near. I'll send out as many more men as I can to join those already out on the search. Is there any information Mattie may have given you about her past that may be connected somehow? Anything at all?"

Rachael was shaking her head with slow deliberate movements. Jackson was trying to think but all he could do was picture his Mattie's fear and her desperate need to get away.

Jackson's heart was breaking with each beat because the real danger of losing Mattie was palpable. Her mental coping skills may not save her this time. The thought of it made him sick to his stomach and as the bile rose in his throat he had to bolt for the door. Leaving all those present to stare at his retreating back.

Rachael meant to follow him but Lyle halted her with his hand on her battered arm. It was as if she were in slow motion as she glanced up to his handsome face. He was shaking his head in a negative fashion and spoke to her softly. "No Rache. He is hurting too much now to talk or need for comfort. Just give him some time. Ok?" Rachael could only nod her understanding. Lyle bent and kissed her softly. The lump in her throat was too huge to speak around.

Lyle was thinking of the information Blake had given them and spoke to him directly. "Listen this stepfather of Mattie's, did he have any relatives that would want revenge or that other guy that was there? Some retaliation for Mattie's survival and their deaths?"

"Well we can sure check into it to see if it could be an angle." Getting up he opened his office door and barked at someone to get on it. Within ten minutes Blake had a name and possibly the oldest motive for revenge and murder known to man. Money and lots of it. According to what officer Jones had found out Mattie was hip deep with it.

"It appears Lyle you aught to go into detective work. Apparently there was a son the stepfather had from another relationship. He had been left out in the cold when his old man bought the farm. It also appears that Frank, the stepfather, took out life insurance policies on himself and Elizabeth a year before their deaths, naming Mattie the beneficiary."

"What are you saying?" Jackson questioned from the doorway. He had heard every word. "Mattie has no money. Hell she's at college because she won scholarships and she works part-time."

"See that is the strange thing here. Mattie didn't know about the policies or repressed it. According to these figures Mr. Woods your Mattie is very well off." He stated as he scanned the papers on his desk not missing the shocked stare on the young mans face. Blake had pretty well ruled Jackson out as a suspect but he was definitely sure he could now. No one could fake that blank look no matter how good they were.

"If that's the case," Lyle spoke, "then how does the guy think he will get his hands on the money if it belongs to Mattie?"

Damn he liked how this young mans brain worked. "Ah, now that is the million-dollar question isn't it? Let's assume Ray, which is his name, has got it in his head that if Mattie were out of the picture then he being the only living relative that he could collect on all that money. It's my guess Mattie doesn't know the guy exists or she would list him as next of kin on her records. Of which she doesn't. I'd say that puts a new wrinkle in it wouldn't you?" Blake jumped up, and headed for his office door. "Boy's we got a name and we got a motive, how are you on the location?"

"Working on it boss." A young rookie spat out.

"Find it, get a warrant, and make sure everything's ready roll." Blake felt his blood roaring in his ears as it always did when a bust was within reach. He couldn't help admire the young Indian and the way his mind worked. He would be a benefit to the force if he chose. Blake decided to talk to him in the very near future.

Twenty minutes later the break came. "Boss the van was spotted heading toward Hawthorne rise by some local fisherman. Seems some strange men in a white van were spotted up at a friend's old cabin. Since one of those friends happen to be related he knew those guys were uninvited and immediately reported it to one of our boys who was cruising the area. My guess is it's time to rock and roll. Huh boss?"

"Let's do it!" Blake was grateful for snoopy neighbors on rare occasions as it was now. Nothing would keep Jackson from going short of locking him up which was a thought. Blake being who he was felt a wave of pity for the newlywed and agreed he could go, but he was to stay in the car until the area was secured.

Blake felt he might need the young man with Mattie once they got her back. Unethical and not allowed of course, but Blake had always been the rule breaker so why change now? He was uneasy because they didn't know what lay ahead. He couldn't guess what might be waiting for them up there. Lyle and Rachael refused to be left behind, and threatened to go it alone if he didn't let them go along. So they were given the same rules as Jackson had been given.

Jackson couldn't focus on one damn thought. Mattie consumed his entire mind. He refused to believe his life, as he knew it, would be over. He tried to listen to his mother and father's advice when he spoke with them, but his heart hurt and his head wouldn't function right. Everything was a blur. His constant was his Mattie's smiling face. He kept pulling it into focus and repeating her name. She had to be all right. Jackson feared more than her sanity and her health. He feared for his own as well.

Rachael grabbed Lyles and Jackson's hands as they sat in the back of Blake's car. Her heart was in her throat. Rachael had never had so much fear in her life and she couldn't begin to imagine how Mattie survived the first attack. Now she would have to survive a second. Jackson was her lifeline. Mattie loved him so much it was evident in every glance, every word, and every smile towards him. Mattie would survive with Jackson there. Lyle and she would help. They were family and she refused to give up on family.

Lyle held on to Rachael, supporting her battered body, she refused to go the hospital so it was his duty to keep an eye on her. He was also trying to keep his own fear in check by holding her.

They were taking the same path Rachael had been forced to take in a van tied and gagged. Not knowing what was going on. Yet she got away and ran through the woods for help. She just reacted and it probably saved her life in more ways than one. The thoughts that threatened to take over were too full of dread so Lyle pushed them aside. He held her closer and gave silent prayers of thanks.

As it turned out the cabin wasn't far, but it was secluded enough to be missed without proper directions. There were so many police around; it looked like a cop convention. Armed men in uniforms and in black flight suits circled the cabin. It was all set to go down.

Blake made his way as close to the cabin as he could without being seen. He gave signals to the men to prepare. Sweat trickled down his back along the waist of his jeans. The adrenaline made his metabolism run into hyper-drive. The police made their way to the outer walls of the cabin. The windows were open. The breeze was light. The quiet was deafening. When niggling doubt began to work into the equation regarding the right location Blake's doubts were squashed when he heard a loud male voice. The male voice that screamed inside the cabin caused the police surrounding the cabin to freeze in their positions.

"Damn you! I will get satisfaction if I have to cut you to pieces. You'll not cheat me of it Mattie. I've waited too damned long and I won't be denied what's mine. I want to hear you scream and beg. I want you to plead for me to stop. Let's hear it damn you!

The sounds of hard slapping broke the silence that had followed his demands. Angered by no response he mumbled to himself. "Blank eyes, blank face, nobody home Ray. I guess dear old dad did a number on you already didn't he sweetheart? Leave it to the old man to get everything first." He started laughing a twisted, sickening laugh that had those listening cringe with disgust. "Don't worry my precious, ole Ray will still enjoy seeing you die and live it up after the money rolls in. I'll be number one then. Not you. You will be worm bait." He laughed at his own sick joke.

It didn't take a genius to figure out that this guy was beyond crazy. Blake heard all he needed to hear and gave the signal. All hell broke loose in a matter of seconds.

Ray was swarmed with cops at every turn. Bowie knife in hand dripping of fresh blood from the cut he had just executed on Mattie's abdomen. Crazed was a mild description of the total insanity that gleamed within the empty, soulless eyes of the man standing before them. "What the..." was all he managed as the resounding clicking of hammers being thrown back on the multiple guns pointed directly at him.

"Freeze right there you sorry excuse for a human. You're under arrest." Blake was going to love seeing this waste of flesh go down. His gaze went to the cot where the sickest sight he had seen in many years police work greeted him.

The cruelty of it made his stomach lurch. Mattie, he assumed it was her, was bound hand and foot naked to the bed. She had been beaten beyond recognition. Blood trickled everywhere form the cuts running over her arms, legs, chest, and stomach. He feared they were too late. She hadn't even flinched when all the commotion broke out in the room. He hoped she was only in shock, but in his gut he feared it was more than that.

The absence of her chest rising and falling was ominous. Blake could see the sickened stares that crossed his men's faces. This was a cruel destruction of a beautiful young woman. Mattie had her entire life ahead of her with people who loved her and Blake's fear was that it had all ended in the most brutal of ways.

This girl didn't resemble the photos he had looked at earlier and it made him feel sick to his stomach. Knowing the perp was restrained and cuffed Blake made his way to the cot. Mattie's skin was still warm he felt his heart quicken with hope. But when he felt for a carotid pulse along her neck, he didn't find one. A sick dread swept through him as the reality of her death hit him full force.

Mattie was too young to have suffered as she had in her short life. How was he going to tell Jackson? Motioning for the Medics to check her over they confirmed what he already knew to be the truth. She was gone. They had been too late to save her from the cruelty and death that followed it.

The men in the room went still as the reality of the young woman's death was made clear. Death wasn't easy as it was but such a senseless waste of a young woman who never hurt a soul was hard to deal with. The officer's thoughts went out to the three young people who waited outside. The only family this poor girl had. The young husband was going to be devastated. That part of the job was the absolute worst as far a they were concerned. How did you explain this?

Blake didn't have time to react to the heavy footfalls that landed at the cabin door. Too late. "Damn it get him out of..." He didn't finish the words as the soul wrenching scream broke the silence of death that overwhelmed the room. Jackson sounded as if he was dieing right in front of them and God help him he probably was. Never in all the cases where he had to deliver the news had he ever heard such anguish. When he delivered such horrible news the receivers of the news hadn't seen what was done to their loved ones. He wished to God it hadn't happened this time. The sound of such pain and loss from Jackson's mouth cut through his soul like highlander's broadsword.

Jackson's heart stopped when he saw the cops rush the place. He couldn't stand waiting so he leaped out of the car and bolted for the door. The site that greeted him stole his breath away.

He stopped dead. "Dead." He whispered. His Mattie dead. "God No! NO! NO!" He never knew when his feet moved. He stood near the cot looking at Mattie's abused body. His hands shook as he reached for her. He had to touch her. He had to feel her warmth under his fingers. Before his hand graced her pale skin he barely registered a shrilling scream cutting into the cold empty space.

Rachael was at Lyle's side and frozen in agony at her friend's body being lifeless and she swayed as if pushed into Lyle's arms. The blackness took her as Lyle cradled her in his arms, but his thoughts were who was going to catch him? He had to be strong, because Rachael needed him to be. He just didn't know how, when his heart felt like breaking.

To see Mattie like that would take more than Lyle had in him to cope. He backed out of the cabin with the motionless Rachael in his arms. He was numb. No thoughts would come to replace the cold empty dread that was all consuming. Not only for Mattie and Jacks but the selfish, sick knowledge that he was relieved that it wasn't Rachael lying there as well.

He carried her small, limp body to a grassy area and sat with her tightly cradled in his arms. Lyle rocked her while the tears he never shed escaped his blank stare. He cried for the loss Rachael would always suffer, the loss Jackson would never heal from, and for the loss of the light that Mattie had brought into their lives. That light was gone and their worlds would be forever dark

Ray started laughing. "She ain't so pretty now is she lover boy?" "What's that?" "Cat got your tongue?" "Hey, rich kid, are you listening to me?" He taunted with his sick words.

Jackson faintly heard the sick sonofabitch behind him. He refused to acknowledge that he had heard anything. His focus was on his wife, his life. Mattie couldn't be dead. He wouldn't let her. She promised she would always be with him. She had promised to stay with him always. Till death do us part, she had promised the day they were married.

"NOoooooo!!" He screamed and jumped up to face Ray. The look within his eyes was past hatred.

Ray actually flinched as if he had been hit and realized he was trembling.

White-hot rage poured from Jackson. Never in his life did he want to hurt someone as much as he wanted to hurt the scumbag that destroyed his life. The bastard had ripped his heart out and stomped it into nothingness.

The look on Jackson's face didn't go unnoticed by those who were close enough to witness it.

"Back off Jackson." Blake warned. Even though he would love to join him in the task of ripping this piece of shit into tiny shreds; unfortunately he knew he couldn't. It wasn't often Blake witnessed that look but he had seen it, experienced it, and knew no good would become of it.

Jackson whipped around to face his bloody wife's body. "Give me a knife. I won't have her disgraced any further. She's very shy and I refuse to let her be exposed like this. I want her cut free dammit!" Tears flowed as he spoke.

Blake new it was totally against rules, but this wasn't the typical scenario. He would answer for it later it wouldn't be the first time he had his ass chewed nor would it be his last. He nodded to the young rookie who offered his pocketknife to Jackson.

Jackson's eyes blurred and he sank down next to Mattie as he began to saw at the tightly anchored twine that had cut into Mattie's skin. Blood trickled down her damaged wrists making its path down her pale arms. Jackson never felt the nicks he cut into his own fingers as her tried to free his wife of the bonds she had suffered under.

He never heard Ray get carted off. He didn't notice a soul in the room. His focus was on his wife. Once he had her arms free he started on her ankles. He pulled the blanket over her nakedness knowing she would want to be covered. His Mattie was special that way. She would never forgive him if he didn't give her some dignity. Once he freed her, Jackson flung the knife across the floor, to land in a corner of the cabin. His tears had gone unchecked. He didn't notice his own anguish.

Jackson bent and gently lifted Mattie's lifeless body into his embrace whispering his love to her. She felt so warm in his arms. She couldn't be gone. She was so full of life. Wasn't it just this morning she laughed with me after making love? God she couldn't be gone. How was he supposed to live without a heart to beat? Not hearing her laugh or sing. Not having her to love. He would not survive it. God even his soul hurt. Why her? Why? Jackson had no idea there were no dry eyes in the group of officers that surrounded him. He didn't know he had streams of tears coursing down his cheeks.

The cabin was so quiet you could hear heartbeats. Everyone watched. No one moved. Thoughts were consumed with loved ones. Wives, daughters, granddaughters, nieces, sisters, and even cousins. Sometimes life was too unfair and death was too greedy.

Jackson hugged Mattie tighter to his body and he swayed with her in his lap. He sat on the edge of the cot and rocked her. He let out such a moan of raw, all consuming pain it was unbearable to witness.

Chapter Thirty-Seven

"Mattie, honey?" Liz softly spoke to her daughter.

"Yes momma." Mattie felt weightless and detached.

"Mattie it's over now. Your safe and Jackson is waiting for you baby. The game is over now and you need to let him know you are all right. His heart is breaking honey. Give him a sign. It's ok to move now. Hurry baby." Urgency laced Liz's voice. Time was running out. "Gracie tell her. Tell her now before it's too late."

"Mattie girl. You need to listen to your momma and move now. Jackson is waiting for you. Don't keep him guessing girl. You're safe now. Get going child time is wasting. Do it now!"

"OK." Mattie relented. "Will you stay until I go?"

"We will always be with you sweetheart. Now get on with you. Jackson needs you now more than ever."

Mattie's head was cradled at Jackson's neck as he held her in his lap. Rocking her was as natural as loving her had been. The ache that consumed him couldn't be compared to anything he had ever experienced. His life was here in his arms and now she was gone.

Without realizing it Jackson continued to hum to her as he had in the past when he held her. The site of Jackson holding Mattie was hard to see and the emptiness in his soft humming was overbearingly hard to deal with. The sadness he felt bled out into the song he was now singing softly to his dead wife.

The sadness became so unbearably thick within the small room it could be tasted in the air. The misery was overwhelmingly evident to all those who stood in silence around the lifeless girl and the man who held her tenderly within his arms. Hearts were so heavy they struggled to beat out a normal rhythm. The surrounding officers were openly shedding tears and didn't give a good damn who witnessed it. They didn't care. They were human too. Blake heard Jackson singing and watched him stroke Mattie's butchered hair. He kissed her forehead and whispered for her "Oh Mattie, my heart, I can't stand it without you. I love you."

The weeping overtook him in great racking sobs. Holding Mattie so close to his body, Jackson could almost imagine her warm breath on his neck,and her heart beating against his. He wanted those two things so badly he felt as if both were occurring. He groaned as he spoke. "God please don't take her from me." He held her tighter and imagined the warmth of her sweet breath sweep over him again. So consumed with grief he didn't here the soft hush against his skin. Grief had him in knot.

A soft sigh escaped Mattie's lips against Jackson's neck and he knew he had felt it. It wasn't his imagination was it? Had he gone over the deep end? His heart stopped and he froze.

Blake saw the abrupt change in Jackson and wandered what had suddenly gone through his mind. He didn't want to imagine. It couldn't be good.

Jackson sat motionless. Stone moved more than he did and he waited holding his breath. Then, whisper soft, it happened again. It wasn't his imagination. Mattie let out a small unnoticeable breath that only Jackson noticed because he was holding her so closely. Holding his own breath he waited and it happened again. She did it again and then again. Dear God in Heaven thank you. He jerked his head up and locked stares with Blake.

Blake saw the look of shock cross his face and was quickly followed by excitement. The boy must be going into shock. "What is it Jackson?"

Before Jackson found his voice to answer a soft, barely audible, "Jacks" was whispered into the room. The place became tomb quiet. Everyone froze. Who the hell spoke? There weren't any females in the room except one and she was a dead one. Nerves jumped like water in hot oil.

Jackson froze as the soft whisper of his name filled the quiet room. He knew it. Mattie was with him. The sudden joy he felt at that very moment couldn't be measured on any scale known to man. Never in his life had he loved the sound of his own name but at that particular moment it was heavenly. "Mattie, honey, I'm here. I'm here baby. I've been waiting for you"

"Good," was whispered on a heavy sigh.

Mattie was not dead. God had given her back to him. How could he ever repay that kindness? Gratitude washed over him in waves. He smiled.

Blake was almost frozen in place. When he got a grip on himself he moved toward the couple and felt for a carotid pulse that he knew wasn't there before and was shocked to feel it pounding against his fingers. That steady thumping only went with life and that meant she would need medical attention. He jumped up and ran out the door like lightning. "Medics get your asses in here. She is still alive damn you. Alive!" He couldn't help but smile at the shocked look on their faces as well as his men's faces. A hushed whispering could be heard in the room while the medics checked the patient's vitals. Mattie Woods was definitely alive.

Jackson refused to let go of his wife. His miracle. Never again would he let her go. He walked with her toward the ambulance and spotted Lyle. With all his breath he yelled one time which was enough to get his friends attention. Lyle turned to Jackson's voice with a puzzled look on his face.

Lyle saw Jackson caring Mattie's lifeless body. She looked like a rag doll in his arms and he was smiling. So were those beside him. Lyle jumped up and drug Rachael with him. "Jacks?" Lyle questioned as he made his way to the ambulance.

"She is alive. Lyle she is alive. Do you here me? Alive." Jackson was ecstatic. "We are going to the hospital. Get there!" Jackson was already in the ambulance and on his way.

It wasn't a request. It was a demand. Looking to Blake for some assistance in the transportation department he gestured toward the car they had ridden up here in.

Blake grinned and headed for the car without a word passing between them. This was a day he would never forget. Mattie was a dead as dead could be and he knew it. Her coming back was a miracle and he was witness to it. His faith was renewed and the power of love was moved up notch or two in his estimation.

At the hospital Mattie was rushed into surgery for extensive repairs and blood loss. She not only suffered contusions, cuts, and serious bruises. She had suffered several fractured facial bones and ribs. The situation was very serious and her condition was guarded.

The story broke the evening news and Rachael had been deemed the soul reason Mattie was still alive due to her get away. Her own recovery would take a while. She had managed all this time with two broken ribs and fractured wrist. Bruises and cuts not withstanding. She was Jackson's hero. Lyle could only love her more and support her.

Rachael didn't care about any of it. She just wanted her soul sister back with her and healthy. The surgery went on for hours with only periodic reports from a surgical nurse. The information was scarce but at least Mattie was holding on. The local police also set up a vigil consisting of those who were there at the time of discovery and the arrest of a complete psycho. They couldn't walk away from the young woman who had defied the odds and survived. They were involved and sometimes they needed closure in a case too. They also prayed for her. Every little bit helped.

Jackson's parents arrived shortly after he had called them with the news. Blake picked them up on his own time to bring them to the hospital.

Jackson collapsed in his mothers and fathers embrace as soon as they were in the waiting room. The whole family wept for the injustice to such an innocent, sweet person and the insult to their family.

Lyndal waved Lyle and Rachael over and the group hugged and cried for the pain they all shared. They comforted each other as much as they could; knowing that the situation was still a serious one. Mattie may have not had a family when she came here but now she had more than she could have imagined. Jackson prayed she would live to know the amount of love she had now. He silently wept for the woman who meant everything to him.

Jackson's mother watched her son and it broke her heart at the empty cold look his eyes held. Joyce sat beside him and spoke softly. "Want to talk Jacks?"

Jackson searched her face for the sincerity of her request and was moved by the look he saw in her eyes. "You shouldn't be here worrying mom. Your health." He whispered to her.

"My health couldn't be any better. Now talk to me Jacks. What happened to our Mattie?"

Jackson liked how she referred to Mattie as 'our Mattie' and it gave him the courage he needed to recount what had happened.

Joyce spoke softly after hearing a story that made her want to retch. "Jackson, honey, don't give up. Mattie needs all our thoughts and prayers. Do you want to go to the chapel with me?" Joyce waited for a response.

Jackson whipped his head around in his mother's direction. Surprise noted on his expression but he didn't hesitate in his answer. "Yeah, Yeah, I think I do."

Lyndal smiled as he approached after hearing their conversation and gently laid his hand on his wife's shoulder. Facing his son he told him they could go as a family. After three hours of no news regarding Mattie's condition the chapel was less stressful and quiet.

Jackson needed the piece for his thoughts were consumed of Mattie. He prayed, like he never prayed in his life, for his wife and her speedy recovery with his parents at each side. He felt loved and supported more than he ever had before in his life. He just wished it were under better circumstances.

Mattie felt like she was drifting on a bed of clouds. She was weightless and floating along with Liz and Gracie. She didn't want to leave the pleasantness of it and so she stayed with them unaware of any problems or concerns. She felt at total piece for the first time in her life and she embraced it with all her energy. Mattie smiled and enjoyed the ride.

Rachael was exhausted. Never had she been so exhausted and drained. She was so thankful Lyle was with her and holding her. This was one time she didn't fight it. She was glad someone else was taking care of everything. Without Lyle she would have sunk into a misery she feared she wouldn't be able to escape. Mattie had died. The words bounced around in her thoughts without purpose. Tears coursed down her cheeks in tiny rivulets that went unnoticed.

Lyle felt the change in Rachael and he knew she was crying again. "Poor baby," he mumbled into her ear. He had never been any good at comforting females so he felt useless. All he could think to do was to hold her tighter and let her cry out her grief. He had heard a faint sob from her that sounded like,

"I failed." Lyle couldn't believe what he thought he heard. "What?" He waited and yet no answer came. "What did you say Rache?"

"I...I failed her Lyle. I was too late. Too...slow." Rachael began to earnestly cry.

"Rachael. My God sweetheart. You half killed yourself trying to get help. Mattie would be lost forever if you hadn't moved as quickly as you had. I don't want to hear you say that again. You didn't fail. You are the strongest female I know. My little powerhouse. Don't you realize how different things would have been if you hadn't gotten away? Where would you be? I couldn't stand the thought of losing you. I love you. You were so brave and strong and Mattie was lucky you were there for her honey. Don't blame yourself." Lyle held her tighter if that were at all possible.

"Oh Lyle" With that she held onto him for all she was worth and silently wept for her friend until sleep claimed her in the safe haven of Lyle's arms.

After six and a half hours of surgery Mattie was wheeled into recovery. Jackson and his family had returned to the waiting room earlier and sat among friends praying for just a scrap of news regarding Mattie. As if on cue the double doors opened and an older man with white hair appeared wearing surgical scrubs and a weary face.

Feeling exhausted and dreading the conversation to come he searchingly asked for Mr. Woods. When he spotted a young man rising he made his way across the room to him. "Mr. Woods?" He inquired again.

"Yes Sir. How is Mattie? How is my wife? Is she all right? When can I see her?"

"Would you like to speak privately or is this fine?" He gestured at the waiting room.

"Here is fine. We are all here for Mattie. What news do you have?"

The surgeon noted the hope and love in the young mans eyes. He felt damned awful to tell him the news he had regarding his wife. Sometimes in these situations he hated this damned job. "Mr. Woods." Better to get it over with he thought.

"Jackson," the young man corrected.

"Jackson, may we sit? I have been on my feet all day." Making his way to an available chair he lowered his weary bones on the cool vinyl with a small sigh of relief. He felt all eyes on him. That always unnerved him and this time was no exception.

Jackson moved like he was wearing cement shoes. He could feel dread pouring from the older man and he couldn't stand it any longer. "What is it doc?

"Well son. Your wife's condition was pretty grave and we were touch and go there for a while. Her injuries were extensive. I repaired as much damage

255

as I could and the plastic surgeon has done his best with her busted nose and shattered cheekbone. We replaced the blood loss she suffered and we stitched up the massive amount of cuts on her body. However..."

Jackson couldn't stand it anymore so he interrupted the surgeon and demanded the final report on Mattie. He better than anyone knew what she had suffered.

"Listen Jackson. Your wife's injuries were, and still are life-threatening. I know what I was told about the accident and her...well...her death. She is very lucky she survived this long. A miracle is what you've got with your young lady and with a strong will to live."

"I know," he whispered.

The doctor droned on. "My concern is her mentality. She took several damaging blows to her face and head and at this point her brain has begun to swell. It began that the minute she endured the blows she received."

Even after hearing the indrawn breaths of those around them the surgeon continued. He wanted Jackson to know it all. "I think we stopped the bleeding and we are monitoring her intracranial pressure. We have to make sure we keep her pressures down or she will suffer irreparable damage to the brain. The skull doesn't allow for any swelling and in that is where the danger lies. It's not only that son but...well she is in a coma as well. The problem here is we want her to wake as soon as possible. The longer she is in a coma the worse her chances are of coming out of it. Mattie's body has suffered greatly and now we wait and keep her as comfortable as we can."

"What?" Jackson's voice broke the silence. "You're telling me she has survived hell and now she may not even wake up?"

"We don't know that and neither do you. I'm laying all the cards on the table so you will know all the possibilities. I don't know how long she will be in this condition or if she will ever come out of it. All we can do now, is wait and see. It is up to God and Mattie now. Medically we have done all we can."

"Oh my God!" Jackson growled out as he ran his fingers through his hair and dropped his head and wept. His parents encircled him and the bystanders stared in disbelief and shock. The room that had been filled with mumbled excitement fell to a hushed silence.

The surgeon wasn't finished and he didn't know how to continue with the news he still had to deliver. Taking a lung full of air he spoke. "Jackson?" He waited for the young man to look up. "There is more I'm afraid and it is just as serious as everything else I've told you so far."

"I don't know if I can take anymore." Jackson managed to force out.

"Well I don't know how to say this to you. If you had known I'm sure you would have told us, but since you didn't we assumed you didn't know. When we did Mattie's blood work we also ran a HCG test. We routinely do this on young females before treatment. Just in case."

"What the hell is HCG mean?" Jackson's nerves were raw. He wanted this over with.

"Oh. Forgive me. The test is a Human Chorionic Gonadotropin and we use it to determine if...well...Damn I hate this. The test is used to determine if a woman is pregnant. Mattie's was positive Jackson. She is pregnant. The ultrasounds estimation is she's about six to weeks along. Mattie probably didn't even know." If the waiting room was tomb quiet before, it was death silent now.

"How in the hell am I going to handle this too?" Jackson's thoughts were as random as a ping pong ball on a concrete floor. Pregnant? Mattie is pregnant and she was near death and in a coma. Could things be any worse? Yes. She could be dead.

"The thing is Jackson we can wait to see if alls well with Mattie and limit the drugs as much as we can for the babies sake or we can abort the fetus. The choice is up to you and needs to be made soon so we can focus on the treatment of your wife." This job really sucked sometimes. The anguish on that young mans face would haunt his dreams for some time to come and he knew it.

"I couldn't kill our baby. I couldn't do that to her. I couldn't take her baby. God. My baby. We didn't even know. I can't. Don't even ask me to do that. I just can't." Jackson stumbled as he jumped up and staggered to the stairs. He couldn't wait for the elevator. He couldn't breath. His heart hurt. The tears streamed unchecked down his unshaven cheek. He wished someone would pull the hot poker out of his chest.

"Mattie," he groaned as he weaved from side to side in the stairwell. Lack of sleep and tear-filled eyes prevented seeing much of anything. Jackson made his way to the hospital gardens. He openly wept for everything. For Mattie, for himself, for the future, and for the unborn child he now knew Mattie carried. He cried until no more tears would come. "God? Hasn't she suffered enough?" He turned his face skyward as he waited for answers. "Why can't she just be happy?" Jackson was so empty he was surprised his thoughts didn't echo.

"Jackson?" Lyndal was standing near the bench waiting. His son had the weight of the world on his young shoulders and there wasn't a darn thing he. He waited for him to look up letting him know he'd heard him.

The pain and anguish he saw in his son's eyes was like that he had witnessed during the war. He didn't know what to do for his men then and now he stood facing his son still not knowing what to do. He did know he would support him. No matter what he decided.

"Dad what am I going to do?" Hesitating he admitted his own despair. "I can't think straight. Just knowing Mattie is fighting for her life was hard enough but to know there is a little life growing and I'm supposed to decide who to choose. How do I do that? Mattie's heart would break if she knew I had decided to end a precious gift and I don't think I can do that dad. I don't know anything anymore. I'm empty and so damn tired." Jackson dropped his head, slumping his shoulders, and cried anew. He looked beaten.

Lyndal embraced his son in a tell-all-hug. He had no answers but he would not let his son go through this alone. He and Joyce would give him all the love and support they could.

"Jacks I want you to listen to me. Mattie is a fighter. She has proven that time and time again because she has had to deal with so much. More than most ever have had to deal with. She won't quit, she won't give up, and she will need you to be strong for her. If I know Mattie, and she knew about that baby, I have no doubt that she would fight even harder."

"I know dad. I know it here," he tapped his chest, "it's here," as he tapped his head, "I'm having trouble with. I can't think straight. I'm just so confused."

"Jacks, I don't have any answers but I will go to the chapel with you. We can pray for God to do his work because it is up to him now. I love that wife of yours son. You couldn't have chosen a better person to share your life with. If all I can do is lend my strength by being here or praying, then that is what I will do."

"So will we Jackson." Lyle added.

Jackson had never known Lyle to pray for anything and the offer of it touched Jackson's heart. He looked up to his friend and found his entire family there. Yes, Lyle and Rachael were his family too and his heart fluttered with the knowledge they were there. He wasn't alone in this. Would Mattie ever know how these people loved her? Yeah. Mattie would. She is that kind of person.

Gathering his strength he said "Ok, let's go. Mattie needs everything we can give her." The small group headed for the hospital chapel and Jackson abruptly stopped when he focused on several police officers that were bent in prayer. Jackson felt blessed with such concern for his wife. The small group gathered and began their vigil for the young woman who was struggling for her life and the life of an unborn child she didn't know she carried.

"Mattie?" Liz spoke softy to her daughter.

"Mattie, girl. Are you with us honey?" Gracie spoke in a soft tone as well.

"I'm here. Momma, Gracie where did you go? I was getting scared being here all alone."

"We only left for a little while honey. We are staying with you this time until you're healed up enough to wake up. Your body has been hurt pretty bad and you need to rest so you can heal. You have to get better so you can take care of your baby."

"Baby?" Mattie was puzzled at what her mother had just said.

"Yes honey, a baby. You have my grandbaby in there," as she patted Mattie's belly, "and we need to get you better so you can take care of her. That's right honey. A little girl is growing inside of you and she is going to need you to take care of yourself, for her sake, as well as your own."

"A baby? A baby girl? Oh momma. I didn't know. Jackson doesn't know either. Are you sure?"

"Honey, we got out information from the higher ups. We were told to stay with you until it was time."

"Time? For what?" Mattie curiously asked.

"Well, time for you to wake up for Jackson and the people who love you, of course."

"Ok, can I rest now? I am kind of tired."

"You close your eyes honey and we will keep you safe while you rest."

"All right. I'm just so...tired." She yawned as she fell into a healing sleep cuddled in her mother's warm embrace.

The day's drug on, from one endless misery right into another. Jackson couldn't rest, couldn't eat, couldn't think, and couldn't even focus anymore. The ICU would only let him stay for a few minutes at each visit no matter how much he begged, threatened, or attempted to bribe. He was always there when the time was allowed for him to sit with Mattie.

He wiped her pale face being mindful of her bandages and stitches. He held her limp, cool hand in his while he talked to her. He monitored each assisted breath she was given and the heart monitor that told him she was still with him. Her expression was so peaceful that it gave him some peace of mind. She didn't seem to be in pain, thanks to diligent nurses, and wonderful pain meds. Mattie had more bandages than exposed skin.

His stomach still gripped when he looked at her short hair, the result of the attack and then the surgery. She didn't resemble his Mattie except for his ring on her finger. The pleasant reminder, that she was his. Jackson was very pleased that there hadn't been any further brain swelling and the doctors seemed to lesson that as a priority.

Jackson was apprehensive. Today the doctors decided to attempt removal of the breathing tube. They said the sooner she got off the device the better for her in the long run. It had been told to him that some people were unable to breathe without it after a time. Jackson had to believe that wouldn't happen to his Mattie. The numbers were in her favor and she was stable now. If they could get her off the ventilator and she stayed stable a few more days then they may be able to move her to a private room. Jackson wanted that. He would be able to spend as much time with her as he wanted to. That thought brought a smile to his bearded face. He might take time to shave then, but not until then. He wouldn't lose a minute of time he could spend with her, on his own looks. He didn't care what he looked like.

"Well Jackson," the doctor boomed as he entered the small curtained room, "are you ready to get this show on the road? Are you ready to see if Mattie is ready to make a step up?"

"If you think she's ready, then yeah."

"We've been weaning her from the machine for brief periods and she has responded well, so everything looks very good. What do you say we give her a chance to prove her stuff?"

Everyone, friends and family alike, waited anxiously lounge. All thoughts and prayers were for Mattie. In the cubicle the doctor on one side and an ICU nurse on the other. Mattie's hands had been restrained to prevent involuntarily pulling the breathing tube out, but Jackson still held her hand. The machine was shut off and they waited.

Jackson held his breath and sat frozen. It felt like hours when it really was only seconds. A gasp broke the silence. Then a pause and another gasp. The cycle continued and Jackson sighed when he saw her breathing on her own and when the doctor grinned at him he knew she was ready to graduate.

His relief to see that piece of equipment removed was immeasurable. The doctor explained the need to assist her oxygen with a mask until she became more stable and that was fine with Jackson. She still had packing in her nose from the reconstructive surgery so a mask made more sense to him anyway.

The nurse was going to give Mattie a bath but Jackson convinced her he could do it without all those tubes in the way. The nurse even allowed him the extra time to do the deed.

It was the first time for him to see all of Mattie since that day at the cabin. He didn't know what to expect but he felt he could handle it. He removed her gown with the nurse's help getting around the IV's and she gave him instructions on the chest tube and other paraphernalia that invaded Mattie's body. He had to be real careful with her bandages.

Jackson had brought Mattie's entire bath supply from home for when she could take a bath herself, but he wanted to treat her to it now. He wanted her to smell like his Mattie; not a medicine cabinet.

Jackson gradually bathed his battered wife. He took note of the bruises that were turning a sickly yellow and ugly purple. The cuts were stitched and healing well. He saw the scabs on some cuts. That was a good sign he told himself. His stomach rolled as he viewed her upper torso. There were very few places that didn't sport a bruise or a cut.

"How you must have suffered Matt," he whispered as he continued with her bath. Being mindful of the chest tube he knew it was to keep her lung from collapsing again and he didn't want to mess with that. He made his way to her belly and realized he hadn't given much thought to the little life they had created that was living in there.

He was thankful he hadn't had to make any decisions on that score, because Mattie's body was doing all the work to keep the little one safe. The baby was growing but he couldn't think rationally about that yet. He had all the worry he could handle just focusing on Mattie. He loved his baby but he couldn't make himself think of anyone but his wife. Not yet. Mattie was his number one priority.

Her beautiful long legs were cut more than bruised. She didn't have too many stitches there. Mattie wouldn't care how they looked as long as she could run. At least that was his hope. The bath being completed and her new gown in place she looked as if she were merely sleeping.

Jackson felt a little lighter now. She was getting better. If only she would wake up. He was ushered out of her room as soon as he was finished. He went willingly this time. She was growing healthier, and that alone gave him hope. Just the flicker of hope, but it was hope, just the same.

Jackson walked into a crowded waiting room of anxious faces. If Mattie could see this he thought. He couldn't hide the pleasure he felt and broke into a face splitting grin. He hadn't told them the news because he didn't want to lose the time with Mattie by coming out here. He almost felt bad for not letting them all know sooner. To stay and bathe her was worth it.

"Mattie is breathing on her own now. The vent is not needed anymore." The whoops and hollers that information elicited warranted a reprimand from the nurses. That didn't lesson the mood or the excitement everyone felt. After weeks of no changes this was a giant leap. Mattie was holding her own, for now and that warranted a shout of cheer.

Everyone knew she had a long way to go yet but this was a positive step in a basketful of negatives. The news would spread be it by word of mouth or by the paper.

The papers had followed the story since day one and the outpouring of support was over abundant and welcomed. The renewal of faith and hope would continue to grow with this news. Mattie would hate to be the center of attention but she would love knowing she was responsible for people helping each other in a time of need. That was how his Mattie was. Jackson smiled with the thought.

Joyce and Lyndal sighed with relief at the news. Now they could enforce some R&R on their son. He had dark circles under his eyes. He had lost weight because he didn't eat. He was a shadow of himself. They knew he hadn't slept except for bits and snatches here and there. Well, things were going to change and they decided it was up to them to make sure he did what he was told for once in his adult life.

Besides he was too tired to argue the point. Lyle was in full agreement and they were ready with their plan.

"Jackson, now that Mattie is better and she is stable, why don't you try to get some rest?" Joyce used her most pleading tone she could muster up.

"I can't Mom. I won't leave." His words were meant to be strong but they were a weak as cooked pasta.

"Jacks. You are going to be in bed right beside Mattie if you don't take care of yourself. She is going to need you even more as time passes son. You're not going to be able to keep this pace up much longer before you collapse. Your health is suffering. Just what do you think Mattie would say if she knew what you were doing?"

"I can't...I can't go back to the apartment Mom." He whispered. "It won't be the same without her there. I just can't go there."

"Come home with me Jacks." Lyle spoke up grabbing his attention. "It wouldn't be the first time you bunked at my place. Come on man, your beginning to stink and you're starting to look like a wild man with all that facial hair. Quite bluntly you look like hell." Lyle thought some humor wouldn't hurt. He was pleased he had scored a response.

Jackson half smiled up at his friend. "Always the charmer, huh Lyle? Since I offend your nose so much maybe I should continue with this new look and odor. It could grow on you after a while."

This was more like it. "There already is something growing on you and I don't dare try to figure out what it is. For that matter I don't want it to grow on me. You smell and you need some food."

"I could use a shave. I don't want Mattie to throw me out because I reek. Ok. Mom I'll go with Lyle for a while but you have to promise to call me if there is any news."

"Now Jackson you know I will." Joyce was pleased with this turn of events. Apparently Lyndal was too if the pressure he was putting on her hand was any indication. The room of people seemed to sigh with the relief that Jackson was going to get some rest and a well-needed meal. He hadn't left the hospital since Mattie had been brought in.

Lyle stopped by the local Steak-n-Shake on the way home. He took it upon himself to order two of the largest meals on the menu for each of them. It may not be healthy but it was food and that was all that mattered right now.

Pointing Jackson toward the shower and handed him a change of clothes as he went. Lyle set about getting the table ready for the impromptu meal.

Jackson did feel better after the shower and shave. In fact he hadn't felt good in a long time. It was a good thing Mattie hadn't seen him. He looked down right scary.

The meal was harder to choke down. He wasn't hungry but realized he hadn't eaten much in far too long and he was wasting away.

Lyle spoke as he watched Jackson choke down his food. "Mattie is going to be ok Jacks. I know it. I can feel it."

"I know she has to Lyle. I can't lose her. I wouldn't survive it. It's amazing how much my life was lacking until she came into it. Right now I feel like half of me was ripped away and I can't function as half a person."

"Don't worry Jacks. Mattie is a fighter. My God she has managed it all so far. She's not a quitter and she won't give up. If she knew about the baby she would fight even harder."

"A baby Lyle. We didn't know and now..." he couldn't finish his train of thought.

"Listen to me Rich kid. No God would be so cruel to take her and the baby from you. He has allowed her this much time and the baby is in perfect health according to the ultrasounds they keep doing on her. She wouldn't make the progress she was if weren't meant for her to come back to us." Lyle knew he had to make him think positively or his friend could slide into a depression that could take him away.

"Yeah. You could be right, but..." he hesitated, "Damn Lyle I'm so tired I can't think straight."

"Would you quit flapping your gums and eat the food I slaved over just for you so you can hit the sack? And before you ask it. Yes, I will wake you if there is any news. Now eat."

"Thanks Chief." He smiled at his lifelong friend and began to eat in earnest. Amazing how he managed it but the whole meal disappeared and the sleep began to wage its war on his exhausted body. Jackson began to nod off at the table.

Lyle smiled at him and stood pointing to the bedroom. "Hit it before you hit the floor."

Jackson got up and staggered his way to Lyle's side and placed his hand on Lyle's shoulder. "Thanks friend," then he headed for the bedroom. Without undressing he fell on the bedspread and surrendered to the blackness that invited him. He didn't dream, he didn't move, he only slept.

After a couple of hours of uninterrupted sleep Lyle checked on him to make sure all was well. "Good," he whispered as he looked upon the prostrate form still deeply sleeping. Just what he needed.

Lyle backed out of the room and picked up the phone. He knew Joyce would want to know how Jackson was doing. At least he had eaten and was catching some much-needed sleep.

"I'm so glad to hear it Lyle. Thank you. You have been there for Jacks since you were boys. You have always been there even when we weren't. I'm glad he has had you for a friend."

"Jackson is the brother I didn't have Joyce. There's nothing I wouldn't do for him."

"We appreciate everything. I'll call you if anything changes here."

"Ok. Keep me posted." Lyle hung up feeling he was accepted and it was a rather good feeling. Especially after all the years he hadn't been. Some good things do come out of bad situations.

Jackson stretched like a cat and groaned at his stiff back. He slowly opened his eyes. The room was dark as pitch and for a minute he didn't know where he was. Reality came in a flood. "Oh damn," he muttered in the darkness. "Lyle what time is it?" He demanded as he made his way to the side of the bed.

Focusing on the red numbers on the clock he groaned. It was nine thirty. How could I have slept so long? He jumped off the bed and staggered like a drunk as he grabbed for the door facing. The apartment was dark and quiet. He spotted Lyle in the kitchen and made his way over and leaned into the counter. "Any word? How's Mattie?"

"Geeze Jacks are you trying to cause me to have a heart attack? Dammit man don't sneak up on people like that. It's unnerving!"

"Sorry, any word?"

"I called the hospital. Your mom says no change."

Jackson's shoulders slumped. No change meant no worse. Which was good. However that also meant no better.

Lyle saw the changes in his friend's posture and the frown that creased his brow. Knowing Jackson as he did Lyle felt he would make the only suggestion that he would accept. "Listen, let's say we eat this grilled cheese and some soup and we make tracks for the hospital?"

That elicited the response he wanted. "Great."

The days continued to pass. It would seem that one ran into the other and another like ripples a stone makes breaking the surface of a still winter pond. An unspoken number of shifts were created for visits, baths, and quality time to be spent at Mattie's side. Jackson made sure she was never left alone and if she was it was too brief to mention and even then he kept the radio going.

One morning during his routine rounds the doctor informed Jackson that the chest tube could be removed. The chest x-rays looked good and Mattie's lung had returned to normal functions. After the successful removal of the tube and a dressing was applied the doctor told Jackson that Mattie would be able to go to her own room that day. He saw no reason to keep her in Intensive Care when she had improved so much.

Jackson was relieved and a little nervous at the same time. He had been wanting Mattie in her own room for a long time so he could stay with her but then again he was afraid she wouldn't get the same one on one attention she got here. "Are you sure?"

"I couldn't be surer. Jackson she has held her own for some time now. Mattie may still be in a coma but her body is healing rather nicely. I couldn't begin to tell you how pleased all of us are with the progress she has made. And besides you'll be granted unlimited visit time with her in a private room of her own. You even stay the nights with her on a monitored floor."

"Great! When can we move her then?"

"Just as soon as we get it all arranged. We will still need to keep her heart on a monitor and since she has the head injury I want her transferred to the Neurological floor. That way if there is any change it will be detected a little earlier than if she was on a Medical floor.

The nurses will let you know when it's all set. Now don't worry so much. That little lady is the strongest willed person I have ever had the pleasure to work with. Mattie has a guardian angle on her shoulder."

"Ok. Thanks Doc." Jackson shook his hand before the doctor left. He knew what the doctor said was true but he still felt like he should ask all the questions anyway.

Within three hours a bed was available for Mattie and she was transferred to Neuro. It was exactly what Jackson wanted. The move meant more freedom to be with his wife, without someone tapping their wristwatch like he was in some competition.

Mattie never wanted for company. Her days were full of stories; music, one way conversations, and physical therapy followed by a lotion rub down. Jackson should be certified by now he had gotten so adept at the treatments.

Rachael read her poems from her little red book. Lyle played any CD he could find, and Jackson took care of most everything else. Jackson's mom and dad also took turns with the various entertainment selections. If only Mattie knew how lucky she was. All she had to do was open those tiger-eyes and see the love people had for her.

Physical Therapy continued to exercise her muscles to prevent wasting from lack of use. Her bruises were fading to only hints of discolored areas. The stitches were dwindling and her cuts were healing. Her nose wasn't swollen as much and the bandages were all gone from her head. The road to good health kept getting smoother. Mattie didn't need oxygen anymore but she still had her IV's and her catheter that drained her bladder. Which noting the color didn't resemble Hawaiian punch anymore was a real good sign her kidneys had survived the bruising they took.

The baby remained healthy and continued to grow. The Obstetrician who saw her said everything looked real good from her standpoint. Her only concern had been the medications Mattie had been treated with over the past couple of weeks.

The coma was the largest concern at this point. They needed for her to come out of it. Soon.

One night Jackson sat at her bedside holding her hand as he had countless times in the past and spoke soothing words telling her his desires. "Mattie, I sure miss you. I miss your laugh, your voice, and having your body next to mine. I want you home with me. I want us to be together. I want us to watch our baby grow inside you. I don't know if you heard me talk to them about the baby but the doctors say everything is ok. We just need for you to wake up now. Life is so empty and boring without you in it. I want us to be a family again. Please honey. Wake up." Jackson waited for some response. He didn't receive one.

The only responses he did get were periodic twitches that he was informed occurred in coma patients. Sighing he raised up and kissed her forehead.

"I love you. Please come home to me," he whispered against her cool skin. Jackson made his way to the window and gazed out at the dancing twinkling stars. He searched for the brightest one so he could make his nightly wish. Leaning his head against the cool glass he sighed and felt as weary as a man three times his age. How long he stood there he had no idea. He roused himself after a prickly feeling crept up his neck. The kind of prickly sensation you get when someone is staring at you. "Imagination is a powerful thing Jacks." He chuckled at his own thoughts. He sighed again and turned to continue his vigil with Mattie. He didn't make it.

Jackson froze in his tracks. Did he wish it so hard that he was seeing things? Rubbing his eyes he whispered a silent plea that he wasn't seeing things. Nope. He didn't wish it into being.

Mattie was looking at him. Rushing to her bedside he spoke raggedly. "Mattie?" Yes, her eyes were definitely open. One was bloodshot badly but other than that they appeared to be all right. He became anxious with the blank look he saw and the fact she hadn't moved or said a thing. Jackson pounded on the Nurses call button.

Impatience taking over he began to yell for the nurse to hurry up. He stroked Mattie's hair and her cheek as he spoke to her. "Mattie honey can you hear me? It's Jackson baby. Can you hear me?" No response. Her stare was unnerving and empty of any emotion.

"Mattie can you see me? " He whispered. Hope that her sight hadn't been damaged was running thin. Impatiently waiting for the nurse Jackson kept talking to her.

The nurse rushed to the bedside and checked Mattie's pupils for reactions to the flashlight she used and she was pleased to note both eyes had reactive pupils. The nurse checked her blood pressure, heart rate, and temperature so she could report all the changes to the doctor.

"What's wrong?" Jackson demanded. "Why doesn't she respond to me?"

"Jackson I don't have the answers for you but I can tell you any response is a positive one. This does mean she hasn't slipped into a deep coma. Your wife suffered a serious trauma. Let me call the Doc and we'll leave the guesswork to him." She noticed that Mattie had responded to some of her physical examinations with twitches and signs of withdrawal from pain while she was there. That blank stare didn't change and in her opinion this young couple still had a long road to travel before things were any semblance of normal. "Remember to keep talking to her Jackson and let her know your here with her. I'm sure she already knows that but it wouldn't hurt to keep reminding her."

Jackson called his mother with the changes in Mattie's condition and hung up with her promise to notify everyone else. Jackson talked to Mattie with everything he could possibly think of while he touched her and stroked her hair. He had noticed she would flinch when he came near her eyes an unconscious response but a response just the same. He refused to think negatively. He would wait for the doctor's opinion.

The Doctor ran more scans, more x-rays, test after test, as the days drug by with still no answers from anyone. It was a relief to note she was in very good physical health but her mental health was still the main area of concern. As soon as the Doctor entered the room he was hit with a barrage of questions about Mattie. "What's wrong Doc? Why won't she respond to me or for that matter to any of us?"

"Jackson your wife suffered a severe trauma and in order to protect herself she withdrew into the recesses of her mind. I'm afraid there is a chance she may not ever come out of it and then again she could come out of it with no ill effects. The mind is still a mystery to us and we don't know all the intricate detailed workings it is capable of. We have to wait and see. I'm sorry Jackson but that is the facts. Just don't give up hope."

"What about her physical abilities? Will she be able to get up and move around and eat and stuff like that?"

"Well. Yes. Mattie can still function with direction. I know you have continued with her exercises and her muscles haven't deteriorated as some do but she will still need to be introduced to new activities slowly adding a little

267

each day. I'll make sure that physical therapy sees her on a daily basis for walking exercises. Jackson don't give up. Your Mattie has been through hell and back and I have a feeling she's not through fighting yet." With that the Doctor left the room with a hopeful Jackson smiling down at his wife. "You keep fighting honey and I'll be here waiting for you. I love you Mattie and don't you forget it."

The nurse showed Jackson how to feed Mattie liquids when she responded more. At first she wouldn't swallow and the liquid would run out of her mouth but as the days past she began to take some of the broth without choking. Jackson felt a little lighter of spirit just knowing she was improving a little more each day.

Mattie was getting better and he was able to do more with her. Jackson decided that when she was strong enough he wanted to take her to the hospital flower garden for an evening walk. He knew that would brighten her spirits the way she loved flowers and nature. Before he was done feeding her she was probably wearing as much as she ate.

That didn't deter Jackson. He would just get better at it with the more practice he had. Not only would Mattie get some nutrition but the baby would too. He was beginning to accept the baby as a reality now that Mattie was on the mend. He couldn't separate his thoughts before, but now it made him smile to think of their child.

It would be a beautiful little girl just like her momma. Jackson found himself grinning at the mere thought of his daughter being held to Mattie's breast. He was in a better mood and found himself talking to his baby with the affection he now could spare for her. She was important too.

Everyone continued to work in shifts with Mattie. They had her up and moving with a walker as soon as the Intravenous fluids and catheter were removed. It was the first ambulation she was exercised with and then when her strength improved they could hold onto her and walk with her.

She never did anything on her own. She was like a robot. All you had to do was point her in the direction you wanted her to go and guide her into whatever motions you wanted. Her face remained blank and expressionless.

Hope was dwindling but had not been abandoned. Jackson kept everyone positive even when he felt beaten. He knew Mattie would come back to him. He had no other choice but to believe that.

As sleep eluded Jackson as it had most nights he blankly stared at the television not registering what was on. Mattie appeared to sleep calmly. No nightmares. Hell, she barely resembled the living anymore. The days had drifted from one into another and her condition had remained the same. He was exhausted and feeling sorry for himself. He had the right to, didn't he? He felt alone with his thoughts and a restlessness that wouldn't quit nipping at his heels. Jackson made his way to the window as he had thousands of times already and looked into the starlit night. The sky was blue black and cloudless. His thoughts and prayers were centered on his wife and baby as they always were.

Sighing deeply he lowered his head and prayed the same prayer he had since Mattie's attack. To bring Mattie back to him. He knew it was redundant to ask for the same thing and that God would know the prayer before he even opened his mouth but Jackson figured eventually God would get sick of hearing it and let his Mattie come back to him. Lame he knew, but it was worth the effort. He would do anything for her.

Feeling out of sorts he decided a hot cup of cocoa was in order. He had learned along time ago to alternate the bad coffee and the mediocre cocoa to break the monotony. He made his way to the hot beverage machine and punched his selection. Resting his head on the machine while he waited; keeping his mind as blank as he felt.

The nurses knew Jackson was devoted to his wife and they had come to be good friends with the young man. Judy, the Registered Nurse on duty at night had really gotten close to the couple since she had the opportunity to spend some time with them and talking with Jackson during his sleepless nights.

It would appear he was having one of those nights again. He looked so lost standing there using the coffee machine to hold him up. It amazed her the way he took care of Mattie. He was at her side most of the time and had been for weeks. The hours of worry and strain of sleepless nights were beginning show in the lines on his face. The poor man was exhausted and she knew not to say anything it was a useless argument.

"Long night Jackson?" A question she had asked many times before. He looked so drained it broke her heart. They should be enjoying their life together they shouldn't have to suffer with this injustice.

"Yeah. Same-o-same-o. I feel rode hard and put up wet." He smiled a smile that didn't reach his eyes. He was as empty as that smile, sad thing was, even he knew it.

"Don't get discouraged Jackson. I know you hear that over and over, but it's the best advice I've got." Judy smiled sadly for the young man.

"It's very hard not to Judy. I wish the nightmare would end. I can't remember when...Oh never mind. Ignore me I'm just too tired to think straight. So how is tonight? Been as crazy as it was last night?" He had gotten good at changing the subject.

Judy knew the ploy and didn't question it. "It's better tonight since all our beds are full and we can't get hammered with admissions. That makes a big difference especially when we're short-staffed most of the time. Thanks for asking."

"You Nurses work too hard. I ought to know I see it all day and night. If people knew what you all had to do they would be a little more sympathetic and less demanding but we both know that is unrealistic don't we?"

"Yeah. Like you said. Same-o-same-o. The ones who understand are those who spend some time here and see for themselves. That's not the case with most patients since they are in and out so fast. We keep hoping it will get better." Judy shrugged her shoulders giving her opinion with the action. She knew it wouldn't get any better, but yet she kept up the hope that it would.

"Well Judy I guess..." The ear splitting scream stopped him in mid sentence. Jackson stared at Judy.

Surely he hadn't heard what just pierced the quiet night. The scream ripped through the air again and before it was finished he was running. It was Mattie.

He flew into her room focusing on the bed where he had left her and it was empty. "What the hell?" He demanded revealing his nervous confusion at not seeing his wife where he had left her. The room was dark except for the light coming from the TV and the hall. The scream made the hair on Jackson's neck stand on end.

Mattie had scurried to the corner and was huddled there staring at the television. Jackson went to her. He couldn't think or feel. He felt numb. Jackson followed Mattie's line of vision to the TV. And swore at what he saw. How could he be so careless to have left the thing on? "Oh shit. Turn that damn thing off." The scene was so much like what she had gone through no wander she lost it. The hall light illuminated Mattie's face and the fear he saw stabbed him right in the heart.

Granted it was the most emotion he had seen on her face since the attack but if that was what he had to witness he would rather she remained with a blank stare. His blood ran cold at the sight. Jackson squatted in front of Mattie and slowly reached for her. He didn't want to scare her anymore than she was. He didn't know how she would react to his holding her but he was relieved that she didn't scream or pull away from him.

She had gone back to being the zombie she had been for so long he wasn't surprised to see it. Jackson gathered her into his arms and held her as he felt her trembling subside. She felt so good in his arms. He hadn't held her since the day at the cabin when he carried her to the ambulance. He didn't want to risk any set backs by holding her the way he wanted to.

God, how he had missed holding her and showering her with his love. His heart ached for her, for them. The tears ran down his cheeks unchecked. He had cried so much of late, he was surprised he had any tears left.

He was trapped in the misery of his wife's pain and all he could do was let it run its course. He hugged her close, rubbed her back, and talked to her with loving words meant only for her ears.

Judy backed out of the room wiping away her own tears. The sight of Jackson holding onto the shell of his wife as if she were made of bone china was her undoing. How lucky Mattie was to have someone love her so much. Judy sent her prayers up for the couple. It hadn't been the first one or the last.

Jackson didn't know how long he sat there with Mattie in his arms but he knew she was asleep because her breathing had slowed.

He just hadn't wanted to give up the contact. Lifting her slight body he placed her on the bed and covered her with the pristine white sheet. Jackson lightly caressed her face with his palm and kissed her softly on the lips. He really missed her smile and the laughter she had just discovered before it ripped away.

Jackson's eyes followed the curves of her body and noted the changes her illness and pregnancy was taking on her. She was thinner but her breasts were rounder and her belly was swelling more with their child. He removed the top sheet and lifted her gown. He wanted to look at her. Gently, he placed his palm on the swell of their baby and smiled.

Their precious baby was growing and he hoped Mattie wouldn't miss the wonder of it. Jackson kept his hand on her for the sheer pleasure of touching her and his baby. It was the most sensual and relaxing feeling he had experienced in weeks. He kicked off his shoes and climbed onto the bed. Resting his head on the pillow he fell into a sound sleep, cradling his wife in the crook of his arm. Something he hadn't been able to do since his life had been turned upside down.

The doctor came by later that morning. The nurse and Jackson related what had happened in the wee hours of the morning and much to Jackson's shock the Doctor smiled. Was he crazy? "I wish you would let me in on the joke. What the hell is so funny about my wife being scared half to death?" He snapped angrily.

"No Jackson you misunderstand. I'm not happy about her fright. Don't you see Mattie is a lot closer than we thought? If she responded to a television show it means she is close to the surface. Jackson, don't you see, this is a very good sign. The sign we have been waiting for. Mattie reacted to her surroundings the only way she could for now. It is most important, now more than ever before, to talk to her convince her she is safe. Draw her out. Let her know she isn't alone. Just keep doing what you're doing Jackson it must be working or she wouldn't have responded to a mere television show regardless of what it was."

"I hadn't looked at it that way Doc. You mean regardless of how scary it was it's a good thing she reacted? This is good news then. Mattie is coming back to me isn't she?" Jackson smile was like a beacon in a storm. He felt his heart swell with happiness.

This was the best news he had in too many weeks to count. He had to tell his friends and family. Lyle and Rachael would be the first he would call. They were as close as friends could be. His parents would be the next after that he would leave it up to his mom to notify.

He knew the papers would pick it up since they still occasionally wrote about Mattie. That was fine too. It had amazed him how the community supported him and Mattie since the whole mess was made public. This was good news indeed.

"If I were a betting man? I would say Mattie is taking baby steps, making her way back. Now it's up to us too make sure she makes it." The doctor hadn't missed the glow he saw in the young mans eyes. It was the first time he had seen a genuine smile on his face and he realized the young man was rather handsome.

He had known all along how much the kid loved his wife because he hadn't ever seen anyone as attentive as Jackson was. He was so young but he was devoted and diligent something he didn't see in older men. Mattie was a very lucky young lady. If only the rest of the world could have that, it would be a better place to live in.

Shaking Jackson's hand he went to see his other patients. This case was going to end the way it should always be. A happy ending. He saw so few he was thrilled this would end right. His step was lighter and he whistled as he made his way down the hall.

Jackson was so happy. "Did you hear that Judy?" Jackson hugged her and spun her around and around. "Mattie is on her way back. Isn't that the best news?" He put her down and rushed to the nearest phone leaving Judy with her mouth gapping open. Mattie was definitely a lucky woman.

Everyone was buzzing with the news of Mattie's reaction and her prognosis of a full recovery. It was all up to Mattie now. Her friends and family would help as much as they could.

The days that passed didn't seem so heavy and long. Spirits were high and almost tangible. Shifts were created so Mattie would have variety and everyone insisted on Jackson getting more rest. He didn't want to leave her side for fear she would come back and he wouldn't be there for her. He didn't want that. He wanted his to be the first face she saw when she finally snapped out of it. But his friends insisted he take breaks so they could spend some time with her too which was the case one afternoon when Rachael came to visit.

272

"Listen Jacks I know Mattie is your wife and all, but she's my sister and your monopolizing her time. I need to have a little female quality time with her if you don't mind. Now go on. Get a cup of coffee or something. Shoot go visit Lyle for a while or go get some sleep. You look like hell. You'll probably scare poor Mattie half to death with the way you look right now."

Rachael gave him the sassy little smile he had come to love about her. She had turned out to be the best friend a guy could have and that was something he didn't think he would ever be able to claim. A female friend. No wander Lyle had fallen head over heals for the little package. Rachael was an endless supply of energy and support. Yep, he was lucky having her in his life especially considering the rough start they'd had. He smiled back at her. "Are you trying to say something? Well don't beat the bush to death come on out and say it shrimp."

"Well duh. How many ways can a girl say it? You need a bath in a real bad way and you need to shave that facial fuzz. Mattie would run screaming the other way if she saw you right now. Go to Lyle's and get some rest. If not that at least go clean up while Mattie and I have a little female bonding. Go on." Rachael shooed him off like a pesky bug in her way.

"You're a real good friend Rache. Thanks for everything." He surprised her just as much as he had himself when he hugged her. It felt like the right thing to do so he did it. "I think I'll take your advice and get cleaned up. Besides, Lyle needs a kick in the butt. I can't believe he hasn't popped the question to you yet. I know he loves you. Heck a blind man could see that."

Rachael blushed. Something she didn't do very often. Lifting her hand she sported a diamond on her left hand. A diamond Lyle had placed on her hand just the night before on bended knee. It was the most romantic night of her life and much to her surprise and pleasure her parents were thrilled.

Rachael loved Lyle more than she thought was possible. Seeing how Mattie and Jackson were together was a terrific template for their relationship. They were the personification of love. "He already did Jacks." She sighed as she watched the light dance on the facets.

"Well son of a gun. He has got a brain after all. I was beginning to worry about my friend if he didn't start to see what was as plain as the nose on his face. Congratulations Rachael. I think it's time I go rub his nose it in just for the sheer pleasure of it. Remember how he taunted me about Mattie? Now it's his turn. I'll be back in an hour or so, if that's alright?" Jackson turned to walk away and Rachael grabbed his arm.

"Mattie will be our Mattie again soon Jacks. I have a feeling about it, a very strong feeling. Now go get cleaned up." Rachael smiled and turned away. She heard Jackson's "Yes, she will" before she made her way down the hall to Mattie's room.

273

Mattie was dressed in her own clothes. Something Jackson insisted on. Rachael saw Mattie was in need of a trim and a shampoo. It had been cleaned but she really needed a thorough scrubbing now that her incisions were healed well enough and a female needed to do this task. Jackson had done a very good job but a woman's hair was a different matter.

Rachael used Mattie's shampoo and gently washed her auburn locks till her hair shined. She always carried supplies she needed after her workouts and she was thankful she had them with her. After blow drying her hair Rachael set out to curl it and shape up the uneven pieces with her handy scissors.

She giggled at the thought of all the times she had been teased by her friends for carrying everything including the kitchen sink in her backpack. This time she would bet they would be glad she did. Mattie's hair was styled so pretty in curls around her face and Rachael added a ribbon to pull the sides back. She chattered like a magpie the whole time she pampered Mattie.

Finally, deciding she needed some color Rachael applied all the makeup she had used when Mattie sang for the first time at Waves. There were scars now, that were fading, but Mattie was still as stunning as ever and she was sure Jackson would appreciate her efforts. Standing back and viewing her accomplishment Rachael told Mattie how beautiful she was and asked her if she would like to take a walk out to the garden since it was such a beautiful day.

The nurses were lenient when it came to Mattie. She had been there so long they had all come to think of her as a friend and not just a patient. Rachael smiled at the comments of how Mattie looked so pretty today and that the sunshine would do her some good. Rachael looped her arm around Mattie's and they headed for the garden. The sun was bright and the birds were calling to one another.

The garden was fairly empty so they had their choice of places to sit. There was a slight chill in the air, but it was refreshing as they made their way to the bench beneath a budding dogwood. Rachael told Mattie her news of the engagement and continued carrying the conversation while Mattie remained silent. She wished with all her heart that Mattie would snap out of it soon. Poor Jackson was running on empty.

Mattie didn't hear anything except the humming and soft voice of her mother. Liz stopped her singing and turned her head as if listening to someone speaking.

Mattie hadn't heard a word and yet she saw her momma shake her head in agreement of something. "Mattie it's time. We have kept you here long enough. You're safe and your body is healed. It's time to go back. Jackson and the baby need you there and your time here is over."

"You want me to go? Momma, I can't go back. I'm afraid too."

"There is no need to be frightened. Jackson, Rachael, Lyle, and all your friends will keep you safe. There's more for you there than there is for you here. It's not your time to be here. You will have a long life with Jackson and your children. Tell her Gracie. She will listen to you."

"Mattie girl your momma is right. It's time for you to go back and live your life the way it was intended. This is not your time. You need to go to your young man and share your life with him as it was meant to be. Now you go on and know this, your momma and me, we will always be with you and your family. You have a baby to take care of. Heck child you name that young-in after me if you want. I always wanted a grandbaby." The old woman smiled a toothless smile and her love for the girl was evident on her wrinkled, smiling face.

"That's right Matt. You go on now and know we won't ever leave you unprotected. Besides you have a lot of friends and a wonderful family to watch out for you now. Your not alone anymore Mattie and you never will be again. That is my promise to you. Love that baby enough for me. She will be the light of your life as you always were for me. I love you Mattie. Don't ever forget."

Her voice was fading as she spoke knowing Mattie was already on her journey home. She would miss her daughter but it was time for her to enjoy her life. Her time of suffering was going to end. Mattie was going to be happy and she knew Jackson was the best thing that had ever happened to her little girl and she loved him for it. God knew what he was doing the day he put them together. Liz clasped Gracie's hand and faded into the white light that consumed them. They could be heard laughing as they disappeared.

Jackson knew something was wrong or at least different. He couldn't shake the sensation that he had to get to Mattie.

Lyle understood the urgency Jackson felt and rushed in the making of a quick bite for him in the form of a sandwich.

Jackson took a shower that took less than five minutes to complete and was heading out the door as he finger combed his wet hair. He was so preoccupied with his feelings that he didn't even tease Lyle about Rachael. All he managed was congratulation's.

The need to be with Mattie was so strong he was being pulled back to the hospital by invisible hands. By the time he made it back to the hospital he was almost in a panic. He stopped the impending scream he wanted to unleash when he saw her empty room but was relieved when the aide told him they were in the garden.

Without a word he took off at a dead run. He made his way to the edge of the garden and sighed with relief when he caught site of Rachael and Mattie sitting on the bench. He closed his eyes as he calmed his nerves to a low hum instead of the freight train rush he had been feeling.

When he opened his eyes and focused on his favorite women he felt his heart take on a thunderous pounding rhythm. Rachael stiffened at the same sight he had just witnessed so he knew at that precise moment Mattie was moving without any help.

His feet moved on there own and he found himself close to the bench they had been sharing. Dear God in Heaven Mattie had not only moved she stood up. Her gaze was fixed on a woman holding her baby just across the path.

Rachael gaped up at Mattie and when she looked to her left, she saw Jackson. The look on his face was all the conformation she needed to know that he had witnessed the same thing she had. He moved to stand beside her and waited as she did to see what was happening.

Jackson gazed at how Mattie's hair was fixed and she was wearing makeup. She was beautiful no matter what she wore, but the smile that spread across her face was his undoing. She was smiling!

Her focus was on the baby in the woman's arms and he knew then that Mattie was aware of the baby she carried within her. She had heard him all those times he had talked to her. He watched her place her palm on her slightly rounded belly as the tears slide down her cheek.

Jackson began to move toward her just as she began to move in the direction her gaze was locked on. He stopped as he watched intently for Mattie to continue on the path she was taking toward the woman and her infant.

Mattie was so happy she couldn't stand herself. The baby in the woman's arms was so pretty and she just had to get close to her. Her voice wouldn't work when she tried to speak. Swallowing hard she tried again and a hoarse whisper passed her lips. "She's pretty."

"Thank you. Would you like to sit with me? You can hold her if you like."

"Can I?" Mattie whispered.

"Sure," the woman helped her hold her baby and watched the light brighten in the young girl's eyes. She knew who Mattie was from all the publicity and she was becoming part of something miraculous. As the woman lifted her gaze she saw the young woman's husband watching his wife intently.

She knew Mattie hadn't done any of this before. The reports had said she was unresponsive. Well, Mary decided, she was awake now and she had the pleasure of being included in the experience. She saw the young man look at her and mouth a 'thank you' to her. She only nodded because she didn't want to break the spell that had wrapped around them like a soft blanket.

Mattie sat there holding the baby girl, rocking her, and singing softly to her. The tears streaked down her cheeks in tiny rivulets.

Tear filled eyes lifted to the shadow that crossed her lap and she beheld her sun. Jackson was in front of her smiling and crying at the same time. "Oh, Jacks," she whispered as he knelt down in front of her. "I missed you."

"Mattie you don't know how long I've waited to here your voice again, to see your face light up the way it is now, and to tell you and know you hear me say "I love you".

Jackson continued to kneel in front of Mattie as she held the little bundle wrapped in pink. When the baby wriggled Mattie focused on the little bundle again and started to calm her. "We're having a baby too aren't we Jacks"

"Yes, honey we are and we'll talk about that later but for now, all I want to do is hold you. It has been such a long time I don't think I can stand another minute of waiting."

Jackson motioned for the woman to take her baby as he lifted Mattie from the bench and held her close. He buried his face in her neck and began to laugh and spin her around until everyone was laughing. Jackson felt the weight of the world lift from his shoulders as he heard Mattie's laughter in his ear. He lifted a silent thank you to the heavens knowing that was where the true miracle had come from.

He held his family in his arms until his muscles began to protest. Reluctantly, he let Mattie down on her feet and continued to sway with her in his embrace. The outside world didn't exist for them.

Jackson bent his head and kissed his wife for the first time in months getting a response when he did. His heart raced and his breath stilled in his chest. This was what his life was supposed to be like with this woman.

Mattie responded to him as she always had. The response told him just how well she was. Jackson didn't understand what all had happened, all he knew was the torment was over and they could start their life again. "I love you Mattie. I have missed you so much."

"I have been away along time haven't I? I'm sorry Jacks. I had to. You know I wouldn't have stayed away if I had a choice don't you?" She pleaded with her eyes for him to understand.

"I know baby. I know." Jackson kissed her soundly and didn't pull away until he heard someone clearing their throat and then a tapping on his shoulder. Jackson was breathless as he lifted his mouth from Mattie's and turned in the direction of the interruption.

It was a very tearful Rachael. How could he have forgotten her standing there? "Mattie there is someone here that we can never repay for her bravery. Rachael was responsible for bringing help to you. She saved your life Mattie." Jackson released her as she turned to Rachael and grabbed her into a tight hug.

Laughter and tears intermingled as they hugged. A friendship for life was what they had. They had become sisters before and now they were even closer than ever before. "I knew you had made it. Mom told me when you did and that you were safe. Don't look so shocked Rache. I haven't lost my mind and I'll tell you all about it later ok?"

"Yeah, ok. It's so good having you back Matt. I have missed everything about you and so have a lot of others. You, Mattie Woods, are a celebrity and didn't even know it. We will talk a lot sometime in the very near future. Right now I need to make some phone calls to some very concerned people. I love you Matt." Turning to Jackson she pointed her finger at him and smiled when she told him, "and you keep your eyes on her." It wasn't a request but for once he wouldn't argue. "Yes mam." He smiled at her as she turned to make the calls.

"Excuse me." The lady with the baby whispered around tightened vocal chords. "I just want to say thank you for letting me and my daughter be a part of the reunion. It has been along time in coming and I'm glad I was here to share it with you."

"We should thank you. I have tried everything to get Mattie back except the most obvious, a baby. Your daughter was the key to the locked door. We won't forget you." Before she left Jackson got all of her information with plans to contact her in the future. This woman wouldn't be forgotten. Nope good things would come to the single parent Bethany Morris and little Samantha. Jackson's parents had a lot pull and for once he would use it to help the little family that pulled his wife back to him.

Making their way back into the hospital taking slow careful steps, a very shocked staff smiled as they saw new Mattie. The doctor was paged immediately. The examination didn't take long and he was pleased to say she was through her ordeal. He informed her to make a follow up visit but he didn't foresee any lingering problems. One more night in the hospital was all that was required and she could go home in the morning. Nothing sounded any better than home. As the doctor left the room he was quickly replaced with family and friends. Some Mattie didn't know and others she did and had missed very much.

Lyle towered over most of the people in the room and Mattie's eyes found his. She couldn't help but smile at him. Rachael was at his side as he made his way to Mattie. He kept her in front of him with a protective hand on the small of her back.

Mattie didn't miss the gesture. She may be tired but she wasn't blind. When Mattie focused on the clasped hands she noticed the ring on Rachael's finger. She was very pleased that her friends realized what was there all along. They loved each other.

Lyle squatted down so he was eye to eye with Mattie. He looked deep into the shimmering tear filled pools and was relieved to see the life of her there again. Lyle felt his own eyes well up as he faced their Mattie again and not the shell she had been.

Being the type to not show much emotion faded away as he grabbed Mattie's hands and let the tears roll unabashed. "Mattie," he rasped out, "how are you honey?" He wanted her to tell him herself, that she was all right. They had a special bond from the beginning and they understood one another's past for it held a lot of bad times. Mattie and he had talked before as much as she would allow and he wanted her to talk to him now. So he would know for himself she had survived.

"I'm fine Lyle; even better now that I'm going to go home. But somehow I think you already know that don't you?" Mattie looked directly into his eyes and didn't turn away or blink. Her life had changed.

Lyle knew she was fine. Mattie had survived. She held his stare without a flinch, as she wouldn't have in the past. She held her face up and she smiled at him as if she could read his mind. Yep Mattie had survived in more ways than one. It warmed his heart and he smiled back at her.

"You'll do Matt. You'll do." Then as much as a surprise to him as it was to the onlookers who knew Mattie before she reached over and hugged Lyle with a strength that surprised him. He felt her breath near his cheek when she spoke for his ears only. "The ghosts are gone and now I can live. You take care of Rachael won't you?"

Lyle reluctantly hugged her back and whispered for her only. "I can finally live too Matt. You know I'll take care of Rachael. I love her very much." He held her tighter to let her know how glad he was for the both of them.

"I know." Mattie pulled back and kissed his cheek. He only smiled at her as the realization that the past was where it was supposed to be.

The entire scene played out in front of a room full of family and friends and no one spoke. Feeling strangely awkward Mattie brought some lightness to the mood. "What?" She asked innocently as she shrugged her shoulders.

Jackson was surprised but relieved with her reaction to Lyle. He also felt it was time to break the serious mood. He had had enough of that. "You've got your own woman low rent so get lost." It felt good to tease with his friend again. It had been too long.

"Who says a guy can't have two women?" Lyle acted as if he had been insulted.

"I do Mr. and I suggest you get your hands off my sister and put them on me." Rachael joined in the jesting. It was so nice to laugh and joke again.

"All right mighty mouse I got the picture." Lyle hugged his fiancée' and kissed her soundly. That left no doubt who had whose heart.

Jackson saw Joey and waved him over to the group. Feeling a little out of sorts he didn't know how to act. As if Mattie knew the problem she stood on shaky legs and hugged him. "I have missed you boss. You have a job for me?" Mattie was teasing with him and he was pleasantly surprised at the banter. Mattie was whole and it didn't take a college education to figure it out.

"I missed you too Mattie. I'm so glad this is over. I would be a fool to offer you a job because if I did Jackson would hurt me." Joey chuckled. He didn't miss the look on Jackson's face at the mention of a job. Everyone knew full well he intended to keep Mattie home with him especially with the baby on the way. "You just focus on your family and if a time comes when you want a job there will always be one available. Is that acceptable?"

"That is what I hoped for. Thanks boss." She kissed his cheek and winked. For the first time since she had known him, Joey actually blushed.

Sarah sent word she would visit Mattie when she got out of the hospital and they would have a nice long tea date. Mattie was ecstatic to hear the invitation because she hadn't seen her with the others she was worried. Rachael, bless her heart, had already called Sarah and was the one giving her the message.

Mattie smothered a yawn and sat down. Jackson knew she had done too much too soon. He didn't have to say a word to his friends they all knew what he wanted without a syllable passing his lips.

The Police officers who knew the case and had been involved said a quick word and then an open invitation to Waves took the crowd away. A lone man stood at the doorway. Watching and waiting for his turn.

Mattie didn't know him and yet she felt as if she did. That was strange. No one seemed to be concerned with his presence except her so she just sat with Jackson and watched him as he was watching her.

Mattie focused her gaze as he moved into the room. Puzzled with his reaction she began to get a little nervous. Her hand tightened on Jackson's as she whispered. "Who is that man Jackson? It's like I know him but yet I know I don't."

"That's Blake and he is a detective. He was very helpful with finding you and rescuing you. Do you remember him or anything Matt?" Jackson hoped she didn't. It was too painful.

"I don't really. There are some bits and pieces that are fuzzy but no I don't remember." Mattie frowned.

"Blake." Jackson reached out his hand to the man and shook it. "You remember Mattie?"

"I'm sorry for staring Mrs. Woods. I'm normally not so rude but to see you defy the odds makes me a believer in a power greater than the man made

280

stuff. You are one lucky lady and I'm happy to know you." He smiled at her hoping to relieve that worry frown that creased her brow. He hadn't meant to frighten her but he was so shocked when one of the men got the news. He had to come and see for himself. Blake couldn't get over the difference in the dead woman he had helped rescue and the live one he was looking at now. Mattie was a beautiful woman and he knew she was a blessed one. She literally glowed.

"I'm sorry I don't remember you but thank you for all you did. I know how lucky I am and thanks to a lot of caring people my luck didn't run out."

"Your welcome and the next time you need anything feel free to call me. Now I'll leave you so you can get some rest. Take care of yourself and that baby. Jackson I'll see you around."

Blake headed toward the elevator with a new leash on life. If that little slip of a lady could do it then so could he. His life was in for a major overhaul. His step lightened and he whistled all the way to his car.

After hugs and kisses from everyone they all filed out of the room. Lyle and Rachael left just because they knew Jackson and Mattie needed the time together. Alone at last they mutually thought.

Jackson's parents would come in on the first available flight in the morning. They were content enough with a phone call for the time being and a promise to see them as soon as possible. The room went from a quiet roar to a calm silence.

It was just Jackson and Mattie and the empty room. Jackson felt a little awkward. He had imagined this for so long that now it was staring him in the face he didn't know what to do or how to act. He stood at the window looking at her beautiful face. Waiting, hoping, and needing just Mattie.

Mattie didn't think twice. "Come here Jackson and hold me will you? I'm so tired but I want to be with you." She held her arms out to him as he walked into her embrace. He felt so good she could almost weep. Instead she sighed with the contentment he gave her.

Jackson scooted on the bed and pulled Mattie with him. This was how it was supposed to be. His heart swelled with the love he had for her and their baby. Mattie rubbed his chest with her palm and hummed as she had in the past.

Poor thing was so tired she fell asleep as soon as she grew comfortable. Jackson didn't mind. Mattie was back and she was his. She was here in every sense of the word. He hugged her closer just to feel more of her. He must have squeezed her a little too tightly for she moaned.

She must have sensed his thoughts because on a hushed whisper she spoke softly. "I'm not ever leaving again Jackson. Don't worry we have our whole lives to share. That was a promise given to me before I came back and it came from a reliable source." Mattie fell asleep again on a soft giggle. He heard a whispered "I love you" as she drifted off.

Jackson blinked away the tears that crowded his eyes. He knew she spoke the truth and he did loosen his grip. Not much though. He needed to hold her. While the room was dark and quiet Jackson found himself talking to her as he had so many times in the past. He told her of his love for her and the love he had for their baby and he spoke of the future they were to share just as he had before. The difference was he knew Mattie heard him. He tilted her slightly and lovingly gazed into her sleeping face and whispered. "I love you with all my being Mattie."

Mattie's eyes opened and she smiled lazily at him. "I love you too," she whispered as she went back to sleep in his arms. It was at that moment he felt the small life flutter against his palm as he cupped Mattie's bulging belly. Life would continue for them and the love they shared would get them through all the tough times that would eventually challenge their lives. They knew better than anyone that love was a cure. Weren't they the best example after all?

Epilogue

The reception was loud and crowded but it was for his best friends that he had lingered. Jackson was more of a home body and was always anxious to get there to be with his family and today was no exception. Whispering into Lyle's ear as he brushed against the smiling groom he voiced his thoughts. "Who would have ever thought we would be where we are and happy with it?"

"I didn't until my little powerhouse leapt into my life and knocked me into a tailspin. She means more too me than I ever thought another person ever would. I love her more than I thought possible." Lyle said this with his eyes fixed on his new bride and Rachael returned the look with love for him.

Lyle smiled and gifted her with a wink that said more than mere words. How was it he could make her blush with such a small gesture was beyond him but he savored the pink tinting of her beautiful skin. She was his. He was hers. The future was theirs.

"Listen lover boy I'm off to find Mattie so you can make goo-goo eyes at your wife." Jackson couldn't let the opportunity pass to jab at his best friend, wedding day or not.

"I do not make goo-goo eyes at anyone thank you very much. I happen to be lusting with my eyes and my ever-increasing dirty mind. If you will excuse me I believe I'll go lust a little with my hands." Lyle wiggled his eyebrows suggestively with a grin that would dull the sun.

Jackson laughed and slapped Lyle on the back. "Go ahead then pervert. I have my own lustful thoughts of my wife at present but in order to fulfill those thoughts I need the wife to do it."

Jackson strolled off in search of Mattie almost certain of where he would find her. The sun was setting and Mattie had always preferred a spot when she felt the need to get away and watch the gift God gave us at the end of the day. Ever since moving to his childhood home with his parents the family as a whole bloomed and became closer than any they knew.

Mattie still found days of fright with groups of strangers but not the all-consuming kind as she had before. When those occasions happened she would simply excuse herself in search of a peaceful place to 'regroup', as she liked to call it. Making his way to the back of the house and down the graveled path he himself put in for Mattie. Jackson soon caught sight of her.

The sun was setting the sky ablaze with fiery oranges and reds with hints of yellows. With such a background he couldn't miss the silhouettes of his family on the hill. Madonna with child couldn't hold a candle to his women. Jackson stopped dead in his tracks as he took in the sight. Almost afraid breathing would break the spell he remained as still as a statue and drank in the sight like a man dieing of thirst.

"God, what a sight they make," he heard whispered into his ear. Slowly turning his head he looked into the face of his parents and they wore the same expression of awe as he knew he was wearing. He couldn't help but smile in agreement with his parents.

Moving without realizing it Jackson's vision was for his family and nothing else. The slight breeze whispering silent secrets as it brushed his face and hair carrying the hint of Mattie's scent. He would know it anywhere and he inhaled deeply taking her into his lungs. She was his light, his life, and the mother of his child and most of all she was his.

Making his way closer he heard the occasional lilts of singing pass by only hinting at the music it carried. Closing the distance he could make out the lullaby Mattie was softly singing to their daughter. Elizabeth Grace was a miracle in a time of tragedy and a cure for the hurts they had endured. She was their little angel and they adored her.

Mattie was a great mother, as he knew she would be. Mothering was her life and their family would be a large one if she could manage it. All in all Jackson wouldn't mind a large family either but he would wait to tell her that for he was selfish enough to want her to himself for a while yet.

Softly stepping in hopes of not disturbing them and to absorb the sight a little longer Jackson made his way closer. His hopes were dashed away when Mattie, as she usually did, turned knowing he was near and rewarded him with a smile that made the sun dull in comparison.

Turning as he made his way to stand in front of her she swayed slightly with the weight of his daughter in her arms sucking lazily at Mattie's breast. The sight of his wife breastfeeding Liz always made his throat constrict with emotion.

Kneeling down to face his family no words were spoken for the looks that passed between them said more than a mere word ever could. Jackson reached to cup his daughter's auburn head and cradled it in his palm feeling the warmth of it, the softness of it, and the life in her pulse against his palm. Nothing could mean more.

Watching Mattie's face as she stared down at the baby was a sight Jackson would always remember. Elizabeth's tiny fingers kneaded Mattie's breast lovingly stroking her pale skin for the mere joy of touching her momma. When Mattie smiled at the gesture Liz smiled with a milk bubble popping as she gurgled with a relish. God had definitely smiled down on him and his.

Feeling the love wrap around them like an embrace, Jackson leaned over his daughter and placed his forehead against Mattie's.

With a hoarse whisper he told her what was swelling in his heart. "God, I love you two with all that I am. You take my breath away." He let the emotion take him and the tear slid down his shadowed cheek. Mattie had taught him feelings were meant to be shared not hidden. He saw her mouth curve and the tiger-eyes he loved to gaze into, filled with her own tears, as she whispered what was bursting to be said. "I love you with all my heart. You two are the life I never thought I would have."

Leaning in closer to his wife as she closed the distance their lips met. They kissed deeply causing their hearts to soar, while their daughter was cradled in the middle. Placing their foreheads together they jointly looked upon the face of their blessing. As the sun fell into the horizon deepening the warm glowing colors that surrounded them the little family made the perfect picture.

Lyndal and Joyce jointly sighed at the sight they beheld. Turning to leave them in peace Joyce was engulfed in a warm strong embrace as Lyndal whispered his love for her.

"That is what makes life worth living my love," she whispered back before taking his mouth with hers in a kiss of deep passion.

They all had been given the gift of second chances and each embraced it with open arms and full hearts.

E.F. James lives in Kentucky with her incredibly supportive family. Even though wife and mother was a fulfilling role she went to college to become a registered nurse and has enjoyed her career for many years. The desire to write has always surpassed her love of reading and invites you to visit her and her works at www.EFJames.com.